MW01028799

The Quiet Light

The Quiet Light

A Novel about Thomas Aquinas

by
Louis de Wohl

IGNATIUS PRESS SAN FRANCISCO

Original edition published in 1950
J. B. Lippincott, Company, Philadelphia and New York

Cover design by Roxanne Mei Lum
Cover art by Christopher J. Pelicano
Reprinted 1996 Ignatius Press, San Francisco
With permission of Mrs. Ruth Magdalene de Wohl
and Curtis Brown, Limited, New York
ISBN 978–0–89870–595–9
Library of Congress catalogue number 96–83641
Printed in the United States of America

Book One

Chapter I

BROTHER VINCENT WAS READING his office when it happened; it was in the early afternoon, when his mind was at its best and therefore less inclined to wander, and he was alone in the garden. The garden, too, was at its best, growing and glowing and censing the praise of God in robes that put King Solomon in all his glory to shame.

That was when it happened, and the first thing Brother Vincent became aware of was that something was wrong with the shadow of the wall in front of him. It ought to have been a smooth shadow, one long, unbroken line, and it wasn't. There was something there like an excrescence; it disturbed the even flow of the shadow, and it disturbed Brother Vincent's thoughts sufficiently to make him give it a closer look. On a closer look the excrescence appeared to have an absurd shape, almost like the head of a goat—horns, ears, and all. A goat, then. But . . . but since when could a goat climb up a wall, nine feet high?

Brother Vincent knew that he should concentrate on his breviary; somewhere in the deeper recesses of his mind he could hear the thin voice of an alarm bell: stick to your office and don't bother about shadows, excrescences, and goats. He actually went so far as to read the next line; then the temptation to give that shadow just one more look proved overwhelming.

It did look like the head of a goat, and yet it didn't.

And . . . it was moving . . .

Brother Vincent wheeled round.

It was there. It was real. But it wasn't a goat. What . . . what was it? It had a long, melancholic face, yellowish and thin; it had pointed ears and, yes, it did have horns, short, straight horns ending in little knobs; its eyes were half closed. But the most terrible thing about it was that it was growing, growing all the time. Already the head was a foot high over the wall . . . no, it was not the . . . the thing itself that was growing, only its neck, an endless, yellowish neck with strange, brown designs on it.

Brother Vincent stood and stared; with a queer and terrified fascination he saw that horrible neck stretching and stretching beyond the measure of the permissible for man or animal. What he saw seemed to be an evil, goatlike head on the body of an enormous serpent, towering higher and higher above him.

Suddenly a pair of black hands appeared above the wall, and in the next instant a little black man stood there, upright and grinning, his teeth matching his turban and dress in whiteness.

He pointed to the . . . the thing, whose neck was still growing, and said in a squeaky voice:

"Giraffe. Giraffe".

The thing itself had not uttered a sound.

With a deep, tremulous breath Brother Vincent regained control over his mind. *"Apage,"* he uttered, *"apage, Satanas"*. And he made the sign of the Cross. It did not seem to have much effect on either the thing or its black familiar, but it helped Brother Vincent to regain control of his limbs. He made a jump backward, turned, and fled, as quickly as his seventy-year-old legs would carry him, back to the entrance of the monastery.

* * *

Francesco Tecchini, Abbot of Santa Justina, was studying a beautifully made copy of Aristotle's *Organon.* It was, of course, the translation of Boethius, not that Moorish edition with the footnotes of Averroes that of late had become so popular in certain clerical circles—that mixture of Aristotelian truth and Averroist heresy that one fine day would ruin the good name of the Stagirite. If only someone would come to clean that stable of Augeas—someone who would prove to those glib, self-assured Moslem philosophers that Aristotle, if he were alive today, would laugh at their fatalistic interpretations . . .

"Father Abbot! Father Abbot!"

"You can't see Father Abbot now; he is working on . . . "

"I *must* see him!"

"Let Brother Vincent come in, Brother Leo", said the Abbot aloud, and the old man tumbled into the room.

"Father Abbot . . . the devil . . . I . . . I . . . have seen the devil."

"The devil you have", said the Abbot, annoyed to the point of inconsistency as well as flippancy. It was only a year ago that he had had to relegate one of the brothers to the infirmary and have him watched day and night because he believed himself to be attacked continuously by the devil. In the end he had had to call in the exorcist of another monastery, who examined the man and prescribed that he should leave off fasting and vigils for a while and do a few hours of gardening instead. "And that is all?" "That is all, my Lord Abbot. He'll be well again in three weeks' time." He was, too. But it was annoying to have solemnly asked for another monastery's exorcist just for that. Still—Brother Vincent was different: a sensible man, not given to nervous outbursts and the like. In any case there would be no necessity to prescribe gardening for him. For he *was* the gardener.

"It must have been the devil", said Brother Vincent firmly. "He had his familiar with him—or whatever it was, a little black man and *he* said it was a seraph. But that was a lie, of course. That and a seraph! The ugliest, the most horrible thing I ever saw—a seraph."

He fairly snorted.

"And where", asked the Abbot, "did you see . . . umph . . . all this?"

"At the roses", said Brother Vincent at once. "That is: behind the wall behind the roses."

"The natural topography of the gardener", thought the Abbot. "Where on earth do we have roses? But at least it shows that he has not lost his reason." Then only he became aware of the whole significance of the sentence.

"Behind the wall, you say? Then how could you see . . . him, or them or it?"

"The little black man climbed up the wall", said Brother Vincent. "And the . . . the other just looked over it with his head and neck."

"Rather a big devil", murmured the Abbot. Only now he got up, a little heavily. "I suppose we'd better have a look."

"Yes, Father Abbot."

Outside about a dozen monks had assembled.

"You seem to be right after all, Brother Vincent", said the Abbot ironically. "It must be the devil. Look—how much holy work he has stopped." As they scattered: "Show the way to the roses, Brother Vincent."

They reached the place a few minutes later. But the wall behind the red and white glory was empty.

"Are you sure it was here, Brother Vincent?"

"Quite sure, Father Abbot."

"A pity", said the Abbot. "Well—come and see me in my study after Compline. Now I must go back to my work. And if in the meantime . . . "

To the Abbot's dismay Brother Vincent uttered a hoarse cry. "There . . . there! Look, Father Abbot, look!"

The monk's finger was pointing toward the gate.

And there, yes, something was coming there, something that made Brother *Ostiarius* run madly toward the main building; he was screaming, too, but the sound of his voice was drowned by the blast of a trumpet so fierce that it hurt the eardrums. Was that Brother Vincent's devil? There seemed to be an enormous commotion just outside the monastery gates. But this thing, this endless yellow-brown thing, led by a little black man . . .

"That's it, Father Abbot", cried Brother Vincent. "See it now? That's it—and its familiar."

The gate had an arc twelve feet high, and yet the thing had to bend its neck to get through: down it came, as if in a reverential greeting, and raised itself again to its full, incredible height. For a brief moment the Abbot felt inclined to accept Brother Vincent's theory; but then he saw a huge, unwieldly grey mass appear behind the thing, flapping ears, a long trunk—no doubt, that was the animal *elephas;* he had seen a picture of it before, a strange, forbidding sort of animal, but an animal—so that other thing was likely to be an animal as well. "After this," thought the Abbot, "it's easy enough to believe in the existence of unicorns . . . in fact of anything. But what . . . why . . . ?"

It occurred to him that all this was simply a nightmare and that he was going to wake up any moment now. Monks had come out from all the doors; they huddled together, gaping. The animal *elephas* trumpeted again as it managed, only just, to pass the gate. It, too, had its familiar, a dark-skinned pagan in turban and white robes, who patted it on the trunk. And behind it came other animals—lynxes and panthers, at least half a dozen of them, muzzled and bridled, led by more familiars and closely followed by an entire herd of camels, some with one, some with two humps.

"Holy Mother of God", groaned Brother Vincent. "What is it, Father Abbot? Is it real?"

The Abbot gave no answer. He stared hard at the gate, where now, behind the clumsily trotting camels, other figures appeared—human figures, clad in gorgeous, semi-transparent garments of all the colors of the rainbow. Pretty faces, heavily made up. Women. They, too, had their familiars—fat, misshapen creatures in billowing robes. Eunuchs. Dancing girls and eunuchs.

Suddenly the Abbot understood. He became very pale. "Yes, Brother Vincent, it is real—as real as the insults hurled at Our Gracious Lord and of the same intention. Ah—here it comes."

A knight in full armor, on a fully armored horse, rode into the courtyard, flanked by his pages, followed by his varlets—a huge, metallic beetle, surrounded by ants. He looked about, rode on straight up to the Abbot, and halted. His helmetless head, topped by unruly brown hair, seemed curiously small, unworthy of the regal trappings from which it emerged.

"You the Abbot?"

"I am Don Francesco Tecchini, Abbot of Santa Justina. What is the meaning of this unseemly procession, Sir?"

"I am the Count of Caserta", said the knight. "Your servant, my Lord Abbot." He brushed an invisible speck of dust off his cloak of green velvet. "What you choose to call an unseemly procession is part of the court of His Most Gracious Majesty the Emperor, whose subject you are as much as I. Subject and servant, my Lord Abbot—just as all these are his servants, too—two-legged and four-legged, what's the difference?"

"A child could tell you the difference, Sir Count. This is sacred ground."

"I haven't come here to indulge in theological subtleties", interrupted the knight, "but to herald the arrival of my imperial master, who has deigned to choose this place as his temporary headquarters."

"Impossible", said the Abbot with trembling lips. "The Emperor and his nobles are welcome, of course—but if his headquarters includes . . . "

"I regret to interrupt your fine speech, but nothing is impossible when my imperial master commands. He is well aware of the fact that monks should not consort with the beautiful sex. You and your monks will therefore leave Santa Justina without delay . . . in your own interest." The thin, sarcastic mouth under the flat, sensual nose broadened a little, without opening. The keen, dark eyes were bright with mischief.

"Leave Santa Justina", gasped the Abbot. "I . . . I cannot believe that the Emperor will go so far."

"My Lord Abbot! Your age and your habit forbid me to answer you as I would answer another man if he doubted my veracity. Even so . . . "

"I would rather insult you", broke in the old man, now thoroughly roused, "by giving you the lie than insult the Emperor by accepting your words as his truth, much as I regret being forced by such an alternative."

"That's enough", rapped the knight. "I give you exactly half an hour. Any monk who hasn't left by then will be thrown out by his ear. My orders are to clean up this place and make it fit for my master to dwell in it. Such are his own words."

"I understand", said the Abbot, suddenly quite calm again. "If Santa Justina is to be fit for your master, it cannot any longer be fit for mine. We shall leave."

He walked past the knight toward the entrance, where now half a hundred monks huddled together, numb with fear and indignation.

"The Blessed Sacrament," he thought, "the altar vessels and vestments—and just a few of the books and manuscripts. Thank God for the vow of poverty. We shall find refuge at Monte Cassino. There is room enough there for all of us." This would not last forever. Emperor Frederick never stayed very long at the same place. Since his excommunication he was shifting his abode several times a year—as if the very earth were burning under his feet—as well it might.

"Father Abbot . . . "

"Yes, Brother Vincent".

"What are they going to do about my flowers?"

"Our flowers, Brother Vincent."

"Our flowers, Father Abbot. There are some which need water three times a day and . . . "

"I don't know—but I suppose we shall have to build up all over again when we return—starting with the reconsecration." And with a painful little smile: "You were right and wrong, Brother Vincent. Wrong: for the thing you saw was not the devil. And right: for it was the herald of the devil."

Suddenly a silvery bell began to toll. Faithful old Brother Philip, unsuspecting old Brother Philip, was ringing Vespers. Vespers that would never be sung.

Horrified, Brother Vincent saw the face of his Abbot distorted with soundless weeping.

And still the bell tolled.

* * *

Five hours later the Emperor arrived with a suite of about sixty nobles and many hundred servants. It was dark now. But not in the monastery.

The Count of Caserta was ready for his master. Torches were ablaze all along the walls of the courtyard, now crossed by a narrow path of precious carpets. All the bells of the monastery were ringing at the same time. He himself, now dressed in fur-trimmed velvet without armor, bowed deeply, then went over to kiss the Emperor's stirrup and help him dismount.

Frederick II hesitated a little. "Living torches", he said. "By the beard of the prophet, this is very pretty." Every torch was fastened on the head of a dancing girl dressed only in wide oriental trousers and strings of jewelry. "Your taste is improving, Caserta. But do not let them stand there too long. The night is cool, and if they catch a cold, most of my friends are likely to catch one, too. They usually do—I don't quite know why that should be, but there it is."

He acknowledged the respectful wave of laughter with the smile peculiar to all Hohenstaufens—a smile in which the eyes took no part.

"Caserta is a wizard", laughed the Margrave Pallavicini. "However did you manage to change the monks into this, I wonder? And which one was the Abbot? I'd like to meet the Abbot—and I never wished that before in my life."

"The monks?" asked Frederick curtly.

Count Caserta shrugged his shoulders. "Tramping through the night—in a southerly direction."

"But these bells?"

"Ah, the bells, my liege", smiled Caserta. "Perhaps you would like to see how they are being rung?"

"Let's see", said Frederick, dismounting at last. "Come with me, cousin Cornwall—and, you, Hapsburg. Pallavicini? Eccelino? Let's see Caserta's bells. By the Caaba of Mecca, I can sense something extraordinary."

The nobles he had called dismounted, too, and followed him to the bell tower.

"What about me, Father?" cried a woman's voice.

"If I know Caserta, you are too young a man for such a sight, Selvaggia", laughed Frederick without turning his head.

They all laughed. The Princess Selvaggia had dressed as a boy for the ride, and as she was slim and very young she almost managed to look the part. Her face, however, was utterly feminine, with a generous, sensual, very red mouth, pert little nose and the strangely oblique grey eyes of her mother. Eccelino, turning his head, blew a kiss at her, and she answered by showing her tongue like a street urchin. He laughed uproariously.

A very young knight of the retinue of the Earl of Cornwall could not forbear shaking his head a little.

"Does this shock you, Sir Knight?" whispered a mocking voice. "It needn't, you know. They'll marry before the week is out."

The young Englishman looked up. He saw a man of about his own age, no more than twenty, well built and rather tall for an Italian, with a lovely forehead, dark eyes ready for laughter, and a small mouth ready for any girl. The kind of man it was difficult to be angry with—and the kind of man Piers Rudde had always secretly envied a little; they grew that way in Italy and in France, too—elegant, lighthearted men, so well balanced in manners and speech that they could insult a king and the king would give them a golden chain. He had wanted to give a haughty reply. Instead he said: "It is all a little confusing for me."

The young Italian laughed. "I'll well believe that. Nothing of all this could happen in Britain, I suppose."

"Certainly not", said Piers Rudde somewhat primly. "But do tell me, noble sir, what was it I heard the Emperor swear by? Which prophet did he refer to?"

"Oh, that—" the young Italian shrugged his shoulders. " 'By the beard of the prophet', he said: it's Mohammed, of course; although I have little doubt that all the other prophets had beards as well as he. It seems to be a necessary condition. The longer the beard, the better the prophecy. But he did mean Mohammed. Didn't you hear him say, 'By the Caaba of Mecca'?"

"Yes, but . . . what is it?"

"A huge black stone in the heart of the holy city of the Moslems. It's supposed to be the stone on which Abraham was going to sacrifice Isaac, and the Archangel Gabriel kindly transported it to Mecca."

"Does the Emperor believe *that?*" asked the Englishman with wide-open eyes. "Is it true, then, what the priests say, that he has become a Moslem himself?"

"Not quite so loud, Sir Knight", whispered the Italian. "No, I don't think it's true. In fact he said only the other day: 'I haven't shed one chain to be tied with another.' But it's the fashion to swear by Mohammedan symbols. The Emperor introduced the fashion, that is true."

"And perhaps just as well", said Piers Rudde stiffly. "At least the holy names are left alone. This was a monastery once, wasn't it?"

"Until a few hours ago, I should think", was the cheerful answer. "I wonder what the monks thought when the imperial animals made their entry. It was his own idea, you know. He loves playing pranks on them ever since . . . "

He broke off. It was not good form to mention the Emperor's excommunication.

"What animals? These . . . young women?"

The Italian laughed heartily. "Excellent, excellent, Sir Knight—and then they say that you do not know how to laugh in the land of fog and mist." But he caught himself, as he saw the bland surprise on the young Englishman's face. "By all the blessed califs and all the saints—I believe you *meant* your question. Forgive my hilarity, but it was such a very good answer, you know. No, I meant the real animals, all those rare specimens the Emperor has collected from all over the world—some of them are quite unique, and he never travels without them. How is it that you did not know that he sent them off with Caserta?—but, of course, you only joined us this afternoon, so it's all new to you. No wonder you say you are a little confused. This is a very confusing court."

"So it appears", was the curt answer.

"It is not without beauty, though", ventured the Italian. "There is something . . . godlike in this . . . in all this. We are roaming about a beautiful world that belongs to us; wherever we appear we spread joy and fear, hope and despair, love and hatred. Is not that the manner of the gods? One word from the Emperor . . . and a town is razed to the ground. The wise sultans and emirs of the East send us gold, frankincense, and myrrh. . . . "

"This is sacrilegious talk, Sir Knight", frowned Piers Rudde.

"It is poetry, my friend, poetry. I am a poet."

"It is sacrilegious poetry, then."

The young Italian sighed. "Now you are talking exactly like my mother. Oh, *mamma mia.* How often has she told me I will come to a bad end. She, too, cannot see the difference between poetry and ordinary language. What else have you in common, I wonder? She is tall and dark and fiery; she is like a statue of Juno, the Queen Mother of the gods. And you—you are fair haired and blue eyed and probably abominably strong. You are not Apollo, or you would have more appreciation for poetry. You are rather one of those Germanic gods whose very names would break an Italian tongue, they are so powerful. You and Mamma couldn't be more different, and yet you agree about a poor poet. If one more person comes along to tell me this, I shall probably believe it. But they are coming back . . . and it does seem to have been amusing. I wonder what Caserta did do about those bells. I always thought he was an unimaginative ass. . . . "

The little group came nearer. The Emperor seemed mildly amused; Eccelino was grinning all over his face, and so was Pallavicini. The Count of Hapsburg did not seem to know whether he should laugh or cry, and the Earl of Cromwell was looking down his nose in glum boredom. But Caserta was radiant.

"I must hand it to Caserta", cried Eccelino. "The most graceful bell ringers I ever saw, floating about through the air like butterflies."

"Let's see", said the Emperor, "whether he has provided us equally well with food and wine."

"Supper is awaiting you, Divus Augustus", said Caserta at once. "We had to change the refectory a little—it seems these monks really believed in austerity."

"Monks", said the Emperor, "will believe in anything, if they are told to. Where is Mouska?"

The little man appeared as from nowhere and prostrated himself.

"My dear animals, Mouska?"

"All safe and provided for, Invincible Sun."

"It is well. I shall visit them tomorrow morning. To supper, my friends."

The refectory had indeed been changed beyond recognition.

Oriental carpets covered the stone floor and purple cloth enveloped the enormous cross-shaped table. The crucifix above the heavy chair of the Abbot had been removed by the monks. Caserta had replaced it with the imperial standard, a black eagle embroidered on cloth of gold.

A band of musicians played in a corner of the room, and Iocco, the Emperor's jester, was dancing attendance on the nobles, trying to find their seats and giving them all names of his own invention, most of them containing a little drop of bitter truth, though not too much—that would have been unwise, before they had eaten and drunk, as every jester knew. He was a little hunchback with an absurdly long nose between small, black eyes, darting right and left with lightning speed, and his deformity was emphasized by his dress, half red and half pink.

When he called Eccelino "Ecce homo", the Emperor laughed; it was the kind of joke he liked to make himself. But when Iocco addressed the grave Count of Hapsburg as "Sour Uncle", a frown appeared on the imperial forehead. "Sorry", said Iocco immediately. "My master disagrees with me, and as he is so much bigger than I am, I must agree with him for disagreeing with me. I therefore withdraw the title Sour Uncle from you and confer it upon the great Earl from England. You are right as always, Lord of the World; he is much worthier of it than Uncle Underlip."

As the laughter subsided, Piers Rudde heard a voice say: "Well done."

Looking up, he saw that his neighbor was the young Italian knight who had conversed with him before. "What do you mean?"

"Good jester's tactics. Insult one man, and he may get angry. Insult two or more at a time, and they will all laugh together. Dignity is a matter of the individual—a lone goddess."

Actually, Hapsburg had smiled, broadening the insulted underlip, but the Earl of Cornwall sat there with a stony face as if he had not heard anything at all.

Pages in the imperial livery brought in the first dishes.

"Stop", cried Iocco. "I am surprised at you, noble sirs—you seem to forget where you are. Will no one say grace? Then I will do it for you."

He turned to the Emperor, raised his stumpy hands in a gesture of adoration, and proclaimed: "Great and Divine Lord of Animals, we thank you for giving us our daily bread. Some of your camels brought it here on their backs—it is only meet and just that the others should carry it away in their bellies. Amen."

Piers decided that he did not like the fool. It was a fool's business to make fun of everything, but he did not like this fool. The Earl didn't either, he felt. But already Eccelino called out: "Hey, Iocco—you talk so much of camels and yet you are the only one here who's got a hump."

The jester beamed at him. "Spoken truly, noble sir. When the camel's heritage was divided, I was the last to get my share, and so I got the hump. There's a family always very quick at hand when it comes to dividing and I wouldn't be surprised if they got the brain. Now as Plato says . . . "

"To Gehenna with Plato and all philosophers", growled Eccelino, decidedly nettled. "I don't want to think; I want to eat."

"Happy man", sighed Iocco. "He knows his limitations."

"That will do, Iocco", said the Emperor. The jester staggered back, as if hit, dropped on his knees, and crawled under the table.

"You must not mind fools, cousin Cornwall; for if you do, you will end up hating the world. They are useful, too: for what is foolishness but the concatenation of things that do not belong together? And by the elimination of foolishness we find the right way."

"You have been very consistent, then, Your Majesty", said the Earl with the ghost of a smile. "For you have eliminated the fool."

Selvaggia, next to him, applauded. "You see, Father—you never know with these island people. He has got a sense of humor after all."

"And a sense of beauty, thank God", said the Earl with a slight bow to her.

"Our fool called me the 'Lord of Animals' ", went on the Emperor. "There is much to be said for such suzerainty. Few men attain the graceful beauty of a falcon, and none can fly—save Daedalus and his son. I must show you my elephant tomorrow, cousin Cornwall. It is a royal beast. The Sultan Al Kamil gave it to me, feeling certain that I had nothing equal to give him in exchange. But I got the better of him by presenting him with a white bear—you have heard of them, I suppose—they live in the uttermost North, where the sun shines for only a few months of the year. . . . "

"I thought Britain was the foggiest country", said the Earl drily.

"It isn't fog I'm speaking of, cousin Cornwall. There is another reason for it, as my learned men explained to me. Anyway, much to my surprise the whiteness of my bear did not strike my Saracen friends as particularly strange. I found out later that the bears of Kurdistan turn white, sometimes, when they are very old. But when *my* white bear would only eat fish—that did surprise them greatly. *Mash' Allah, mash' Allah,* they could not get over it. The Sultan himself raised both his hands to heaven and with them a diamond worth his own ransom. Ah, Al Kamil, my great friend . . . "

"Your friend?" asked the Earl. "Surely Your Majesty does not consider a poor benighted heathen a friend?"

"He is not that, cousin. He is rich beyond the measure of wealth given to Christian monarchs; he is a deeply learned man; and what, by the Koran, do you call a heathen? To me a heathen, and especially a benighted heathen, is he who blocks his mind to progress and ever-widening knowledge, who leads an unnatural life by abstaining from woman, who believes in magical incantations spoken over a little piece of unleavened bread and a sip of wine or a drop of oil, and who has to all your enquiry only the brain-laming formula: Credo!"

"Credo", said the Count of Hapsburg quietly, and the Earl nodded.

Frederick laughed harshly. "Differences of opinion need not upset us, cousins and friends. If you had seen as much as I have of the greed, the selfishness, and the pigheaded obstinacy of the priests in this country and of my much beloved friend Gregory the Ninth, first and foremost—I venture to say you would agree with me ... You wouldn't? But I forget—you are still in the Holy Father's good books, aren't you? You are not black sheep ... you haven't been excluded from the communion of saints. It has not taken me long to find out that in order to belong to that communion one must be a sheep. And I refuse to be a sheep. I prefer the lion's role." He drank, gave an appreciative look at the beautiful goblet in the form of a golden turret, and went on: "Even so I could not see why the Supreme Shepherd of the Christian God should have anything against me. I reminded him of the time when the lion would lie down with the lamb. It is supposed to be a very good time, in fact the best of all, for they call it paradise. But Pope Gregory would have none of it. What he wanted was sheep only. And there *I* would not comply. I have almost given up hope that he will ever see my point of view. Almost: not quite."

Hapsburg looked up quickly, a ray of hope on his ugly, intelligent face. There was nothing more terrible to him than the position of princes and rulers in a world of divided loyalties. Could it be that Frederick had come to his senses after all? But the expression on the Emperor's face was one he knew only too well. He drank deeply to conceal his disappointment. Perhaps the Holy Father was a little obstinate at times, but that was not the real source of the conflict. The real source of the conflict was that the papacy was a red rag to the bull Frederick, whatever the Pope did.

"I think we shall see him soften up after all" went on Frederick. "He's bound to find out that an excommunicated Emperor is bad business for his own enterprise—in the long run. There may be bad news for him soon."

"He won't give in", said Eccelino. "The only thing that really matters to him is Rome, and ... "

"And Rome, too, may not be as papal as he thinks",

interposed Frederick. "In fact, the news we have from Rome is most interesting in that respect."

"You are not thinking of attacking Rome, I hope", said Hapsburg, horrified.

"It may not be necessary, my pious friend."

Selvaggia leaned forward. "Perhaps all this sounds very strange to *you?*" she asked in a low voice.

Piers Rudde looked up. Surely the Emperor's daughter had not addressed *him,* the very least of all those allowed to sit at this table. But she was looking at him, her oblique eyes narrowed a little, a faintly mocking smile on her full, very red lips.

His thoughts had been chasing each other in circles. What a country was this, where Pope and Emperor were at war with each other! Now the Emperor, of course, though King of Sicily, was Lord and Master of the entire Roman Empire of the German nation, not only of Italy—and he was brother, brother-in-law, uncle, or nephew of almost all the monarchs alive in the Christian world—yet he himself boasted of not being a Christian at all, he derided all things Christian, wore a dress curiously mixed of oriental and occidental styles, swore by the Koran—the supreme Lord of the Christian World, of whom it was said that scarcely half a dozen men in the world could match his intelligence.

Piers thought of the Feast of the Assumption, when King Henry had sent the Earl, and Piers Rudde with him, to the chapel of Our Lady of Walsingham, to offer up three thousand tapers, delivered by the sheriffs of Norfolk and Suffolk, who also had to feed as many poor people as they could find, on the King's behalf.

He had never forgotten the sight of the shrine of Walsingham—somehow the picture of its quiet majesty came up in his mind whenever doubts assailed him, as sometimes they would when God seemed to tolerate things that not even the least of Christian knights would tolerate if he could alter it—as God surely could. It was comforting then to think of Walsingham, for so much beauty could be based only upon truth. But here . . .

Into these thoughts came the low-voiced, faintly mocking question of the Emperor's daughter; they drifted away like ghosts when their hour is up, and he heard himself say: "Yes, most noble lady—and I am not quite certain whether I am waking or dreaming."

"You are in the country of miracles", said Selvaggia slowly. "Everything is possible here, and the impossible most of all." Imps and pixies seemed to somersault in her eyes and in the corners of her mouth. Piers found himself blushing and felt furious with himself for it. She would take him for a boor, a lout, not accustomed to be talked to by a great lady. He pulled himself together.

"There seems only one thing to do, most noble lady—to be ready even for the impossible and meet it squarely."

"I think I like you", said Selvaggia, appraising him as if he were a rare specimen among her father's animals. "Perhaps I shall ask your liege to lend you to me for a while—I have a bodyguard of my own, you know; and their dress would suit you very well, with your fair hair. All the others are dark. Have some more of these peaches in muscatel—" The last words she spoke in a much louder voice. She pushed the dish a little nearer to him.

"Eat", said a low, urgent voice at his side. "Don't look up now, eat."

Mechanically he obeyed. He knew it was his new Italian friend who had spoken. But . . . "What is wrong?" he whispered back. "What have I done?"

"Holy Venus", muttered the Italian. "I did not know you wanted to die so young. 'What is wrong?' he asks. Did I not tell you she is going to marry Eccelino of Romano? You did not see his eyes just now, but your liege did, I believe. Sour grapes for you, friend, not peaches in muscatel. Now if you . . . " He broke off, because the Emperor was speaking again. It was not only the deference due to his sovereign that made him listen as he did. This man, Emperor, monster, hero—Lucifer, Augustus, and Justinian all in one person— was the most fascinating person the young poet had ever encountered; even though he knew this was exactly the impression Frederick wanted to make, on most people, it did not diminish its effect.

"No, no, Pallavicini", Frederick was saying. "I left my guards outside, in the village. They'll find more fun there with the wenches, and I don't need them here. *You* aren't going to kill me, are you? It would please old Gregory, no doubt, but I think you know me to be the better master of us two. But seriously—where could I be safer than surrounded by you, my friends? Besides there are Mouska and Marzoukh, my two little ebony beauties: they always sleep on my doorstep. They can deal with elephants and tigers, let alone with a human intruder."

"Is it true that their little daggers are poisoned, Father?"

Frederick smiled at her affectionately. "You mustn't be so curious, Selvaggia. How do the shorn heads put it?—'The first curiosity of the first woman brought down the world in ruins'; and when she first conceived, she gave birth to a murderer. But poison or no poison, guard or no guard, I shall not die tonight; that much is certain."

"Did your astrologer tell you that?" asked Eccelino with interest.

"No, it wasn't Bonatti—it was his predecessor, Michael Scotus—he came from your country, cousin Cornwall."

"Hardly", said the Earl, stiffly.

"From your island, then. But he was not only an astrologer. He had learned more than the wisdom of the stars in Toledo."

"Toledo . . . the citadel of the dark art . . . "

"The citadel of learning, you mean, Hapsburg. The occult is occult only to the unlearned—young souls, immature, not ripe yet for the real mysteries of the universe. Come, come, you cannot go on having that attitude—worthy of a village priest rather than a ruler. We must learn from people even when their religious beliefs do not coincide with our own. You may think little of the Koran, but mathematics and astronomy, algebra and the occult art of numbers are great enrichments. My faithful Leonardo Fibonacci of Pisa has introduced Arabic numerals on my request, and they are being taught now in many of my most modern schools. They include that wonderful little thing, so insignificant and yet so powerful . . . "

"Do you mean me, Brother Emperor?" asked Iocco, emerging from under the table.

"In a way I do, fool. I mean the zero—a thing of incalculable value to those who keep the accounts in my treasury. It is nothing by itself, but put it behind any other figure and it will increase its value tenfold—put two of them behind a figure and it will increase it a hundredfold. All calculation is simplified and clarified by it. Yet it is nothing. Truly a metaphysical value."

"That's it", said Iocco beaming. "That's what you will be remembered by, Brother Emperor, by all future generations. That is what will remain of your glory and your deeds, the apex of your achievements. Zero, zero, zero. Long live the Emperor Zero."

"I am sorry," said the Earl of Cornwall, "but when metaphysical elements are introduced into my accounts, I feel certain that I shall be cheated."

"Hopeless man," laughed Frederick, "in twenty years no one will use the old system anywhere, believe me. The new is built on the ten and not on the twelve. The decimal system, the innate system of man. Ten fingers, cousin Cornwall, ten toes."

"It will never be adopted in my country", said the Earl with an expression of finality. "This is a foreign thing."

"So is Christianity", laughed the Emperor. "It's a Jewish thing, if ever there was one. Yet you adopted it, and you still adhere to it."

"True enough, thank God", said the Earl drily. "My Greek has never been worth much, but as far as I can remember the word 'catholic' means universal . . . not foreign."

"It isn't universal", said Frederick contemptuously. "Go to Africa—go to Egypt and India and beyond and ask whether anybody has even so much as heard of it. In Egypt, yes—but those who have heard of it will spit when its name is mentioned. In India they will not even spit. That astonishing little man Francis of Assisi was one of the few who really tried to spread it—harangued the great Sultan himself; I could almost like him for it, if it weren't for his insufferable spiritual children, begging their way through life and generally being an infernal nuisance, just as much as the holy beggars of St. Dominic. But even Francis could not get very far. He preached a pretty sermon to be sure and finally launched an ultimatum at the Sultan: 'Become a Christian', he thundered, 'or have me burned at the stake.' Quite shrewd, as you see: either the Sultan would become Christian and Brother Francis have the triumph of his life—or he would burn little Francis at the stake, thereby making him a martyr—and he would have the triumph of his death. It was heads I win and tails you lose, as it invariably is with the Church. But the Sultan was wise. He saw the trap. He complimented little Francis on the fine speech he had made and sent him home safe and sound. One can learn a good deal from the Sultan."

"There I agree with you, Your Majesty", said Hapsburg. "He was a generous man and appreciated a man's greatness even if he disagreed with his views. Isn't it true that he gave orders that from then on to the end of time the Franciscan Order would be allowed to be guardians of the Holy Sepulcher?"

Frederick shrugged his shoulders. "We have heard too much of the Holy Land, Hapsburg, believe me. I was there. I rode into Jerusalem, and I crowned myself in the Church of the Holy Sepulcher."

"The world knows that", cried Eccelino. "And it made the Pope shiver in his shoes."

Hapsburg smiled thinly. He thought of the great Godefroy, the first Christian conqueror of Jerusalem, who had refused to wear even a small golden circlet in the church where his Redeemer's tomb was.

"The so-called Holy Land", said Frederick, "is scarcely worth the effort of so many good men. Jehovah can never have seen my Apulia, my Terra Laboris, my Sicily, or he wouldn't have made Palestine the center of his activity. He overrated it grossly."

Eccelino and Pallavicini crowed with delight, and so did many of the other nobles. Hapsburg and the Earl of Cornwall exchanged a helpless glance.

"If only Hermann von Salza had not died", thought Hapsburg. "The Emperor's good angel—the only one he listened to, at least sometimes, when he pleaded for peace." The death of the great man on that fateful Palm Sunday two years ago coincided with the terrible news of the Emperor's excommunication. The reasons given by the Pope were good enough; indeed, it was surprising that the lightning had not struck earlier. The Emperor had formed a Moslem colony in the very heart of Italy, at Lucera; fourteen thousand Saracens had been sent there, and the Emperor, who had never built a single church in his life, had had mosques built for them. Oppression of the Church and her clergy . . . priests executed, drowned, hanged. It was a long list. The Emperor's reply had been grim. He had hanged all blood relatives of the Pope he could get hold of: "I hate the whole breed—and are we not asked to fulfill the will of the One who hath said, I will visit the sins of the fathers upon their children?" He had destroyed Benevento this very year because it had adhered to the Pope. And everywhere the Eccelinos and Pallavicinis and many of the other great names began to follow his example. A new age of utter ferocity was ushered in. It was said that in a far away eastern country a new Attila had appeared, a khan of the Mongols, as dreadful as Genghis, Batu by name, whose horsemen slaughtered people by the tens of thousand. But then, he was a heathen, a barbarian like his Hunnish ancestor. True, Frederick, though baptized, was no Christian, as he himself would be the first to admit. But he was a knight and the Lord of Knights, the supreme sovereign of Europe. What was to become of Europe under such a ruler?

He was whispering to Caserta now. That ghastly smile again.

"Ah, to be back in Austria," Hapsburg thought, "far away from this court of vipers and adders, to breathe the clean air of the mountains again and the clean air of faith . . . "

"But Scotus", said Frederick, as Caserta slipped out of the room. "We quite forgot Michael Scotus and his prophecies. He knew from a vision or from some secret experiment of his own how he would die: a stone would fall on his head. So he always wore an iron cap. But when we were on our way to Germany, seven years ago, an avalanche of stones came down on the highway we were riding on, and one of them fell on poor Scotus' head, driving his iron cap deeply into his learned brain. *Anangke,* my friends, the goddess behind all gods—'Necessity' to you, cousin Cornwall, as you said that your Greek was not what it should be. So, as you see, I have good reasons to believe that my fate, too, will fulfill itself when the time comes. But it will not be here. It will not be now."

He rose. "I bid you good night, and pleasant dreams." They all rose and bowed deeply as he walked out of the room.

At once Iocco sat down on the imperial chair. "I bid you go on drinking merrily," he cried, "and may never a stone fall on your heads. As for me, I am sure I prefer my fool's cap to the iron one of Scotus."

But most of the nobles retired.

Piers, too, made his way out. He felt a strong urge to be alone for a while, to get his thoughts clear. Too many things had happened, too many things had been said—and this Emperor, despite his sacrilegious remarks, was . . . well, an incredible personality. It was said that men died for him with a smile on their lips, that they dared anything for a smile on his. One could well imagine it. There was something strange about his eyes: it was not only that they never smiled; they never blinked. They had a steady, sharp gaze . . . like an eagle's or falcon's. It would be good to be alone; it was necessary to be alone.

But first he must see that the Earl was well installed . . . and there he was, talking to the Count of Caserta.

Piers drew nearer.

" . . . you are a most observant man, my lord", replied Caserta. "Yes, the Emperor did give me an important order. There is no need for any special secrecy here, though, and even if there were, the order would be carried out before there could be any treachery. I must leave this very night with a hundred knights and two thousand men on foot, to destroy a stronghold my gracious Emperor wants out of the way once and for all. 'Caserta,' he said to me, 'raze that thing to the ground so that it will never rise again.' It is a monastery, of course."

"Again a monastery", said the Earl.

"Yes—a good many of the Pope's spies are said to have fled there. And the Abbot has been not too loyal, either. Besides, the Emperor thinks that the monks of this house here may be on their way to the other place, and it seems he wants to keep them on the run a little."

"What is the name of—that other place? The place that will never rise again."

"Monte Cassino, my lord."

"Ah, there you are, Piers", said the Earl. "My Lord of Caserta, this is Sir Piers Rudde, a young knight of mine and a promising one. He can do with a little more battle experience. Will you allow him to accompany you on your expedition?"

He had taken Piers by the arm when he introduced him. But his grip was so strong that the young Englishman knew he was not supposed to say anything. There would have been no need for that. Piers was far too perplexed to speak.

Caserta gave the young knight a searching look. "Certainly, my lord, if it pleases you. But we may have to be away for some time . . . "

"That's all right, my lord. I have men enough to dispense with him for the present. It means a reinforcement in quality rather than in quantity—he has only one varlet with him."

"There are enough of us for the shorn heads of Cassino", laughed Caserta. Then, to Piers: "Be ready in half an hour, at the main gate. I shall meet you there."

"Very well, my lord", said Piers mechanically, and Caserta nodded, bowed to the Earl, and strode off.

"Quiet, Piers", murmured the Earl. "Let him get out of sight first. Now then . . . we must be careful; everybody is spying on everyone else here. I've done this in your own interest, my boy. The young Princess has been . . . a little forward, and I fear he didn't like it."

"Eccelino?"

"I don't care what Eccelino likes or dislikes. No. The Emperor. He won't take it out on her. He needs her to assure himself of the loyalty of that man Eccelino. But he doesn't need you. Therefore something might happen to you, an accident, you know. They would make a very fine speech to me about it afterwards, but that wouldn't make you alive again. So I think it's best if you disappear. I'm not angry with you, my boy, I know perfectly well you haven't done anything wrong. But there was just a trifle too much interest in you on the part of . . . that lady. So off you go, and take your time; I won't expect you back too quickly. The . . . expedition may be over soon. Travel about a little. You are young—you may learn a good deal, though I doubt whether it will be much good to you. The only thing that matters is that you keep out of the Emperor's way. Have any money?"

"Not too much, my liege."

"Take this; it will cover a few months. I shall be back in England by then. You may join me there any time you like. There is no hurry. I'm sorry about this. Also, it's not the kind of an expedition an English knight can get battle experience from. But it can't be helped. God bless you, my dear boy."

"Thank you, my liege . . . thank you for everything."

The Earl gave him his hand, and Piers kissed it. Then they parted, and Piers made his way to the stable to look for his varlet and his horse. Suddenly a slim shadow appeared behind him. Hurrying steps. He turned round quickly, his fingers closing round the hilt of his dagger.

"Don't kill *me,* friend", said the young Italian poet. "It is certainly not I who means you harm. May I have a word with you? I know you are in a hurry, but it won't take long. You are leaving, aren't you? On . . . on that expedition against Monte Cassino?"

"Things get around very quickly here, it seems", said Piers cautiously.

The Italian laughed. "Caserta has a voice like a trumpet. Even the horses know it by now. Look, friend, you could do me a very great favor. You see, I have a brother at Monte Cassino . . . he's only a boy, no more than fifteen. My youngest brother. He's been a Benedictine oblate ever since he was five. When you take the place . . . will you keep an eye on him and see that he doesn't get hurt?"

"Most certainly I will, if I can", said Piers warmly. "But how shall I recognize him?"

The young poet laughed again. "You can't miss him. He is a very fat boy, surely the fattest of the lot. Ah, but you don't know his name, of course. I haven't introduced myself. I am Count Rainald of Aquino, and my little brother's name is Thomas . . . Thomas of Aquino."

Chapter II

DOWN WITH THE TOWER", roared Caserta. "Stop messing about with the cattle, you filth; let them burn. I'll see that you get your belly full later on. All men to the tower . . . ram it, men, ram it, you vermin, or I'll have your ears cut off. . . . Ears off of everybody who's deaf to my command. Ram it, I say . . . yes, that's better: Down with it."

But the tower resisted. All that was wood was burning lustily; some of the bold, high-vaulted arches had tumbled down; thick black smoke filled the countless stairways, but the tower and some of the main buildings resisted.

"They've built too well, the damned shorn heads. I ought to tell the Emperor that he should use them to build his fortresses for him—instead of mumbling prayers all day long."

Piers, on his horse beside the Count, did not reply. He had seen burning castles before, and fighting was a knight's work, whether in peaceful jousting or in war.

But much as it looked like a castle, Monte Cassino was not the stronghold of a baron or duke. The garrison did not fight back. There were no volleys of arrows, no hail of stones, no burning pitch poured on the invaders. It was a one-sided war, and a one-sided war was not war at all.

He had seen some of the monks fleeing, some killed by falling masonry or suffocating in the quickly spreading flames. But none of them had been fighting back. The Earl was right: it wasn't the sort of expedition from which an English knight could gain battle experience.

Caserta gave him a quick look and laughed. "I didn't like it much either, at first", he said almost good-naturedly. "But it's no good having two masters in the same house, and we can sell ourselves only once. Besides, the Emperor is right: we cannot tolerate that the Pope's spies have such a convenient place of assembly. You'll get accustomed to it just as I have."

"By your leave, Sir Count," said Piers in a hard voice, "I'd like to have a closer look at . . . all this." He dismounted, clumsy in his armor.

"I'd wait a little, if I were you", advised Caserta. "It's hellish hot in there just now. Unless you feel an urge for roast monk's flesh . . . "

"Have I your leave, Sir Count?"

Caserta shrugged his shoulders. "As you wish. But don't blame me for your blisters, young devil."

Piers threw the reins of his horse to his man and began to stalk toward the monastery.

Robin, his man, had caught the reins adroitly. "May I not come with you, sir?"

"Stay where you are", was the sharp answer.

Robin growled something under his beard. Always head on into things, the young master. And this was an unhealthy place, as anybody could see, and an unholy business, too. But then what else could one expect from those foreigners. It was a beautiful country, no doubt, but what good was that, when it was swarming with people who couldn't speak English or Norman—not even Gaelic.

Burning down monasteries was poor sport, and one shouldn't be mixed up with it. Just as well Lady Elfleda had not lived to see it or hear of it, bless her soul; *she* wouldn't have liked to see her only son mixed up in such business, and she would have held him, Robin, responsible for it, too, she would. She'd made that clear enough, when the news came that young Sir Piers was joining the retinue of the King's own brother to accompany him into foreign lands. "Robin," she had said, "you are going with my son, and I make you responsible. You've been my good servant many a year, and you know your place and what you can do and what you can't. You will look after him. He's your master, but he's very young. He is very young, but he's your master. You will know what to do. You're responsible.

That is all." That she had said and not a word more, and he had said, "Yes, gracious lady", and that was all, too. Perhaps it had broken her grand old heart that the young master was leaving for what might well be a very long time—she'd died three weeks before he left, God rest her. So far the old lady had had no reason to look down angrily on Robin Cherrywoode from her place in heaven—she'd be there sure enough by now, as gracious a lady as ever fed and clothed the poor, and having an ear for the least of her servants. He had been looking after the young master all right; there were ways and means how a good man could see to it that the master was kept out of harm's way without forgetting his place, hurting the master's pride, or lying to him too often.

"Stay where you are", he had said. So one had to stay at least until he was out of sight, and that was right now.

Robin dismounted. "Hey, you . . . hold these for me a while, will you?"

The soldier he had addressed looked up to his height of six foot three, with a pair of shoulders to match; he swallowed the curse already on his tongue, put down his crossbow, and took the reins of the two horses.

Robin gave him a friendly nod. "Look after them, little man. They're worth more than you are." And he made his way to where his master had disappeared.

* * *

Piers, meanwhile, had reached the main building. A few times he was forced to take cover to avoid being hit by falling stones. He could still hear the crashing noise of the battering ram; they had not given up their attempts to get that tower down.

Where on earth could that boy be? It was a hopeless task to find anybody in this enormous building . . . especially as he was likely to be doing his very best not to be found. If he was still here at all . . . for some of the monks seemed to have fled before the attack started. Caserta had mentioned that and also that he was going to let the dogs loose on them: "Anyone who flees when the Emperor's men come must have a bad conscience and is likely one of those spies." As if anyone in his senses, spy or otherwise, would not try to avoid meeting Caserta's men.

Impossible to go on here . . . the refectory was a blazing furnace. The stairway to the upper floor was burning, too. What was this? A monk, an old man . . . dead. Suffocated, God rest his soul. He crossed himself. It was a great thing, a very great thing to be the Emperor, but it was healthier to be Sir Piers Rudde, of all good English knights one of the poorest and least.

"I wonder whether he's got a conscience", he thought. "I wonder how he sleeps at night. Here's another one . . . dead, too. I'd better get out of here, or there'll be three in a short while. Piers, my son, that comes from giving promises to strangers." He turned round. There were no less than four different corridors behind him. This house was a labyrinth. Which way had he come? Holy Mother of God, how hot it was. It was the confounded armor, of course . . . a little more of this and it would get red hot, and he would be roasted in it like St. Lawrence. "Help me out of this, St. Lawrence—you know how it hurts." Ah, there was a stairway from which a breath of cool air came up. . . . "Thanks, St. Lawrence, if it was you . . . it's going downward, is it? Down or up, breathing is what matters most. . . . "

He descended the stairs. Yes, it was a little cooler here. And he wasn't shirking his duty either . . . if the boy was hiding anywhere in the building, he would be where it was safe from the fire.

Voices. Decidedly voices. They were coming from somewhere still deeper down. This staircase did not seem to have an end at all. But there was also a voice behind him, and it was calling his name.

"Sir Piers . . . Sir Piers . . . are you there? Are you there?"

Robin. He might have known that the fellow would come fluttering after him like a hen looking for its chick.

"Yes, here I am, Robin."

Tramp, tramp, tramp. There he was, black as a devil from the smoke and with part of his jerkin singed away.

"I think I told you to stay where you were", said Piers, frowning.

"So you did, master, so you did, but the horses are quite safe and this building isn't, and so I thought . . . "

"Shut your mouth now . . . I thought I heard voices down there."

They listened. But all was quiet.

"I'm sure I heard voices", said Piers. "And I've got to find that boy, if it's the last thing I do."

Robin gave him a doubtful look. "It easily might be, master", he said, scratching his head.

"Well, no one asked you to come along. Hey . . . is anybody here?"

There was no answer.

"They must think that we belong to the rabble upstairs", said Robin. "So they won't answer, of course."

Piers gulped. It was insolence to call the Emperor's troops "rabble". But it was the truth, too. It was difficult enough to convince the fellow that something foreign was not for that reason worthless, and Caserta's men were only too apt to fortify his belief.

"Come on, Robin, we must get farther down. This stair must have an end somewhere."

He began to descend again. It was pitch dark here; even the glow of the fire could not get through any more. Dark and slippery.

"Careful now."

"I can see a light, master."

"Can you? I can't. Yes, there it is. Quiet now and softly on those big feet of yours."

Again they descended.

"It's coming from over there, master", whispered Robin. "There must be a door there; it's coming from under it. Your sword, master . . . better be ready, just in case. . . . "

"Quiet".

Robin shook his head. Either these men down there were frightened to death . . . and when a man is in that state he can go fighting mad any moment . . . or this was the place where they kept what mattered most to them, and for that any man will fight. He had taken his master's shield with him. Now he drew a long, serviceable dagger.

Piers did not see it. He was cautiously approaching the door from under which the light was coming. Suddenly he threw himself against it, and it gave so easily that he almost fell into the room. But he had regained his equilibrium even before Robin swung the shield in front of him.

It was a small room, bare of all furniture. An old monk was sitting on the floor, leaning against the wall, his head in a blood-stained bandage. About a dozen or more monks of all ages were standing to his right and left. In the light of an old oil lamp, hanging from the ceiling, Piers could see that their faces were white and drawn. But no one said a word. A long pause followed. For Piers, too, was completely at a loss what to say. In the end it was the wounded old man who spoke first.

"If your orders are to kill, Sir Knight . . . I am the one you are looking for. Therefore let these go their way."

Piers shivered. He felt that he had heard these words before, but where? Suddenly he remembered: the Gospel- . . . the Gospel for Good Friday, read by Father Thorney, the old chaplain of his mother's castle: Christ's words, when they came to arrest him in Gethsemane. When Piers heard them for the first time, he had been blind with rage that the Apostles had not defended him better . . . just one stroke of the sword, and that only cutting off a miserable ear. Now if his father had been there or he himself in a few years' time, or better still, his father *and* he . . . they would never have succeeded in arresting him. He had mentioned that in no uncertain terms to the old chaplain later, at breakfast, and Father Thorney had gently stroked his head: "Don't you know that Our Lord *had* to be crucified, so that you and I and all of us will find the gates of heaven open when the hour comes for us?" He had pondered over that for a long time and then hung his head. There seemed no way out. Still, they might have defended him a *little* better, at least.

And now he was supposed to be one of those who arrested, who killed, one who represented Christ at the altar every day. The terrible words were used against him, Piers Rudde. . . .

He blurted out: "I have no orders to kill. I . . . I don't approve of all this. I . . . I'm English."

"I can hear that," said the old monk with a very faint smile. "It is a long time since I was in your country . . . almost half a century ago. They were just starting rebuilding the beautiful cathedral of Canterbury."

"It is growing," said Piers, "but they have not begun the nave yet."

"It takes a long time to build", said the old monk sadly, "and a very short time to destroy. St. Benedict founded this house . . . the Venerable Bede knew it and St. Anselm and St. Bernard . . . and look what happens to it now." He stiffled a groan and bit his lip. Clearly he was in great physical pain.

"You should not speak at all, Father Abbot", murmured one of the monks anxiously.

The Abbot . . . of course, he was wearing the pectoral cross. The Lord Abbot of Monte Cassino, one of the oldest and most famous monasteries in Christendom. "I am the one you are looking for. Therefore let these go their way."

The entire body of the old man stiffened as he fought the pain and his breath came heavily. "It . . . is all right, my dear Brother . . . He doesn't want me as yet . . . it seems." Then to Piers: "What are you doing here, my son? You said you do not approve."

"I am looking for a young boy, my Lord Abbot: his brother, Count Rainald of Aquino, has asked me to look after him and see that he does not get hurt."

The monks looked at each other.

"If I give him into your care," said the Abbot slowly, "will you get him home safely? The castle of his family is not far away."

"I will get him home safely, my Lord Abbot."

"Here he is", said the old monk. "Come to me, Thomas."

The sturdy, thick-set boy had been in the background, just one more pale face and black habit. Now he approached the Abbot and knelt down at his side.

"Thomas, my son, this has put an end to studies . . . though nothing but death itself can put an end to prayer. I want you to go home and stay at your good mother's house for a while."

The boy bowed his head in silence.

The old monk smiled at him. "I don't know if or when we shall meet again in this world, my son; there is one thing I want you to remember. Your first question, when you came here, five years old, was: 'What is God?' You asked it so eagerly, again and again. Perhaps it is the wish of Our Father in heaven that you should find the answer to that question in such a way that it may be understood by many. Fare well now. *Benedicat te omnipotens Deus, Pater, et Filius et Spiritus Sanctus. Divinum auxilium maneat semper tecum. Amen.*"

The boy's shoulders were heaving as the hand of the Abbot made the sign of the cross over him.

A heavy crash broke the solemn silence, and a gust of hot wind filled the room. The monks stiffened.

Piers turned round, not entirely free of superstitious fear.

"Not so good, master", said Robin calmly. "Part of the upper building has fallen . . . can you hear? There are still stones rolling down our staircase."

"Which means . . . "

"I don't know whether we shall get out of here, master; but if we do, it won't be the way we came."

"Have a look, Robin. It may not be as bad as you think."

The varlet obeyed. But he had made no more than a step outside when he jumped back. A dull, rolling noise, and another, and a third, all ending in a short, resounding crash.

"Stay here, Robin. You seem to be right."

The voice of the Abbot said: "Sir Knight . . . I will show you a way out."

Looking up, Piers saw that a narrow door was slowly opening at the back of the room. It was sliding aside. A secret way out, obviously.

"We may have to use the same way, as soon as I can walk again", said the old man. "You will come out behind the south wall; it is a leafy part of the garden, and you are not likely to be seen."

Somehow Piers could not resist asking: "Are you not afraid that I might give you away to those outside?"

"Fear is a bad adviser, son. You must do as your will and your conscience tell you. Go now. We shall pray for you."

The boy Thomas kissed the old man's hand, rose, and walked quietly through the secret entrance. Piers bowed to the Abbot and followed the boy into a dark corridor, whose stone-paved floor soon began to lead upward fairly steeply. "Are you there, Robin?"

"Yes, master. Can you still see the boy in front of you?"

"No."

Robin muttered under his breath. The old man had looked honest enough, but you could never be sure with these outlandish people, and if this were a trap that boy would disappear and they would fall into a moat or a dungeon.

For a long time they groped their way higher and higher in complete darkness; it was not easy for a fully armored man, and from time to time Piers had to rest for a minute or two. At long last the darkness changed into a shadowy grey . . . light was coming from somewhere. Suddenly the narrow corridor took a turn sharply to the right, and, with a breath of relief, Piers saw the foliage of a tree, no, of bushes, oleander and laurel, and there was air, fresh air, though tinged with a burning smell.

And here was the boy, too, and he seemed to have taken cover . . . no, he was on his knees, praying. Poor child . . . this was a nasty experience for one so young and an experience he was not likely to be prepared for in the quiet, sheltered life of a monastery.

Piers walked up to him. At a distance he could see the pall of smoke hanging over the gigantic building from which he had emerged; there were a detachment of cross-bow men on the crest of a hillock and another marching in the direction of a village . . . he could see the flat roofs of the houses. Of course . . . the expedition was not against the monastery only. Monte Cassino was a little realm by itself, of which the monastery was only the citadel.

The boy was still praying; he did not seem to notice Piers' presence at all. His poet brother was right: he was a fat sort of a boy; "plump" was perhaps the better word, pale faced with a circlet of glossy, dark brown hair round his carefully shorn head. A little monk, even if he had not yet reached the age to take the three vows. There was some sort of vow the parents must have made in his name when they took him to Monte Cassino first, but that was not the final thing. Why had they done this to him? Surely it was cruel to condemn a child to a life of austerity, of "poverty, chastity, and obedience" at a time when he could not possibly know his own mind. He could get out of it later if he wanted, but would he know then what he wanted, if he had not known anything but a cloistered life? Perhaps this involuntary return to his family, to life outside, would be a very good thing for him. How old was he? Fifteen, sixteen at the utmost. Why, so far he had never even consciously seen a woman's face. What did he know of the pleasures of hunting, of tossing up an Icelandic falcon and seeing him disappear in the blue air of the morning, of the happy revelry of good companions and of the overwhelming feeling of strength and power that fills a man when he rides, visor down and lance set straight, against the enemy. All he knew were praying and fasting and reading old books. This happening, terrible as it was, might save him for a life of knightly joy.

He touched the boy's shoulder. "You've done enough praying. Come along now, my boy."

Thomas did not seem to have heard or felt anything. His eyes were closed; he looked as if he were asleep.

Piers shook him a little. "Hey . . . what's the matter with you?"

The boy opened his eyes and made the sign of the cross, with a large, sweeping gesture. Only then he looked at Piers, stood up, and said with a surprisingly graceful little nod: "At your service, sir."

"Come along, then; let's get away from all this."

They had to walk for almost a quarter of an hour before they reached the place where Robin had left the horses. Piers saw with a slight frown that Caserta was still there, too, giving orders right and left to his officers.

They had got the tower down after all, and the main building was still burning.

Now Caserta had seen him coming. "Holy Mohammed . . . so you're still alive. I'd made a fine speech already in my mind to milord of Cornwall. Where have you been? I'm sick of this damned place. The shorn heads don't resist, but I lost at least a dozen men when the tower came down, and a good many more have burns; the leeches are working away with a will. What have you got there, a prisoner?"

"In a way, my lord. He's the brother of Count Rainald of Aquino, who asked me to look for him. He's only a child. I'll take him home to his mother."

"That can't be much fun. Better wait a little . . . we'll soon be through with this, and there are a few villages around here, where the wenches grow as luscious as anywhere in Italy or Sicily."

Piers shook his head. "Duty first, my lord. Can I have a mule for the boy?"

Caserta laughed. "Well, if you'd rather do a nursemaid's work than a man's, I won't stop you. A mule for the shorn child, somebody! I wish you had caught the Abbot instead of this brat. You didn't come across him on your errand, did you?"

"I was only looking for the boy", said Piers coolly and Robin behind him began to chew one end of his thick yellow moustache. The master was still young, very young, but he was learning fast. This wasn't so bad.

"What about you, little monk?" asked Caserta. "Where is this abbot of yours? Come on, speak up; you needn't be afraid. Where is he?"

"He is in the hands of God", said the boy.

"Dead, you mean, eh? I wonder, are you a sly fox or just an innocent?"

"I am an oblate of St. Benedict", said the boy without either pride or modesty.

Again Caserta laughed. "Take your nurseling home, Sir Knight. I have work to do."

Robin had retrieved the horses, and someone had brought a mule along.

"Help this boy to mount, Robin."

But only when he had made his master in his heavy armor quite secure in the saddle did the giant varlet turn to the boy . . . to find him already on the back of his mule. Now he mounted his own horse. It was a huge, strong-boned animal, and it had to be, for it carried, besides a heavy man, all the luggage, which meant practically everything Sir Piers Rudde had taken with him from home. It was not much, but it was enough for a horse already laden with Robin Cherrywoode.

"Do you know the way, my boy?" asked Piers.

"Yes, Sir Knight. My mother is now in Rocca Secca, not in Aquino."

"Does that belong to your family, too?"

"Oh, yes."

"And your mother prefers Rocca Secca in winter?"

"Rocca Secca or the Castello San Giovanni."

Three castles. The Aquinos seemed to be a wealthy little dynasty. The boy's answers had been immediate and polite, but one could feel that they were given mechanically and that his thoughts were still at Monte Cassino. One could see it, too. There were shadows in the corners of the young mouth and around his eyes.

"That was a good answer you gave to the Count of Caserta when he asked you about your abbot."

"It was true", said the boy gravely. "So was yours." Suddenly he turned his face full toward Piers—it was lit up by a smile—warm and round like the sun; joy for all that is good was in it and the sparkle of intelligence; and it conferred an honorable accompliceship.

Much to his own surprise Piers found himself blushing and laughing as if he had been complimented by a very lovely woman or a man far superior to him in rank. Yet there was nothing either girlish or in the least superior about the boy. He was a nice, plump boy, that was all. They were riding through the loveliest country Piers had ever seen in his life. Orange and lemon trees, oleander and laurel and flowers of a richness that made the eye dizzy. Almost one could understand the boast of the Emperor. This was the nearest thing to paradise a man could imagine. One shouldn't wear armor in a country like this; one shouldn't carry arms. But . . . should one shut oneself up in a monastery?

"It is a beautiful world", he said. "You should be glad to come back to it for a while."

"I am," said the boy, "as it is God's will."

Piers thought of the words of the Abbot. He cleared his throat. "Do you think you are going to find the answer to your question: 'What is God?'" But even while he was speaking he thought that he might well get the same answer as before: "I will if it is God's will."

The boy smiled at him again, almost as if he knew that the question was already answered in the enquirer's mind.

Piers raised his chin a little. "It doesn't make much sense sometimes, does it?" he said, and his voice sounded a trifle impatient. "A good God, a perfect God . . . and what we have seen today."

The boy frowned. After some hesitation he said: "If your teacher draws a mathematical formula and you do not understand it, would you say that it does not make sense?"

"I don't know anything about mathematical formulas", said Piers honestly. "But I suppose I would ask him for an explanation."

"Then why don't you ask God?" asked the boy, obviously surprised. "Perhaps he will explain it to you. Of course, it may be that you will not understand the explanation either. Would you for that reason accuse him of not knowing what he means?"

"But you can't ask God questions", said Piers with a shrug.

"Course you can", replied the astonishing boy. "In prayer. But it matters a great deal that it should be the right question. The first question a man asked God was Cain's: 'Am I my brother's keeper?' At least," he added quickly, "it was the first question we know of. Job asked questions, and all the prophets and the Apostles and Our Lady. But we must be careful not to ask as the Pharisees did", he concluded with ecclesiastical dignity.

Piers was amused. "And did you ask questions?"

"Oh, yes. Often."

"And God answered?"

"The right question he is certain to answer."

"How can you be so certain about what God will do in such a case?"

The boy rubbed his round chin. "Do we agree that all that is good comes from God?"

"Yes, I think we agree there", said Piers after a short hesitation.

"Well," said Thomas, "if you ask an intelligent question, humbly and modestly, is that a good thing? If you ask it in the service of God?"

"Well, yes, I suppose it is."

"Then such a question must come from God as the source of all good things. Therefore he himself has raised the question in us. Why would he not answer a question he himself wanted us to ask?"

Piers' eyes widened. He opened his mouth and shut it again. From somewhere behind came a long, low whistle. Turning in the saddle, Piers saw on Robin's face an expression of bland innocence. He turned back again.

"They do seem to teach you dialectics in a monastery", he said a little hoarsely.

"It is part of the curriculum", admitted the boy, beaming with delight.

Piers cleared his throat again. He was thinking hard, so hard that he began to perspire profusely. One couldn't let that little fellow get away just like that. And suddenly he had it. He was so pleased that he could not help grinning.

"I'm afraid your theory's got a hole", he said. "Didn't your Abbot mention that you always asked, 'What is God?' And from the way he went on I gather that he hoped you would find the answer some time. In other words, you haven't found it yet. God has not answered your question. Yet it was a good question, and I'm sure you asked it humbly and modestly. What have you to say to that one?"

He breathed heavily. This thinking sport was as strenuous as jousting. But he had the little devil now.

The little devil had listened very politely. Now he said: "I was a very small child when I first asked that question. . . . God has been answering it ever since. Some of the answers I learned at school: that he is HE WHO IS and that he is Three and yet One from the beginning of time and what he said about himself when he was on earth. He answers also in trees and flowers and clouds and all such things because they are beautiful. But the best answer I got when I first went to Holy Communion."

Piers did not speak. Nor did Robin whistle this time.

After a while the boy said cheerfully: "He is still answering me by making my head grow! You see, Father Abbot didn't mean that he hadn't answered me so far. What he meant was, he hoped I'd get less stupid and then could understand his answers better."

"I see", said Piers. He began to rub the chain mail of his left arm. His armor had become dull and very dirty; Robin would have much cleaning to do. "You're a monk, all right", he said as calmly as he could. "Are there many like you in Monte Cassino?"

"There are seventeen oblates at present", was the naïve answer.

Then the boy's face lit up again with that incredible smile of his, and he said: "It is very good of you to make me talk so much."

"Not at all, not at all", said Piers, bewildered. And it was bewildering, at first, to be transformed from a miserably defeated dialectician to a warm-hearted adult who had simply condescended to make a young boy talk so as to make him forget what he had gone through. Then he began to enjoy the transformation. After all, he *had* made the boy talk. Another man might not have bothered. Or he would have told him unseemly stories. Whereas he had given the boy the opportunity to talk about the subject he apparently liked best. Perhaps that was what made a man become a monk: that he liked best to think and talk about God.

He eased up a little in the saddle. It was not such a bad world, really. He felt good for no apparent reason. This young Aquino was a nice little fellow. He chuckled.

"Hey, Robin! What do you think about our little theologian here?"

Robin Cherrywoode raised his bushy yellow eyebrows.

"He'll end up as an archbishop if he's not careful."

The boy's face reddened.

"I mean it, young sir", said Robin good-naturedly. "No joking."

Thomas shook his head vigorously.

"What's wrong with that?" enquired Piers, smiling. "Don't you want to be an archbishop?"

"Oh no . . . no . . . never."

There was much relief in being able to be amused.

"And why not, my boy?"

"Archbishops have so much other work to do they have no time to *think.*"

"You'll change your mind about that one day", assured Piers. To his surprise Robin appeared at his side and handed him his shield. Mechanically he took it, his eyes already searching the horizon. Something shimmery came up from the laurel groves on the right. Horsemen, armored, and riding very quickly. Five, ten . . . twenty, and more. He gripped his lance. They could not belong to Caserta's men; they came from the opposite direction. Succor for Monte Cassino? They weren't numerous enough for that.

He could hear them now.

"Get behind me, my boy."

Thomas looked up. "They are men from Aquino, Sir Knight. I can see the flag." But obediently he rode behind Piers. "My brother Landulph is leading them", he added after a while.

Piers whirled his lance round and stuck it, point downward, into the soil. He heard the leader of the troop bark a command. In the next moment they were surrounded.

"So there you are, brother monk", said Count Landulph cheerfully. He was a powerfully built young man of about twenty-five, all crude strength and cunning. "Has the Emperor smoked you out? Serves you right, bookworm. We saw the smoke, you know, and Mother got worried, so we decided to have a look, I this way, and Mother is on the other side. Hey, Tonio . . . ride over to the Countess and tell her we've got him, safe and sound; she need cry no more. Off with you. With whom have I the honor, Sir Knight?"

"I am Sir Piers Rudde of the retinue of His Lordship the Earl of Cornwall", said Piers. "Your brother, Count Rainald, asked me to look after your younger brother here when he heard that I had joined the Count of Caserta's men."

Landulph exploded with laughter. "Rainald, too! The entire family is out to save you, brother monk. Are you worth it? Your servant, Sir Knight. But I wonder what made you join Caserta—personally, I'd rather fight half a dozen yokels with pitchforks single-handed than go to war with that filthy hound, begging your pardon if you should be a friend of his. Good of you to look after the child. Will it please you to honor us at Rocca Secca? My mother would never forgive me if I'd let you go, so have pity on me. It is only half an hour's ride now."

Piers accepted politely, and the cavalcade began to move. Little Thomas had not said a single word since the arrival of Count Landulph, but then there had not been an opportunity. How different the three brothers were from each other: the warrior, the poet, and the monk. Landulph was riding at his side, talking all the time. "If Caserta is in charge, it isn't likely that much will remain standing in Monte Cassino. I don't like what he does, but I must admit he does it whole-heartedly."

"I suppose he must obey the Emperor", said Piers vaguely.

"Ah, certainly, we all do. I hope you did not misunderstand my words: if the Emperor wants Monte Cassino destroyed, well and good. I am a simple man; I do not question the actions of the most brilliant man of our time. Had he commanded me to burn down Cassino, I would have done it just the same as Caserta. It isn't the first time it happened. Eleven years ago my own father was ordered to do it, and he obeyed, too, of course. He had scruples, though, poor old father." Landulph raised his powerful shoulders and grinned. "He couldn't sleep well afterward. That's why he offered little Thomas to the Order, as soon as they started building again." Now he laughed outright. "Old men have strange ideas sometimes. But little Thomas seemed to like the idea. I suppose he hasn't said a single word all the way so far, has he?"

"On the contrary; we had a lively discussion."

Landulph gave him a surprised look. "God's wounds: Are you serious? He hardly ever talks at all. What's come over him, I wonder? Mother often said: 'They don't need to make a monk of him. He's one already. A born monk.' I'm afraid she's right. She often is. Well, I don't mind. Why should I? They'll build the old rubble up again; you can be sure of that. And in ten years' time Mother will ask the Pope to make him lord abbot. It's not a bad position. Father had that in mind for him from the start, of course."

"Lord abbot", repeated Piers. And with a little smile: "Has a lord abbot time to think?"

"To think?" Landulph's eyes widened. "What's that to do with it? How do I know? Ah, there we are . . . there's the castle."

Piers gave it a long, searching look. Double walls. The turrets well built and modern. A single way up between steep rocks. Easy to defend even against tenfold superiority in numbers and big enough for a garrison of three hundred, perhaps more. Rocca Secca was the castle of a ruler, not of a simple knight. Foregay, his own place, was a molehill in comparison.

At their approach a wicket was opened and the drawbridge fell.

About fifty men with pikes and crossbows gave the salute to the young master returning. Another fifty were standing in readiness on the second wall. They didn't take any chances at Rocca Secca, it seemed.

"Welcome home, Sir Piers", said Count Landulph good-naturedly. "Niccolo . . . lead our guests to the green room, prepare a bath, and have a set of clothes put out for him as befits his rank. Will it please you to meet us in the hall in half an hour's time, Sir Piers? With your permission, I take my leave now."

* * *

The bathtub was of well-polished copper; the Emperor himself would not have a better one, and the two buxom maids who scrubbed him, put hot and cold compresses on his face, and massaged his feet, legs, and arms had the natural, self-effacing manner good bathmaids must have. It was wonderful to relax and to leave everything to Niccolo, a grey-haired Sicilian with the graceful movements of a cat. Robin and the horses were well looked after, that was certain. And Niccolo brought a beautiful tunic of French camelot—silk and wool interwoven—and an overtunic, sleeveless, of dark blue *tiretaine:* Niccolo arranged his hair, combed it, perfumed it; Niccolo brought a goblet full of red Sicilian wine of the kind that would make a dead man jump on his feet again. In less than half an hour Piers was a changed man. Rid of his heavy armor, clean, and most elegantly dressed, he sauntered down the staircase to the large shadowy hall to meet his host.

There was only one solitary figure in sight in the hall . . . the figure of a girl in a long, honey-colored robe. She stood with her back to him at one of the windows leading to the courtyard, and she was saying with a little laugh: "Well, Landulph, where is your guest? Marotta and Adelasia are looking after little Tommaso—two are enough for him. I am most curious about whom you've brought in, Landulph. . . . Is he very old and ugly?"

Had he been five years older, perhaps Piers would have been amused. As it was, he did not know what to do; the weight of his silence made her turn round, and thus it happened that he first saw her face as a small ivory oval surrounded by glossy dark brown curls; he was not aware, and would not be for some time, of the black eyes, whose fire gave them the luster of the darkest wine; the proud, small nose with its sensitive nostrils; the mouth perfect for love and hatred, joy and contempt; the little round chin; the exquisite texture of the skin, yet innocent of powder and makeup.

He stood and gaped. He heard her speak, but not a word of what she said came to his understanding. Never, to the very end of his life, was he able to say what her first words to him had been.

Not until he grasped the one word "mute" did the spell diminish sufficiently to enable him to bow, his face all scarlet, and he said in a curiously hoarse voice: "I crave your pardon, noble lady. If I were a better Christian than I am, I would be grieved for every mother's son who is not blessed as I am by meeting you."

It was a compliment permissible in an age adoring beauty, and she said with a graceful nod: "You do not speak badly . . . for a mute." Then she laughed. "You are an Englishman, Sir Knight, are you not? They say that you are most reticent in your country to acknowledge the very existence of anything that is not grave and serious. Would I have to be grave and serious in your country, Sir Knight?"

"Yes, noble lady," said Piers, "unless you should wish to have the entire country at your feet by smiling as you do now."

Again that graceful nod of appreciation. But her tone and expression were different as she said: "I know you have been most kind to my little brother Tommaso. It is his mother's privilege to thank you for it, but I would like you to know that you have won his sister's gratitude as well."

Something like an invisible barrier came up between them . . . a barrier that only the surprise of the first moments could neglect. The barrier of rank. There were at least eighty knights of the rank of Sir Piers Rudde at the beck and call of the rulers of Aquino.

"I did nothing at all", said Piers with a polite bow.

He had to repeat these words a few minutes later, when the Countess had returned to the castle with no less than a hundred men on horseback. She was a tall, gaunt woman of forty-five and still beautiful in an imperious way. Her movements were quick and energetic, and her voice just a shade louder than was usual for a lady of rank. There was little doubt that she was accustomed to make herself obeyed wherever she was.

"In thanking you, Sir Knight," she said, "I am thanking also the Emperor, my most gracious liege, for sending you out to look after my son. It is good to know that he does not forget his friends and their children, even if he has to destroy their abode."

"With your leave, most noble lady," interposed Piers, "it was not the Emperor who asked me to look after Count Thomas; the Emperor knows nothing about it. It was Count Rainald, whom I had the pleasure to meet at . . . errh . . . imperial headquarters."

The Countess bit her lip. "So that is how it happened. Rainald is a good son and a good brother. I hope you have not been bored too much with my youngest son's company. Ah, there they all come. Niccolo! See to it that supper is ready soon—I am ravenous."

No more than half an hour ago she had heard from Landulph's messenger that Thomas was safe, thought Piers. "Tell her . . . she need cry no more", Landulph had said. Only now he understood that this had been irony. The Countess did not look at all as if she had cried. In fact, it was difficult to imagine that she had ever cried.

Landulph came up to them, and with him Thomas and two young girls, both in honey-colored dresses like . . . like the apparition from whom he had by no means recovered. Her sisters, then.

Landulph introduced them, in his own way. "Sir Piers Rudde . . . an English knight who's just taken brother monk out of the frying pan . . . my sisters Marotta and Adelasia . . . you seem to have met Theodora already. The youngest and the most forward. All right, all right, you need not glare at me, my beautiful, the most forward does not mean much in your sisters' company, does it? You still owe us the story of how you got brother Thomas out, Sir Piers."

"There is no story", replied the young Englishman. "I went in and fetched him."

"You forgot to say that the building was burning", said Thomas, and for the third time today Piers saw his incredible smile; now it reminded him strangely of his youngest sister . . . no, it didn't . . . yes, it did. It was the same and yet different. A queer comparison besieged his mind: it was like the same dress worn inside out. Stupid. But he knew what he meant.

"Sir Knight," said the Countess with unexpected warmth, "I will not sit down at my own table until I have suitably rewarded you. Choose your own reward."

"But, most noble lady . . . "

"You have risked your life for a stranger. But he was an Aquino. By Our Lady, I will not have it said that we do not know how to repay our debts."

Piers gulped. It was a mad thing to do, a hopeless thing; it would make him suffer all the pains of damnation itself. But he did it.

"Most noble lady, as you insist: my liege, the Earl of Cornwall, has given me unlimited leave. Will you permit me to join the knights of your household?"

The Countess was too surprised to answer at once.

Landulph laughed.

"A good idea, Mother. He looks as if he could be pretty useful in case of trouble."

Piers carefully avoided looking at little Theodora. It was the most difficult thing he had ever done; it was the beginning of countless difficulties to come. "I really am completely mad", he thought.

Now the Countess had made her decision. She had banned from her mind as unworthy the suspicion that this young man might have good cause to hide himself from somebody or something behind the colors of Aquino. He did not look like that sort of man, even if one could never be quite sure in these times.

"My house will be pleased and honored", she said politely. "You have brought your own men with you?"

"Only one varlet, Robin Cherrywoode, a very trustworthy man".

"You will have two more, as all our knights have. There

will be ample time to discuss everything else. You will swear fealty tomorrow."

"This is happy news", said the boy Thomas warmly. Piers smiled back at him.

"A small reward for a great service", laughed Landulph. "My brother Thomas was born the year that Pope Honorius died . . . , and St. Francis . . . and Genghis Khan. Perhaps he was born to make up for one of these. Which shall it be, brother monk?"

"Your joke is in poor taste, Landulph", said the Countess severely. "An Aquino can be neither an infidel nor a beggar. Not even a holy beggar."

Niccolo appeared. "The most noble lady is served."

Chapter III

EVERYWHERE THE TREES were blossoming. The very earth seemed to breathe luxuriously. From the ringwall of Rocca Secca a man could look straight into paradise itself, white and pink and flaming red and all shades of green. Every peasant girl walking up the narrow causeway with a pitcher on her head looked like a Greek statue. It was hot, but pleasantly so, and the wind mingled the salty freshness of the sea with the fragrance of millions of flowers. The little green lizards were out, and butterflies of incredible beauty. The two men on watch on the wall in their heavy armor seemed utterly out of place.

"Two years", said Piers.

"Two years, one month, and eleven days, master", said

Robin Cherrywoode grimly. "That is, since our arrival here. It's almost three years since we left England."

"What have you to complain about?" asked Piers, frowning.

"Nothing, master. I've got accustomed even to the stuff they call food in this country. When I go home, I shall be almost a foreigner myself."

"Not you, Robin", smiled Piers. "You would be as English as a chalk cliff if you stayed here for the rest of your life."

"Heaven forbid."

"You're ungrateful, Robin. Admit that you never had a better life. We are serving a great name, there is jousting, there is good company, there are witty minstrels and troubadours, wine and food are plentiful . . . what more can you ask for?" And Piers sighed heavily.

"Yes, master."

There was a pause. "Are there no pretty girls in England?" thought Robin. "Must it be that little devil whom he cannot get, even if he stays here another twenty years? Why not the Emperor's daughter or the Sultan's . . . he might just as well sigh for *them.* And talk of the devil . . . "

The three young countesses came fluttering out of the hall and started a ball game.

The young knight did not seem to notice them. He was in command of the watch on the north wall. Two years . . . over two years since the day he had knelt before the Countess, his mailed fist on the blue flag of Aquino, saying the oath; for one year he had bound himself, and since then he had renewed the oath twice. Many things had happened . . . and nothing.

Four times Theodora had declined marriage offers even a lady of her rank would consider very suitable. She was supposed to have said to her mother that she would probably never marry at all. It had given him both pain and joy. Even the young Tiepolo, the son of the Doge of Venice, she had refused.

The Countess had not interferred. It was said that she did not like the idea of a very early marriage, and Theodora was the youngest of the three daughters.

But why think such thoughts? What could it be to him whether or not Theodora refused a suitor? He could never be a suitor . . . not even if he performed a deed for which he was raised in rank. Nor did she herself pay much attention to him. He was just one more knight of the household. She talked to him occasionally; she was friendly and kind . . . usually, at least. But that was all, and it was all he could ever expect.

She had consented to be his "lady" on his solemn request when he had won the tournament a year and a half ago. He was allowed, then, "to devote his heart and the fame of any action he might win" to her. The least of all knights was entitled to choose the highest-born lady of the country for such sacred purpose . . . just as any boy might choose any saint, and even the Queen of Saints, as his patroness on the day of his confirmation.

Near and gracious and yet unattainable, like the saints, was Theodora of Aquino. More than once, of course, he had played with the idea of going back to England. By now the Earl of Cornwall was surely home, and he could return without people saying that he had been sent home for some mistake, or even crime, he had committed. They were very quick, as a rule, in saying things like that. He could return. And yet he couldn't. He had known from the start that he would have to suffer. Only to look at her was an exquisite kind of torture. But not to be able to look at her at all . . . that was impossible.

"A knight and his retinue, master", said Robin.

Piers looked. "Blow the trumpet", he commanded, and the man next to him in the small watchtower obeyed.

From the guardhouse ironclad men hastened up the steep stairs, clanging in their armor.

The three ladies had interrupted their game, and Adelasia shouted up: "What is it, Sir Knight?"

"A visitor, noble lady. I cannot see his colors yet."

The three came up in a flurry of velvet and silk. It was a sight that justified a man's suffering. "As if God had tried to create perfect beauty", thought Piers, "and had succeeded in the third attempt."

"Where is it, where is it?"

They stared, gazed, giggled, and guessed, until Marotta cried. "It's Rainald. . . . Holy Mother of God, it's Rainald!"

Far down, in the valley, the knight was waving his hand.

"We must tell Landulph. . . . We must tell Mother."

Down the stairs went the flurry of velvet and silk.

Even Piers gladdened a little, although his lady had not given him so much as a single look when she stood next to him. Better Rainald than another of those inevitable admirers of Theodora. Besides, he rather liked Rainald; when he was present the entire castle became less formal, and he invariably brought news of what was going on in the wide world. Only when he was a little drunk, he could become a nuisance and overstep the mark in more directions than one. But that did not happen too often. In any case Rainald was a better companion than Landulph, who gave himself airs as the ruler of all the Aquino estates—whenever his mother was not present—and bowed to her and cajoled her when she was. There is little or nothing as exasperating as the condescending attitude of a coarse man.

The only one who ever seemed to feel it was the boy, Thomas, if one could still call him that . . . he was seventeen now. Landulph never missed an opportunity for a jibe against monks, priests, and monasteries in general and his "monk brother" in particular. And Thomas missed every opportunity to pay him back. He just sat there, saying nothing at all. Sometimes one could not even be sure whether he was awake. Was he indolent, after all? Or was he still suffering from the shock of having lost his little hole in Monte Cassino? In any case, it was just as well that the Countess had sent him to Naples, where he was now studying whatever they did study at the University of

Naples—he was among boys of his own age and was seeing something of the world. It would do him good.

Robin had discovered a strange story about him from old Maddalena, who had been his nurse. The Countess had had seven children, and one day Thomas had been playing in the room where Maddalena was sitting with the newborn baby, little Maria, on her lap. There had been a thunderstorm, and suddenly a streak of lightning lit up the whole room. When Maddalena came to her senses again, she found that she could not move her left arm; it was lame. And little Maria in her arms was dead. Thomas remained untouched. It had taken several years before Maddalena regained control of her left arm. Was it possible that this incident had in some way influenced the character of the boy? There was a little girl in the village of Foregay who had lost the power of speech because she had seen her drunken father attack her mother. Such things could happen. Perhaps it was that which had made Thomas so utterly different from his brothers. Perhaps the early encounter with death had something to do with his religious leanings. Perhaps it made him shy and silent and awkward in the presence of noisy, cheerful people.

The university would do him good.

And here came Rainald with his retinue, the three girls around him, of course, and Landulph . . . even the Countess.

Half an hour later they were all sitting together in the large hall, drinking. Piers and half a dozen other knights of the household with their ladies were allowed to participate: Rainald had insisted on that. "They're all thirsty for news about what is going on, Mother." He liked a big audience.

"Lend me thy lute, Homer," he began, "that Ulysses the Much-traveled may relate all he has seen and suffered. But there is someone missing . . . ah, our little monk. He was here when I came last time. Back to the university? Oh, well, they will spoil him there completely. He will be neither monk nor knight after they have had him in their clutches. The jurists will teach him how to let the big fish escape and hang the small fry instead, the leeches will teach him the only science whose final failure is guaranteed beforehand, and his master of rhetoric will die from exhaustion. Imagine our Thomas making a speech. During my last visit here I believe he spoke twenty-three words in two days and a half. And when he . . . "

"Never mind Thomas", interrupted the Countess impatiently. "Thomas is not important. The news, Rainald."

Rainald looked about. Upturned faces everywhere. "It is against all the laws of the dramatic art," he said, "but I will give you the great secret at once: *Habemus papam.*"

At last half a dozen voices said, "At last", "Thank God", "Blessed be the Virgin." But the Countess asked: "Who is it? Who?"

"Cardinal Sinibald Fiesco".

"A very good family", said the Countess. "And the Emperor likes him, I believe."

Rainald laughed. "I wouldn't hope for too much, Mother. Do you know what he said, when he heard it? I was present. 'I have lost a friend in the Cardinal, but I have gained an enemy in the Pope.' And the new Pope has chosen the name of Innocent IV. That isn't exactly a good omen, is it? It was Innocent III under whom the trouble with the Emperor started."

The Countess pressed her lips together. "Frederick is very fond of a witty sentence," she said, "just as you are. I think it is good news. Sinibald Fiesco has always been such a sensible man. And it was time that this happened. The papal seat has been vacant for too long. The things that have been going on lately: beggar monks everywhere, preaching as if tomorrow would be the Day of Judgment; if I want a sermon, I go to Mass. It is simply revolting to hear these sweaty vulgarians shriek at everybody in the market places. I hope the Pope will re-establish order."

"Well, in any case it can't be worse than it was under Gregory", said Rainald. "I don't think the Emperor ever hated anybody so much as he hated him. You remember when we were going to attack Rome, or rather when we set out to take Rome . . . there was no need to attack it; the Emperor had pumped so much money into the city that almost every other citizen was bribed. We heard from our agents that the imperial colors were being worn quite openly by thousands of people. . . . And old Gregory? Made a procession through the city with the relics of St. Peter and St. Paul and declared on the Piazza that he now left the protection and preservation of Rome to them, as the citizens had forsaken their cause. It must have been a grandiose spectacle, a scene worthy to be described by a poet. The imperial colors disappeared, the citizens manned the walls, we heard the reports, and . . . Rome was not taken by us after all. Then the Emperor prepared the matter even more thoroughly, directing all the propaganda against the person of Gregory himself as the only man responsible for the feud, for the war, for all the misery in Italy. And again we approach. It was masterfully prepared, I must say. And what does old Gregory do? Goes and dies. Just like that. And there we sat with all our beautiful propaganda running dry, with no Gregory to fix it on. But worse still: we no longer had any pretext for taking Rome. We were beaten by our own words. The Emperor was beside himself. 'He has cheated me in life, and now he has cheated me by his death', he said." Rainald laughed heartily. "You know, this is like the climax of a dramatic play. If only I had the time I'd write it one day. The old Pope, trying to shield his Rome against the Emperor all by himself . . . like Leo when he warded off Attila single-handed."

"Rainald!" The Countess was seriously annoyed. "You will not compare the Emperor with Attila in this house."

"Sorry, Mother." Rainald bowed to her. "Poets are irresponsible people, you know. But I'm not so sure the Emperor would not have been as pleased as you are annoyed. And it would be such a good play."

They all laughed now. One could never be seriously angry with Rainald for long.

"Let me have my lute . . . I'd much rather sing to you what I've composed than go on telling you about what happened at court. Believe me, my music is better than theirs. . . . Thank you, Marotta."

He began to play and sing. " 'You were made for this hour, you with your eyes like stars . . . ' "

"Stop your nonsense", said the Countess. "You will have all the time you want for that. I must know what happened."

Rainald sighed, played a last chord, and shook his head. "How human you are, Mother dear. To be human means invariably to ask for trouble. Very well, then. Young Tiepolo is dead."

"Pietro Tiepolo?" cried the Countess aghast. "But he was in excellent health only a few months ago."

"I know", said Rainald with a furtive glance at Theodora. She had refused young Tiepolo, but one could never know a girl's mind. However, she showed no more regret than her sisters. He made his thumb run across the lute and added calmly: "The Emperor had him hanged, you know."

"Hanged? The son of the Doge? A Tiepolo?" The Countess forced her voice into obedience. She sounded almost indifferent as she asked: "Why, Rainald?"

"Della Vigna had found certain letters, they say. The Doge had been parleying with the Pope . . . with Gregory. It was some sort of retribution."

"Della Vigna . . . I might have guessed it. He is the Emperor's black angel."

"Della Vigna did not order the hanging, Mother", said Rainald with a shrug.

"He might have been Theodora's husband", thought the Countess. She had in fact been in favor of Pietro Tiepolo; she had spoken for him, but the girl would not hear of it. Poor little Pietro.

"Just as well you didn't marry him, little one." That was Landulph, of course, and of course he received no reply.

"Dear Landulph . . . " Rainald smiled ironically. "I have a message for you, by the way. We must leave together tomorrow morning. You see, Mother, there is *not* much time for my new poems. Somehow there never is. The Emperor wants us both. Something is brewing; I don't know what. I think we may have to go to Genoa."

For a short moment the Countess held her breath. Then she smiled, regaining her composure. The Emperor was hard, terribly hard against his enemies. But the Aquinos had been for him, without a single break, during his entire reign.

"How many men do we take?" asked Landulph simply. He did not mind going at all. Rocca Secca had been boring lately.

"Fifty each. I have no orders about that."

"I'll take de Braccio with me and you, Sir Piers", said Landulph.

"Better leave our English friend at home", advised Rainald. "The little incident at Santa Justina may not yet be forgotten."

"What incident?" asked the Countess.

"Have I never told you that?" Rainald laughed. "It was on the day we met. Princess Selvaggia made eyes at him; she talked about taking him on as one of her personal guards. Eccelino was blue in the face, and the Emperor did not like it, I suppose because he likes Eccelino. Holy Mohammed, it's two years ago and may be entirely forgotten by now. But one can never be sure. The Emperor has got such a damnably good memory."

"There was no incident", said Piers firmly.

Rainald shrugged his shoulders. "Dear friend, I know it wasn't your fault. No one can possibly help it if Princess Selvaggia chooses to make eyes at him. It could have been I; fortunately it wasn't. You didn't tell me, but I feel certain that your joining the expedition against Monte Cassino had something to do with it. The Earl of Cornwall is not only a great nobleman; he also has open eyes. It was an excellent solution to get you out of harm's way so quickly, excellent especially because it enables us to be together now. Let's drink on that, shall we?"

"There was no incident", repeated Piers stonily.
"You'd better stay here, though", said Landulph.
Rainald was playing softly. " 'You were made for this hour, you with your eyes like stars . . . the promise of your lips . . . ' What is the matter with you, Theodora?"
"Nothing at all."
"Nothing at all . . . and you look as if you'd erupt any moment like Vesuvius. Listen to this song, pretty one. They're singing it all over Parma and Siena and Florence. Personally I don't think it's my best song at all, but they love it. 'The promise of your lips . . . ' "
Theodora got up and left abruptly.
"What have I done now?" asked Rainald, frowning.
"She didn't like your song, it seems", said Landulph.
"Fools", said their mother acidly. "Will you never grow up? I must talk to you two alone."
"I will listen to your song later", said Marotta kindly. Adelasia laughed and drew her sister away.
"A poet, like a prophet, does not amount to much at home", said Rainald with a wry face. "I'd still like to know what I've done."
The Countess watched her daughters depart and the knights and ladies of the household with them. Piers' face was very pale.
When the heavy door had closed behind them she said icily: "When you have news of such importance, Rainald, I would rather hear it alone. In these times you cannot implicitly trust even your own household."
"Yes, Mother", said Rainald. "But what *is* the matter with the child?"
"Santa Madonna," exclaimed the Countess, "why bother over the game of a girl? Sir Piers has chosen her as his lady, and she thought fit to show her displeasure at your story about Princess Selvaggia, that is all."
He blinked and grinned. "How stupid of me. He's a fine figure of a man—do you think the little one might care for him in earnest?"
His mother rose, her eyes blazing. "Your life at a disso-

lute court has had a bad effect on you, son. There is a difference, I trust, between the manners there and at Aquino. We here do not forget who we are. If the Princess Selvaggia chooses to be interested in a little knight without rank and standing, it is her affair. Theodora is a headstrong girl, but she will never overstep the mark. Neither will Sir Piers, I'm sure. He was entitled to choose her as his lady, and she has accepted him as her knight. That is all, and I forbid you to talk loosely about her."

She paced up and down the room. The two brothers exchanged grins of embarrassment.

"Neither of you has many brains in his head", the Countess went on. "I am not very lucky with my sons. A simpleton of a soldier, a versemaker and woman chaser, and a dumb monk. At least Thomas will be Lord Abbot of Monte Cassino in a few years. That I can get for him. But you two? I cannot deal with the della Vignas and Eccelinos. You will have to do something about it yourselves. But what? And in the meantime the Emperor is surrounded by snakes and scorpions, and things are allowed to happen that make one feel ashamed of loyalty itself."

"You are beautiful, Mother", said Rainald enthusiastically. "By all the houris and saints, you are a match for any woman at court."

She stopped in her tracks. "Nothing but nonsense in your silly head." But she smiled. The filial compliment was true, and she knew it was true. "I'm a cantankerous old woman. But you haven't known the Emperor as I have. He is my second cousin. I have seen him rise from his early days in Palermo, when he had to beg a meal from strangers because no one cared about the Hohenstaufens until Pope Innocent III established Frederick. I have seen him rise till the day when he was crowned—till he crowned himself in Jerusalem. I've heard Pope Gregory call him the 'beloved sapling of the Church'. The most beautiful, the most elegant, and the most intelligent man of his time he was then, and when he entered a room the very air seemed to brighten.

He was the devoted friend of Elizabeth of Hungary, a saint if ever there was one. He was a builder, not a destroyer. The kingdom of Sicily blossomed under his hand. No one but he could unite the German princes, and he did. He still is the vital center of Europe and the world. He is what Caesar was and Augustus and Justinian . . . the ruler of the world. And he is what none of them ever was: the head of the nobility of his time. As that he has a claim to our allegiance. For a nobleman to be against him means to break his own coat of arms. That's what we must remember when we hear that he has done terrible things. Such things cannot have grown in his own soul; I refuse to believe it. They come from the della Vignas, the Eccelinos, and similar upstarts. It is sad, very sad, that he is continuously fighting with the Pope. Let's hope it will be better now under Fiesco's rule in Rome. But our place is with our imperial cousin. We have no choice. An Aquino has no choice."

She sat down, exhausted. "Wine, Landulph . . . thank you. Well, you've heard *my* story now . . . an old woman's story as grey as her hair. Where's your lute, Rainald?"

"No, Mother", Rainald sighed a little. "After your epic my poor lyrics would not sound well. You're made of sterner stuff than we are. I don't see it all as you do. . . . I see it as a man who is reading a book or listening to music. It is not the reader's fault when the hero commits a crime, nor can he stop him from doing so. He just reads on. . . . But I've never had any idea of leaving cousin Frederick's cause. There's no need to worry. I won't be hanged like poor little Pietro Tiepolo. Neither will Landulph."

"Oh, be quiet, Rainald!"

To his horror and bewilderment the Countess burst into tears.

* * *

"What is the matter with Sir Piers?" asked Adelasia, laden with curiosity. "He has scarcely spoken a word all day."

Theodora laughed curtly. "I did not speak to him at all."
"But why? What has he done?"
"He? Nothing. If he wants to ogle that Selvaggia woman, he's welcome to."
"But he didn't. It was she who . . . "
"What does it matter who started it? I don't care. But he's always so righteous, so stolid, so . . . English. He . . . he bores me."
"He's a very handsome man", said Adelasia.
"Do you think so?" Theodora yawned delicately.
At night Piers made up his mind to return to England as soon as his year of allegiance was over.

* * *

The imperial University of Naples was in more than one sense a symbol of the time. In fact, it was a sort of microcosm of Europe. Here the young scholar could study medicine under teachers who had graced Toledo and Salamanca; he could learn the complexities of jurisprudence, while his teachers did their best to keep up with the exceedingly numerous new laws the Emperor proclaimed at ever shortening intervals; he could acquire the art of rhetoric in proportion to his talent and knowledge of grammar from no less an expert than Walter of Ascoli, who was working on an etymological encyclopedia. Roffredo of Benevento gave the courses on civil law, Bartholomeo Pignatelli on canon law, Master Terrisius of Atina lectured on the arts, and Peter of Ireland on natural science. Thus Naples catered to everybody. It was the Emperor's answer to Rome, which stuck to theology, and to Bologna, which had acquired the reputation of being rather "freethinking". In Naples you could study whether you believed or disbelieved. And as there was no attempt at synthesis, the result was that the scholars emerged with a number of totally different and entirely contradictory views dancing in their heads.
"Let them", said Frederick, when della Vigna drew his

attention to the fact. "At least they will have open minds and will not be sworn to one thing and no other."

Della Vigna murmured his admiration. So far all the universities in Europe had been founded by the Church and staffed by the Church. It was supreme wisdom on the part of the Emperor to enter into competition; it was essential if the type of man was to be formed who would be useful for the Empire. But why in such circumstances lectures on canon law? Why such teachers as Pignatelli or Peter of Ireland? Why not a citadel of free thought, surpassing even Bologna?

Frederick smiled, and della Vigna understood at last. "My great Emperor, I am a fool, as we all are in your presence. Of course you want Naples to be a new center for the best intellectual forces, and therefore you do not wish to deter anybody. You do not want to convince the convinced. You want fresh blood, virgin brains . . . and no one must be able to point out to a pious father or a bigoted mother that Naples is godless."

"That", said the Emperor, "is part of my idea. Besides, you cannot do these things with one stroke. Gently, della Vigna, gently. Do you think it would not have amused me to ask my friends in Syria and Tunis and Egypt for a few of their first-rate men to teach the wisdom of the East? But they are bigoted there, too, in some ways and would have assailed that fantastic confusion we call theology by pointing out that Christianity is a polytheistic religion. We must leave the fun for later, perhaps not much later. Naples is a beginning. It will stir them up; it will confuse them—so much the better. We want no fixed lines at present. Thus the Trinity is safe . . . for the time being."

And Naples grew. As in every other university, no one was refused on account of nationality, race, or birth. The scions of famous and wealthy families sat next to half-starved boys whose enthusiasm for knowledge was their only asset. After each lecture, discussions took place, and students were asked to analyze what they had learned and to comment on it.

* * *

Magister Pignatelli had spoken on the thoughts of St. Augustine. The large lecture room was buzzing. Pignatelli was a master at presenting the old in a new form, and his hearers exchanged their views as was their right until the lecturer should call up one of them to comment on what he had said.

"This is not really canon law, you know."

"Obviously not. But canon law was formed more than once on the basis of old Augustine's statements. The Church Fathers . . . "

"You can say what you like; this is Pignatelli's subtle way of introducing theology pure and simple. In other words: you must be simple to swallow it pure."

"I don't know. I hope he doesn't call me up. I really wouldn't know what to say."

"You're not alone there. Look at *him.*"

"At whom? Oh, he . . . you know, I've never seen anybody quite like that. I've been observing him for months now. He never opens his mouth at all. Just sits and goggles. He's an Aquino, isn't he?"

"Yes, the youngest son. They couldn't make a soldier out of him; he'd cut a fine figure on a horse, wouldn't he? See him in full armor attacking the infidel . . . a sight for the gods. *Arma virumque cano . . .* "

"Bit weak on the brain, too. And slow . . . it takes him half an hour to get up or sit down."

"But why did they send him here, then? He's a Benedictine oblate. Look at his habit. Why not leave him in whatever monastery he was in?"

"Don't you know that? He was at Cassino. Well, they're building there now, so he should be able to go back and play saint or something."

"*Sancta simplicitas!* He is an Aquino. He doesn't need to

go in for sanctity. They'll have him installed there as lord abbot before you and I have earned our first pieces of gold at the law court, rest assured of that. There, now . . . he's writing something. You know, I have never seen him make a single note so far. Almost wondered whether he *can* write. Look, Tolomeo's sitting down next to him."

"And starts explaining something . . . poor Tolomeo. That comes from being charitable."

"Charitable? Tolomeo? Ha, ha, ha. All he wants to do is to shine!"

* * *

"It is really quite simple, you know", said Tolomeo d'Andrea. "I saw you try and make notes, so I gather you *want* to understand."

Thomas opened his mouth to speak, but already young Tolomeo was sailing into his explanation of Pignatelli's lecture. "What you must understand first is that old Augustine regarded Plato's philosophy—suitably re-interpreted and embellished by Plotinus—as the absolutely perfect type of rational knowledge. He set out to interpret it again: no, he set out to interpret Christian revelation *by* Platonic knowledge—in Plato's terms, rather. Got that so far? You needn't make a speech, I know you are not the talkative type. Got it? Very well, then: his main principle was that the best way to reach truth was not the one that starts with reasoning and goes via intellectual certainty to faith, but the other way round: you start with faith and go from there to revelation and from that to reason. Or as Augustine himself put it: errh . . . 'Understanding is . . . ' errh . . . 'Understanding is . . . ' "

" 'Understanding is the reward of faith' ", said Thomas gently. " 'Therefore seek not to understand that thou mayest believe but believe that thou mayest understand.' Yes, beautiful. But I love the other passage: 'If to believe were not one thing and to understand another, and unless we had first to believe the great and divine thing which we desire to understand, the Prophet would have spoken idly when he said: "Unless you believe, you shall not understand." ' "

"Good Lord", said Tolomeo d'Andrea, taken aback.

By now Thomas seemed to have forgotten all about him. The magnificent sentences of Augustine erupted inexorably: " 'Furthermore, Our Lord said to those who were already believers, "Seek and you shall find." For what is believed unknown cannot be called found, nor is any one capable of finding God, unless he first believe that he will eventually find him. . . . That which we seek on his exhortation, we shall find by his showing it to us, so far as it is possible to such as us to find this in this life . . . and we must surely believe that after this life this will be perceived and attained more clearly and more perfectly.'[1]

"I call that bursting the Platonic frame", Thomas said joyfully. "Just as the Word of St. John is too big a thing for Plato's Logos." Now, only, he turned to Tolomeo. The young man was gaping at him in complete bewilderment. The fire in the large, round, black eyes died down. "I am sorry", said Thomas. "I'm afraid I interrupted you very rudely."

Tolomeo stared hard. No . . . not the faintest trace of irony. He opened his mouth, shut it again, and finally said: "That's all right", peering out of the corner of his eye to decide whether anybody could have seen or heard. To his relief he saw no one grinning at him.

But something like a wave of cheerful excitement seemed to go over the room. What had happened? Only when Pignatelli repeated his name did Thomas know that he was called upon to give an analysis of the lecture.

Obediently he stood up. There were a few sniggers. He did not hear them. He was calmly arranging the analysis in his mind.

"Eh, Tolomeo", whispered a voice. "Did you brief him?"

[1] Quotations taken from Augustine, "On Free Will", II, 2, 6, trans. E. Przywara, *An Augustine Synthesis* (London: Sheed and Ward, 1936).

"Brief him?" Tolomeo gave a short, hoarse laugh. Then he quoted St. Paul in reverse: "Professing himself to be a fool, he became wise."

"What did he say?"

"I didn't hear it. Called him a fool, I think."

"What else? But Lord Abbot he will be, mark my word."

"Hush . . . I don't want to miss the fun."

He didn't. No one did. The first surprise was the timbre of the voice, clear, metallic, and yet warm. It did not seem to belong to the plump, awkward figure. After the third sentence the room grew quiet. Within the space of a quarter of an hour Thomas gave a summary of Pignatelli's lecture of over an hour, so complete in its lucidity that the master asked himself why it had taken him so long.

From Plato to Plotinus, from Plotinus to Augustine, from Augustine to Anselm of Canterbury, who had condensed the Augustinian principle to the formula *"Credo ut intelligam."* And from Anselm and his ontological proof of the existence of God to today, when faith and reason were divorced so completely that they were like parallels in mathematics.

The only way Christian philosophers could save themselves from an open clash with theology was to state that their conclusions were necessary . . . but not necessarily true. This, of course, made the word "truth" itself meaningless.

Therefore it was to be hoped that reason and revelation would both cease to be one-sided, that in a new order harmony between the two great gifts of God would prevail.

But the immortal merit of St. Augustine remained insofar as he had first introduced Plato to orthodox theology. The philosophers were the most perfect natures of ancient times. This by itself gave reason for the hope that the cleavage between faith and reason would not be permanent, now that a higher world had been reborn in Christ. For the higher always encompassed the perfection of the lower.

Thomas bowed respectfully and sat down.

Pignatelli's fine old face was flushed. "That was not a

student's way to talk", he said vehemently. "It was a master's way."

Awkwardly Thomas scrambled to his legs again. "I am extremely sorry, sir," he said helplessly, "but I know no other way to treat the problem."

Pignatelli glared at him. Then he grinned. For once, almost in a lifetime, he had given praise . . . and it was taken for a reproach. Still grinning and shaking his head he left the room. Astonishing. Astonishing. One knew that type, of course; it sits and sits and doesn't open its mouth, and all the time it sucks up everything, like a sponge.

But there was more than that here. How old was he? Never mind.

That end bit about the potential harmony between faith and reason was nonsense, of course. Try it and before you know where you are, you're a heretic. Averroes tried and became one even according to the tenets of Islam. And Maimonides tried, of course, and got into trouble, too. There was precious little likelihood of a solution. But it was amusing that this chubby cherub demanded a solution, earnestly and categorically. The best thing the pagan times had produced was the philosopher. Quite right. Now we are living in a higher world, the Christian world. Therefore our world should encompass philosophy as the most perfect thing of the lower, the pagan world. How did he put it? "The higher always encompasses the perfection of the lower." Where did he get that from?

Here was Master Peter, Petrus Hibernicus, just the man he wanted. He put the sentence to him. Was it correct? Was it true in the light of natural science? Master Peter thought it over. "Something to it", he said. "Look at us: look at the other kingdoms: mineral, vegetable, animal, man. There is mineral stuff in the vegetable kingdom, which by itself is the higher of the two. There is vegetable stuff in all animals—and mineral stuff as well. And all three realms are in man. Your bones are mineral in origin, your hair is a plant, and there is hardly any need to mention the animalic heritage, is there? And look at mathematics: a cube is a thing of three dimensions, but it carries within itself the straight line of the first and the square of the second dimension. Metaphysically I'm not so sure.... Angels are higher than men, but does their nature encompass the perfection of human nature?"

"It does in a way", mused Pignatelli. "They're pure intellect and pure will..."

"Which is more than can be said about men..."

"Which is the perfection of the best in man. You know, I believe the boy is right."

"What boy?"

Pignatelli told him, and Peter of Ireland's eyes widened.

"Not that dolt, surely!"

"Why do you think he is a dolt?"

"He just sits there and gazes into the void. Never asks questions. Never makes notes."

"Ever asked him a question? Ever asked him to speak? No? I thought as much. Try once and see what happens."

The "dolt", in the meantime, had left the lecture room and the university. He was deep in thought, on lines somewhat similar to Master Peter's, and thus utterly unaware of the curious looks he received from a number of fellow students in the corridors and on the piazza. As usual he went to the Dominican convent near by, entered the church, and prayed for a while.

As he rose, he saw Friar John standing beside him, smiling. He bowed to him, and they left the church and entered the convent itself and Friar John's cell, a fairly roomy cell with a heavy desk, two solid chairs, a straw mattress, and, as the only ornament, a crucifix on the wall opposite the desk. They sat down. Face to face they sat a while without speaking, as strangers may or intimate friends.

Friar John smiled again, suddenly. "I am thinking", he said, "of how we met first, we two."

Now Thomas smiled, too. On his way to Naples, riding his mule and followed by three soldiers on horseback—his mother had insisted on such escort—he had seen a friar in the Dominican habit surrounded by a number of street urchins, dancing around him and yelling at the top of their voices: "Magpie . . . magpie . . . "

The friar had walked on calmly, so they proceeded to throw things at him, and for once Thomas had become angry. He had spurred his mule, and the brute, entirely unaccustomed to such treatment, had jumped forward wildly.

This had a double effect. The street urchins fled hastily, and Thomas lost stirrups and reins, fell heavily on the mule's neck, and was rescued by the friar to whose rescue he had come. It had made them laugh a little, but then the friar said: "It is not a good sign for a Christian country when youth dislikes the sight of a beggar or the sight of a priest. But if they do, it is only logical that they should doubly dislike a priest who is a beggar."

Thomas had offered the tired man a ride on his mule, but he declined politely. "It is against the rule." Whereupon Thomas dismounted and began to walk beside the friar, who was also going to Naples. He had never talked to a Dominican before, and he was not going to let this opportunity go by. Thus their first talk had lasted four hours, and the men of the escort became rather sulky.

Since then they had met a good many times. The Dominican convent was conveniently near the university, where a few of the friars were actually teaching, and more than once Thomas had seen Friar John in the lecture room. The corona of hair that the monastic clipping left was grey, and his face wrinkled, but so mobile was it, so illuminated with intelligence, that no one would have thought of calling him an old man.

Fifty-five? Sixty? Even more? It was impossible to say. The strong, aquiline features were those of a Roman officer rather than a friar. But the eyes were blue.

"We've gone a long way since then", said Friar John tranquilly.

"But only part of the way, my Father."

"I, too, have only gone part of the way, son. Besides, I very much doubt whether there is an end to the way altogether."

"But death ends activity as we know it."

"As we know it! Never in this life can we be as active as we shall be in the next. There is nothing more active than contemplation. There is nothing more active, even here, than contemplation. And here is the great command of our Order: *Contemplat aliis tradere.* We must not keep for ourselves the result of our work. We must pass it on to others, to our neighbor. For too long, monks have been shut up in their monasteries. It was necessary, assuredly it was. Just as it was necessary for St. John the Baptist, perhaps even for Our Lord, to withdraw into the wilderness for a time. But then they broke forth to preach their wisdom to the common man. The time is ripe and more than ripe. For the enemies of God have got hold of knowledge and have done what they would do: distorted it, twisted it so as to fit it in with their purpose. We shall answer them with the knowledge of truth." The wrinkled face broke into a boyish smile. "No wonder they call us a nuisance—we are . . . to them. And we are more than that, please God."

Thomas took a deep breath. "My Father . . . do you think I . . . I could be of use in your Order?"

Friar John closed his eyes for a moment. When he opened them again his voice had once more a casual tone: "Oh, certainly." And with a humorous blink: "What about the solution of the problem of bringing faith and philosophy into harmony?"

The young man flushed scarlet. "You know about that, my Father?"

"I was in the lecture room."

"My Father . . . you said that your Order might have use for me . . . "

Friar John raised his strong eyebrows. "It's a hard life, Thomas. Much harder than with the Benedictines. Our fasting lasts from the Feast of the Exaltation of the Holy Cross in September to the end of Lent: one meal a day within that time. Wherever we go we walk. And we are beggars. The life of a mendicant is not for everybody."

"Will you consider talking to the Father Prior about me?" asked Thomas simply.

Friar John did not seem to have heard. "The Church is universal", he said as if to himself. "She must provide for all types . . . for all men. Cardinals, archbishops, lord abbots . . . citadels of prayer and castles of learning . . . High Pontifical Mass and the prayer of the hermit: each has its proper place. But St. Dominic, yes, and St. Francis, too: they revived primitive Christianity. It is not a reform. It is taking up a thread again, a very precious thread. It is the acceleration of the Mystical Body of Christ, which is the Church. It is the quickening of its pulse, a faster movement toward God. *Creasti nos, Domine, ad te* . . . "*Towards* thee thou hast created us, O Lord." Toward thee . . . not for thee. It is the strengthening of the vertical beam of the Cross. And it is the vertical beam of the Cross that matters first and foremost, for the horizontal is carried by it."

He got up and began to pace up and down the cell. "Our best men are working on the problem you talked about today, Thomas. They are hungry and thirsty for knowledge, but not like the dabblers at the Emperor's court, who wallow in that peculiar modern mixture of scepticism and Eastern mysticism. For they know that science must try to read the will of God from nature."

Now Thomas, too, stood up.

"I am ready, my Father", he said. "Tell me where I can humbly ask for the habit of your Order."

Friar John stood still. His face was very grave.

"You are young, Thomas . . . not much more than a boy. You are enthusiastic now . . . but after a few years of the kind of work we are doing, you may lose your enthusiasm completely. You do not know, you cannot know, what you are letting yourself in for. And then, yours is a great name; it might well estrange you from your family. In fact, I am almost certain it would. It would cause great bitterness and sorrow to your mother. She has not raised you to become a beggar of God. It is an open secret that a very exalted and, as I am the first to admit, a very sacred office is in store for you at Monte Cassino. St. Benedict has the first claim on you. You will be in charge of many souls, and you will wield great power. The good you can do there is immense. Why should you break, irrevocably, with all your past? Why, if you took this step, you would in all likelihood become a fugitive . . . for they would not take it lightly at Rocca Secca, and the arm of temporal power is long and strong. No, my son, I do not think that the habit of our Order is for you."

Thomas had turned very pale. His hands shook. But without hesitation he bowed deeply and walked toward the door. In the door he stopped, for Friar John had called out.

"Thomas, my son, will you admit that my arguments are convincing?"

"No, my Father", said the young man softly.

The Dominican made a step forward.

"Will you admit, at least, that they are strong enough to make you think things over for a while . . . say, for a week? No? For a day, then."

"No, my Father", repeated Thomas, as softly as before.

Friar John's eyes narrowed.

"And on what, if I may ask, do you base this attitude of yours?"

"On the words of our Lord", said Thomas, entirely unruffled. " 'I have come to set man at variance with his father and the daughter with her mother and the daughter-in-law with her mother-in-law; a man's enemies will be the people of his own house. He is not worthy of me, that loves father or mother more.' "

"And why", thundered Friar John, "did you not say that when I asked you whether my arguments had convinced you?"

"Because you did not ask me for my reasons, then, my Father."

A flash of lightning came from Friar John's eyes.

"Friar Thomas: you will have the habit this very day."

"You will speak to Father Prior for me?" asked Thomas, his voice tremulous with joy.

"There is no need for that", said Friar John gently. "I am the Master General of the Order."

Chapter IV

NICCOLO! Twenty men on horseback; my horse and that of Sir Piers. We ride at once."

"Yes, most noble lady."

"Off with you. And this must happen now . . . now, when neither Landulph nor Rainald is at home. They're never here when one needs them and always when one doesn't. Don't stand there like an antique statue, Sir Piers, if you please; get ready. We shall take no food with us; we'll find all we need on the way, if that's what you were going to ask."

The young Englishman withdrew without a word, but at the door he had to step aside. The three sisters came rushing in.

"What's happened, Mother?"

"I have no time for explanations. Where is Nina? Where is Eugenia? *No* one is here when I need somebody. I must change my dress. I'm riding."

"We'll help you, Mother."
"We can do it better than the maids."
"But you must tell us what's happened."
"The dress is over there in the black cupboard . . . no, not that one, the blue riding dress with the blue cope, yes. . . . Help me out of this thing, Adelasia."
"Mother, please, what happened? Bad news from Rainald?"
"Rainald? No . . . Thomas, that idiot . . . "
"Has the Emperor burned down the university?" There was a streak of logic in Theodora.
"I wish he had . . . no, I don't. I don't care what he has burned down. He's got nothing to do with it. It's Thomas, I'm telling you. The fool. I knew he was going to get himself into trouble one day, I knew it. But this I did not expect. I'm glad his father did not live to see it."
"But what has he done, Mother?" They had got her out of her dress now. Half naked, her eyes blazing, she looked like a very angry pagan goddess.
"What has he done? He's dishonored us. They'll laugh at the name of Aquino from one end of the kingdom to the other. He's joined the beggar monks!"
"No!"
"Don't stop and gape at me; get me into the riding dress. Hold it tighter, Marotta, and for heaven's sake don't fidget. Yes, the beggar monks. The Dominicans. He's a fool and backward and clumsy and anything you like—but he still is an Aquino, and an Aquino is not a beggar, monk or otherwise. There are limits. An Aquino wandering through the streets, begging for alms . . . an Aquino making vulgar speeches to the scum of the cities! Great God in heaven, what have I done to deserve this! Can't you see that the button is further up, Marotta? Up, not down, up! The girl doesn't even know what up and down is. A beggar monk. In a black and white peasant dress. It is insufferable. But I'll show them."

"But, Mother, how could he do such a thing? He's a Benedictine, isn't he?"

"Only an oblate. But now he's taken vows. At least it looks as if he has. Carlo came back from Naples. He was buying things there for me, and he saw it all, saw it with his own eyes. How I wish I'd gone with him. He saw it, I tell you: they made a feast out of it, his beggar brothers. I don't blame them for that. One doesn't catch an Aquino every day. The story was all over Naples at once, of course. They escorted him into their wretched little church, beggars right and beggars left, and there they gave him . . . what was it? . . . the badges of penance and of submission and their confounded habit. Sounds nice, doesn't it, for a boy with imperial blood in his veins? Penance and submission and a beggar's dress. Carlo saw it all. He couldn't stop it, of course; he was alone and he had no orders. But he had the good sense to stay there for a while and observe, and he found out that they were taking Thomas to Rome."

"To Rome? Why?"

"Sparrow brain! Why? Because they know perfectly well that I am not going to let that happen, and Naples is not exactly safe ground for them. Never mind; I'll find them in Rome just as easily. I'll find them. And God help them when I do."

"The men are ready, most noble lady."

"Right. My whip. I'll be back in three days at the latest." She stormed out of the room.

The three girls looked at each other, horrified.

"I didn't think Thomas could be *so* stupid", said Adelasia.

"Men are strange creatures", said Theodora. "You never know where you are with them."

* * *

They made the sixty miles to Rome in little over four hours. When they sped through Terracina a local procession had to scatter in all directions, and in Anagni two dogs got themselves ridden over, and an old man very nearly suffered the same fate. At the gates of Rome the papal guard insisted on disarming the men from Aquino before allowing them to enter. Piers alone, as of knightly rank, was permitted to keep his sword. The Countess' temper was not improved by that incident. She forgot all about the plan she had made during the ride: to get in touch with her cousin, Paolo Orsini, and to approach the Dominican authorities through him, who was a man of great influence in clerical circles. Instead she ordered: "To the convent of Santa Sabina." It was the first Dominican convent of the city, near the church of St. Sixtus II. It was as good as certain that they had taken Thomas there, to their citadel.

At the convent door she dismounted and rang the bell herself.

The *Ostiarius* opened his little window. When he saw the Countess and behind her an armed knight and twenty armored, if unarmed men, he swiftly closed it again.

"Open at once", commanded the Countess, enraged. As she was not obeyed, she began to knock at the door with the knob of her riding whip. Then she rang the bell again. And again. And again.

"Open, you rabble", she shouted. "Open, or I'll have my men smash this door."

The little window opened again. She could see the face of a friar, and it was not the same man as before: it was a grey-haired man with a strong face.

"What is it?" asked the friar.

"Open the door."

"This is a Dominican convent. I cannot open to a woman."

"Open the door, I say. Open it at once."

"Impossible."

"I'll have it smashed by my men if you don't, my good friar."

"Do that," said the friar perfectly calmly, "and you will be excommunicated *ipso facto.* This is consecrated ground."

"How dare you talk to me like that! I'm the Countess of Aquino."

"You are no more than any other human soul here."

She managed to gain control of herself.

"You are wrong . . . Father. For I am also the mother of Count Thomas of Aquino, whom you have taken here, a mere boy, against my will. Give him back to me: that is all I have come for."

"There is no Count Thomas of Aquino here. And Friar Thomas has made his own decision."

"You admit, then, that he is here", she snapped at him. But once more she regained control. "It isn't the Countess of Aquino who is talking to you now, Father . . . it is simply a mother who wants her child. Let me have my child, and there shall be peace between us."

"I repeat," said the friar, "your son has made his own decision before God and the Order. This decision cannot be undone. There is no reason for you to be unhappy about it; there is no higher honor than to give one's son to the service of God. You will certainly see him again, but you cannot see him now."

Her patience was exhausted. "I will see him if I have to turn Rome upside down", she shouted. "And what is more, I shall get him back to my house. No one has the right to stand between a mother and her child, least of all a herd of religious rabble rousers. Believe me, you will rue the day on which you tricked my son into your hateful community."

"May God forgive you as I do, my daughter", said the friar stonily, and the window closed.

For a moment she stood motionless. Then she turned sharply.

"I wish to mount."

Piers himself helped her up and gave her the reins.

"To the Lateran Palace."

* * *

Sinibald Fiesco, Count of Lavagna, newly elected Pope under the name of Innocent IV, was a man of medium height, very elegant, with polished manners. He was not a towering figure of almost superhuman energy like Innocent III, and he had none of the do-or-die tenacity of Gregory IX. His profound study and knowledge of law had made him more elastic rather than more rigid . . . the study of law can have either effect. He was far too intelligent not to know that he was not a great man. And he was fully aware that Emperor Frederick II was just that. He had accepted the papacy with a heavy heart. He knew that Innocent IV could not condone what Cardinal Fiesco had, well, not condoned but not interfered with—if only because he knew that no interference would have been of the slightest use. Now it would have to come to either an arrangement or a clash, and his whole nature longed for an arrangement.

Again and again he told himself that there were good traits in Frederick's nature, that the right way of handling him might well have excellent results. He could not revoke the excommunication, of course, as long as the Emperor would not show repentance. But there were, perhaps, ways and means to let the Emperor know that the excommunication could be revoked, *if* he showed repentance. As for reparation . . . it was to be feared that the entire lifetime of Frederick would not suffice to make good what he had done. Too many towns, villages, castles, and monasteries were in ashes, too many people had died . . . some of them in a very terrible way. And yet, there was always hope. He thought of the Church's teaching on hell. The Christian had to believe in hell . . . for Christ himself had mentioned its existence no less than six times in the Sermon on the Mount, as everyone would know if they'd only take the trouble of reading on a little further than the Beatitudes. But no one was allowed to say that any particular person was actually in hell. Not even Nero. Not even Judas Iscariot, despite his dreadful epithet of "Son of Perdition". Hell existed . . . but perhaps, perhaps there was no human being in it. There was hope, then, also for Frederick. And if there was hope for him before that ultimate court from which there was no appeal, it was safe to say that there was hope for him here, too.

Heaven knew he didn't make it easy for the successor of St. Peter.

The specter of divided loyalties looming all over the empire was a terrible thing. It was intolerable. It had to be exorcised, and nothing but the return of the Emperor to the fold could ban it.

They all came to him, to the Pope, with their very justifiable complaints and accusations: the Abbot of Santa Justina, whom Frederick had driven out of his monastery; the Abbot of Monte Cassino, whose monastery had been burned and pillaged with eleven monks dead; the cities in Lombardy, which had to bear the imperial onslaught year after year; the towns around Lucera, Moliso, Termolo, Foggia, whose girls and women disappeared without a trace . . . until they turned up again in the harem of some Saracen in the Emperor's Islamitic colony of Lucera.

They all came to the Pope . . . for they dared not go to the Emperor. And the Pope could do nothing. The patrimony around Rome was slender territory, its army small, its revenues shrunken. As a temporal ruler there was not the slightest possibility of combatting the "Wonder of the World", the *Stupor Mundi,* as he was called. And as the spiritual ruler: well, Frederick did not belong to his jurisdiction any longer . . . he was cast out into the horrible freedom he seemed to enjoy—though no one could enjoy it for very long. Compassion and prayer were all the Pope could give to Frederick's victims. There was no end in sight, either. Frederick was relatively young, only a little over fifty; and his sons, Enzio perhaps excepted, already showed signs of becoming, if anything, worse than their father. Once more, as in the times of Nero and Diocletian and Attila, people were whispering of the Antichrist.

If only Frederick could make a move to return to the fold. The Pope had seen to it that certain people should drop a hint to him about it. He, too, could not enjoy the unnatural state of affairs. He had suffered much from his excommunication; whatever went on in his soul . . . and no one but he himself knew that . . . there was no doubt that he had suffered bitterly.

Such was the situation and such were the thoughts of Innocent IV when, fairly late in the evening, the visit of the Countess of Aquino was announced to him in his small study, which in its bareness was not unlike the cell of a monk.

Aquino. Aquino. A family entirely and unrestrictedly proimperial. At least two Aquinos were serving in the Emperor's army. He had met old Count Landulph once, but never the Countess. Her name had never been mentioned to him in connection with political affairs. What could lead her here, at this hour? Was it possible that the Emperor used her, perhaps had even sent her in some unofficial capacity? It was highly unlikely. But nothing was impossible with the "Wonder of the World".

He gave orders to have her shown in.

She was calm now and very dignified; she knelt, kissed the Fisherman's ring, and apologized for her spontaneous visit at an unseemly hour. She gave an account of what had happened, quite accurately, to the best of her ability, and asked for his help.

By now he saw fairly clearly that there was no connection whatsoever between her and Frederick and that she was simply a great lady, accustomed to being obeyed and quite incapable of seeing her wishes thwarted. It was obvious to him, too, that she did not have too much respect for the character and intelligence of her son Thomas. In that she could be right or wrong, but one had to give her the benefit of the doubt. In any case he could not very well comply with her idea of taking the Dominican Order to task merely because her son had seen fit to join it. How old was the young man? Nearly eighteen. Certainly an age in which a young Italian had learned to think for himself, if he was capable of thinking at all.

But then she mentioned that the Emperor was certain to grant her the Lord Abbotship of Monte Cassino for her son in a few years' time and that this was the main reason why she could not countenance his absurd wish to be a beggar monk.

So far he had not interrupted her rapid speech at all, except once to inquire the age of her son. Now he said with firm politeness: "It is not for the Emperor to decide who will be Lord Abbot of Monte Cassino. And so far he has not shown much interest in the well-being of the monastery, to say the very least."

She began to breathe heavily. Only now she realized that her visit to the Pope could easily be misunderstood at the imperial court. She had put herself in a dangerous position, directly between the two warring powers.

She decided to make an end to the audience.

"I see that you cannot help me, Your Holiness."

"On the contrary", said the Pope, smiling gently. "I am quite willing to help you as best I can." There was no reason, at present, strongly to oppose the Emperor's idea of giving Monte Cassino to Thomas of Aquino . . . if it really was his idea. There was, on the contrary, every reason to comply, once one had made it clear that this was a matter for the Lateran and not imperial headquarters. One would have to have a look at the young man, of course, and he would need a very efficient prior in any case. Besides, there was no hurry.

Theodora stood up quickly. "You will help me? Thank you, thank you, Your Holiness. One word from you and that terrible Order will give him back to me, and he will be able to take up the position fitting his rank."

The Pope raised his thin, beautiful hands in polite protest. "It is not quite as easy as that, my daughter. I shall make inquiries. Something, after all, depends also upon his own wishes. He cannot be *forced* to leave the Order, except in certain circumstances, which, fortunately, do not apply here. But as far as Monte Cassino is concerned, there we shall be able to do something, I trust, when the time is ripe for it. But not at the age of eighteen, my daughter; surely you understand that."

Silently she knelt to receive his blessing.

Five minutes later she rejoined her escort, waiting for her outside the palace. "Sir Piers? I am sorry to have to ask this of you after our long ride, but it cannot be helped. The audience was not successful. Take your own men and ride with the utmost speed to Ciprano. There you will find my sons. At least I hope they are still there. Tell them what has happened. And tell them that I expect them to bring me back my son Thomas. Not to Rocca Secca. To my fortress of Monte San Giovanni. And I will not set eyes on either of them until they bring Thomas back. He may have been smuggled out of Rome by now. But he cannot be far. Tell them to get him . . . never mind how."

* * *

They were waiting on a hillock, near the village of Acquapendente. The place was cleverly chosen. Not only could they see the old Roman road, stretching out between rows of cyprus trees, irregular as the teeth in the mouth of an aging giant—but they themselves had perfect cover behind the thick oleander bushes. It was near midday.

"See anything, Landulph?"

"No."

"Well, keep it up . . . your eyes are better than mine."

"Perhaps we missed him after all."

Rainald looked impatient. "We can't have missed him. Not after all the precautions we took."

"You never know. It's like trying to find a needle in a haystack anyway."

"Brother Thomas is a very large needle, Landulph. Besides, he can't be alone. And until we came here, almost to the very gates of Rome, we had every road watched for black and white friars."

"Yes", said Landulph drily. "It's just like a boar hunt, isn't it?"

"Comparisons abounding . . . " Rainald laughed a little angrily. "What do you think, Sir Piers?"

"He hasn't passed yet", said the young Englishman curtly.

"What makes you so sure about that?" asked Landulph.

"It's not only because of the net you've drawn. The quarry may slip through any net, if it's only wide enough. But the friars wouldn't let him leave Rome as long as the Countess was there. The only place where he was safe then was the convent. And I and my men have been very quick on our way to you. So I think you will catch him here."

"Confound these Englishmen", thought Rainald. It was a perfectly sensible explanation, given perfectly politely. But the tone . . . the tone suggests a mixture of disapproval and . . . well, almost contempt. Or was he just being over-sensitive?

"I can see something", said Landulph.

"Where? Yes . . . they're monks all right. And, wait a minute . . . black . . . black and white. Dominicans. Got 'em. Five of 'em. Two round ones and three thin ones. And . . . one of the round ones . . . the big one on the left, that's him, that's brother monk. On our horses, Crusaders . . . the infidel is here. Bear yourselves with Christian fortitude and valor."

"Oh, shut up", growled Landulph.

"Now we shall be able to go home to the fleshpots of Mamma", sang the irrepressible poet. "To horse, to horse . . . "

Frowning, Landulph allowed himself to be helped into the saddle. Piers and Rainald followed his example. They had thirty men with them. More than sixty were watching other roads, but this had been the most likely place.

"Give the order, great general," said Rainald, "and we shall sail into them like Achilles, Hannibal, and Caesar, rolled into one."

"Come on, men", said Landulph. He was very angry, although he would not have been able to say exactly why. He spurred his horse and broke down onto the road.

Rainald, Piers and the men followed. No more than a minute later the five Dominicans were surrounded.

"Now then," said Landulph sulkily, "you talk, Rainald."

The poet bowed to him with an ironic smile and said: "Pious friars, please understand that we have nothing whatever against you. All we want is our little brother Thomas, whom you have . . . errh . . . shall we say annexed? We want to take him home to his mother and his sisters."

Friar John remained silent. The Friars d'Aguidi, St. Giuliano, and Lucca remained silent. So Thomas himself spoke. He pointed to the others and said gravely: "These are my mother and my brothers and my sisters."

Piers drew a sharp breath. He knew where those words came from. Once more, the defense against violence was simply a word of Christ. The only defense, perhaps . . . but one that made one feel, well, as he felt when the Abbot had used the same weapon against him in Monte Cassino, years ago. There seemed to be such a sentence ready for every opportunity, and it put a man completely in the wrong; no . . . it made a man aware of *being* completely in the wrong.

But now Rainald leaned forward. "Look here, Thomas," he said sharply, "I don't know what you were thinking when you did this thing, and I don't care. But you're coming with us now, d'ya hear?" He beckoned to two of his men, who dismounted and seized Thomas' arms. He did not resist. But when they tried to drag him to a spare horse, two huge shoulders and arms got into extremely swift motion, and the two baffled men found themselves tumbling back with such vigor that one of them toppled over and sat down heavily on the road. Their comrades laughed outright.

"Get him", yelled Rainald, pale with anger. "Get him, you stupid cowards."

But it was Landulph who brought about the decision. He had made a mistake by allowing Rainald to talk. Talking was always a mistake. It got a man nowhere. He saw that the grey-haired friar was producing a crucifix, and he knew instinctively that in the next moment they would hear some solemn anathema if they went on with this. He didn't want any anathemas or crosses. He wanted action. "Stop, men", he roared, and he rode up to Thomas himself and seized him. "The other arm, Rainald, and be quick about it, you fool." Instinctively Rainald obeyed, and as soon as they had got hold of him they spurred their horses. Even a giant could not have resisted the tug of two horses. In vain Thomas struggled between them as best he could.

"Leave the friars alone. Follow us", bellowed Landulph to his men.

They had Thomas out of the dangerous black and white circle now. Twenty yards further on Piers brought up the spare horse. The brothers heaved Thomas on it . . . some of the men helped . . . they took the reins, and Landulph ordered a sharp canter. Off they went, in the direction away from Rome, leaving a mighty cloud of dust behind them that reached and enveloped the silent group of the friars.

Friar John of Wildeshausen, Master General of the Order of Preachers, called by most the Dominican Order, turned abruptly and walked in the direction of Rome. He swallowed hard before he said: "We shall pray for the transgressors." They did, as was their duty. But at least old Brother St. Giuliano knew his Magister General well enough to be certain that the matter would not rest at that, although he realized better than most what it meant to be up against the Aquinos. An hour later they were back at the convent, where Friar John wrote immediately to the Pope.

In the meantime the victors of the encounter had left the road and were now traveling in a half-circle, so as to bypass Rome, picking up the men they had left to watch other roads toward the north. Three hours later they had reached the southern precincts of the city and were speeding down the Via Appia on their way to the fortress of San Giovanni, in a compact mass, with the prisoner in the middle. Two trumpeters, giving piercing signals, formed the vanguard. The blue flag of the Aquinos was flying.

Chapter V

THE LITTLE FORTRESS was perched on top of the mountain like a bird of prey. It was said that on particularly fine days one could see the sea from the watch-tower facing west, but that was not true. All one could see was an endless realm of blue-green, green, brown, and grey hills, meadows, and groves.

Landulph was stretching his muscular limbs in the hall—a tiny replica of the hall of Rocca Secca, all wooden beams and heavy chairs.

"This is going to be extremely tiresome", he growled.

"What?" asked Rainald, emptying his goblet of wine. "And why?"

"Monte San Giovanni is a damned poor exchange for Rocca Secca . . . or for Aquino. It's so small. Scarcely a dozen servants for all of us . . . no music, except yours, of course . . . "

"Thank you for nothing."

"No minstrels, no feasting, most of our friends miles and miles away . . . why, one would think we were in a state of siege."

"And so we are, brother", said Rainald cheerfully. "So we are. It's obvious. We are at war. And our enemies are numerous: the entire Dominican Order. I don't know how many hundreds or thousands of fierce warriors in black and white and maybe the Pope and his army of ecclesiastics: everybody is after us because we have stolen their priceless jewel, the pride of their eyes, the indispensable, the incomparable brother Thomas."

"You can never be serious, can you?"

"I refuse to be serious. Everybody else is. It's precisely the seriousness of the place that gets you down, Landulph. And perhaps also your bad conscience."

"Bad conscience? I haven't got a bad conscience. Why should I have?"

"Because you have stolen the priceless brother Thomas and put him into a little bottle of copper and closed and sealed it with the seal of Solomon. And now you are under a curse: you must watch the little bottle of copper lest the *Djin* get out somehow; and if there is anything more tiresome than watching a bottled-up *Djin* I still have to learn what it is. No wonder you feel bored."

"We could have taken the boy to Rocca Secca just as well."

"No, Landulph, we couldn't. It is not a very nice situation to keep a member of the family in a dungeon in the castle of his ancestors."

"Dungeon? A very comfortable tower room. A far better room than the cell they would give him in one of their confounded convents or monasteries."

"As usual you miss the point that matters most, *carissimo.* In his cell is where he wants to be. The room where he is now is where he does not want to be. In his cell he may have little freedom, but he has sacrificed his freedom voluntarily. Here we force him to live the way he is living. The point you missed so elegantly is the little matter of freedom. But what I was driving at is this: Mother doesn't wish this matter to be talked about more than is inevitable. Therefore quite consistently she chooses Monte San Giovanni, where we receive no guests. Have some wine."

"Thanks. You know what occurs to me?"

"No, but I'm sure you will tell me if I ask you nicely."

"I'll tell you whether you ask me or not. What occurs to me is that we are just as much prisoners here as Thomas is."

"Of course", said Rainald, grinning. "Prison guards always are. But something can be done about that, I think."

"Damn the young idiot", said Landulph angrily. "I should like to give him a proper hiding for all the mischief he's caused us. I'd like . . . "

He stopped as the Countess entered with one of her ladies.

"Ah, here you both are . . . very good. I wish to pay a visit to Thomas now. He's had a week to think his decision over alone. That should be sufficient. But I refuse to meet him as long as he is wearing that absurd beggar's dress. I have brought decent clothes for him . . . give them to Count Landulph, Eugenia, please. Take those, Landulph, go into his room, and ask him to change into these. Have the black and white rags burned. And if he resists, force him."

Landulph looked at Rainald. "Well . . . perhaps he will resist," said he hopefully. "Thank you, Mother, your orders will be carried out punctiliously."

Grinning, he stalked out of the room.

"You know, Mother," said Rainald, "you really are an admirable person. I very much doubt whether any other mother could have waited one full week before going to see Thomas. But I wish you would let the girls take his food to him and not Landulph and me. It does look a little silly."

"Very well. I'll tell them. What you really mean is, of course, that you want to have more time for yourself- . . . that you want to ride out and stay out for a night or two."

"Mother, you're a genius."

At that moment a noise as of breaking wood could be heard and then Landulph's voice, strangely muffled, but definitely shouting for Rainald.

"Seems he's run into a bit of trouble there", said the poet. "I suppose I'd better have a look."

He sauntered over to the tower room. But the noise went on for quite a while. At last it abated. The brothers came back.

"Santa Madonna," exclaimed the Countess, "what has happened?"

Landulph's nose was red and swollen, and he painfully rubbed his head where another swelling seemed to be forming. His hair and clothes were in complete disarray so that Eugenia could not help laughing. And Rainald had the beginning of a large black eye.

Both were panting and exhausted. But between them they carried what once had been a Dominican habit.

"General," said Rainald to his mother, "here is the trophy. We got it . . . but at what a price."

"You mean to say that Thomas . . . ?"

"What a monk—" Landulph was still panting. "I've never seen anything . . . like it. He hit me over the head with . . . the back of a chair."

"He got the worst of it, poor Landulph did", said the poet. "I found him in pretty bad shape when I went in. Thomas was on top of him, and he couldn't get up. So I got busy, but Thomas hit me in the eye . . . have you got a mirror, Mother? I must be a fine sight. We've all been quite wrong, Mother. Father was and you were: he should never have become a monk at all. He's made for the two-hander. I'll bet anything he could split a Saracen from head to foot with a single stroke. My eye hurts."

"And all that", gasped Landulph, "because I wanted to take these rags off him as you said I should."

"That'll do, Eugenia", said the Countess, and the lady of the household stopped giggling. "You may go now." Then to Rainald: "Is he hurt too?"

"Frankly, I don't know", said Rainald. "We were much too busy fighting."

"I hope he is", said Landulph grimly.

Without a word she turned and left. The tower room was near by, a fairly large room. The key was in the outside of the door.

"Nice", said Landulph. He had thrown himself into his chair and was pouring himself a fresh goblet of wine. "I've never been so surprised in all my life. A monk. And lays about like a berserker."

"But how did it start?"

"Well, I asked him for those rags."

"Nicely?"

"Well . . . "

"I see."

"Confound it, I *wanted* to give him his hiding."

"Had I known that," said Rainald, "I would have left you to stew in your own juice."

"He's merited a hiding, hasn't he?"

"Perhaps", said Rainald. "But you got it. And so did I. I don't think he got much. *Per Baccho,* the boy's an ox. And the worst is . . . "

"What?"

"Well, I tried to wheedle Mother into having him served by the girls. She agreed, too. I wanted to go to Naples and see little red Barbara again."

"And who the hell is little red Barbara?"

Rainald's one healthy eye became dreamy. "The loveliest girl in Naples . . . an exquisite specimen of lusciousness. Unfortunately, I am not the only one to have found that out. She's seen to *that.* In short, half Naples is at her little feet, and I very much fear not only at her feet. She has more to give than that, and she gives it, brother, she gives it in abundance. Tomorrow night I hoped I would be able to see her at that little pink house just above Santa Agnes'. And now I can't."

"Why not?"

"Look at me! This'll take three or four days at least before it settles down, and even then it will still be all the colors of the rainbow. She'd laugh at me."

"Well, I don't know . . . if she's a whore, she'll take your gold even if you have a hump like the Emperor's jester."

"Landulph, Landulph . . . " Rainald was morally indignant. "You have no right to talk like that about little red

Barbara. She will take gold, certainly. But she will not prostitute her aesthetic sense. Not little red Barbara. And I wouldn't dream of showing myself to her like this."

"From which I can deduce two things", said Landulph. "First, that she has gold enough to be choosy if she feels like it. Secondly, that it isn't her aesthetic sense that matters here but yours. Or rather you're too damned vain, that's all. Where did you say her house was?"

"In . . . oh, I see. No, brother mine, you look even worse than I do. In fact, you looked worse than I do now, even before brother Thomas gave you a nose like a plum, watery eyes, and a tumor on your head. Ah, little red Barbara. What a fool I was to save you from the wrath of the friar, Landulph. She's so versatile . . . sometimes she is like a little lizard in the sun, quiet and lazy and when you touch her, hush . . . she is gone. Sometimes she is passionate and fiery like Astaroth of the Phoenicians, ready to devour you alive in the flame of her love. And she gives you the feeling that you and you alone matter, that there is no other man in the entire universe and that her heart would break if you left her. It was she who inspired me to write my 'Lamento', and that's one of my best, you know:

Gia mai non mi comforto
Ne mi vo' rallegrare
Le navi sono al porto
E vogliono collare
Vassene la piu gente
In terra d'oltra mare
Ed' io, lassa dolente
Como deg' io fare?"

"Pretty", said Landulph.

"Murder and pestilence", broke out Rainald. "And now I can't go and see her and embrace her, because brother friar has hit me in the eye."

"In this case," declared Landulph, "it was his business to

do so. He prevented you from mortal sin, master poet." And he grinned.

Rainald gave him a look of surprise. Then he frowned. "That's not a very good joke."

Suddenly they both looked up. The Countess reappeared, pale and angry, her lips pressed tightly together. Without a word she swept past them and disappeared in the corridor leading to her own apartment.

Rainald smiled significantly. "Despite black eye and swollen nose", he said, "I think we did better than Mamma."

* * *

The three sisters had had a prolonged debate about who was to take the prisoner his meals. In the end they had decided that they would all take their turn and that Marotta as the eldest was going to take the next, the midday meal, in to him. She had fought for it for a long time, and energetically, but now that she received the plates from the kitchen she became a little frightened. "You don't think he's going to hit me, too? I mean, he seems to have changed so much; who would have thought . . . ?"

"Nonsense, Marotta; if you're afraid, let me."

"No, no, I was only asking. I'm going. I'm going."

And in she went with her plates, into the den of the wild friar.

It was quite a comfortable den with a good bed, a fairly large window, and even with a fireplace. The nights could be very cold at this time of the year.

The wild friar was sitting in a huge armchair, reading Aristotle. Willynilly, he had had to put on the clothes the Countess had chosen for him—a long green tunic with a belt of gold-embroidered leather and green velvet shoes.

He looked up. "Marotta? It is good to see you."

She smiled, her eyes searching his face. "They didn't hurt you, did they?"

"Hurt me? Oh, that." He looked very embarrassed. "I

did a terrible thing, Marotta. I forgot . . . I entirely forgot that I mustn't . . . I fought, you know."

"I know." Her eyes sparkled. "You did very well, too."

"No, no . . . it was a disgraceful thing to do. But Landulph came and tried to tear my habit off me. It was only a few days ago that my prior had given it to me, Thomas Agni di Lentino, a saintly old man . . . you would love him, Marotta . . . and it meant so much to me. And there he was, just tearing it to pieces, and I . . . I fought him. It has taught me something, though."

"What has it taught you, Thomas?"

"Why I am here, Marotta. Why God has permitted this thing."

"You should eat now, Thomas. It will get cold."

Obediently he ate. But she could see that he did not know what he was eating. He had become very strange, she thought. It was as if he were talking to her from a great distance, and that distance in some inexplicable way frightened her a little. She drew nearer and caressed his glossy dark brown hair, the circlet of it that his Order had left him. What an enormous head he had.

"Tell me, Thomas . . . what do you mean? Why has God permitted what? I want to understand."

He looked at her gravely. She was the oldest and by far the gentlest of his sisters, and she resembled him in a peculiar way: it was as if his own shy gentleness had been poured into a dainty feminine form with deep, pensive eyes and a pale, firm little mouth.

"I'll tell you, Marotta: we were walking to Paris, the other friars and I. I have never been so happy in all my life. I was going to work and study, and either word just means collecting treasures to the honor of God and of the Order. Then they came and stopped me and forced me back. And though I prayed, 'Thy will be done', I could not help a question surging up in me again and again: Why did God permit this thing?"

"But surely that often happens, Thomas . . . that we do not understand why God permits this or that to happen?"

"Yes. But I do understand now. It is not just because of Mother's indiscretion or because of Landulph's and Rainald's violence. It is because of my own imperfection. God does not want me as yet."

There were tears in her eyes.

"One of us is behaving very foolishly", she said in a wavering voice. "I think it's me."

Then she fled.

"He didn't hit you, too, did he?" asked Adelasia curiously.

Marotta ran past her without answering.

Blinded with tears, she almost crashed into Robin Cherrywoode as he came up from the basement to go on watch.

"Anything wrong, noble lady?"

"No", sobbed Marotta.

"I see", said Robin. "Wouldn't be such a bad thing, perhaps, if you'd tell it to an old war dog. There may be a remedy . . . you never know."

She shook her head. "It's my brother Thomas. They've taken his habit away, and now he's . . . he thinks God doesn't want him. Oh, Robin, I've never seen such unhappiness in anyone's face as when he said that God didn't want him."

"Hmmm, hmmm . . . and where is that habit now?"

"Oh, it's all in pieces. . . . Adelasia has it. It's finished . . . rags."

"Hmmm, hmmm . . . tell you what . . . you get me those rags; yes, yes, I know they're beyond repair, but get them for me all the same. And if something can be done . . . will you promise to keep silent about it? Good."

An hour later on the ringwall Piers saw something black and white sticking out of the armor of his varlet. "What have you got there, Robin?"

"A friar's habit, master."

"Don't tell me you are going in for that now, Robin?"

"Not exactly, master. It's *his* habit, you know . . . they tore it off him." Robin chuckled. "He gave it to them good and proper, master. Wouldn't have made such a bad soldier after all."

"It's a damned shame, Robin. I wish we hadn't been on that business of getting him back."

"No, master. If a man wants to be a monk, why not let him be one? A man will be good only at what he likes. They shouldn't have torn his habit off, either. It's like breaking a knight's sword. It isn't done."

"Quite right, Robin. And I shall be glad when our time here is over."

"It couldn't have happened in England. But seeing that it has happened, perhaps, if I may . . . I mean . . . "

"What exactly do you mean, Robin?"

Robin hummed and hawed. The rags were beyond repair. But there should be more like it where these had come from, shouldn't there? And there was a curious black and white speck down there, to the left, just behind the oleander bushes. He had seen it before . . . there! But of course they were having the watch, the master and he.

Piers gave a sharp look in the direction Robin had mentioned and began to understand.

"Of course", he said in a casual tone. "We are having the watch. I think I'm going to have a look at the other side." And he sauntered off.

Robin chuckled. As a stickler for form, he waited until his master was out of sight. Then he produced the habit and began to wave it wildly.

After about five minutes the black and white speck behind the oleander bushes began to move nearer. Robin went on waving.

The black and white speck became a Dominican monk, looking up curiously. It was still too far away for any other method of communication . . . nor would any other method have been advisable in the circumstances.

Robin went on waving for a while. Then he showed the habit to the friar . . . see . . . all worn . . . all rags . . . and he dropped it over the wall. To his joy the friar came and picked it up. Now Robin began to make gestures of such classic simplicity that even a child would have understood them. He stretched out his enormous hands as if he wished to have the habit back . . . he looked up to the sun and then showed the monk both his hands with the fingers stretched widely apart . . . ten, yes, ten . . . and one more, the thumb . . . eleven. Again the gesture of trying to get the habit back.

To his immense satisfaction he saw the friar smile and nod and then depart very quickly. A minute later he had disappeared in the bushes.

A little later Piers came back, leisurely.

"Nothing new to report, master," said Robin, beaming.

Piers saw that the black and white thing was not any longer sticking out from under his armor. The black and white speck behind the oleander bushes seemed to have disappeared too.

"Very good, Robin", he said calmly.

* * *

It so happened that for several days Robin would have the watch on the ringwall late in the evening . . . up to midnight. On the third evening he saw what he had been waiting for. He gave a sign with a torch. A few minutes later he recognized the shadowy, moving form. The Dominicans . . . two of them . . . slowly raised a very long pole, at the end of which something black and white was attached. Up and up went the flag of God until it appeared on the ringwall.

* * *

Landulph, rather pale around the gills, stormed into the Countess' room.

"Mother, I don't like it."

"What is it?"

"I've just inspected Thomas' room. He . . . he's got his habit back."

"What?"

"I'm telling you, he's got it back. He's dressed in it. Do you think . . . do you think it's sorcery?"

Rainald, who had been sitting in a corner fingering his lute, began to giggle.

"Worse", said the Countess. "It's treason." She reached for her little silver bell. Who was it? The girls? Most likely. In any case, they were bound to have seen it when they brought him his last meal. No one else had been in his room since then. And they had not reported it to her. So most likely the girls. They were hanging around the tower room all the time anyway. Call Sir Piers, have a couple of men sent into the tower room and the second dress taken off Thomas just like the first? And three days later the same thing again? No. She put the little bell back. "Let the fool have his fool's dress if he's so fond of it", she said with an angry smile.

"Splendid", said Rainald from his corner. He played a short cadenza on his lute. "Your nose is still swollen, Landulph, isn't it? And my eye is now in the brown and yellow stage. And all that for nothing. You know, Mother . . . I think we made a mistake. We ought to have let him go and do what he liked."

"Never", said the Countess.

"I don't know . . . I have a strange feeling about all this. Good old Landulph isn't so far out with his idea of sorcery. We've got him back from his good-for-nothing Order, true. But it has changed all our lives. Instead of sitting at ease in Rocca Secca, we must bury ourselves here on Monte San Giovanni with a minimum of comfort. And everything we do somehow seems to turn round that tower room. We never used to pay much attention to Thomas. Now he is the center of all our activities. And I tell you, Mother . . . when we brought him here, I had the most extraordinary feeling. It seemed so silly then that I didn't talk about it. But now . . . now I better tell you. I felt we were bringing in the Trojan horse."

"Idiotic", said the Countess. "He'll change his mind."

"Mother, you have talked to him a dozen times now . . . well, half a dozen. Has he given in one inch? No, he sits there like a benevolent frog and says nothing and doesn't budge. The girls have been talking their heads off. No result. You can't keep him here for the rest of his life, can you?"

"I shall never consent to this madness, Rainald. And I am the head of the family. As a matter of fact, I am glad about what Landulph has just told us. It's a good sign. It means that Thomas is still a child. All he wants is his Dominican habit. We shall give in on that point . . . he will give in on the point that really matters. I shall write to the Pope, tell him about it, and ask him to grant him the right to go on wearing the silly habit as Lord Abbot of Monte Cassino."

* * *

Sinibald Fiesco, Count of Lavagna, Pope under the name of Innocent IV, received the letter of the Countess of Aquino a week later in his small cell-like study at the Lateran. He gave it to his secretary. "We grant this", he said. There was something very much like exasperation in the tone of his voice.

"Very good, Your Holiness".

The secretary withdrew, and the Pope began to think again the thoughts the Countess had interrupted for a brief moment. Peace . . . peace after all. For weeks and weeks there had been conferences with Frederick's men, with della Vigna, with Thaddeus of Suessa, with the Archbishop Berard.

Horrible negotiations with smooth, ironic men whose courteous manners only very thinly veiled their deep-seated enmity. Oh, not only enmity. If only it had been nothing more than enmity. But there was treachery underneath it all, subtle and mocking, a live thing that one could grasp, almost, with one's hands.

Agreements, treaties, with such men . . . what were they worth?

It was bad enough to have della Vigna expounding the manifold advantages of peace, counting them on his fingers one by one and perverting them all by doing so; della Vigna, black bearded and slant eyed, a man who would inspire a great painter for the figure of Judas Iscariot, but the most faithful of Frederick's creatures, to whom the Emperor was a saint and more than a saint. He talked of Frederick as a Mohammedan talked of Mohammed, with a faith as admirable as it was misplaced and with a badly concealed contempt for the unbeliever. He would break any oath without the slightest compunction if it furthered the Emperor's cause. To listen to della Vigna was bad enough.

But the worst, easily, was that great, big, lumbering mass of flesh, Archbishop Berard of Palermo, who had sided with Frederick from the beginning and shared his excommunication. Here at least one should have expected true repentance, caused by attrition at least, if not contrition. But he would bargain with God and St. Peter as a disgusting old man would try to bargain with the priest in the confessional about his pet vice. Couldn't he keep this, at least, or perhaps that? Must he give it all up? Of course, the Emperor had made him "head of the Church of Sicily", as if he had a right to give away what belonged to the Holy See and no one else. He was afraid of a "reduction in rank" instead of being afraid for his soul. High ecclesiastics like that made one believe more strongly than ever in the necessity of the mendicant orders. It was said . . . and on good authority . . . that his great namesake, Innocent III, had dreamed of St. Francis holding up, like a Catholic Atlas, the entire Church and Palace of St. John Lateran and that he had regarded this dream as prophetic. Perhaps it was.

How fortunate for a man to be a Franciscan or Dominican, to praise God all day and study and write to his glory instead of having to deal with these vipers and adders. And yet: peace was the dire need of the century. One could not sacrifice principles. But one could and must go to the uttermost limit to bring about peace.

Already a truce had been declared. And the negotiations, thank God, seemed to progress toward a solution. There was hope. At long last there was hope. . . .

Quietly he began to pray.

* * *

Somehow the three sisters never became accustomed to their prisoner brother. To slip into the tower room for this reason or that was always a sort of event, although as often as not he would simply go on reading his book. It was not a deliberate hint that he did not wish to be disturbed. He was utterly unaware of another presence.

Theodora could never tolerate that. She would talk to him until he answered. Or she would simply take the book out of his hand and command: "Tell me a story", as if she were a child and Thomas her grandfather. He would comply gravely and tell her what he had been reading. After a few minutes she would give up.

"You are too deep for me, brother monk."

But he would never accept that. He started again, put it in a simpler way until she had to admit that she had grasped it after all. Adelasia, too, was subjected to excerpts from Aristotle and Peter Lombard.

With Marotta, however, it was different, although she came more frequently than the other two. Usually she sat down beside him on the bed or even on the floor at his feet and stayed there for half an hour or longer without saying a single word. Adelasia, who had observed her more than once, asked her point blank why she did that, and Marotta answered without hesitation: "Because there is peace there."

But sometimes he talked to her, and she listened, wide eyed and solemn, her gentle little face preternaturally grave.

Then she asked questions, and usually they were very much to the point.

He told her about St. Dominic and St. Francis. When he talked about St. Benedict, she thought she could detect an undertone of sadness in his voice.

"Aren't you sorry that you have left him, Thomas? I like him best of all the saints you've told me about."

There was a long pause. "No, Marotta, I don't regret it. But I wish . . . "

"Tell me", she urged softly. "I . . . I feel I ought to know."

"I didn't choose to become a Benedictine, Marotta. Father chose that for me when I was five years of age. Since I have learned what the Dominican Order stands for, I've discovered that that is where I belong. There is much more to it, but these are things I cannot talk about even to you, my dear. I am where God wishes me to be: a Dominican, not yet reunited with his brothers. All the same, there is a gap in the ranks of the children of St. Benedict through my leaving, and *that* is what I regret."

After a long while she said: "It must be very difficult to be a monk . . . or a nun."

He smiled at her. "Do you think so? Most girls try to be beautiful from without, and to achieve that they renounce being beautiful from within. Whereas the nun tries to be beautiful from within and, through doing so, achieves the beauty of the whole."

She shook her head. "Surely to be a monk or a nun means striving for sanctity. And one must be terribly virtuous to be a saint."

"It's the other way round, Marotta", said he, suddenly very serious. "Sanctity is perfect love. All virtues are only consequences of that love."

They were silent for a long while after that.

Then Marotta got up. "I could never be a nun", she said almost fiercely and ran out of the room.

He looked after her, a little surprised. Then he took up his book again. In a moment he had forgotten all about her.

* * *

A few days later his mother paid him a visit.

Triumphantly she presented to him the answer of the

Pope. He had granted Thomas the right to go on wearing the Dominican habit even as Lord Abbot of Monte Cassino.

Thomas stood in silence, his eyes fixed on the floor.

"Well . . . what do you say now? Aren't you satisfied?"

He looked up. "Mother . . . I'm not wearing this habit because it pleases me. I am wearing it for what it stands for. I am a Dominican friar."

She stamped her foot. "Your famous vow of obedience doesn't seem to count for much, I must say. Here you go, resisting even the Pope's orders."

The gross unfairness her sentence contained escaped him completely. He had known nothing of her letter to the Pope, whose answer was a drily worded grant of her request "as soon as the occasion should arise".

He said slowly: "If the Holy Father commands me to do something, he will do so through my superior in the Order."

"Thomas . . . Thomas . . . "

"It is the rule, Mother."

"You are more than I can stand", screamed the Countess and left the room, trembling with rage.

Later she had a long discussion with Landulph and Rainald, in which she did most of the talking. "It's no good your sitting here doing absolutely nothing about it", she concluded. "Why don't you go in and tackle him? I can do no more. I know I am treating him wrongly, but this stubborn silence of his makes me lose my temper every time. I can't help it. It's your turn now. But no more fighting, if you please. Rainald, you call yourself a poet: you should be able to put into words what I mean . . . what we all mean. Go and talk to him."

Rainald sighed deeply. "The poet against the saint. Cheerful jousting. Landulph will make the background noises; I mean he'll be the chorus: get that quite clear, Landulph, you personify the three *Erinyes,* the Eumenides, threatening the culprit with the everlasting anger of the gods and with eternal unrest if he goes on resisting the will of his mother."

"I am . . . what?" Greek mythology was outside of Landulph's little realm.

"You are three old ladies with snakes in their hair. Never mind. Just sit there and make appreciative noises when I make my points. We'll attack him tomorrow, Mother, if that's all right with you. It's fairly late now, and he goes to bed very early. He is up early, too. In fact, I believe he is sticking very much to the same sort of life he would have in his convent."

"I know", nodded the Countess grimly. "And I know also that it was a mistake of mine to let him keep this habit. It seems to be something in the nature of a union between him and his Order. More than just a fancy. But that can't be helped now that the Pope has granted my request. Very well . . . do it tomorrow."

They visited Thomas the following afternoon. Rainald spoke well. He spoke of their father and his eager wish that Thomas should be at Monte Cassino to atone for his sin of storming it in the old days. He spoke of the very real and deep-seated grief of their mother.

Did the name of Aquino really mean nothing to him? No one was trying to force him to become a worldly man. They all respected his vocation for the priesthood. But was not St. Benedict as good a saint as St. Dominic?

It was an intuitive shot in the dark, and he saw, good observer that he was, that it had been effective. He began to harp on it, to embroider it.

Had Thomas ever thought on what St. Benedict's opinion was of all this? Surely he had the first claim. Was it right, was it godly and pious, to desert him to follow another saint? Could it not be that his family's—and especially his mother's—resistance was a direct sign from St. Benedict? And contrariwise, if it were his vocation to desert St. Benedict and follow St. Dominic, why should he, Rainald— and Landulph here—have succeeded in interrupting his journey? Surely he would have got through somehow and would by now be studying in a Dominican convent somewhere in northern Italy or in France?

Landulph fairly gaped with admiration of his brother's ingenuity.

Thomas had listened patiently, with round-eyed gentleness.

"You are right in one point, Rainald: St. Benedict has lost one of his children."

"There you are . . . "

"But God will see to that, in his own good way and in his own good time. I was only an oblate. Now I am a Dominican friar. That means that I have surrendered my will to my superiors. They, not I, decide about me."

"In other words," said Rainald quickly, "I may go and see your superiors and tell them that you are quite willing to leave the Order if they will permit it?"

"No", said Thomas with great firmness. "I shall stay a Dominican unless they chase me away."

"Brother," said Rainald, "you are the most obstinate mule I've ever seen." He laughed angrily. "Well, if we must have a beggar monk in the family, we shall see to it at least that our shame will not become public. You can stay here another twenty years for all I care."

"You are a great nuisance to us, Thomas", said Landulph suddenly. "The Emperor loathes the mendicants. And we depend upon the Emperor."

"But the Emperor", said Thomas calmly, "depends upon God."

"I doubt very much whether he thinks so", laughed Rainald.

"If that is true," said Thomas, "what makes you so proud of serving him? If you serve a man who does not serve God, how can you serve God yourselves, except in the way even the worst sinner serves God despite himself? Are you still not tired of siding with this man who has persecuted one successor of St. Peter after the other?"

"Popes come and go", said Landulph with a shrug. "But the Emperor remains. He's still young."

"As the opposite from what you say is true, your statement must be erroneous", said Thomas.

Rainald laughed. "Don't you try and fight this dialectician, Landulph. Never mind that, Thomas; you're still wrong, and I can prove it. You don't know the latest developments. A courier arrived this very morning. There will be peace between the Emperor and the Pope. And the excommunication will be revoked on the sixth of May. In Rome. The Emperor is going there in a few days' time. So we have not backed the wrong side after all, as you see."

He got up. "Well, think it over once more, brother monk. Try and find out whether your association with professional beggars is really so much more important than your father's vow and the honor of your family. Good night."

He gave Landulph a sign to leave with him.

Thomas had no answer for him. He was thinking of the great and holy joy all his brothers in the Order would be feeling over the news of peace. They had been longing for it, and now it was coming.

"Once I thought I had got him, you know", said Rainald outside. "When I mentioned that he had deserted St. Benedict. He admitted it, too."

" 'But God will see to that' ", quoted Landulph with heavy sarcasm. " 'In his own good way and in his own good time.' You just can't do anything with him. He's mad."

"What's going on there?" asked Rainald. "Mother is shouting at the top of her voice."

"Yes, at Marotta, it seems. The girl's been away all day, and she was worried."

They entered the Countess' room.

"Sorry to add to your bad temper, Mother, but there is no change. Landulph here will confirm that I have talked with angels' tongues."

The Countess was very pale.

"You may felicitate your sister Marotta. She has secretly visited a Benedictine convent and had her name inscribed as a postulant. She wishes to become a Benedictine nun."

The brothers looked at each other, stupefied. Suddenly Rainald gave a hoarse laugh. "By all the Furies, St. Benedict has got his substitute. You just quoted brother Thomas to me, Landulph, didn't you? Do it again now, will you? Just do it again."

"Nothing you may say will alter my decision", said Marotta.

"Give me wine", said Rainald. "She's got the same expression on her face as Thomas. Give me wine. I feel faint."

* * *

The Countess retired very early that day. Marotta had been sent to her room, but everyone knew that this was no more than a gesture of anger on the part of her mother. It would not last. In fact, she might have welcomed the decision of her eldest daughter if it had come in different circumstances. But as it was, it would only fortify Thomas' obstinacy. Adelasia and Theodora had been forbidden to go near Marotta, but as soon as the Countess went to bed, they slipped into Marotta's room, where they spent hours whispering together.

Rainald had suggested a drinking bout in the hall with Landulph and Piers. But after an hour or so Piers had made his excuses and gone to bed. He did not care much for heavy drinking.

"Damn the fellow", said Rainald. "Don't you go to bed, too, Landulph; I need company tonight. I refuse to be alone."

"You know, I believe he's bewitched you, too", said Landulph.

"What, our Englishman? They have no magic in England. That's the trouble with the country."

"Not Piers, idiot. Thomas, of course."

"Don't mention his name", begged Rainald. "I can't bear it. 'In God's own good way and in his own good time', eh? And Marotta goes and makes herself a nun. Who is next, Landulph? You, perhaps. Or I."

"What *do* you mean?"

"What I mean is that you are very likely quite right in a way. He's bewitched us all. Have you ever seen Mother like she is now? Marotta a nun . . . and I distinctly remember Adelasia quoting something damned pious the other day. We know now where she picked that up, don't we?"

"Mother should not have allowed the girls to look after him. They're too susceptible."

"You be happy, my boy, that you don't have to do it. Or by now you would be a confounded monk yourself."

"Don't be an ass, Rainald", said Landulph uneasily.

"I'm not an ass. I'm just a little drunk . . . not very much. Just in that stage when one begins to see things clearer. The Trojan horse, Landulph . . . I told Mother so the other day. We've taken him away from his confounded convent, so he's making a convent out of Monte San Giovanni. Aren't we living like monks and nuns already, all of us? Just give him another few months and see what happens. And there he sits, round and cheerful and completely unabashed . . . what am I saying? Unabashed? Serene and victorious! And everything turns out just as he wants it." He got up. "It's too much for me, brother. I won't stand it any longer. I'm going."

"Going? Where to?"

"I'm getting my horse out. I'm going to Naples. I want to see little red Barbara. Just as well she isn't here, or else he'd turn her, too, into a nun . . . holy Venus!"

"What is it now?" asked Landulph, bewildered.

"I have an idea", said Rainald. "I have a glorious idea. Yes. It's the solution of everything. It'll break the spell. Landulph, your brother Rainald is a genius."

"What do you mean? What's your idea?"

"I won't tell you", said Rainald with immense satisfaction. "Not yet. But listen carefully. I shall be back . . . let me see . . . on Friday night. But keep that a dead secret, understand? Tell them you have no idea when I'll come back. I shall arrive very late . . . shortly before midnight. See to it that you have the watch yourself. I don't want to be cross-examined by the Englishman."

"He wouldn't dare . . . "

Rainald laughed. "He might, in the circumstances. In any case, I rely on you having the watch. And in that night, brother mine, we shall break the monk's spell. He'll eat out of our hand after this."

"You mean . . . you are really going to use magic on him?" asked Landulph.

"Very real magic, Landulph. Very expensive magic, too. Just leave it to me. And remember: not a word to anybody."

* * *

"But why?" asked little red Barbara. "Why do you want me to do that?" She was looking at herself in the beautiful Venetian mirror . . . the present of a distinguished man she knew under the name of "Carlo", although that was not his real name, of course. She had never enquired what his real name was. It didn't pay to be curious, or rather, sometimes it did pay, but she had had the feeling—not without justification—that in Carlo's case it might have been dangerous.

"Why?" Rainald caressed her white shoulder. "Why, my soft-winged dove, my purgatorial fire, my gorgeous idol? Because I am sorry for my poor little brother. Don't you think it is a shame that he is eighteen years of age without ever having tasted the sweetness of woman?"

"He's virgin?" asked little red Barbara not without interest. "That's rare these days, I should think. But why me?"

"That's an easy one, my scintillating little serpent, my sweetly scented flower of paradise. Because only the very best is good enough for my little brother. That's why I have come all the way to Naples; that's why I am willing to incur heavy expense . . . "

"You've haggled long enough", said little red Barbara. "What's *wrong* with that brother of yours? . . . that's what I would like to know. You say he's eighteen and virgin. . . . I wouldn't like to find out, when I get there, that he's some disgusting old man or that he suffers from some horrible skin trouble . . . or something."

"Have you no confidence in me?" asked Rainald reproachfully.

"None whatever", said little red Barbara.

"Very well; I'll tell you. The only thing that's wrong with him is that he's a monk and thinks he'll die on the spot when he sets his eye on a pretty girl. I swear he's got no other blemishes."

Little red Barbara was amused. "We won't let him die, poor little thing", she said. "We'll be kind to him, so kind he'll think he is in heaven already."

"Mind you," warned Rainald, "he's just the kind of boy who'd leave his cloak in my lady Potiphar's rosy fingers and run away. Well, he can't run away very well, because he's locked in. But still . . . "

"Locked in?" interrupted little red Barbara, all her suspicions aroused again. "Why is he locked in?"

Rainald groaned. "Here we go again. Very well then: Mother has locked him in because he wants to join the beggar monks, in his holy zeal. It's so silly, it makes me cry. The only thing I'm worried about is that you may not be able to . . . make him look at you. Even you may fail . . . "

She gave him a look of amused contempt. "He's flesh and blood, I take it."

"Lots of both. A plump boy. He'll be fat one fine day."

"Then," said little red Barbara, "you needn't worry. If I fail, you'll get your golden augustals back . . . all of them. No one's done that to me since I was fourteen." She rang a little bell, and after a while a grizzled old man poked his head into the room. "You rang, my lady?"

"Yes, Matteo. Get my carriage ready. We travel to Monte San Giovanni. It's . . . how far is it, Rainald? About sixty-five miles, Matteo. See to all that is necessary."

"Very well, my lady." The old man disappeared. There

were not many people who knew that he was her uncle or that her maid was really her far less attractive sister. Little red Barbara had her family pride, too.

* * *

"Hey, Landulph!"

"Come in, Rainald." Landulph opened the door. "Did you get what you need for . . . whatever it is?"

"Certainly."

"What is it? A powder or an incantation?"

"It's a *succuba.*"

"A what?"

"It's got two admirable little white breasts, sweet lips, and masses of lovely red hair, and it's called 'little red Barbara'. She's waiting in a carriage outside."

Landulph gaped at him. "Are you completely out of your senses?"

"Keep quiet", warned Rainald.

" . . . to bring a whore into Mother's house . . . "

"Quiet, I say", blazed Rainald. "Do you want to awaken the whole house?"

But Landulph was very angry. "Have as many amours as you like. I'm not a saint either. But don't drag them here, where . . . "

"Will you keep your mouth shut, brainless? She's the remedy for Thomas, don't you understand? Once he's been in her arms, he'll forget about his holy beggars. He'll have to. They take that sort of thing rather seriously."

"Oh . . . " A silent laughter began to shake Landulph's sturdy body. "Now I understand. You're a devil, Rainald. Why didn't you bring her with you straight away?"

"And let her hear you call her a whore and make a song about the purity of the house? I know you, Landulph. Besides, I had to find out first whether they're all asleep. Are they?"

"Yes. Everybody is except myself. Go and get her."

"And keep your paws off her, brother. You mustn't

covet your brother's little red Barbara. All right, all right, I'm going."

It was not difficult to smuggle her past the two men at the drawbridge, not after each of them had received a couple of gold pieces.

A minute later the veiled young woman was inside the main building.

"Landulph, hold her cloak—no, my sweet, this is *not* my brother Thomas; it's my brother Landulph. Nothing virgin about him. All right, he'll be for another day. Now follow me on tiptoes . . . we're going straight to his room. Stay where you are, Landulph . . . if *you* go on tiptoes one can still hear it through the entire building."

"What a girl, brother . . . "

"Shhh . . . "

They mounted the stairs and reached the door; Rainald very slowly and carefully unlocked it. "He's in bed . . . asleep", he whispered. "Now then . . . in you go."

And in went little red Barbara.

On the bed lay a chubby young monk in a white habit. His black cloak covered him as a rug. The real rug and the silk cushions he had thrown out as he did every night. He was sleeping peacefully on one side, with both his fists covering his face, as most children sleep.

She wondered what his face was like. Very softly she seized the fists, easily double the size of her own overslim hands with their long, tapering fingers, and drew them toward herself.

And he woke up.

She saw a powerful young face, with strong, arched eyebrows over round, black eyes gazing at her in quiet benevolence. Then this benevolence changed, slowly, to surprise and to bewilderment.

"Quiet, my sweet", she whispered, smiling her best smile.

But he sat up, and she found her hands flying aside right and left.

He was still gazing at her, but no longer in bewilderment. It was not anger; it was not contempt. It was as if he recognized her, clearly and unmistakably, for what she really was. And for the first time in her life she became aware of what she really was, and that all her triumphs had not been hers at all. . . . She was a bundle of painted flesh; she was crawling with vermin; she thought she could see pity in those black eyes, which saw her as she was, as she was, as she was . . .

He rose from the bed. He was enormous, towering. She could not bear his eyes any longer; she knew that she had to act and act swiftly. She smiled up at him and with a desperate effort took a step toward him, displaying a beauty that had never failed her. The splendid contours of her body were lit by the red glow of the fireplace.

Without a word, without a sound he made two long steps. He snatched a huge, burning log from the fireplace and walked toward her with the quiet determination of a man who is going to put fire to a heap of rubble and rags.

Little red Barbara gave a piercing scream and turned and ran for her life. For one horrible moment she thought she could not open the door, and there he came, the giant with the fiery log; but then it did open, and she ran out, shrieking, past Rainald and down the stairs and toward the main door.

Landulph tried to stop her, to ask her what had happened. She pushed him aside with incredible force and rushed out.

Upstairs, the door to Thomas' room closed with a sound like thunder.

Rainald was cursing. The worst had happened. After the very first scream the door to Theodora's room had opened, and she had come out. She was bound to have seen the girl passing by. One look at her face and he knew that she had not only seen but also understood.

He stared hard at her. "If you tell Mother, I shall say you're overwrought. Tomorrow I shall explain it all to you."

She looked at him with unconcealed contempt.

The voice of the Countess came from the other side of the corridor. "What's happened?"

Theodora called: "Nothing, Mother. I'm sorry. I had a very bad nightmare."

They waited. But her answer seemed to have satisfied her mother.

"Thanks", said Rainald. He wiped his brow.

"I want no thanks from you", said Theodora. "You are the most contemptible person I've ever known. It's too bad that you should be my brother. Thank God that Thomas is, too. He makes up for you."

She went back into her room.

* * *

Thomas had closed his door with a quick movement of his foot. He now raised the fiery log in his hand, and with an almost ceremonial gesture he scorched a huge, black cross into the wood. He strode back to the fireplace and put the log exactly where it had been before. Then he went back to bed.

Two or three minutes before he had been fast asleep. Had he ever woken up? Had he ever left his bed? Was he awake now? That black cross on the door, was it real?

He thought it over slowly and calmly and came to the conclusion that it very likely was real and that he had not dreamed the incident but that it did not matter much whether it was so or not. What mattered was that he had been attacked, waking or asleep, by one of the archenemies of monastic life and that by the Grace of God he had been able to repulse the attack.

Clasping his hands together in great and urgent prayer, he invoked God to spare him such temptations so that he could use all his energies unhampered in his service.

The clouds of unconsciousness came down on him as he was still praying, and out of the clouds came what seemed to be a wave of light, iridescent in all the colors of the rainbow and flowing together to one single beam of white. No, it was a cone, a white-hot, fiery cone, and it came nearer and nearer, exhaling waves of heat. Down it came, inexorably; and under the pain of its approach he groaned like a man dying.

Deep in the ultimate recesses of his mind he knew that he himself had called it down on himself, that a cross, black and blistering, would have to be burned into him, and with a firm movement of his will he accepted it.

And then the fiery cone touched him, and he screamed under the terrible, unbearable pain that drew a glowing circle around his body, like a belt, a girdle of fire.

Once more they all awoke.

But there was no other sound. On the bed a chubby young monk was sleeping peacefully on one side with both his fists covering his face, as most children sleep.

* * *

When Theodora came up the steep stairs to the ringwall, Piers knew that she wished to speak to him. He knew it instinctively as lovers will, and his heart began to beat very fast.

"Sir Piers . . . "

"Your servant, noble lady".

"Sir Piers, you have once done me the honor to declare me your lady. I have never made use of your services so far."

"And I have always regretted it."

"I beg you for your services now, Sir Piers."

His childish anger was forgotten. "They are yours, my lady."

"What I tell you now must remain a secret between us."

"It will be."

Her eyes sparkled. "Sir Piers, my brother Thomas has been treated most unjustly and dastardly. Forgive me if I do not tell what I know. I must not accuse members of my family to anyone. But I wish he were free to join the brothers of his Order."

"You want him to escape?" asked Piers in his most matter-of-fact voice. "I think that can be done."

She was so happy that she pressed both his hands. "I shall be grateful to you as long as I live."

He knelt down to kiss her hand. "I've had my reward", he said simply. "Did you make a plan, or shall I make it?"

She laughed happily. "We're all working this, you know . . . Marotta, Adelasia, and I. We are in touch with the Dominicans. They say if we can only get him out, they would certainly see to it that he is not captured a second time. But we can't get him out with all the guards about."

He nodded. "Impossible to get him past the watch at the drawbridge. They are not under my command. But I remember a very holy man who once left a city hostile to him by being heaved over the wall in a basket."

She laughed. "Who was that?"

"St. Paul, if I remember rightly. That's how he escaped from Damascus. But then, he was a slight man, and three girls could have done the work. It won't be quite as easy in our case, I'm afraid."

Again she had to laugh. "I came here all anger and hope, and all you do is make jokes."

"That's our way in England, when things are really serious, my lady."

"And when they are not serious?"

"Then we are very grave and solemn about it, my lady."

Her eyes danced. "Then I must conclude, as brother Thomas would say, that you did not take anything very seriously at Aquino."

"I take you very seriously, my lady", said Piers, grinning all over his face.

"Really, I don't know what I would do without you . . . " she felt that it was time to come back to the issue at hand. "You are quite right; we need a few strong men to get Thomas over the wall."

"My man Robin is just what you need, my lady. When do you expect the men of your brother's Order to come for him?"

"All I need to do is send them a message. Tomorrow night?"

He nodded. "I shall see to it that no one else is around on this side of the wall. Robin will provide basket and ropes. You must provide the Dominican friars and . . . your brother."

It was all so natural, so simple; he did not seem even to consider the possibility of an obstacle.

She beamed at him. "I'm glad", she said vehemently. "I'm very glad you've chosen me as your lady."

As if she had said too much, she turned away and ran down the stairs.

"I'm a fool", thought Piers. "She comes to me because she needs me. But, oh, my God, give me a few more of such moments, and I'll take all the rest without complaining."

* * *

"Rainald . . . wake up. Rainald!"

"What is it . . . you, Landulph?"

"Get your sword and come outside. They are trying to get Thomas to escape."

"They? Who? What did you say?"

"Wake up, I tell you. Thomas is escaping. The girls have got him out, and he's up on the ringwall. Someone dropped something; I woke up and looked. Be quick."

"Thomas is escaping, eh?" said Rainald. He sat up with a jerk. "That's the best bit of news I've heard for a year."

"Are you mad?"

"Sleep, brother mine. You haven't waked up. You're still sleeping. Take it from me, that's what you are doing."

"Very well, then I must do it alone. I'll get the men from the guardroom."

Rainald jumped up and seized him in a grip of iron. "Oh, no, you won't. You fool. Don't you ever know when something good is happening to you? Must you spoil it?"

"Let me go . . . You're mad."

"I was mad . . . and so were you, for ever bringing him here. Landulph, if you are going to yell, I'll hit you over the head. Listen to me: Do you want to go on forever jailing your own brother? Do you want Adelasia and Theodora to become nuns, too? Do you wish to feel as I feel, that you are a particularly contemptible sort of ruffian? Let him go, I say."

"But Mother . . . she'll order us to pursue him again."

"Then we shall pursue him. But we won't catch him. Not if I can prevent it. Good night, brother Landulph. And if you feel as I do, it will be the first good night you have had for a long time."

Book Two

Chapter VI

DRUMS AND FIFES and trumpets; a cavalcade of knights; an endless procession of armored soldiers; the imperial animals, led by their dusky guards on chains wound with flowers; the imperial dancing girls under the supervision of their eunuchs; soldiers again and knights again; the imperial legal council; the officials of the treasury; the nobles, each with his own retinue, starting with those of lowest rank and rising slowly to the heights of barons and counts; the German bodyguard, all of noble blood, young giants in chain mail from head to foot on heavily armored horses . . . every man a battle unit by himself and almost invincible; the imperial councillors for political and military matters; forty exquisitely beautiful young girls with baskets of flowers.

The Emperor, on his black horse, Dragon. He was dressed in purple velvet; his helmet and cuirass were of gold, his sword hilt set with rubies. He smiled and nodded continuously and graciously whenever the Imperial Progress passed through a village or town, while twelve pages behind him threw gold and silver coins to the people.

The imperial flag, gold cloth with a huge black eagle, carried by a man of almost seven feet. The cavalcade of the "inner council", the Emperor's closest friends, including Archbishop Berard of Palermo, Chancellor Piero della Vigna, Thaddeus of Suessa, and the Count of Caserta. Iocco, the jester. And again a detachment of the German bodyguard, followed by a stream of soldiery and hundreds of wagons and carts.

Wherever the Imperial Progress passed, the populace shouted with joy, and, for once, not only because of the silver and gold coins thrown at them. For they knew that the Emperor was going to Rome, to make peace, at long last, with the Holy Father. The bells were ringing peace. Men embraced each other with tears in their eyes. There was no town, no village that had not suffered, and suffered heavily, in those terrible years that had now come to an end. No one had been safe; on everyone had been the leaden pressure of deadly uncertainty. A denunciation, true or untrue, of having harbored "spies" of the Pope, and suddenly the Emperor's troops would sweep in and burn and loot and kill. And now there was peace. Now they would be able to sleep in their beds without fear. Now the faithful knew that in the future they could serve the Emperor's Majesty without the qualms of conscience that had haunted them so often in the past for serving a man who had been exiled from the Mystical Body of Christ and thus was worse than a heathen.

In all churches a Te Deum had been ordered for the sixth of May, the glorious date to be remembered by generations to come . . . the date when in Rome the Holy Father would embrace the Emperor and take him back into the fold, back into the company of all Christians, living and dead and to come, back into the company of the saints, of the Apostles, of Christ himself. Heralds were riding into all the countries of Christendom to proclaim the news. Ships were carrying it across the seas to Britain and Norway and Sweden, and in the Orient the richly bejeweled turbans of sultans and amirs would be raised in anxious concern: for peace and unity in Christendom meant that their continuous work for the expansion of holy Islam was going to be resisted more strongly than before, and it might even mean a new crusade.

Now the Imperial Progress had passed the western shore of the large lake of Bolsena and was heading steadily in a southeasterly direction.

One could relax a little. The Emperor beckoned his friends, and they rode up to him.

"Let's shorten the way", said Frederick, smiling, "by letting our minds play a little. Thaddeus, my friend, tell me: What do you think the Pope is thinking at this moment?"

Thaddeus of Suessa, lean, cadaverous, and cleanshaven, assumed an air of pompous ecclesiastical dignity. "Now I shall get my Peter's pence again without interference", he said.

Frederick laughed. "Not unlikely. You, della Vigna?"

"He's bound to have thought that long ago, great Augustus. But now he's gnawing his fingernails, asking himself whether he hasn't made too many concessions and whether he couldn't have got a cheaper bargain."

"Not bad. My friend Berard?"

The Archbishop raised his fleshy chin. "I'm no good at this game, dear master, and I have no wish to be presumptuous."

"Berard, Berard, . . . our peace with the Pope threatens to make you a boring companion. However, I'll tell you my opinion: he thinks, 'Now I am greater than Gregory, greater even than the third Innocent: for I have managed what they could not manage . . . to make the eagle eat out of my hand.' "

The Archbishop smiled thinly. "That is what he would think if he had the Emperor's character. The fourth Innocent is not so ambitious."

Frederick laughed again, but he was not too pleased.

"We shall have to comply with a great many church ceremonies", he said, "you can trust dear Innocent for that, at least. There will be a procession and Mass and Te Deum and the gods know what else. There . . . there's a one-man procession . . . one man and a boy . . . "

They looked. A priest in surplice and stole was quietly walking across a field preceded by a tiny acolyte.

"Carrying the last sacraments to someone dying in one of those houses over there, I suppose", said the Archbishop. He crossed himself.

Frederick pressed his lips together. "I wonder . . . I really wonder how long that nonsense will go on."

"Please, please", said Berard; it did not sound like a protest but rather like a weak and kindly mother trying to quiet a boisterous child.

The Emperor sighed. "I know we cannot ask for the enlightenment of the people as quickly as we would like. These things have been drummed into them for over a thousand years. Amazing, though, how they stick to it, and not necessarily out of cowardice, I'll grant you that. It only shows the greatness of the truly great impostors."

They looked at him, questioningly.

"... the three greatest impostors the world has ever seen", said Frederick. "Moses, Christ, and Mohammed".

"Magnificent", exclaimed della Vigna enthusiastically. "This will be remembered throughout the ages as one of the boldest sentences ever spoken by anybody."

Thaddeus of Suessa cackled with laughter.

The Archbishop said nothing. It was regrettable, of course, that the Emperor liked to make that kind of remark, but anything one might answer ... and, of course, there was a good deal one could answer ... would only arouse his love of "bold sentences" more and more. Also, he might lose his temper altogether, and there was every reason to see to it that he did not lose his temper just now. Not only because of the sixth of May, only two days away, but also because they were approaching a dangerous place, a place whose very name was anathema to him. Over there, behind the soft hills, aglow with sunlight, were the walls of Viterbo.

"It is no laughing matter, Thaddeus", said the Emperor. "I mean every word I said. These three truly great impostors had the same idea, the plan to form millions and millions after their own image. Millions of little Moseses and Christs and Mohammeds carry on their own personality throughout the ages. I do not blame them ... in fact, it is perhaps the only way in which a great man can achieve immortality. The small man has only the way of reproduction. He sleeps with his wife to produce another dear ego. The great man forces generation after generation into the mold of his own personality. I must talk to Bonatti about this. It may be one of the keys of the great arcana."

"Who should find them, if not you", said della Vigna, his eyes shining. "To Gehenna with this peace. Why should we tolerate the Pope, when the unique spiritual leader of our time is in our very midst, the coadjutor of God, versed in divine plans, ceaselessly illuminated by the eye of God."

"He means it, too", thought the Archbishop. And when one came to think how Frederick had made his way from nothing to the very head of the civilized world, it was difficult not to agree with him . . . within certain limitations, of course. But let him, let them all go on praising . . . it would keep him in an even temper. And he was far too great a statesman to endanger this peace, so carefully worked out, because of anyone's flattery. Viterbo . . . that was another matter. If only no one mentioned it.

"There is much in what you say", said the Emperor calmly. "And my life is ample proof of it, I believe. But there is still the hope that Innocent IV will be intelligent enough to understand it, too; perhaps his ardent wish to make peace with me is the beginning of such understanding. You all know about the Indian belief that a man's soul is incarnated time and again until it reaches perfection. I could almost believe that myself . . . almost. Not quite. For it is inconceivable to me that one day the soul of Frederick should join the Allsoul as the drop joins the ocean. It would mean that I would cease to be I. And I cannot cease to be I, ever. I prefer not to believe in the existence of the soul at all."

"But, logically . . . " began the Archbishop.

"The Emperor is above logic. Divinity is above logic", cried della Vigna.

"You understand me at times, friends", said Frederick. "I am grateful for that. It is very lonely . . . where I am. And that which is human in me suffers from it. When I was younger, I often thought that the souls for a thousand men had been crushed in the crucible of God to make a soul for me: my love and my hatred, my thinking and feeling . . . they all surpassed mere human limitations. In fact, there were moments . . . and there still are . . . when it seems to me that there are no limitations in me at all."

He spoke with the urgent, red-hot vehemence of a poet, and there was a strange, frightening beauty about him, the heritage of the Hohenstaufens, that had won them many a day. And in his own, terrible way he was a poet . . . a poet of action, creating and obliterating, forming and destroying on the spur of the moment. Very rarely he spoke so openly . . . usually he shielded his thoughts behind that spare, faintly mocking smile in which the unblinking eyes had no part.

"Today", he went on, "I doubt that there is such a thing as the soul, and it is typical of the distance between me and poor Innocent that he should think I am making peace with him to save a soul in whose existence I do not believe. But genius as such is immortal, without doubt."

It was then that the little incident occurred. Something looking very much like a little hill of iron came clanking down the road, passing the nobles, passing the flower girls, and halted in front of the group around the Emperor. It was Willmar von Zangenburg, section leader of the imperial bodyguard, twenty-three years of age, blond, blue eyed, the idol of the girls. Frederick looked at him affectionately.

"What is it, my son?"

The young knight reported that there was a crossroad ahead, one arm leading directly to Rome, the other to Viterbo, and as Viterbo would not see the sacred person of the Emperor if one went directly to Rome, he permitted himself the question of what the Emperor's orders were.

The Archbishop had paled. "Surely, young man," he said severely, "you had your clear orders for today's march. We are not passing through that town."

Willmar von Zangenburg gave a brief glance at the

huge, excited man in ecclesiastical robes and looked back to the Emperor. There was a very faint smile on his face. He knew he had the entire bodyguard behind him: they were all bored with the snail-like procession of the last days. Viterbo, as everyone knew, had refused to receive the Emperor in its walls before peace was actually concluded . . . and that for good reasons. It would stir up things a little if one went through Viterbo.

"Viterbo?" asked the Emperor. "Viterbo." In a flash he knew the meaning of the sullen, unformed thoughts of the last days; the origin and cause of that sneaking feeling of frustration when everybody was bawling about the beginning of the golden age. Viterbo had deserted his cause when he had been weak. And its desertion was unavenged. The town could boast—and would—that against it the Emperor had proved to be powerless. They would smirk and wink at each other in Viterbo when he signed a peace that forced him to forgive those who had not even asked for forgiveness. Viterbo was the stain on his shield and on his name.

He stopped his horse. Horrified, the Archbishop saw him gaze in the direction of the walled town, only a few miles away; it was the gaze of an eagle, of the archetypal eagle. He had lived too long at the Emperor's court not to know that gaze. With the courage of desperation, he began to plead. Surely, surely the Master of the World would not bother about a little town gone astray? Surely not at this hour, with all Christendom awaiting peace. Surely he would not change his plans because of the words of a youth, itching for mischief.

"I hear you, Berard", said Frederick, his eyes glued to Viterbo's walls. "Poor soul, poor soul, trembling for your peace, are you? What has the Pope promised you in private that you should be so keen? Zangenburg has asked for my orders, and you answered. Do I then need a guardian?"

The Archbishop began to stammer apologies. They were cut short.

"Zangenburg, my poor man, is nothing but a thought of my own—one of my thoughts, just as you are another. No one makes decisions for me. You tried to banish Viterbo from my thoughts, didn't you, Berard? Because you knew that we were passing it. Tell me . . . does hate suffice to give the soul power to return after death . . . if there is a soul?"

The Archbishop was almost in tears. "My gracious Emperor, I beg of you, I entreat you . . . you are on your way to heaven. Don't let this wretched town upset things infinitely more important."

He stared, open mouthed. For now Frederick was looking at him, deadly pale, black fire in his eyes.

"Berard . . . if I had one foot in paradise, I would withdraw it to take vengeance on Viterbo." He turned to Zangenburg and began to shoot orders at him in clipped military language. Young Zangenburg saluted and rode off, beaming all over his handsome face.

"Caserta," said the Emperor, "have the entire Progress stopped. Quarters must be found for my animals and my women. Get the colonels together. Six riders without armor will gallop to Orvieto to fetch the two thousand cavalrymen we left there. They must be here by midnight." Off went Caserta.

"We'll attack at dawn tomorrow morning, then", said della Vigna.

"No, Piero".

"Perhaps you will ask them to open their gates first", ventured Thaddeus of Suessa.

"Never. I attack now. Why wait until they get suspicious? Where is Count Brandenstein? I want the carts with the crossbows and the Greek fire rolled out. Just as well I thought of taking them with us in case there was foul play. Get the girls off the road. Berard, old friend, don't look so dejected. Believe me, your Pope will be ready to receive us in Rome the day after tomorrow just the same. This is what history calls a regrettable little incident. He will receive us because he must. There is no other way for him.

His smile when he greets us will be a trifle more acid, that is all. But Viterbo's hour has struck. Brandenstein, there you are at last: look, I've been studying these walls a little just now. The weakest point from the west is between the third and fourth turret. Get the defenders off with the Greek firepots and try to storm the gate. Take my Germans for the task; they're eager for action anyway. Pirelli . . . the left wing. You hold back until Brandenstein's men have made a breach. Almarane . . . the right wing. Keep the men on the walls busy with your crossbow men. I shall see to it that they cannot make a sortie against you, but don't attack, just play them, do you hear? Play them . . . "

* * *

They were winding garlands round the pillars of the court for the reception of the Emperor when the messenger from Viterbo arrived at the Lateran Palace.

The Pope read the letter in the presence of a dozen people . . . the architect surveying the preparations, the leading florists of Rome, the Bishop of Perugia, and several prelates. They saw him blanch and his right hand go up to his heart.

"Good people," said the Bishop of Perugia, "you must leave the Holy Father alone for a little while. He will see you later. All of you."

They withdrew hesitatingly, even the prelates.

Innocent IV's hands trembled. He tried to speak, but the words would not come. The Bishop of Perugia closed the door himself. He was a grizzled old man with a strong chin and lively dark eyes under bushy brows.

"Etiquette has been upset all day, Holy Father", he said. "It is only natural, with so many preparations to be made. May I commit another breach, then, and ask what has happened?"

The Pope looked up. His face was suddenly that of a very old man.

"The worst", he said. "The Emperor has attacked Viterbo."

"No!"

"Without warning . . . and there was a solemn truce, a solemn truce. He broke it and attacked."

"If I know anything about Cardinal Rainer of Viterbo," the Bishop's eyes gleamed, "the Emperor won't have had it all his own way."

"He didn't. The attack was repulsed. The wind changed direction and blew the Greek fire back to the attackers. Fighting was still going on when this letter was sent off. Frederick has attacked our town of Orte, too, allegedly because they would not give him all the support he wanted."

"He is mad", murmured the Bishop. "And God forgive him if he isn't."

"No, he is not mad. Only foolish", said the Pope tonelessly. "He is not mad, for he knows exactly what he wants. And he is foolish because he has shown his hand too early. He struck at Viterbo. He will strike at Rome."

The Bishop was aghast. "You think all his peace talks were just a feint? That he always intended treachery?"

"No", said the Pope, his eyes far away. "No, I don't mean that. He is a creature of the moment; it will flash through him to commit treachery, and in the next instant he will drop everything and commit it, thinking himself inspired. He will not call it treachery, either. He thinks himself above such things . . . as Lucifer did. Oh, I know him; I know him so well; I have fought with him during so many bitter nights of sleeplessness. I don't think he planned it at all. But I do think that he is planning it now. He may not even have thought of it when he gave the order to attack Viterbo. But since then he has tasted blood again, and it has gone to his head. Why content himself with Viterbo if he can have Rome? The conditions of the treaty would change very quickly if he could lay hands on the successor of St. Peter."

He rang the bell.

"But what is to be done?" asked the Bishop, dumbfounded. "We counted on peace. There are scarcely any troops in the patrimony, and until help can come . . . "

"Exactly", said the Pope. "I shall be his prisoner, and he will enact any law that strikes his fancy . . . in my name. But I have prepared for such an emergency."

A prelate entered.

"All carriages available must be ready in two hours", said the Pope. "Take this list. And that one. The persons mentioned in the first, the things in the second will accompany us on our journey. As many spare horses and mules as possible. Those who travel with us will not communicate with others about it. Please hasten."

The prelate withdrew without a word, but his excitement was obvious.

"In the name of Our Lord", whispered the Bishop. "You are leaving Rome, Holy Father? Rome? What will become of the Church?"

"The Church is where Peter is", said Innocent very quietly.

"But where, Holy Father, where are you going?"

"To Genoa, first", said the Pope after an almost imperceptible moment of hesitation. "Then to Lyons."

The Bishop of Perugia hung his head.

"Dear Bruno", said Innocent softly. "Dear old friend. Do you think it is easy for me to take this step? Gregory was made of sterner stuff than I am, and yet the Emperor hounded him to death. I must be free in order to think and act. Forgive me for going, Bruno."

Looking up, the Bishop saw tears in the eyes of the Pope. He went down on his knees and kissed the Fisherman's ring.

* * *

Several hours later the long cavalcade left Rome, traveling in a northwesterly direction.

Toward evening they overtook a small group of Dominican friars who had to walk for a long time in the clouds of dust the carriages left behind.

* * *

When the news of the Pope's flight from Rome came to the Emperor, he broke off the siege of Viterbo at once and returned in forced marches to Parma. The Pope's action had brought about an entirely new political situation. There were rumors that he was going to convoke a council of the Church. If true, that could well be dangerous. One could stop most of the Italian bishops from taking part, of course; there were always ways and means for that. Pressure could be exercised also on the Hungarians and on most of the Germans. It would not be too much of a council then. But the English would come, and the Spaniards and Louis of France would not stop the French bishops from coming either.

The rumors became almost a certainty when news came that the Pope had left Genoa, his natal town, for Lyons.

He had been received in Genoa with open arms; Genoese troops had met him to protect him against a potential attack by the Emperor.

Angrily Frederick wrote to his faithful town of Pisa: "I was playing chess with the Pope and was about to take a castle when the Genoese burst in, swept their hands across the board, and wrecked the game."

Lyons, however, was worse. To go to Lyons, so near the frontier of the empire, meant that the Pope was about to strike back hard. From there he could act with impunity. It was a masterly move, there was no doubt about it.

Black clouds were rising on the horizon. Something had to be done and done quickly, and quick action was the Emperor's strength. He convoked a diet to Verona. But many of the German princes politely excused themselves. He decided to marry young Gertrude of Austria and wrote to her father. Austria was the cornerstone of Europe. It was an important move.

But here in Italy, too, his position had to be buttressed. There were a number of important families of whose loyalty he did not feel sure enough. The best cure was of course to exterminate them, but for that the moment was anything but favorable. He wrote to the head of the most powerful of them, Count San Severino de Marsico, that he had always wished to have his family closer to his heart; that therefore he had decided to suggest a marriage between Count San Severino de Marsico's son, Ruggiero, with Countess Theodora of Aquino, the youngest daughter of the late Count Landulph of Aquino and his wife, born a Countess of Theate. He mentioned that the Aquinos were particularly dear to him not only because of their blood relationship but also because they had been loyal to him without fail in all the difficult times of the past. And he invited the San Severinos to Parma, where the wedding would take place, "if his dear and much-respected friend found himself in agreement with his suggestion".

Then he wrote to the Countess of Aquino in very much the same vein. She too, with all her family, was invited to join him in Parma.

When soon after that all bishops were solemnly invited to come to Lyons for a General Council, Frederick despatched Piero della Vigna and Thaddeus of Suessa to appear there as his ambassadors extraordinary.

"You are both intelligent", said the Emperor. "Therefore there is little need for instructions on this mission. I want nothing dramatic to happen in Lyons. You must convince the Pope that I never dreamed of marching on Rome. Swear by anything you like. All I wanted was to settle my old account with Viterbo. The attack on Orte was nothing. The overzealousness of a little commander in the field. The whole thing was a regrettable incident, no more than that. The Church is clamoring for her legitimate head. We hope and pray—don't forget that—we pray that His Holiness will return at his earliest convenience. He *must* return. He is a constant danger to me as long as I cannot have him under my thumb. Spare neither promises nor gold; make any concessions you like. If you promise enough you might even get me rid of that absurd excommunication after all. It is really ridiculous that he should take Viterbo so seriously. After all, what is Viterbo! Surely it is more important that Empire and Church are at peace with each other. We appeal to his reason. But do not forget promises and gold. The promises are less cumbersome luggage, but the gold may have the stronger effect, at least with some of the bishops. Read the dossier of each of them carefully and act accordingly. There must be *some* who are susceptible, however much they may pray not to be led into temptation. And don't forget the other side of the picture: too much obstinacy on the part of the holy men might have most regrettable consequences. It is all very well for the Spaniards, who are far away. But my arm may reach even them, and we are related to both the King of France and the King of England. We expect wisdom from the wise."

"To hear is to obey", said della Vigna. It was the formula used by the subject's of the sultans of the East.

"*They* must learn that formula", smiled the Emperor. Then the smile disappeared as suddenly as it had come. The unblinking eyes stared into the void. "They must. And if they do not give in to me, by God and by Lucifer, I shall assemble against them an army such as the world has never seen, and I shall assume to myself the countries of all rulers who are trying to give them refuge, just as I have assumed to myself the spirit and the imagination of all men around me. Go, my friends. Go."

Chapter VII

JUST A FEW more steps," said Friar John. The little group of Dominicans reached the crest of the hill. And there was the city that was their goal; in the blue mists of the morning, a fairy city of tightly packed streets, spires, pinnacles, cut in half by the silver band of the Seine and crowned by the towers of Notre Dame.

"The city of St. Geneviève", said Friar John. "And perhaps one day she will be called also after the man who rules her now. For King Louis is a very saintly man. Is it not like God to call to sanctity at the same time a king and a beggar, Louis and Francis of Assisi? I do not say that this city is free of vice and crime; it is not. But it is ruled with justice and mercy. The King never dines without feeding four hundred beggars at the same time. He himself speaks justice, and one of his great friends was our beloved brother in the Order, Friar Vincent of Beauvais, whose works fill an entire library and one of whose books is called *How to Be a Just Judge.* We have left Italy, ruled by Frederick, who takes greedily what God has given to others. We have entered France, where Louis gives passionately what God has given him. The Sieur de Joinville said it exactly: 'As an author when his book is done adorns it with Red and Blue and Gold, so King Louis illuminates all his kingdom.' "

The Friars d'Aguidi, San Giuliano, and Lucca listened with dutiful deference, but the youngest of the friars seemed far away in his thoughts.

The Magister General touched his shoulder. "It is a beautiful city, is it not, Friar Thomas?"

"Very beautiful", said Thomas softly.

"What would you do", pursued Friar John, "if it belonged to you? If the King gave it to you as a present?"

"I would not know what to do with it", said Thomas truthfully.

Friar John smiled slyly. "You might sell it back to the King and build a great many Dominican convents with the gold he would give you, don't you think?"

Thomas frowned heavily. He was quite obviously grappling with the problem. "I would much rather have St. Chrysostom's treatise on the Gospel of St. Matthew", he decided.

"And that," thought the Master General, as the friars laughed, "and that is the man they wanted to make Lord Abbot of Monte Cassino, to spend all his life on administrative work."

He made up his mind not to tell the future teachers of the young friar what he thought of him . . . not even Master Albert, whom many liked to call "the Great". Let them find out by themselves what acquisition the Order had made. There would certainly be much raising of eyebrows if they knew the Magister General himself had postponed his journey to France no less than ten months for the sake of a novice. He made a mental note to instruct d'Aguidi, San Giuliano, and Lucca accordingly. Thomas, however, should be told what kind of a man was going to train him in the service of the Order.

As they were walking downhill toward the city, he began to talk slowly, as was his wont, about the convent of St. Jacques, on St. Geneviève's hill, the first Dominican priory in Paris. "It is more than thirty years ago that our father, St. Dominic, founded the Order, with sixteen men: eight Frenchmen, six Spaniards, one Portuguese and one Englishman. Five years later there were sixty convents. There are hundreds now. But in none of them would you find a teacher of the importance of Master Albert. The builders of Notre Dame were great men, but they built in stone. Albert is building a cathedral of thought. That is the man I have chosen for your teacher."

The young friar's eyes shone. He felt that he was walking on air.

* * *

The Emperor's letter found the Countess of Aquino back in Rocca Secca. Now that Thomas had escaped, there was no reason why one should put up with the inconvenience of life at Monte San Giovanni. She had not given an order to pursue the fugitive. It was Marotta who had brought her the news, and the Countess had spent the whole day alone in her room afterward. When she emerged, the next morning, she was her usual self, but by no word did she allude to Thomas and his flight. That same day Marotta left for her Benedictine convent. Then the family returned to Rocca Secca. Somehow neither brothers nor sisters had dared to question Marotta about how their mother had taken the news and why she did not have Thomas pursued. The brothers knew that it would have been asking for trouble, and both Theodora and Adelasia felt that she did not want to be asked... not then, at least. Much later Adelasia risked it and received the astonishing answer: "I was wrong about Thomas. I was wrong about him all the time."

Life in Rocca Secca had been quiet until the Emperor's letter came. It shot into the castle like a sharp arrow, like a shower of arrows rather... for it seemed that scarcely anyone remained unhurt.

Several hours went by before the Countess could bring herself to call for Theodora. She had read and reread the letter. It could not have been more courteous and friendly. All the same, it was an order and nothing else. She would have to give her youngest, her loveliest child to Frederick's latest favorite, another of those Eccelinos and Casertas. She? No... it was he himself who did it, he who gave Theodora to this San Severino as if she were a title or an estate.

"I do not matter at all", she thought, her first numbness changing into bitterness and hurt pride. "He commands, and I must sacrifice my child." But this was Italy. It wasn't Carthage or Tyre, where they had sacrificed children to Moloch.

Moloch . . . She began to chide herself for exaggerating things grossly, for being a clucking hen of a mother. No one was going to kill Theodora, and no one was going to sacrifice her. The Emperor, her cousin, had very graciously encouraged a marriage between her and the son of one of the oldest and most influential families of the kingdom. Surely, that was not a crime.

But somehow she knew very well that this train of thought was weakness, the wish to go the way of least resistance. She knew that Frederick was no longer the man he had been, that power had corrupted him, that he had knowledge at least of some of the crimes that had been committed in his name, and that he had himself committed crimes.

She knew that his environment was poisonous and that men and women in high positions trembled for their lives all the time, because any denunciation might mean sudden death. This was the atmosphere into which he wanted to transplant Theodora.

She did not know the young San Severino. . . . What was his name? . . . Ruggiero, like his father's. She remembered having met his father many years ago, a great lord without doubt, dark and suave and enigmatic. No doubt he had rendered certain services to the Emperor—and Theodora and her dowry were Frederick's reward for the San Severino family. And he seemed to be in a hurry about it, too. The invitation to Parma meant, of course, that he himself wished to be present at the wedding, that this was an official matter altogether. No doubt San Severino was going to live close to the Emperor, if he was not doing so already. And that, to her, was almost the worst of it.

She admitted to herself that her loyalty to Frederick was not what it used to be, just as he was not, and perhaps for that reason. Here in Rocca Secca she could be loyal. But at court she would never be able to keep silent. The Aquinos weren't courtiers, never had been. There would be trouble; inevitably there would be trouble. On her own ground she would not tolerate a word against the Emperor. At court she would tell everybody what she thought of him. She was a country bumpkin, and so was Theodora, so were all her daughters.

Rainald was the only one who could play the courtier, and it was a trait she disliked intensely in him, though she felt that it was probably due to his being a poet. Poets could always adapt themselves to anything. They were glib people and in some way not quite human. Rainald was never really *in* things; he always seemed to sit on a fence and observe the actions of others as if they were the amusing antics of fools. Even when he himself had to join in for some reason, he seemed to be playing a part in a tumbler's performance. He did not take even his own actions seriously.

He might well be delighted about the news in Frederick's letter. It would mean going to court and being in the foreground of a grand ceremony. Yet he, even he, had shown sometimes that he did not agree with all the Emperor had done.

Never mind Rainald. This matter concerned first of all Theodora and herself. She had to tell her . . . although she had a fairly good idea of what her reaction would be. Such was her mood and such were her thoughts as she sent Eugenia to fetch Theodora.

* * *

The result was even worse than she expected.

She had given the girl the letter to read without making any comment.

Theodora read. Then she dropped the paper as if it were an unclean thing and said: "You know, now I believe what people say . . . that the Emperor has become a heathen or Moslem or whatever they call it."

"What do you mean, child?"

"The Arabs teach that a woman has no soul, don't they?

That a woman is not really a human being at all; only the man counts. That must be what he thinks, or he would not ask me to marry a man I have never seen."

"Child, it has happened very often that a marriage was arranged . . ."

"Mohammedans, heathens, pagans. I am a piece of merchandise to be sold, and who would dream of asking the merchandise whether it wished to be sold."

"The San Severinos are a very old and respected family."

"I don't care what they are. I have no wish to be sold. I shall marry the man I love, or I shall not marry at all. You can tell him that."

"You know perfectly well that I cannot tell him that. And you are not quite just: it is true you have never seen Ruggiero de San Severino. But then, he has never seen you either."

"That", said Theodora hotly, "makes it very clear to me that I could never love him. A man who is ready to marry just any woman because the Emperor says so, because anybody says so, is not a man at all. He is either a slave or a brute, and I will marry neither."

"My darling, you know that I have always respected your feelings in this matter. I have never tried to force your hand . . ."

"No, Mother, you haven't. But you knew that I could not be forced. You thought Thomas could be forced, and you found out that he could not either. Yes, yes, I know all about the loyalty we owe the Emperor; you have mentioned it often enough. Aquinos are loyal. But they are loyal because they are human beings, and therefore they should be treated as human beings. This letter is inhuman, and the whole matter, for me, just does not exist."

"Thank you", said the Countess drily. "That is of course a most helpful attitude. For you the matter does not exist. Unfortunately I shall have to answer the Emperor's letter, and I doubt whether it will do us all much good if I say that we are, of course, much honored, but that the matter does not exist for my daughter Theodora."

"I thought we were nobles, Mother", said Theodora bitterly. "You are telling me that we are slaves."

"In any case we shall have to go to Parma", said the Countess with a shrug. "We cannot afford to refuse *that.*"

"The only sane and human people in my family are Thomas and Marotta", said Theodora and burst into tears. Before her mother could reply, she ran away.

She had to pass the hall before she could reach her own room, and Landulph and Rainald stared at her in amazement. Neither of them had seen her in tears since she had grown up. They got up and without a word went to see their mother. She was sitting strangely huddled up in her armchair, and even the coarse Landulph realised suddenly and with a confused sort of pain that she had aged . . . that she was very nearly an old woman.

"Are you ill, Mother?" he asked awkwardly.

Rainald picked up the letter from the floor. A minute later he knew all that had happened. He gave the letter to Landulph.

"This is not an easy situation", he said. "I think I know how you feel about it, and I have seen the girl's face."

"Who knows", said Landulph, fingering the letter. "He may be a nice fellow, that San Severino." But it sounded very lame.

"Nice or not nice," said the Countess, "she will never marry him. I have been very foolish. I should never have shown her that letter."

"But what else could you do?"

"Tell her that we are invited to Parma and then see what happens when we got there. At the worst I could have begged Frederick to change his mind about the marriage."

Rainald sighed. "Excellent, Mother. But just a trifle late. We are too impetuous to be good diplomats. Never mind. The Emperor would not have changed his mind anyway.

Don't you see it? He *needs* this marriage. He is buying San Severino as an ally. At least that is what he thinks he is doing."

"I don't like it", said Landulph.

Rainald laughed. "Who does, brother mine, who does? Frederick is in a bad way, Mother. Thomas was quite right, and I was quite wrong. The Pope is too much for him. The flight to Lyons was a masterpiece. The Emperor has been aswim ever since. And now little Theodora must help him out. It's not exactly what she's been reared for, Mother, is it?"

The Countess stretched out her hands and drew her sons toward herself. It was an instinctive movement; she felt utterly weak and for the first time in need of protection. Yet as she sat, flanked by the strong young bodies of her sons, she felt a current of power go through her, and she raised her head with a confidence surprising even to herself.

"Something will happen," she whispered, "something must happen. We shall all go to Parma together."

Perhaps none of them would have admitted it: yet in their minds thoughts were racing for the first time that would have horrified them at any other stage of their lives. They were unformed, primitive; they had no definite aim. But they had been touched by the wing of conspiracy.

* * *

It was decided to leave for Parma in ten days' time.

Theodora received the news with stony silence. She refused to discuss the matter with anyone. Six new dresses were being made for her; she did not look at the precious materials, and the seamstresses, coming for the fittings, found her door locked. The dresses had to be made without fittings. Her brothers discussed the matter of retinue with their mother. It was decided to take only one hundred armed men. More might have aroused suspicion, and as Rainald put it, "We can't take thirty thousand with us anyway, and the Emperor has at least that many." Sir Piers and a sturdy young Sicilian, de Braccio, would lead the men.

The many preparations to be made kept the minds of the family occupied, and yet the atmosphere of Rocca Secca was one of black gloom.

Robin Cherrywoode, standing beside his master on the ringwall, said suddenly: "There's at least one good thing about this journey of ours."

"Is there?" asked Piers between his teeth.

"Well, nothing has been much fun since the night we heaved the young friar over the wall, . . . "

"True enough", said Piers with a pale smile.

" . . . but there may be fun in Parma."

"There'll be no fun in Parma, you fool", said Piers.

Cherrywoode rubbed his chin and began to chew one end of his moustache. "When it comes to war, master, or to politics and the like, that's a man's world, and a man can foresee what's likely to happen. But when it's all about marriage, it's a woman's world, and the one thing you can feel sure of is that you cannot be sure of anything. Emperors and kings, master . . . in marriage a woman will always get the better of them. And the little lady does not want this thing to happen, and . . . "

"Shut up and go away", said Piers.

Robin Cherrywoode shut up and marched off, not in the least dissatisfied with himself. He had said all he had wanted to say.

On the evening before the departure Piers saw his lady slip out of the women's wing and ascend the stairs to the ringwall. There she stood for a long time, gazing down into the valley.

He went over to her as quietly as he could in his armor. She did not look up.

"My lady," he said, "please forgive your servant for talking where he should be silent. But it is the wish of my heart to put your mind at rest. I shall kill the Count of San Severino."

She turned round and looked into his eyes. And she knew that he would do what he had said.

Chapter VIII

THE EMPEROR was alone. When the letter from Austria arrived, a short while ago, he had opened it, read the first few lines, and ordered everyone out of the room. He had sat down in one of the beautifully carved chairs and forced himself to read it all, sentence by sentence.

The day was hot; the scent of ten thousand fully blown flowers wafted lethargically into the room, where it remained hanging, an invisible cloud of voluptuousness. August was sultry in Parma.

A refusal. Oh, the most polite, the most charming wording. Trust the Duke of Babenberg for that. He could see him with his shrewd little face, with his expression of suffering indulgence: What can you do, cousin Emperor; I cannot very well force the girl, can I now? And she doesn't want to marry. She is frightened. We are simple people, here in Austria. We are not accustomed to the grand atmosphere of an imperial court. We are peasant nobles, really. And Gertrude feels she would be clumsy and unpopular; she would not know how to be the wife of the Master of the World.

Very touching. Probably quite true, too. But certainly not the whole of the truth, Babenberg. She is frightened, all right, the wench. Frightened because my wives have had a habit of not living long. Frightened because of the stories whispered all over Europe about the manner in which they died. They had all whelped before their deaths, hadn't they? And he had shown a fatherly care for the young ones, all of them, Enzio and Manfred and Frederick of Antioch, Conrad and Henry, Richard of Theate and . . . a good many others. Nothing to complain about, Babenberg. They all got their share. How much better such matters were arranged in the world of Islam, where even an ordinary man may have his four wives at the same time. But the princesses in Christendom were pious; they insisted on being married singly. What is a man supposed to do, Babenberg? The Church has made life difficult as usual. And behind your letter, Babenberg, is again the Church. It stinks of incense. Perhaps it's only some blockhead of a pater confessor, some confounded Austrian village priest, warning little Gertrude against the half-pagan Hohenstaufen, against the enemy of the Pope. Always and always the Pope. Whenever one stretched one's hand to grasp life in its fullness, the Pope was sure to screech about sin or crime or outrage.

Babenberg was much too intelligent to mention anything of the kind, of course. He had even refrained from exhorting him to make peace with the Church, as he had done in every other letter. All the same, his letter stank of incense. Hapsburg was likely to have had a hand in this, too. The Babenbergs were dying out, and Hapsburg was ambitious, as ambitious as he was pious.

If only one had one's hands free. But then if he had his hands free, Babenberg might not have risked refusing him, the old fox.

He laughed grimly. Wait, old man. Just let me finish this business at Lyons, and I *shall* have my hands free. Then we'll see.

He tore the letter into little pieces, rose, and walked into the adjacent room, where the servants had just put the finishing touches to the throne and canopy. He gave one short look at their work and became as pale as a sheet.

"Who gave the order for that?" he rasped, pointing to a garland of exquisite roses attached to the canopy.

They stood bewildered.

"The flowers", he shouted. "Who put those flowers on the canopy?"

The head official, numb with fear, began to stammer something about the beauty of the roses.

"Guards", roared Frederick. "Guards to me."

In a moment the door spouted armored men.

"Seize the man", ordered the Emperor.

The head official hung between them, an almost lifeless little bundle of silk, flesh, and fear.

"Speak, man", said Frederick. "Who told you to put those flowers up there?"

"N-n-no one, Your Majesty, no one, I—I—thought . . . "

"Take him away. Let Marzoukh give him the bastinado on the soles of his feet until he tells the truth. And tear those confounded roses down, somebody."

They obeyed. He looked on until the flowers were down.

"Throw them away", said Frederick. "And never again, do you hear me? Never again will I have flowers over my head. Get out, all of you. Call my retinue in and let me have the list of audiences."

They ran. And again for a short while the Emperor was alone. He mopped his brow. Now they would talk of another strange and tyrannical act of the Emperor. Let them. Let them. They did not know. They could not know. It was many years ago now that Michael Scotus had told him that he would die *sub flore.* Under the flower. He had not read it in the stars . . . he had found it out in a different way, by necromancy. Only the dead knew about death. He had made Scotus swear to keep it secret, and he was the kind of man to keep an oath . . . certainly the kind of oath he had sworn, by all the powers of the occult, by Hermes Trismegistos and Ashtaroth and Ashmodeus and the Tetragrammaton itself. And now Scotus was dead, and he had talked only to one other man: Bonatti the astrologer, himself an eager student of the Cabbalah in his time, at Toledo. Bonatti had confirmed the verdict. And since he had known this, never had he set foot in Florence, and nothing would induce him to enter that town. It could easily mean Florence. But it could also be taken literally. What hellish devil had influenced that fool of an official to fasten those roses on the canopy? Or was it really only some fancy idea of his own? He would soon know. But from now on he was going to be careful. Orders must be given that no flowers were to be used for decoration, when he entered a town or palace or castle. He had not thought of that before. Just as well he had thought of it now.

He sat down on the throne. "Fate, destiny, Ananke, whatever your name may be, we'll cheat you yet. We are only fifty. We are good for another twenty, another thirty years and more. And who knows . . . if we avoid Florence, if we avoid the deadly flowers over our head and keep the curse away . . . who can say whether life will ever end?" Prester John, the ruler of the East, had sent him, in an emerald bottle, an elixir supposed to be the elixir of life itself, conveying immortality. He had given one drop of it to a pigeon . . . it might have been poison after all. But the pigeon lived. Then he had taken a dagger and cut the pigeon's throat with it, and it had died, elixir or not. But perhaps only a man could become immortal through it. However . . . no one said that it conveyed eternal youth as well, and to live on and on as a wrinkled wreck, hairless, and toothless . . . no. One had to be careful with occult presents. "*Sub flore.* Not yet, fate. Not yet. Not for a long time."

They were coming in now, glittering with gold and precious stones and forming the semicircle that the pikes of the guards indicated with a massive sort of courtesy.

Someone gave the Emperor the audience list. He was just beginning to glance through it when an official interrupted him, whispering that the bastinadoed man had confessed that he had been paid to put those flowers on the canopy.

"By whom?" asked the Emperor quickly.

The official was somewhat embarrassed. "He said, 'By whomever the most gracious Emperor wishes', Your Majesty. Then he fainted. He has not recovered consciousness yet."

"Send him home", said Frederick wearily. "I don't want to see him again." This was not a good day. First Babenberg's letter, then this. What next?

The Podestà of Parma, Teobaldo Francesco, rotund, mercurial, and submissive, danced attendance; very well, we know you have been doing your best to receive us worthily in your good town; the Countess of Aquino and family . . . stay here, Podestà: we shall be giving a marriage feast, you will see that it is suitably arranged; for the Countess we rise and come down the steps and kiss her cheek, she has become old, look at those wrinkles, but then women do age so much faster. Count Landulph and Count Rainald, Countess Adelasia, pretty enough, and Countess Theodora, very pretty indeed; San Severino will appreciate it, or should anyway; what does the Countess whisper, a private audience; what is the matter; why not now? Most regrettably the bridegroom has not arrived yet, his is the longer way, but he may be here any hour now . . .

Final? The marriage he had just announced; surely she had heard him? His explicit wish, this marriage; she knew that. No obstacle, he hoped? The young Countess Theodora was free, was she not?

"Free, but for the wish expressed by her Emperor", said the Countess. "Free entirely if you will give the word, my liege. She does not want to marry."

Frederick frowned, but only for a moment. "Your daughter will have to learn the sweetness of submitting herself as a woman should. I will have no objections and obstacles. No, dear old friend, I will hear no more about it. But let me assure you . . . "

He broke off. A herald had appeared in the door, and behind his richly colored coat the figures of two men became visible, both in travel-stained clothes.

"Come in, my friends", cried Frederick. "Step aside, herald. These two need no announcing."

His eyes were greedy for news. Della Vigna and Thaddeus of Suessa, at last, at long last. "Come forward."

The Countess of Aquino, her lips tightly pressed together, bowed ceremoniously and stepped back; Landulph, Rainald, Adelasia, and Theodora followed suit.

Everybody in the room knew the two men who now marched up to the Emperor: della Vigna, large, black-bearded, with deep-set black eyes, and Thaddeus of Suessa, slender and elegant, with the face of an intelligent ferret. Everybody understood that their news was of the utmost importance . . . so much so that they had not even thought fit to change their clothes before appearing before the Emperor. Their faces did not convey anything; they were masks.

Frederick alone saw through them. Before a word had been uttered, before they had reached the end of the semi-circle round the throne, he knew that Babenberg's letter and the flowers on the canopy had been no more than the forerunners of calamity and that here it came. His brain conceived all the possibilities . . . and there were many. His will steeled itself for the blow.

"You are very welcome", said he loudly. "Make your report at once."

And then he saw from their reaction that their news was the worst possible. No secret wave of fear tingled through his bones; there was nothing in him of that strange, tormenting desire of self-surrender, so common to men when they know their fateful hour has struck. There was only a vast intensification of the will and the continuous and masterful work of the brain. With elaborate ease he stepped up the steps of the dais and sat down on the throne.

"Master of the World," said della Vigna solemnly, "we beg to be allowed to speak to your ear alone."

"You will speak here", said Frederick. "And now. There is nothing we wish to conceal from our loyal friends and subjects." The dramatic had always appealed to him, but that was not the main reason. By now he thought he knew the gist of what these two stormy petrels had to say, but the people here did not. Let them hear it all in his presence. Thus he could not only study their reaction but also direct their minds instead of letting them think it over by themselves.

"What is more," said Frederick, "you will omit nothing. Begin, della Vigna."

And della Vigna began, haltingly at first, then quicker and quicker. "We were under orders to try and re-establish peace with His Holiness the Pope; we were to ask him to return to Rome and reoccupy the chair of St. Peter's, free and unmolested, and to spare no effort to bring about a favorable solution of our mission. But when we arrived in Lyons, we found the Pope unapproachable. He would not see us. He refused even to see friends who tried to mediate. A young prelate went so far as to tell one of these friends that the Pope had heard quite enough from the Emperor and that now for a change the Emperor would hear from the Pope."

"This is probably a lie", thought Frederick. "Otherwise he would have mentioned the name of the prelate. He is playing up our cause."

"We had to wait until the General Council had started", went on della Vigna. "There were many rumors, of course, but no tangible and authoritative information was available. The Spanish, French, and British bishops had arrived; all the Italian and Hungarian and most of the German bishops were absent. Thus there were only about one hundred and fifty participants in the General Council. We were informed, however, that its decisions were nevertheless valid. On its last day, July the seventeenth, we were asked to appear in the cathedral of Lyons to hear these decisions. All we knew up to then was that a letter from Cardinal Rainer of Viterbo had arrived and had been discussed at length. In that letter the Cardinal accused the Emperor of charging proudly against the Lord, of having killed his own consorts by having them poisoned when he became tired of them, of being guilty of the death of Pope Gregory the Ninth, having shortened his life through constant persecution and terror, and of countless other crimes and outrages. In this letter the Emperor was compared with Herod, Nero, and Julian the Apostate."

A deep groan went through the assembly.

Frederick, icily calm, let his eyes wander from one frightened face to the other.

"We succeeded in talking to a number of bishops before the seventeenth", said della Vigna. "But they would not answer any questions of ours. They asked us a good many questions, though, about a great many things. For instance, whether it was the Emperor himself who had given the order to attack Viterbo two days before he was to be released from his excommunication; whether it was true that he kept Mohammedan dancing girls of loose morals in his entourage and whether he had the habit of blaspheming Christ and the sacraments of his Church. We were asked also many questions about the Mohammedan colony at Lucera. We answered all these questions to the best of our knowledge and truthfully."

"Of course", said the Emperor with a shrug.

"When we were led into the cathedral on the seventeenth of July, we found the entire General Council there enthroned, in robes of state. Before the Pope and before each bishop a burning torch was installed. There were prayers. There was singing. Then the Pope himself read out a decree, to which we listened in mounting sorrow and anger. It stated that the Emperor, our august sovereign, was guilty of perjury and breach of peace committed through his attack on Viterbo. That he was guilty of sacrilege for attacking with the ships of his fleet a number of ships carrying bishops and prelates and sinking many of them, with the result that a great number of high dignitaries of the Church had drowned while others had been taken prisoner and kept in the Emperor's prisons."

"It is very regrettable that they did not all drown", said Frederick calmly.

"The Emperor was also accused of heresy in many ways and respects. It was stated that he had adopted a number of habits unworthy of a Christian prince and deriving from the customs of Islamic countries, such as having his consorts guarded by eunuchs and allowing Mohammed to be proclaimed as a prophet in the heart of Italy and even in the very temple of Christ in Jerusalem. He was accused of having innocent people assassinated, of having celebrated the sacred mysteries while under excommunication, of the destruction of churches. It was stated that the Emperor had never during his entire reign built a church, chapel, or cloister; that on the other hand he had built mosques for the Saracens in Lucera and that he kept a harem like a Moslem and altogether despised the morals and manners of a Catholic prince; also that he had built no hospital or any pious building whatever."

Piero della Vigna made a short pause, fingering his throat as if that which he now had to say refused to be said.

"My Emperor has commanded me to deliver a full report", he said finally. "It has been difficult enough for me so far; it becomes intolerable now. Friend Thaddeus here was weeping and beating his breast as he witnessed it, and I was cursing; I daresay our feelings were exactly the same. The Pope declared the alleged crimes and outrages of my gracious sovereign as proven and proceeded to read a decree of deposition. The imperial throne, he said, was now vacant . . . "

This time there was no groan, no outcry. The assembly was horror-struck.

Frederick's pale, unblinking eyes were phosphorescent, like those of a wolf at night. His long, sinewy hands clutched the arms of the throne as if to ascertain that they were still there.

"Then the Pope extinguished the torch before him," went on della Vigna, "and all the bishops followed his example. It seemed like a magical ceremony trying to drain the very life of my august master. We could stand it no longer and left the cathedral and the city of Lyons, to return here as fast as we could."

He bowed his head. Many people were weeping now;

no one dared look at his neighbor; some cursed; others prayed silently or aloud.

Frederick raised his hand. "The Treasurer will bring our crowns into this room", he ordered in a trembling voice.

There was a limit to any mortal man's self-control; della Vigna's news went beyond that limit. Frederick forgot to look for the reactions of others. He listened to himself instead. Once again, as so often before, he saw himself, a lean little boy, raised to kingship and the imperial crown by that gigantic hand of Innocent the Third; a pope had raised him, and a pope now tried to depose him. And all his fierce struggle with the papacy—with Innocent the Third, Gregory the Ninth, and now Innocent the Fourth—had at its very root his loathing of having to owe anything to anybody but himself. As if these arrogant priests were not simply the instruments of destiny, as if the third Innocent had not been born to help the greatest ruler of the century, the greatest ruler since Augustus and Justinian, to the throne that was his due. Not he, but Innocent the Fourth, was the heretic, if he thought that he could depose the Emperor.

They brought in the crowns. Two pages carried the crown of the kingdom of Sicily; another two the ancient iron crown of the kings of Lombardy; and two the imperial crown, glittering with priceless jewels and so large that it would not fit the head of mortal man . . . it had to be held over the emperor's head like the diadem of Jupiter of old.

Frederick seized the crowns of Sicily and Lombardy and had the imperial crown held over his head.

"You see, my good people," he said in a ringing voice, "I still hold what is mine by right. And of that right no man will ever deprive us. But they have cut us to the heart, and we shall not forget it. We shall wield the sword of vengeance; and the hate that consumes us will be slaked only by the utter annihilation of our enemies, wherever they are. We have been anvil long enough; now we shall be the hammer, and as the hammer of God, as the scourge of God, we may be remembered by history... as Attila was before us." Throughout his life hatred and revenge had been virtues to him. And the theatricality of words and gesture became awe-inspiring through the power behind it.

Frederick rose and stepped down. "We are leaving this our good town of Parma this very day", he said. "There can be no more audiences. This, if any, is the time for action." His glance fell on the Countess of Aquino; her face was bloodless, and there were tears in her eyes. "We regret that we cannot be present at the wedding", he said. "The Podestà of Parma will represent us. It will take place no later than one day after the arrival of the bridegroom. Francesco, you are responsible for that. Count Brandenstein!"

The huge German stepped forward. "My Emperor?"

"We leave you in charge of the garrison of Parma. We want you to be present at the wedding, too. Not a word, fair cousin of Aquino. It is high time that our wishes are respected everywhere. We shall see to it that they are."

Walking quickly past bowed heads and backs, he disappeared.

And so shattering had been the impression of the last half hour that the assembly dispersed without a murmur. Everybody hastened to get home, so as not to be faced with a discussion in which it would be almost impossible to avoid committing high treason in some way.

Landulph and Rainald escorted their mother and sisters to the wing where the Emperor's guests were accommodated in accordance with their rank and station. The Countess walked with difficulty, Theodora and Adelasia had to support her. She was unable to put her thoughts into words, but what she felt was that the first great love of her life had turned into a demon. Her entire world had fallen in pieces. She felt exhausted and ill. As soon as they got her to her rooms, she went to bed.

Eugenia fluttered about with water, vinegar, and smelling salts. Later a physician had to be called in. He felt for the pulse and heartbeat, shook his head, mentioned very long Latin names, and prescribed a medicine which Eugenia was to fetch from the nearest apothecary.

When he had gone, the Countess called out. "Theodora . . . "

"Yes, Mother. Here I am."

"You were right, Theodora—we are not noble women. We are rightless, helpless slaves. We . . . "

"Hush, Mother—you must not get excited."

"That there should be a day when I must tell my own child that I cannot protect her . . . "

"Try and sleep, Mother darling—we'll talk about it tomorrow."

But it took another half hour of pleading until Eugenia came back with the medicine, which the Countess took in a goblet of spiced wine. Soon afterward she fell asleep.

Theodora left on tiptoes. Outside she stood for a while in the strange, giant castle that seemed to breathe hostility. She saw streams of servants pass by, laden with bags, boxes, and cases. The Emperor was leaving—and they were left behind, little better than prisoners. Rightless, helpless slaves . . .

"My lady . . . "

It was Sir Piers, erect, very calm. He had not talked to her more than was absolutely necessary since that last evening at Rocca Secca—and they had never again been alone together.

"My lady, I know what happened. I just heard. Please rest assured—you will not be forced into anything you do not wish to happen. Not as long as I live."

It was not the kind of language becoming to a knight of the household. It was exactly the language she needed at this hour.

Once more, as on that last evening, she saw in his face a quiet, grim determination.

"He is like a rock", she thought. She stretched out her hand.

"You are indeed my knight", she said. "If ever I marry—I pray that my husband will be a man of your courage and devotion."

"You could not have given me a better word on my way, my lady", said Piers hoarsely. "I'll try to merit it. God bless you, my lady."

He went silently, as he had come.

For a long time she stood immobile, gazing in the direction he had gone, oblivious of everything around her. Suddenly a little frown appeared on the lovely forehead.

"Don't be foolish now, Theodora of Aquino", she said severely.

Her tone was surprisingly like that of her mother.

* * *

Landulph and Rainald had ordered themselves some wine and were drinking steadily and in silence.

"That man Brandenstein", said Landulph suddenly. "He's a malevolent ox. Did you see the smirk on his face as the Emperor made him commander of Parma? As if he were going to say: Don't worry, I'll keep them in order for you." He took another sip. "I wonder what he would look like with his face bashed in", he added thoughtfully.

"Who cares about Brandenstein?" shrugged Rainald. "What do the minions matter? The Emperor matters." How they had all felt—it was amazing—that the man was possessed. Possessed. Mother had felt it . . . he had seen her shiver and look away. The girls had looked like their own ghosts. There was something very great and terrible about della Vigna's report, a casting out of paradise into the nethermost pit, and it had been accepted not with horror and fright but with stark pride and even something akin to triumph by him who had been cast out. What a poem it was, what an apocalyptic poem. It would need the mind of a master to create it; the flight of eagles was in it and the hissing of serpents, the owl's lonely cry and the gleaming eye of the tiger; the piercing scream of a mother whose son was to die and the silent tears of old men who had seen their all go up in the flames of war; it was the rebellion of Adam and the deed of Cain; it was the fall of Satan from heaven to earth like lightning, and it was the flaming sword brandished in the hand of an archangel. It was the poem of the entire century and the symbol of all poems and all centuries. For here was the division that God had tolerated even before the beginning of the world, when Lucifer revolted and with him a third of the heavenly host; here was the song of hell and purgatory and heaven to be sung by him who dared to sing it.

Could *he* dare? The lament of a deserted girl, the joy of love, the bravery of knights; he had sung about all these, but could he dare to sing of heaven and hell? He would have to withdraw from everything just as brother Thomas had withdrawn from everything. Thomas . . . *he* had it; he had that oneness of purpose, that straight aim from which nothing and no one could deflect him; even as a prisoner he had stuck to it and defended it, firebrand in hand. They had laughed at him, shrugged their shoulders over him, despised him for not being knightly, when he had been a knight all the time, a knight in a friar's habit, fighting it through to the very end. "Here's to you, Thomas, brother and knight and monk and all. You have done what I should have done; you have chosen the better part", Rainald lifted his glass in a silent toast. "Can I withdraw now, to create the poem of our time? Heaven help me, I haven't got the strength. Months and months of filing a single rhyme, piling Pelion on Ossa and perhaps still not reaching Olympus. It is in my blood, though; I can hear it singing, I can feel it waving up and down . . . but it is too late", he thought. "Perhaps it will be sung one day by one who has not spent his life as I have, a man of a single great, overpowering love . . . "

"We may have to fight that man, you know", said Landulph slowly.

"Fight? Whom?"

"Brandenstein. He's in command, he and his Germans."

Brandenstein. Landulph seemed not to be able to get his thoughts away from that massive fool of a German. But . . . but he was right . . . good old Landulph, he was right. How like the born soldier he was, to cling to the soldier's business on hand. And what was more, he had seen farther ahead than his clever brother. To him there was nothing apocalyptic and mystical about the matter. He knew that now that the Emperor was deposed, one had to fight him, and as he himself was leaving, one had to fight his representative, and to Landulph that would never be the oily Podestà Tebaldo Francesco; it was the soldier in command who mattered. All these thoughts and cogitations he had jumped over, to come forward with his solution: we may have to fight that man Brandenstein. Indeed we may, brother Landulph. Forgive your brother who was dreaming, as poets will, of heaven and hell instead of concentrating on what had to be done now.

"You've made up your mind, then?" asked Rainald. "I know nothing about the law in such a case, you know; whether or not the Pope *can* depose the Emperor and . . . "

"He was crowned by the Pope", said Landulph; the inflection of his voice seemed to indicate that he was just a trifle surprised at the denseness of his usually so intelligent brother.

Rainald laughed. "Right again, brother Landulph. So he was. Well, that settles it, I suppose. Except of course, if Frederick gets his hands on us . . . or one of us. I don't think your logic will convince him as easily as it convinces me."

"War is always dangerous", stated Landulph simply. "And it's a General Council of the Church *and* the Pope. I'm not a saint, but I don't want to fight the Church. I said once, popes come and go but the Emperor remains, and Thomas said it was the other way round. Well, it looks to me as if he was right. Besides, I didn't like the way he treated Mother: the Emperor, I mean, not Thomas. And I don't like to see little Theodora unhappy. It's just as well we must stay here for this wedding, or else we would have had to go with him straight away, and it would have become very difficult."

Rainald nodded. "You're a paragon of wisdom today, Landulph. I don't know what's come over you. What do you think he's going to do next?"

"Go to Verona. Most of the army is there. He must secure that first. That's why he leaves today, see? And then to Lyons."

Rainald whistled softly. There was genuine admiration in his eyes as he looked at his brother. "Verona to collect the army. Lyons—to take the Pope a prisoner . . . or worse. He may well succeed, too. In fact he will succeed, unless the Holy Father manages to escape again . . . or . . . unless something else happens."

"What?"

"Well, when the cat is away, the mice will start dancing. And there are plenty of mice in Italy. We are not exactly the only ones who have a grudge—shall we say?—against . . . Herod; or Nero, if you prefer it. How many people in Parma alone will be whispering about what we are whispering about now? And the news will spread like wildfire; that sort of news always does. There are garrisons in most of his cities, of course. But are they reliable? All of them? Will they still be reliable when they know what we know now? This thing may become very big, brother mine . . . too big for you and me. But we'll be in it all the same. When we were fighting for him we often thought of that possibility . . . and so did he. And now we are on the other side of the wall."

"The garrison in Parma . . . the Germans here, I mean . . . are about two hundred strong", said Landulph. "And we have only one hundred. And these damned Germans are good. I've seen them in action. So have you. I loathe their guts, but they're good. What do we do?"

"I'll tell you what we must *not* do: look about for allies too openly. If we do, we shall be denounced to our dear cousin Frederick before he even reaches Verona. We must take first things first. We can't start a war against him alone, Aquino against Hohenstaufen. It's absurd. But we must think of what we shall do when San Severino turns up . . . Santa Madonna di Napoli . . . "

They both sat up with a jerk as the shadow of a man in armor fell across the room. Neither of them was a coward, but it took an effort for Rainald to turn round. He sighed with relief when he recognized Piers instead of an officer of the German guard.

"We're not very good at this game yet, brother mine", he said to Landulph. "We didn't even think of closing the door. Come in, Sir Piers, come in. Anything on your mind? You look as if there were."

"May I speak frankly?" asked Piers abruptly.

"By all means, Sir Piers", said Landulph attentively.

"I was told by Messer de Braccio of what happened at the audience this morning . . . "

"Trust de Braccio for knowing it even before it happened", grinned Rainald. "What did he tell you? He's very good at mixing truth and fantasy."

"I don't think he did that in this case . . . he was too excited about it to be able to invent much. The petition of the most noble Countess was refused by the Emperor . . . "

"Surely," interrupted Landulph haughtily, "that is neither de Braccio's concern, nor . . . "

"Nor mine", said Piers coldly. "I am aware of it. But I did ask for your permission to speak frankly."

"So he did", said Rainald. "Don't be an ass, Landulph . . . I mean, let him say what he's got to say."

"Very well", said Landulph curtly.

"The Emperor insisted that the wedding take place as soon as the Count of San Severino arrived and put the mayor of Parma and the commander of the German guards in charge of this matter, as of all matters of importance in Parma."

"Correct", nodded Rainald.

"The audience was interrupted by the arrival of the Emperor's ambassadors to Lyons, who announced that he had been deposed by the Pope, and the Emperor decided to leave Parma at once, apparently in order to put himself at the head of his army."

"The world tumbles down around us," said Rainald, "everything is going to pieces, it's the end of an age, the very soil of Europe is atremble . . . for a true Englishman it is a little matter of one dry sentence. Will there ever be an English poet, I wonder?"

"I take it that your family, my lords, is still opposed to the idea of this marriage", went on Piers, entirely unruffled.

"What?" asked Rainald in mock indignation. "Despite the explicit command of the Emperor?"

"To oppose the Emperor's wish is as good as to oppose his command", was the calm answer. "Besides, there are many now who will doubt the validity of that command."

"Very likely", said Rainald cautiously.

"In any case," said the Englishman, "I suggest that it would be a good thing if the Count of San Severino did not arrive in Parma."

"It would be an excellent thing", muttered Rainald. "But who's to stop him?"

"I shall stop him", said Piers simply. "But I shall have to leave Parma to catch him before he enters the town. That's why I have come to you now."

"By the biceps of Hercules," said Rainald, "the man's found the solution of the problem. It's a brilliant idea. No bridegroom, no wedding. Nothing could be simpler. I can't understand why I didn't think of it myself. But San Severino is likely to travel with a strong retinue."

"Fifty men will do", said Piers.

"And if you succeed . . . what can we do with him? I mean, where shall we take him? All the way back south to Rocca Secca? You'll never get through."

"There'll be no need to take him anywhere", said Piers stonily.

"Holy prophets", said Rainald. "No half measures, eh? Have you ever met the man?"

"No, my lord. May I take the fifty men and leave now, my lord?"

"I'd like to go with him", declared Landulph, chuckling.

"But you can't, brother dear. Don't forget your friend Brandenstein is bound to keep an eye on you and me. If you disappear it will arouse his suspicion at once. No, friend Piers here must do it alone. And no flag, Sir Piers; we needn't expose ourselves too much *at the present stage.*"

For the first time Piers smiled a little. "I understand, my lord."

"Splendid", said Rainald quickly. "Splendid. There are things about which one can be in complete agreement, but which are better not talked about too much before the time is ripe. Take your fifty men and do what you like."

"No", said Landulph, surprisingly. "He's a reliable man. He should know where he stands. Sir Piers, I want you to understand that this is the beginning of greater things to come. You are not alone in this. We stand behind you . . . even if the plans of someone very high should be completely upset by your action. The wind has changed in Italy."

"It's very good of you to tell me that, my lord", said Piers. The little shrug he added meant clearly "but it makes no difference to me."

He bowed and clanked out of the room, closing the door behind him.

"A very good man", said Landulph. "And I wouldn't like to be in San Severino's shoes if he gets hold of him."

"Neither would I", drawled Rainald. He emptied his goblet, deep in thought. Suddenly, in a flash, he understood. He frowned. "Poor fellow", he said.

"Who? San Severino?"

"No. Not at all. Piers."

"Why?"

"Never mind. Give me some more wine. Poor fellow. It could never be, of course. It would be a good poem, though."

Chapter IX

It was not entirely a coincidence that Piers met Messer Giacomo di Barolo at the tavern of the Seven Saints six miles southeast of Parma.

He had to make his headquarters somewhere south of Parma, not too near and not too far, and the tavern was just right for his purpose. He had only too much opportunity to observe a good deal of what was going on in the tavern, for all he could do now was to sit still and wait for news from the dozen or so patrols that guarded every highway toward Parma from the south.

They had orders not to get themselves involved in any trouble but only to keep a sharp lookout for San Severino's approach; as soon as they had sighted him, they were to notify Piers. The crest and flag of the enemy were known to every single man.

The enemy . . . that was Piers' simple way of looking at the matter. San Severino was the enemy of his lady, and that made him his enemy. He had promised his lady that she need not worry, and he was going to keep his promise.

It was all a good deal easier now: they did not seem to mind so much resisting the Emperor, although it was very natural that they preferred not to do it too openly.

So far he had been entirely on his own, except for Robin, of course, and that meant that though he might succeed, he would not be able to escape the consequences. He could not challenge a man so far his superior in rank as San Severino. He could only pick a quarrel with him and resort to the sword. With a bit of luck he might kill him, but there was no chance of escaping the swords of his retinue. Naturally he had never talked to Robin about it, and naturally Robin knew it all, though he tried his best to conceal his knowledge and to go about with an air of having no worries at all. Good old Robin. It was a shame to drag him into this.

But now things were different. Now he had a chance of escape, and a pretty good chance at that. There were signs of unrest, even in Parma itself. When Brandenstein had to send his German guards on an errand, he had to send at least six or seven, although each one of them represented a redoubtable fighting unit. They were very unpopular, and not only because they were foreigners. They were arrogant, very proud of their superior physical strength, and full of contempt for the Italians. They walked about with the air of conquerors, and even when they tried to be polite, they adopted an intolerably patronizing attitude. The very day after the Emperor's departure, three of them had been found with their throats cut, and Brandenstein could not find any witnesses. No one seemed to have seen anything. He would have to resort to reprisals, and that, in turn, would cause more hatred.

But far more interesting than the sporadic unrest in Parma was what Piers could observe and had observed during the last three days at the tavern of the Seven Saints. There was a constant coming and going of people who did not seem to fit in with the ordinary life of a tavern. Peasants with astonishingly well kept fingernails; little groups of inconspicuously dressed men, meeting in the upper rooms, with a couple of sturdy varlets keeping watch at the door. And at one time the stable of the inn contained no less than thirty-six excellent horses, guarded by a dozen stable boys who were dressed in rags but looked as if they belonged in well-cut livery.

And there was Messer Giacomo di Barolo, who said he was a merchant . . . spices and oil were his main trade . . . and who looked rather like a man whose ancestors had been knighted a very long time ago. Messer Giacomo di Barolo was forever asking questions and never seemed to mind that he got very few and curt answers. Also he received many guests . . . other merchants, of course, with whom he engaged in serious and prolonged business talks.

Piers had not been long enough in Italy to know the

differences between the various dialects; an experienced man would have known that the accents of Cremona, of Florence, of Genoa and Venice were all prevalent at the tavern of the Seven Saints. But he knew at least that there were people here who came from different parts of the country.

One day Messer Giacomo's unfailing friendliness suddenly changed. He seemed suspicious and preoccupied, and when they were alone for a moment, he said point blank: "How long are you going to stay here, noble sir?"

"Until my business is concluded", answered Piers.

Messer Giacomo laughed angrily. "Let us hope, then, that this will soon be the case. The air here is not too healthy for those of Aquino."

"Why not?" asked Piers, without batting an eyelid. Obviously the man had his sources of information. To ask him how he knew was to invite his scorn. To deny it would only increase his suspicion.

"It is a very loyal family", said Messer Giacomo with a slight shrug. "Doubtless that is a great virtue . . . in some cases." And he caressed his beautiful black beard with its slight sprinkle of silver, looking less than ever like a merchant.

"Yes", said Piers drily.

"But you," said Messer Giacomo, "you are a foreigner here—why should you be concerned with our politics? Why don't you get out and back to whatever country you belong to . . . and if you want to do a work of mercy, take all the German knights with you. We are just a little tired of you all." He said it extremely politely, and he went on caressing his beard.

"An oath is an oath", replied Piers. "And the house of Aquino has not been excommunicated or deposed. So my oath stands. Also I am not a German. I am English."

"It is a great pity", said Messer Giacomo, "that your masters or lieges, or whatever they are, do not have your fine understanding for what makes an oath invalid. If they had, it might save their lives."

"Their lives?" Piers stared at the strange man.

"But as it is," went on Messer Giacomo, "they are not likely to survive another week, I'm afraid. However, it may comfort them that they will die in what they must consider very good company. Parma will be purged of all friends of the great blasphemer."

"Well, well," said Piers, "you certainly fill your mouth pretty full, Messer merchant. You must be very sure of yourself. I don't care what you do to the German knights in Parma or to anybody else, but I will not stomach any threats against the house of Aquino, whatever *your* true rank may be."

"My true rank is not your concern, Sir Knight. You may guess as much as you like. But it must be clear even to a simpleton like you that I cannot allow you to return to Parma to repeat there what you have heard here."

"I have no intention of returning to Parma as yet", answered Piers, still with great composure. "But if I wanted to return, who's to stop me?"

Messer Giacomo smiled. "This good tavern is surrounded," he said, "and seventy knights with their retinues are perhaps a little too much even for you, though I admit you look as if you could deal with one or two of them. Your own fifty men are dispersed in little groups and can be dealt with easily. You don't seriously think I would talk as frankly to you as I have done this last quarter of an hour if I didn't know that you cannot damage our cause? Give me credit for some intelligence."

Piers rose and walked to the window. Groups of armored men with their horses, near the entrance of the tavern, near the little brook, and to the right and left of the main road. He had had two men posted there; they seemed to have disappeared. "I shouldn't have let Robin go with the patrol yesterday morning", he thought. With Robin here this would not have happened. The fellow had an uncanny sense of danger, like an animal, bless him.

He walked back to the table, where Messer Giacomo di Barolo was sitting, smiling haughtily. He felt just a little angry. He remembered the way in which the Italian had started the conversation, and he understood now that he had done a good deal of talking so as to give his men the opportunity to surround the tavern. He understood now also that the tavernkeeper and his people had been taken care of.

"Very neatly done, Messer merchant", he drawled. "It seems that you consider me a prisoner here."

"You are", said Messer Giacomo coldly.

"Ah, but I remember that at the beginning of our conversation you expressed the wish that I should leave here as soon as possible."

"And so you will—as my prisoner—as soon as you have answered a few more questions. Exactly how many men have the Aquinos in Parma apart from you and your fifty?"

"By the Blessed Virgin," exclaimed Piers, "you seem to know very little about English knights. They may be simpletons, but they do not commit treason."

Messer Giacomo smiled ominously. "Whatever they do or don't do, they are flesh and blood, and there are ways and means of making a man talk. All I need to do is to call in half a dozen of my men and . . . what are you doing?"

Ever since Piers had looked out of the window and seen the trap, he had started undoing the straps of his chainmail. Now he slipped out of it altogether and stood in his undershirt and drawers.

"Making myself lighter", explained Piers. Suddenly he jumped at the Italian, seized him in a grip of iron, and drew a foot-long stiletto from his coat. "Quiet now, Messer merchant, or you'll taste your own dagger—my, what a lovely piece of art it is; sapphires on the hilt. Seems to be well worthwhile being a merchant in—what was it?—spices and oil, wasn't it? Quiet, I say."

"You're mad", breathed Messer Giacomo. "My men will tear you to pieces . . . "

"That may be so," nodded Piers, "but only after your death. I swear it. An oath is an oath."

"But what good does this absurd attack do you, you fool? You can't possibly escape."

"That remains to be seen. What do you think I made myself lighter for? I saw a very good horse held by only one man about fifteen yards from the window. You most kindly gave me credit for being a match for one or two of your men. All I need to do is to throw him, take the horse, and gallop back to Parma. All your men are armored . . . they'll never be able to catch up with me. But now I have an even better idea, Messer merchant: I'll take you with me to Parma. And Count Landulph of Aquino won't have to ask you how many men you have with you, because you have told me that already. Still, I presume he will enjoy your visit all the same. I shall march you out of here, and unless your men give way . . . well . . . "

"You wouldn't dare", snapped Messer Giacomo. But he was pale now.

"I have nothing to lose", said Piers. "Get up and march in front of me. I mean it."

"By my faith, I believe you do", said Messer Giacomo, shaking his head. "I hope they haven't got too many like you in England and, if they have, that they stay where they are. It's a pity we must fight on different sides. Kill me, if you must. But that will not save Parma for the ex-Emperor, and it will not save him from his ultimate defeat either."

Only now was Piers certain that the man was really against Frederick and not a decoy. He released his grip and made a step back. "What makes you so certain that we are on different sides?" he asked quietly.

Messer Giacomo stared at him. "Everybody knows that the Aquinos are for Frederick. They never wavered."

"The Emperor is deposed now", said Piers.

Messer Giacomo gave him a sharp look. "You mean . . . impossible. Not the Aquinos. Why, he's so sure of them that he wants to win over the San Severinos by marrying the young Count to an Aquino girl."

Piers frowned. "That marriage is not going to take place."

Messer Giacomo's eyes narrowed. "No? Why not?"

"Because the house of Aquino refuses to be used as a pawn in the Emperor's political game."

The merchant's face brightened up. "But they did go to Parma for the purpose of the marriage, Sir Knight."

"The Countess of Aquino", said Piers stiffly, "informed the Emperor that her daughter had no wish to marry."

"You surprise me more and more, Sir Knight", said Messer Giacomo. "And the Emperor?"

"Insisted on his wish. And left Parma the same day."

The merchant's face was tense. "You swear that what you say is true, Sir Knight?"

"God's truth," exploded Piers, "why should I tell you all this if it weren't true?"

Messer Giacomo rose. "Sir Knight . . . you are free."

Piers gave a cheerful laugh. "You forget, Messer merchant, that it is you who are my prisoner."

Now the Italian laughed too. "Very well, then—I shall buy my freedom with the dagger you took from me. Here is the sheath as well."

"It's a princely ransom", said Piers, hesitantly.

"And if ever you should leave the service of the house of Aquino, I think I know another house that will have good use for a man of your courage."

"You are very kind, Messer merchant." Piers grinned. "I'm glad you believe me, anyway."

"Yes . . . I believe you. When one has come to my age, one must have learned the art of trusting the right man, and a very great art it is, Sir Knight. The ex-Emperor has never mastered it . . . nor could he; his mind is warped . . . he thinks of himself in terms of divinity and of others only in terms of their usefulness to him. He has sucked the minds and the strength of all those around him like a giant vampire. Loyalty to him is based on fear. He has ravaged my beautiful country with his continuous feuds, town against town, castle against castle; he has polluted it with his jeers and jibes at things we hold holy. At long last the Vicar of Our Lord has declared him unworthy of his high office. We shall see to it that the Holy Father's verdict is executed."

"With seventy knights?" asked Piers. He had come to like the man. There was something clean and noble about him. But by now the Emperor must have arrived in Verona, and there twenty-five thousand men were waiting for him . . . including many hundreds of German knights with their retinues, each a little fortress, a moving hill.

But Messer Giacomo smiled. "Why worry?" he said. "We die only once. But rest assured, Sir Knight, my seventy knights are not alone. This thing is bigger by far than the house of Aquino or the house of . . . the house which I am serving. I must leave you now, but permit me to introduce you to . . . a staunch friend of mine, Captain Bruno de Amicis: he is in charge of the seventy, and it is to him that I shall give the sign when the hour of attack has come. May I call him in?"

"By all means", said Piers without hesitation.

Messer Giacomo walked to the window and gave a peculiar whistle.

A minute later a large, heavy knight entered, fully armored.

"Bruno," said the astonishing merchant, "this noble knight is in the service of the house of Aquino, and it seems that we have been wrong in our opinion about that house."

"You know best . . . Messer Giacomo", grunted the knight, appraising Piers in the manner of men at arms. "You don't want me to seize him, then? I have six of my men outside."

"On the contrary", smiled the merchant. "I want you to be friends, I have received most valuable information, Bruno.

So valuable that I shall go to Parma to meet our friends there. You will get the decisive message from there."

"It is a great risk", warned the knight.

"It is no risk at all, as things are. The risk begins when you get my message. You will find this English knight a very valuable help when it comes to the hard work. Until then I hope you will keep good company."

"Easy now, Messer Giacomo", protested Piers. "I cannot join you in your plans without the explicit orders of my liege."

The merchant nodded. "Of course not. But you will have them . . . I have little doubt that you will have them soon enough. In three days, perhaps. I don't think it will be much more than that. The parole remains the same, Bruno. Just one more word, Sir Knight: I take it you will not move from here before you have heard from your liege . . . is that agreed upon? Very good. God be with you, friends."

"And with you, my . . . Messer Giacomo", said Bruno de Amicis.

"He was going to say 'my liege' ", thought Piers. "Well, it's clear enough that he is a man of high rank. Whoever has seen a knight so deferent toward a merchant in spice and oils?"

"Let's have some wine, Sir Knight", he said aloud, when the merchant had quietly slipped out. He felt very joyful. Parma was going to be stormed in a few days' time, and the attackers had friends within the walls of the town. He would have to send a messenger to Count Landulph to inform him about all this, of course . . . and it would have to be done secretly. This man de Amicis looked like something of a suspicious bull. It would not be too easy, but it would be done. But the main thing was: whether San Severino arrived or not, there would be no marriage. That was certain now.

* * *

Theodora came out of her room just in time to see it happen. But then, as Adelasia said afterward, that would be so. "You have a knack of turning up when things happen, *carissima;* yours is the shortest nose in the whole family, but also the best. *Dio de mi alma,* that's how it is with you." She saw Landulph and Rainald almost tumbling over each other as they hurried along on the sentinel's urgent call. She saw the two very elegantly dressed men—one oldish and black bearded, the other very young—whose visit had caused all the stir. She heard Rainald ask, breathlessly: "Your name, most noble sir, is . . . ?" and she heard the older man answer: "San Severino de Marsico, at your service." Rainald gulped before he was able to introduce himself and to present his brother. He had not seen her, or perhaps in his excitement he forgot all about her; she was standing at some distance anyway. Then the black-bearded man introduced the younger one: "My son Ruggiero," and added, "may it please you, my lords, to lead me to the Countess of Aquino. I wish to present my respects to her." She was rather pleased, later, remembering that she had thought, "This is going to upset Mamma terribly; I hope they won't do it" . . . thinking of her, although she was naturally very upset herself; after all they wanted *her* to marry young San Severino and not Mamma; or rather they didn't. And selfishness was usually her worst point when she had to go to confession. She knew that her brothers had made efforts to prevent the San Severinos from coming to Parma . . . her mother had alluded to that without mentioning how such a thing could be done . . . and she understood therefore that they had somehow failed. But all this was only in the uttermost back of her mind. She did not think of it. She was simply aware of it.

Now they had agreed, it seemed, to lead the count to Mamma; he turned to his son, who was standing with his back to her all the time, and said something in a low voice; he smiled, and it was a nice smile, despite the black beard slightly sprinkled with silver. And he turned again and walked away with Landulph and Rainald, and now she would never know what the young one looked like. If only he had turned round once, only a little . . .

And then, as if he had felt her wish, he did. And he saw her.

"Madonna", she thought. "He is blushing like a girl." And there was something almost girlish about him. Long, black curls framed a sensitive young face with very large, dark eyes and a small mouth; it was not a weak mouth, however, and not a weak chin either; the hand, resting lightly on the golden sword hilt, was white, but it had character. He wore a long, blue coat of heavy silk, with a silver belt.

Her next thought was: "He can't be more than eighteen- . . . and my, how frightened he is."

It was not Theodora's way to have two thoughts in succession, without putting at least one of them into words. And she said: "What has frightened you so badly, my lord?"

"I . . . I am not frightened, most noble lady", said the youth, and now she saw that he had tears in his eyes.

She shook her head. She had wanted to ask him what he looked like when he really was frightened, but she suddenly knew that he did not merit ridicule, and her voice was soft and almost maternal as she asked: "But what is it then, my lord?"

He took a deep breath. "Never in all my life have I seen anyone so beautiful."

She bowed a little, but this time there was a tinge of irony in her voice as she replied: "You are very young, my lord."

"Only once before", he said, "have I felt anything like this . . . "

She raised her eyebrows quizzically; she said nothing.

"I was five years old then", he went on. "It was when my mother showed me the statue of the Holy Virgin at the Church of Marsico."

She frowned a little. "This is very wrong of you, my lord. One does not compare the Queen of Heaven with a sinful girl."

"I know", he admitted innocently. "I suppose I shall

have to confess it. But it's quite true. And painters sometimes choose a lady they know when they want to paint the Madonna . . . if they feel that they respect the lady very much and if she is very beautiful. I . . . I do paint sometimes. But I don't think I would dare . . . "

At that moment it occurred to her that this was the man her entire family had sworn to defend her against, the blood-stained favorite of the Emperor, reckless, blasphemous, and dissolute.

"You are laughing at me", he said a little reproachfully.

"No", she replied hastily. "Not really. But you see . . . I thought you would be so different. Oh, I can't explain it, but that's what I thought."

"I see", said Ruggiero, who had not heard a word of what she had said. But his thoughts were the same as hers. "Theodora of Aquino", he said slowly. "Theodora of Aquino. How often I tried to imagine what you were like, all these weeks . . . "

"How do you know I am Theodora?" was the laughing reply. "We are three sisters . . . one of us is now a Benedictine nun, but the other two are both here, Adelasia and Theodora."

"And are you your sister?" asked Ruggiero, quite overcome.

Peals of laughter. Again he blushed. "I know I said a stupid thing; you must take me for a fool. I wish you were a little less beautiful. No, I don't. But you are not Adelasia, are you?"

"No, I'm Theodora." She became serious now. "But it doesn't make much difference which of us I am. They are all against this . . . this idea of the Emperor's, you know. All my family, I mean."

He nodded. "I know. Father told me yesterday. You, too, are against it, of course."

"Of course," said she hastily. "But . . . but I don't think you are a fool. I think . . . I think you are . . . I don't think you are a fool at all."

"Father is against it, too", said Ruggiero, playing with his belt.

"Why?" asked Theodora, decidedly nettled.

* * *

By this time the Countess of Aquino and her sons had recovered from two shocks—the first that San Severino had managed to bypass Piers and his men, the second that he, too, was opposed to the Emperor's plan. A fairly lengthy bit of verbal skirmishing followed, in which neither of the two parties seemed willing to disclose much about his own ideas, while rather eager to find out exactly where the other stood. It was San Severino who put an end to it, with a little laugh. "I've done too much of this kind of fencing lately", he said. "Faith, I do not blame you for being cautious in times like ours, but one of us must come out of his shell if we want to get anywhere. Very well then: our problem is a twofold one: it is political, and it is personal, and both these facts are closely linked. Now the Council of Lyons has brought about a decisive change. Do we agree about that? We do? Excellent. Now the power of the tyrant is waning. He cannot subsist long with the curse of the Church on his head. He must strike and strike quickly . . . against Lyons. To do so, he has gone to join his army at Verona. Both patriotism and piety demand that we protect the Holy Father and get rid of a tyrant. Italy will rise, and to Parma falls the honor of being the first to act."

"The Parmese are good fighters", said Landulph. "But the Emperor has left the town in the hands of two of his staunchest supporters: Tebaldo Francesco, the mayor, and Count Brandenstein."

San Severino smiled. "Tebaldo Francesco has been won for our cause", he said. "Brandenstein and his Germans are practically the only men the Emperor has in Parma. Until recently I very much feared that he also had the Aquinos and their retinue. I need not fear that any longer, I believe."

"You need not", said the Countess grimly. "I have been loyal to my cousin Frederick long enough."

San Severino nodded. "When I heard that you had opposed his wish that your daughter should marry my son, I knew that even your patience was exhausted."

"I hope you will not misunderstand my opposition, my lord", said the Countess. "Political marriages between ruling houses have happened very frequently. But in this case it was all a matter of fortifying Frederick's position . . . not ours. Besides, my daughter resented having no choice in the matter, and I did not relish the idea of her living at court."

San Severino laughed outright. "So you thought that I was a partisan of the ex-Emperor, and I thought you were. I am enchanted with your daughter's attitude—she sounds a very spirited young lady. Frederick's idea was, of course, to bind my house to yours, of whose loyalty he felt so sure that he did not even mind overriding your petition at your audience."

The Countess bit her lip. "He has changed a great deal", she murmured. "I used to think that his environment had caused all the harm, but now I am not so sure."

"Every ruler", said San Severino gravely, "has the environment he deserves, just as every country has the ruler it deserves. We do not deserve Frederick, I feel, and we shall rid ourselves of him. But his idea to link up our houses has succeeded after all, it seems . . . we are now linked as allies against him. At least, I hope we are."

"You are a very courageous man, my lord", said Rainald, before the Countess could reply. "What if we retained you here until Count Brandenstein made his appearance? He's summoned easily enough."

"Quiet, Rainald", said the Countess. "A thing like that should not be said even in joke. My lord of San Severino, I very much fear that your zeal surpasses your means. Even as allies we cannot hope to resist the Emperor. He has thousands where we have hundreds, and no one can dispute that he is a great soldier. Parma may fall . . . but how do we know that Italy will rise?"

"This list", said San Severino, producing a thin sheet of paper from his cuff, "will show you that we do not stand alone."

The Countess glanced through it. "Genoa *and* Venice", she exclaimed. "But they are inveterate enemies of each other."

"Yet they have agreed to a truce until the tyrant is laid low. And Pandulf of Fasanella in Tuscany; Jacob Morra, governor of the March; Orlando di Rossi; to say nothing of Cardinal Rainer of Viterbo . . . "

The Countess nodded. "You are sure of them, I take it?"

"Upon my word as a Christian knight, I am sure of them. We have all sworn by the sacred Host. Now . . . are we allies?"

"We are", said the Countess simply. "I never dreamed that it would come to this one day. There was a time when I was very fond of the Emperor." She banned a sigh. "What is your plan, my lord? What do you want me to do?"

"How many men do you have in Parma, Countess?"

"Fifty only. Another fifty are in the neighborhood under the command of Sir Piers Rudde."

"I know that", nodded San Severino, smiling. "He almost killed me when I wanted to take him prisoner."

"As a matter of fact," said Rainald, "I was most surprised to see you here in Parma, my lord. Sir Piers had orders to look out for you . . . "

"For me?" San Severino broke into hearty laughter. "Now I begin to understand. Faith, you went to great length to prevent this marriage, I must say. But then, you see, he never met me . . . only the merchant Messer Giacomo di Barolo, though I daresay he knew I was not what I said I was. As I said, he almost killed me. I hate to think what he would have done had he known who I was. I wanted to take him prisoner because I was convinced that you were on Frederick's side at that time, and he turned the tables on me. If I hadn't been able to convince him that I had given up the idea of arresting him, I believe he would have taken me to Parma by force, single-handed, despite the fact that I had seventy knights with me. It's a good man you have there, Countess. Well . . . now he and his fifty will be welcome reinforcement for my men. It will be best, perhaps, to leave him where he is."

Landulph grinned. "I'm glad he behaved well", he said. "And you will find him useful when the hard work is to be done. But when will that be?"

"Soon enough", said San Severino. "Your brother mentioned Count Brandenstein. He is a clumsy man, but by now . . . certainly in a few hours . . . he will know that I am in town. That means he will organize the marriage ceremony. I can stave him off a few days by saying that my retinue has not arrived yet, but that is all I can do. We must strike within three days. All you need to do is to hold yourselves in readiness."

"You have seventy knights with you", said Landulph. "With their followers that should be about four hundred men at least."

"A little over five hundred to be joined by your fifty under the Englishman and the fifty you have here. And now I can also tell you: I visited Tebaldo Francesco before I came to see you. When I give the sign, he will come to our aid with three thousand townsmen."

"That settles Brandenstein", said Landulph appreciatively.

San Severino rose. "My respects, Countess. I'd rather have you as my ally than any number of townsmen. By the way, I left my son Ruggiero outside. May I present him to you? I'm sure he will be inconsolable to hear what trouble he has caused your daughter."

They all walked with him, and Rainald opened the door. "You'll find him rather shy and reticent", said San Severino. "I often thought . . . " He stopped abruptly. They all stood still and stared as if they could not trust their eyes.

Yet what they saw was a very charming picture.

A very young man and a very young girl were embracing each other.

His hands held her waist, not possessively, not passionately, but in a rather uncertain way, as though they could not believe their good fortune. She was looking up at him—just a little, for she was almost as tall as he was—and she was holding his face between her hands. And thus they stood, entirely and completely oblivious of anything else in the world. They had a conspiracy of their own, and it excluded all others.

"Theodora", said the Countess breathlessly.

They both looked at her and at the others; they stood transfixed.

Smiling, San Severino caressed his black beard. "My dearest Countess," he said, "I think this demands a slight alteration of our plan."

* * *

Captain Bruno de Amicis was tiresome company. The only things he seemed fond of were dice, heavy drinking, and the singing of ribald army songs. Piers avoided his company as much as possible. He had sent a messenger to Parma with a report on the situation, who came back a day later with a letter from Count Landulph. It was very short. "Thank you. Follow de Amicis' instructions in everything. Nothing else matters." Short as it was, it conveyed a lot. Messer Giacomo must have succeeded in winning the confidence of the Aquinos, they must have made common cause, and they regarded that cause as too dangerous to mention in a letter that might be intercepted. "Nothing else matters" obviously meant that he need no longer look out for the flag of the San Severinos. Unfortunately it meant also that he had no longer any pretext for avoiding de Amicis' company.

But in the afternoon of the same day, the Captain walked into the tavern, grinning all over his face. "Get your men together, Sir Piers. . . . You have? Good. Tonight's the night."

He sat down, his armor clanking. "There's only one drawback", he went on. "We won't be able to drink a single drop. At least I never do before serious work, and you can trust the Germans for giving us that."

"The Germans?" asked Piers.

"Yes. We're taking Parma tonight. There's nothing much to it. We'll find the gate wide open for us, and most of the town is on our side. Only the Germans will give trouble. Two hundred knights and their men, about eight hundred heads when all is said and done. But most of them will be very drunk."

"How do you know that?"

"There's some festival going on", said de Amicis. "I suppose that's why tonight was chosen. Now listen carefully: our plan is very simple, but nothing must go wrong."

* * *

The main hall of the castle of Parma was lit by a thousand candles.

Count Brandenstein had made his speech, in which he mentioned the Emperor seven times in as many minutes—"the soul and heart and mind of the feast", "continuously occupied in spreading happiness and good fortune among his subjects"—himself three times, and the bridal couple once. He was "a simple soldier who did not know how to juggle with words and just said what he thought". What he thought took the form of army wit—the obvious, ancient, and clumsy jokes about bridegroom and bride.

"You should listen with more respect", whispered Rainald to Landulph. "There is no older tradition than that of vulgarity." Landulph snorted.

The Count of San Severino frowned and smiled. "His frown", thought Rainald, "is for the present—the smile is for the future. Let's hope that the smile survives."

But time and again his eyes, greedy for beauty, returned to the young couple. He was too much of a poet to take his sister's beauty for granted, as brothers often do. Tonight she was radiant, and so was he, as he admitted with a strange little grudge, of which he was well aware, though he could not really understand it. Perhaps it was because it had all gone so quickly—absurdly, insanely quickly. They had only met five days ago—and now they were married.

But—what a pair! They were both dressed in white; the bridegroom with golden embroideries on coat and tunic, the bride with silver veil and heavy silver flowers all over her dress, from the neck down to her feet. Their beauty matched to perfection. It seemed a marriage of elfin spirits rather than of human beings. Surely they had flown into the room and would fly out again when they felt like it.

Theodora had thrown her proud little head back at Brandenstein's stupid allusions. Ruggiero had looked aside, as if he felt embarrassed more for the speaker than for himself.

That and their incredible beauty—perhaps also the fact that they were both dressed in white, although that was by no means unusual—made Rainald suddenly think of two brides, and he smiled at the quaintness of the idea.

Ruggiero was young and almost too good looking for a man, but he came from a family renowned for vigor and courage.

It was just as well that the two young people knew as little of what was going to happen tonight as Brandenstein and his men. It was going to be pretty noisy a few hours from now—but if all went well, it would be over before they had so much as guessed the truth.

There—the little bride was receiving a nod from her mother: time to retire. The quiet, self-assured elegance of it—laughing in response to a friendly word of San Severino—a little bow to the formidable old lady with the pink pearl on her bosom, he had forgotten her name—and all the time she was withdrawing gracefully toward the door.

Then the little bridegroom had to leave, equally imperceptibly—and within half an hour or so all the ladies would follow suit and the real drinking could start. If only the friends remembered that they must not get drunk—if only the Germans drank as much as they usually did—it was quite incredible how much wine they could pour into those huge bodies before it really had an effect on them.

San Severino saw the Countess looking at him stonily, and he smiled.

"I wish I had your equanimity, friend", said she in a low voice.

"You wish for the impossible", he whispered back. "I haven't any."

"But you appear quite happy."

"And I am."

"Poor children", said the Countess almost inaudibly.

"Happy children", said San Severino aloud, raising his goblet. He added in a whisper: "What couple ever has had a more fitting wedding night than this—the night when Italy rises to become free. I told him after all—he has a right to know."

A weary smile passed over the face of the Countess. "I told her, too", she said. "She would never forgive me if I had concealed it from her—as we planned."

He leaned back. He laughed delightedly. "If that generation equals ours, Countess—Italy will *stay* free."

* * *

"You knew, little queen", said Ruggiero an hour later.

"Yes, I knew. Stop kissing me—I want to see your face."

"You shouldn't have been told. You should know nothing about anything harsh and ugly—"

"Darling fool—I must know. It makes—all this—still more wonderful. What is harsh and ugly about it?"

"But, little queen, in an hour or two men will shriek with pain—and die of horrible wounds."

"And my country will be free of tyranny. I'd die for that gladly. I could envy you for being a man."

"You ungrateful creature," he said, "the heavens have

showered beauty on you and grace and the most exquisite femininity . . . "

"I am not ungrateful. I love being a woman. I love you. It is only—tonight—that I would like to be a man, like you—to be able to *do* something myself—to be in the fight. Even as I am, I would like to go with you."

"Go with—me?"

"Yes. Yes. When you go out of this room to fight them—when will it be?"

"I—I don't know for sure. We'll hear it. But . . . "

"Yes?"

He shook his head. "Nothing . . . "

Suddenly he bent over her and kissed her, again and again and again.

But she felt his body trembling in her arms, and she knew instinctively that he was afraid . . .

* * *

The attack started two hours before midnight, but for the better part of half an hour no fighting developed at all.

Gate after gate opened silently as by magic for the chainmailed mass of de Amicis' knights and for Piers and his men.

The streets were dark, and there was no moon, but, even so, little groups of armed men could be seen, marching quickly to strategic points of the town. They were all wearing armlets of straw, so as not to be confused with the enemy, and so did de Amicis' and Piers' men.

Podestà Tebaldo Francesco showed himself as a man of imagination. He had bands of musicians posted within earshot of the two main danger points: the citadel and the castle, and they played for all they were worth to make the noise of hundreds of armed men and horses approaching inaudible to the garrison.

Thus de Amicis succeeded in forcing the very gates of the citadel before the alarm was given; and hundreds of Brandenstein's men—varlets, knaves, and stableboys, most of them, but also a number of knights—were slaughtered before they had time to get into their armor. Some had gone to bed; others were dead drunk; they had been celebrating a little feast of their own. This also was Tebaldo Francesco's work: he had sent a few casks of heavy wine to the citadel, "so that all the soldiers should be able to enjoy the feast."

Piers, with his fifty men and a hundred given to him by de Amicis, had made straight for the castle, where the other fifty men from Aquino would be waiting his arrival before taking action. He had insisted on being given that task. His lady, her mother, and sister were living at the castle, and the inevitable fighting could easily endanger them. He knew, of course, that Landulph and Rainald would do their best to protect them. But he could not bear the idea of not being present himself.

All the windows were lit. There would be sentinels and a guard. Brandenstein was sure to be at the castle, and where he was, there was discipline.

Piers sent six men to overcome the sentinels; it was not likely that they would give an alarm at the approach of six men, as they were sure to do if they saw a hundred and fifty. He gave the six exactly a minute and then raised his mailed hand and rode forward. He arrived just in time to save his six men from the onslaught of a dozen or so of Brandenstein's varlets who had come to the help of the sentinels. Fortunately the gate was still open.

"At last a man gets something to *do*", muttered Robin Cherrywoode as he clubbed a German over the head.

"Ten men to stay here at the gate and another ten with the horses", commanded Piers. "You are responsible for it that nobody leaves the castle."

A red glow, about a mile away, showed that fire had broken out in the citadel. That was certainly not as planned. Perhaps de Amicis had found more resistance than he had expected. But behind de Amicis came the townsmen by the thousand; he could not be in any real danger, and even if he was, there was nothing Piers could do about it. He had to concentrate on his own objective.

The skirmish at the gate could not have remained unobserved, of course. And it was not. A number of officials and servants came running with torches and broke into a howl of terror as they saw what was happening. And behind them the gleam of armor became visible: the guards. The German guards.

"Leave the unarmed men alone.... Attack the guards", shouted Piers.

Then the Germans arrived, about fifty of them, and the game started in earnest. The terrible sweep of the attackers threw the guards back a few paces, but then they stood their ground, and iron clashed with iron; the high-arched corridors of the castle echoed the deadly sound. In the thick of the fighting Piers was aware, strangely, of the music still playing in the main hall. "Flutes", he thought. "Flutes."

In the main hall Count Brandenstein raised his head and sniffed like an animal, the gleam of sudden suspicion in his watery blue eyes. As the representative of the Emperor, he had presided over the banquet for no less than five hours, and he had drunk a very great deal, but without much visible effect, except that his ruddy complexion had become ruddier still. He had been in the Emperor's service twenty-five years and had fought on twice as many occasions. Fighting was in his blood, and he could sense it as the hound senses its quarry. Moving his heavy head from side to side, he peered sharply at the faces of his guests. The Count of San Severino was sitting bolt upright, caressing his black beard. Landulph of Aquino was staring straight ahead, and his brother was smiling a little. But the mayor of Parma, Tebaldo Francesco, was pale and sweating profusely.

A long-drawn scream came from somewhere far away and then a noise as if a number of kitchen boys were throwing iron pots and pans about.

"No", said Brandenstein incredulously. He still did not

get up, but his huge, hulking body had become taut. He began to speak, in a low, rumbling voice. "And what have we here? Treason? By God . . . so that's why the women went to bed so early."

"The ladies", said San Severino, "went early because your jokes were not exactly in the finest taste, Count Brandenstein."

The German laughed. "How many of you are in this, I wonder", he said. "You, of course, Mayor . . . I can see it all over your damned yellow face. My Emperor will give you your own entrails to eat as soon as he's got hold of you, and he will, Francesco, he will. Who else? The noble lords of Aquino, perhaps? And you, my lord of San Severino? Both of you? The hawk and the buzzard against the eagle, eh? Well, the eagle will show you."

The din became louder and louder. In vain Rainald tried to make the musicians play again. They were in the grip of fear. Most heads were now turned toward the main door of the banquet hall, the direction from which the noise was coming.

Brandenstein jumped to his feet so that plates and goblets danced on the oblong table. "Get your swords ready", he shouted in German. "Treason! Get your swords. Woelffingen, Rauterbach, Burckheim, Traunstein—up with you and form a block. Stand together, men. Up, I say."

But not all the Germans in the hall obeyed, for many were very drunk by now and others did not know whether their leader was serious or not.

But then the main door crashed open, and in spouted the men from Aquino, with Piers at their head. At once San Severino, Landulph, and Rainald drew their swords and jumped up, pushing their chairs between them and Brandenstein.

The German drew his sword, too, and swung it round his head in a glittering circle.

"So that's how it is", he shouted. "You know, I suspected it long ago, right at the beginning. But when this marriage was celebrated after all, I thought I had been mistaken. You foxed me neatly there."

Piers had heard him. He disengaged from the German he was fighting, leaving him to the loving care of Robin and a grizzled soldier from Rocca Secca, and stared at Brandenstein. Marriage? Had he said marriage?

Brandenstein turned to Francesco. "Perhaps the priest who read the nuptial mass wasn't a priest at all, eh?"

"Indeed he was", screamed the mayor. "We are not given to blasphemy like you and your infernal master."

"I'll pay you for this", said the German and picked up a heavy pitcher of wine to throw at the mayor, who ducked instinctively. The pitcher crashed against a pillar, bounced back, and hit San Severino's shoulder so hard that the sword dropped from his hand.

"One is as good as the other", jeered Brandenstein. "A joke in the finest taste, San Severino. Where's the bridegroom? I want to give him the wedding night he deserves. But I suppose he prefers to stay with the bride and do his little bit of fighting there."

"You are wrong, dog", shouted Ruggiero, appearing as from nowhere. "Take this as my answer."

"Keep off that wild boar, son", exclaimed San Severino with horror. But already the blades clashed. Only once . . . and Ruggiero's light sword flew across the room and landed point downward on the wooden floor where it stuck, trembling violently.

"Good night, bridegroom", laughed Brandenstein. Down came the heavy sword—but not on the young man's head. A triangular shield took the blow, and between Ruggiero and the German stood a man in full armor and helmet. His visor was up; in a young face, the color of parchment, the blue eyes shone unnaturally bright.

"Don't fight children", said Piers. "Fight a man."

Brandenstein scowled at him. "*Your* courage, of course, is admirable . . . you're armored from head to foot. Iron against velvet. Never mind—I'll teach you to interfere with me."

"Catch", said Piers and threw his shield lightly at the German, who caught it instinctively. Calmly Piers unfastened his helmet and let it drop to the floor. "Satisfied now?" he asked unsmilingly.

The German seized the shield firmly. There was a glint of respect in his eye, but then he sneered. "You would have done better to keep this and your helmet, too, though that wouldn't save you either." And he lunged out wildly. Piers parried, parried again and again. His sword was lighter than the German's, but the strength behind it soon convinced Brandenstein that he would have to make use of all the skill he possessed to finish off his opponent. He did not relish the idea. It was foolish to have involved himself in this bit of brawling when he ought to have tried to hack his way out of this confounded trap with as many of his men as possible. He threw a quick glance over his shoulder at the fighting in the hall, and only Piers' shield saved him when its former owner rushed to his first attack.

"Not bad", muttered Robin Cherrywoode; he knocked down a yelling German with his twohander. "Can't you let a fellow enjoy a fight, you ass? Keep off, you . . . give way . . . that's better." He gave an appreciative nod when Piers parried three wild lunges in quick succession. But Brandenstein's sword had grazed Piers' forehead; blood was flowing, and Robin began to chew the end of his moustache. His long, horny fingers twitched round the hilt of the twohander.

The German began to breathe heavily. Five hours of banqueting are not the best preparation for a fight with an opponent of one's own class.

Piers wiped the blood off his forehead and attacked, his sword raised high above his head. Brandenstein threw the shield up—but in a split moment Piers' left arm shot up; he threw the sword into his left hand, and down came the left arm.

A hundred and more voices screamed at the same time, in terror, anger, joy, and triumph, drowning the crash of Brandenstein's fall. The blow had almost cut him in half.

Pandemonium broke out. The surviving Germans attacked, howling with rage. Robin hit out like a madman to protect his master. At the head of about thirty Aquino men Rainald and Landulph rushed from one side of the hall just as de Amicis' hundred streamed in through the main door, all armored and fresh. The issue was no longer in doubt. After a few minutes Rainald took Piers by the arm.

"That will do, I think. We can safely leave it to Landulph now. He'll do the cleaning up. He never gets enough of this kind of game. Come with me, Sir Piers."

The banquet hall was a picture of devastation. A few of the Germans surrendered; others fought on stubbornly against impossible odds. It was sheer butchery now.

Silently Piers followed Rainald to the corridor, where they met a cheering mass of townsmen surrounding a messenger from de Amicis, who was shouting at the top of his voice "Message for the Count of San Severino—message for the Count of San Severino . . . "

"He is in there", said Rainald, pointing to the banquet hall. "What's the message?"

"From Captain de Amicis", said the messenger. "The citadel is in our hands."

Rainald nodded. The cheering of the townsmen made inaudible what he said. He took Piers' arm again and drew him to a side door. It led to a terrace. Treetops and the roofs of houses were visible in the dim starlight. From the banquet hall still came the noise of fighting. It sounded thin and remote, the wrangling of pygmies, unimportant, unreal even.

"Sir Piers," said Rainald gently, "you have done wonderfully well. Ask for whatever reward you wish; if it's in my power to give it, it is yours."

"Brandenstein spoke of a marriage", said Piers tonelessly. "I take it, it was the marriage of the Lady Theodora?"

"Yes", said Rainald quietly. "She married young San Severino this morning."

Piers clenched his teeth. "You sacrificed her to this political game?"

"I forgive you for thinking that", said Rainald gravely. "For I know how you feel. It was not a sacrifice. She fell in love with him as soon as they met . . . and he with her. It was like magic."

"She loves him", said Piers. There was no bitterness in his voice, but rather something very much like awe. It was as if Rainald had told him, "She has ascended to heaven."

"Yes", said Rainald. "And her happiness is what we must have first and foremost in our minds . . . you and I."

"He has courage", said Piers dully.

"You are a most honorable man, Sir Piers", said Rainald warmly. "Let me explain the part that must still be incomprehensible to you. The man you met as Messer Giacomo de Barolo was the Count of San Severino, Ruggiero's father. He was as opposed to the marriage as we were. He is one of the heads of the general insurrection against the Emperor. He turned up here at the castle a few days ago, spoke openly of his plans, and made an alliance with us. There was no question of a marriage then. But the two young people fell in love with each other. They now wanted to marry. There was no object in opposing them, and Count Severino himself suggested that the marriage feast should also be the occasion of the beginning of Italy's liberation from the tyrant. You understand that we could not let you know all this . . . our messenger might have been intercepted by one of the Emperor's agents."

"Quite so", said Piers mechanically. "I understand."

The noise from the banquet hall had ceased. It was almost unbearably quiet.

"She loves him. She loves him. They had only just met, but she loves him. Ah, yes. When I had set eyes on her first, I loved her. She loves him. He was very near death when he engaged Brandenstein. And at the back of my mind when I interfered was: if this is young San Severino it is I who will kill him . . . though I hesitated for one short moment whether I should let the German do it. But she loves him. Her happiness is what must be first and foremost in our minds. If I had let Brandenstein kill him . . . if I should go now and kill him . . . but by now he has returned . . . to her . . . "

He took a deep breath. "My lord . . . you mentioned a reward for my services."

"Yes", said Rainald. He had waited patiently. The last stanza was coming.

"Then I ask to be released from my allegiance to the house of Aquino", said Piers, "and to be allowed to leave . . . tonight."

"I was afraid of that", said Rainald. "I shall miss you . . . and not only I. But it is granted. I am the younger son of the house, as you know, but I shall set it right with the Countess. We shall never forget you—*none* of us will. Just one question . . . though I have no right to ask it: What are you going to do? Are you going back to England?"

There was a moment of hesitation. "No, my lord . . . I . . . I don't think I could stand the peace and tranquillity at home. King Louis of France is taking the Cross. Perhaps he has use of a blade more."

Rainald nodded. "If we must lose you—he's the best man to lose you to."

Their hands met.

"God bless you, my lord", said Piers hoarsely. Then he turned away and strode off.

Rainald remained where he was, gazing at the pale light of the stars.

"And that is the end of the poem", he thought.

Chapter X

THE CELL IN COLOGNE was very much like the cell in Paris: small, quadrangular, chalk white; a table; a chair; a locker. A few books, a picture of St. Dominic, another of Our Lady. The crucifix in the middle, the first thing to see when one looked up.

In the cell the young monk was writing; his huge body in the black and white habit seemed to fill the room, seemed to press against the walls—it was as if at any moment now they would have to recede, to give way to the pulsating, throbbing life whose chrysalis they were.

Friar Thomas of the Order of Preachers was writing a treatise on *The Divine Names* of Dionysius the Areopagite. He had changed a good deal since the days of Rocca Secca. Despite his youth, the hair had begun to recede at his temples, and thus the narrow circlet left to him after the fortnightly clipping and shaving was interrupted on both sides of the forehead, except for a forelock in the middle, the "St. Peter's forelock", as they called it in Cologne, from the many statues and pictures of St. Peter showing the saint with a similar adornment.

There was no doubt that Friar Thomas had put on weight. Part of that was due to heredity . . . his father had been a very heavy man . . . and another part to lack of physical exercise and to the coarse, starchy food of the refectory, served only once a day—at midday—in the fasting period of the Dominican Order, from the middle of September to the end of Lent. Many of the friars simply had to overeat a little, to keep the body going for the next twenty-four hours. Thus Friar Thomas had at least the beginning of a double chin and the very definite beginning of a paunch. Strangely enough, it suited him. It might have been different had he been a smaller man. But as it was it gave to his towering height a softening note, almost a humorous one. Without it there might have been something terrifying about this enormous body and its heavy head with the strong, black eyebrows, the round, owl-like eyes, and the strong, aquiline nose. There might have been something aggressive and intimidating. Instead, however, there was an impression of rubicund jollity when he was talking to others or of something very much like somnolent placidity when he was not. And there was something true in each impression, and it was just that which made his appearance so misleading. For it was not the whole of the truth. It had tempted novices to make him the butt of their jokes more than once, first in Paris, then in Cologne . . . novices are novices everywhere. They had dubbed him the dumb ox of Sicily . . . until the experience of the students of Naples repeated itself. They played pranks on him and his unshakable calm and ready trust. Only once did he hit back. They had shouted up to his window, from the courtyard: "Brother Thomas! Brother Thomas! Come quick and look . . . a flying ox!" Obediently, he came to the window, to be greeted with loud laughter. "He believed it . . . he believed it . . . " "Simpleton, simpleton . . . " Said Thomas, totally unperturbed: "I'd rather believe that an ox can fly than that a Dominican could lie." And the laughter broke off. It hit them much harder than Thomas ever knew, just because it came from such an unexpected quarter. But a proverbially peaceful man is dangerous when forced to fight, and it may be less risky to tease a wild elephant than to tease a cherub once too often.

But all that was long past now. The novitiate had ended. He had taken the vows. And he had been ordained a priest. Never to the end of his life would he forget the night before his ordination. People did not know what it meant to become a priest. Even the Queen of Heaven, even the Mother of God, had conceived Christ and borne Christ only once . . . whereas the priest, uttering the divine formula, called him to himself every day of his life. Perhaps it was that which had filled St. Francis with such horror at the very potentialities of pride that he steadfastly refused to be ordained and remained a simple religious all his life. The power to call down God from high heaven—to admit others into the Mystical Body of Christ—to remit or retain their sins . . . what was mere man that such power should descend on him?

He had rehearsed the sacred words of the Mass again and again . . . and each time he came to the words "This is my Body", he burst into tears under their impact.

Yet when the day came and the appointed hour, all had been different. There were no tears. But he would never talk about "how it was" to anybody. Not even to Reginald of Piperno, his closest friend among the friars, a gentle, affectionate soul on whose loyalty he could rely. Perhaps it was what Reginald of Piperno called "the chastity of his soul". Perhaps he was not allowed to talk. There had been a new expression on his face ever since, a new and different warmth, almost maternal. And as if his own Mass was too personal an event, as if this close contact with Christ demanded that he should step back into the crowd of humble listeners, he invariably heard the Mass of another priest after his own.

The treatise about the Divine Names was his first . . . and he wrote it on the order of his direct superior, Master Albert. "Would it be true", asked Dionysius, "to say that we do know him but not according to his nature?"

What is God? He had asked that as a boy, five years old. What is God? For a short moment the venerable face of the Abbot of Monte Cassino loomed up from the past, a bandage circling his white hair. What is God?

"The solution", wrote Friar Thomas, "is that we know God, but not by his nature, seeing as it were his very essence, for that essence is unknown to creatures and surpasses not only sense knowledge but every human intellect and the mind of every angel operating with natural power and vigor and cannot be known to anyone otherwise than by the gift of some grace."

He stopped. As from afar he heard his own voice saying, *"Hoc est enim—corpus—meum—"* and felt the wild and sweet upsurge of his heart as his knees gave way under him and he adored, and at once he tore himself away from such feasting in the hour of work. The quill began to race over the paper, the beautiful paper from the new factory at Hérault in France. "We do not, therefore, know God by seeing his essence but from the pattern of the whole universe. The entirety of creatures is set before us by God, that thereby we may know him; for the ordered universe has some likeness and faint resemblance to the divine nature, which is its pattern and archetype."

In the cell next to that of Thomas, Reginald of Piperno stood before Master Albert, as usual not without a certain amount of fear. He could never quite rid himself of that, however much he tried to persuade himself that it was entirely illogical and unnecessary. True, the Master could be extremely severe, when one had not kept the rule, for instance, but he was just and even kind when one stayed on the right side of the fence.

The frightening thing about him was the intellect behind that enormous dome of a forehead. It was uncanny for one man to know so much about so many things. He was in his fifties—could not be more than fifty-five at the utmost. Yet he had written scientific books about mineralogy, botany, zoology, physics, alchemy, astrology, and astronomy. He had given lectures about many of these subjects to the friars, and some of them at least were rather terrifying. That there were at least five different kinds of eagles, four kinds of swallows, five of wild geese, and sixteen of falcons; that the sounding of bells had a definite effect on fish; and that certain she-dogs gave systematic training in wolf hunting to their young; and a thousand and one other such things one could marvel at and understand.

But when he began to explain that the earth was bound to be a round ball in shape and that such a horrible thing could be proved from its own shadow, visible at the time of eclipses of the moon and deduced also from an influence of the earth called *gravitatio* "because all parts of the earth were drawn toward its center"—that was indeed terrifying.

The worst came the other day, when the Master stated categorically that the beautiful and mysterious white curtain half across the night sky was not a cloud but a mass of stars so enormous and yet so far away that they seemed to be a cloud. No, not even that was the worst. Coming back in one mad rush from that milky cloud to the earth, he had frightened the wits out of some of the friars by telling them in all seriousness that the southern part of the ball that was the earth was very likely also inhabited by men. How could they live there without falling off? And if they could because in some magic way they were accustomed to it, how would the friars fare when they went down there to preach Christ? For that they would have to do sooner or later. However, perhaps it was no worse an end than to die from a Saracen arrow.

No wonder, though, that the simple people, not only in Cologne but everywhere all over Germany, had come to regard Master Albert as an adept in the magic art, as a wizard. He was not a wizard, of course. He was a very great and very holy man and the finest teacher any friar could hope to find. But . . . but it was terrifying all the same.

Friar Reginald had no idea why he had been called to see Master Albert, but at least he knew that there was nothing on his conscience except an uncharitable thought against Friar Paul when Friar Paul had made the remark that Friar Thomas was so absentminded that one day he would eat his own thumb for dinner without being aware of it until next time he crossed himself. And wizard or not, Master Albert could not know of his uncharitable thought. It was not a very bad uncharitable thought anyway: he simply did not like it when they talked like that about Friar Thomas; *he* wouldn't defend himself, of course, he'd just not listen; but someone had to stand up for him sometimes and not only in thought.

"Friar Reginald," said the metallic voice to whom they listened spellbound in the lecture rooms, and he came back from his thoughts with a rush, "you are, I believe, on specially friendly terms with Friar Thomas of Aquino."

So that was it . . . personal friendships were frowned at in the Order . . . in all religious Orders, not only because in some cases they might lead to inordinate affections and temptations, if only in the world of thoughts, but mainly because human affections could easily deflect a man from the love of God and thus lead to lessening of the spiritual level.

"You seek his company when it is possible, and you are of assistance to him where you can be."

"Yes, my Father", said Friar Reginald sadly. How was Thomas going to get on with no one looking after him? He *was* a little absentminded, Friar Paul was not wrong there; it was only the way he had said it.

"You know we do not encourage anything in the way of personal friendships, Friar Reginald."

"No, my Father. Yes, my Father."

"But in this case I want you to look after him to the best of your ability. There is no question of alleviating the rule, you understand: but keep unnecessary obstacles out of his way and see to it that he gets what he needs for his work and . . . look after him. We need him."

"I will, my Father", stammered Friar Reginald. "Most certainly, I will."

"That is all, Friar Reginald", said Albert with a friendly nod. He watched the friar's beaming withdrawal. Here was a born secretary, and that was exactly what Thomas needed. And it could not have been done officially.

Thomas . . . He chuckled a little when he thought of the time, not so very long ago, when some of the novices loved to tease him, young asses, because they thought he was stupid. The dumb ox of Sicily. Until one day one had to put them right.

Albert chuckled again. From the pulpit of the lecture room he had thundered at them: "You call him the dumb ox—but I tell you his bellowing will be heard one day to the ends of the world." He had said that in sincere anger—to put an end to that tomfoolery. He did not know, then, that Thomas did not need protection at all; that he defended himself better than anybody could defend him . . . when he wanted to, but that he preferred being taken for a fool as a spiritual exercise to combat the ever-present danger of pride. He had not only fooled the novices but Master Albert as well, and there were not many people who could say that of themselves. He did not need protection. But he did need to be looked after.

Master Albert leaned back and looked through the narrow window into the garden, where a few lay brothers were planting seeds. Behind them the wall and behind the wall the joyful bustle of the streets . . . they were feasting today in Cologne, and it was a good occasion, too: this very morning work had started on the choir of the new cathedral, a thing of such beauty . . . it was a pity he would not live to see it finished. At least he had seen the model as well as the plans. The audacity of that building and yet the deep humility of it! Spires reaching up to God's throne so that we might partake in his divinity, as he partook in our humanity . . . and man himself dwarfed by the size of it all. Holy Mass in stone, that's what it was. And buildings of equal beauty were shooting up in all Christian countries now . . . they were building cathedrals in Reims, in Amiens, in Rouen and Basle, in Canterbury and Chichester, in Lincoln, Litchfield, and Salisbury, in Durham, Southwark, York, and London; only three years ago they had started the most glorious abbey at Westminster, smaller but scarcely less beautiful than the gigantic cathedral of Canterbury; and Siena and Santiago de Compostela . . .

"God is drawing us beyond ourselves", he thought. "He is inventing through our minds." He hummed, his voice cracking a little with sudden emotion. "I have loved, O

Lord, the beauty of thy house and the place where dwelleth thy Glory." The psalmists had it in their prophetic poetry; the architects have it in thoughts of stone. And we . . .

There was still another realm left. There also cathedrals could be built. Cathedrals of the intellect.

They have started their choir today. I shall start mine, too. And this is the hour. They are planting seeds in the garden. I shall do likewise. And this is the hour.

He rose and left the cell, a little man with quick, jerky movements, and he entered the adjacent cell, where a young giant tried to raise himself from his chair and was gently pressed back, and there was a long silence.

"That last page", said Albert suddenly. "May I see it?"

Obediently, Thomas handed him the sheet, and the Master read: "Again there is another very lofty manner of knowing God, by negation: we know God by unknowing, by a manner of uniting with God that exceeds the compass of our minds, when the mind recedes from all things and then leaves even itself and is united with the superresplendent rays of the Divinity."

The ink was quite dry. Several minutes, at least, must have elapsed since he wrote that. He was pale, too, and his eyes . . .

"I have come too early", thought Albert. "If this had happened to me, I would be most upset. I might have known how this would affect him." But his voice sounded casual as he said: "Can you detach yourself from your present work, my son, and listen to me with the whole of your intellect?"

"Certainly, my Father." There was a tinge of surprise in Thomas' voice; Albert noted it with intense satisfaction. The return from genuine spiritual experience is always a quick one. But he did not even seem to be upset; he took it all in his stride. The ordinary was God's present as much as the extraordinary.

"Then let me ask you, my son: Which is the most important rational faculty of man?"

"The faculty to discern the truth." The answer came at once.

"There are those who think that man is unable to discern truth."

"They are to be refuted by the fact that they cannot make such a postulate without contradicting their own hypothesis. If man cannot discern truth, then they cannot state as *true* that man is unable to discern the truth."

"Besides, we would never be able to recognize an error as an error," said Albert, "though at times it can be difficult to recognize it. What is it that makes an error so often credible?"

"The amount of truth it contains in proportion to the untruth."

The simplicity of the Master's questions did not deceive Thomas for a moment. He knew that Albert liked to start a serious theme by a series of questions any student of philosophy of six months' standing could answer. It was like oiling an athlete's body before the fight.

It never occurred to him, however, that in this case the Master simply wanted to give him time to recover from the experience he had gone through just before Albert had come in.

"Aye," said Albert, nodding his heavy head, "truth and untruth mixed . . . that is the danger. That is the danger we are confronted with. That is what threatens to overcome the world, smash all our beautiful new cathedrals, and drive the Faith back into the catacombs. Unless . . . we liberate the giant."

"Liberate the giant, my Father?"

"None of those alive in the flesh—" Albert flung back his head—"not even Frederick the Second, however powerful he may appear to those whom he is crushing at this moment. He is roaring up and down Italy like a mad beast, seeking whom he may devour. But he and his little wars will be forgotten soon enough . . . except by those whose kith and kin have lost their lives through his cruelty. I hope this does not concern you, my son? Your family is still in Italy, as far as I know."

"My two brothers may be in danger", said Thomas. "But at least they are fighting on the right side. I have been praying for that ever since I left Rocca Secca." There was a slight tremor in his voice.

"You have had news, then?"

"The last I had was several months ago."

"Your family was strongly opposed to your entry into the Order. Are they still?"

"Yes . . . but not as much as they used to be." An unexpected smile lit up the huge face. "I think they are getting accustomed to it."

"Good, good, good . . . " Albert's thoughts were already racing back. "I did not mean Frederick, the soon forgotten. I did not mean Louis of France either, though *he* will not be forgotten. My giant is not flesh and blood, though he was that, once. And those who lured him out of limbo are not flesh and blood either, though once they were, too."

Thomas waited, patiently.

"I'll tell you a fairy story, my son", said Albert, grimly. "Once upon a time there was a camel driver far out in the lands of the East who believed that God was talking to him through the mouth of the Archangel Gabriel. And such was the zeal of this man and that of his disciples that they convinced first hundreds, then thousands that the camel driver was the greatest prophet God has ever sent to earth and that it was their duty to spread the new religion all over the earth, not by persuasion and charity but by fire and sword. And the new religion spread all over Arabia and Egypt and Turkey and the entire coast of North Africa and from there into Spain and France, where at last, by the help of God, it was stopped and defeated and driven back by Christian knights and soldiers. But still today the green banner of the prophet Mohammed is raised over large parts of Spain, as it is at the very doors of the city of the great Constantine. The emblem of the new religion is the crescent

. . . and, shaped like an immense crescent, the Mohammedan lands are encircling Christendom, ready to strike at any moment. And some time ago, a new danger arose."

"Now", thought Thomas. He knew the story of Islam, of course. And he sensed at least some of what was coming. But he knew also that the Master was not telling him this "fairy story" without a good reason.

"The crude faith of Moors and Saracens", went on Albert, "could never be a spiritual danger for Christendom. But then came the new danger. First Al Kindi in the ninth, then Al-Farabi in the tenth, and Avicenna in the eleventh century of Our Lord began to invoke the shadow of a giant who had died three centuries before Our Lord walked on earth. There was, at the time, no idea of claiming Aristotle as a forerunner of Islam. Al Kindi, Al-Farabi, and Avicenna wanted to *know.* Nevertheless, under their magic touch, the giant began to change, to be transformed. They filled his shadowy limbs with the air of the East; the mystics of the Orient began to creep in like a subtle perfume, and strange concepts of Neo-Platonic as well as Pre-Platonic origin darkened the brilliancy of his mind. More and more he began to look like an oriental. He might have been born in Baghdad, in Khorasan or Marrakesh. Then, just about a hundred years ago, Averroes made his appearance."

Thomas listened quietly, leaning forward, his elbows on his knees; all that Albert had said so far he had known, and Albert knew that he had known it. It was really like listening to a fairy story, heard before, not once, but many times.

"With Averroes," said Albert, "the birth of Mohammedan philosophy was completed. It was not an original philosophy. It was, to put it bluntly, a garbled and orientalized Aristotelian philosophy. But . . . "

The Master's wrinkled face became grave.

" . . . but it was a philosophy. And it contained enough Aristotelian truth to carry oriental errors right into the heart and intellect of Christendom. At last, at long last,

Islam had a weapon against the Christian Faith, a weapon of such sharpness that it drove our own philosophers to the terrible admission that there must be two truths . . . that of revealed faith and that of philosophy. And in the souls of intelligent Christians doubts are being raised for which theology has only the one answer: 'Leave philosophy alone and stick to faith.' In other words: the Trojan horse is within our walls, and its name is the philosophy of Islam. What the vast armies of the camel driver could not do may be accomplished from within by this Trojan horse, by the spirit of the giant Aristotle, led by the spirit of Averroes. They say Frederick the Second is aping oriental customs in many ways, swearing by Mohammed and the Caaba, and making all things oriental a fashion. It is a sorry sight. But it isn't a tenth as dangerous as oriental doctrine fogging our best ecclesiastical brains. And why is it that they are captivated by this thing? Because behind Averroist error is Aristotelian truth. Truth and untruth mixed . . . that is the danger. Unless . . . we liberate the giant."

"We . . . " said Thomas incredulously. "We . . . ?"

"You and I. I have cast about; I have been casting about for years to find the man who can do it. My own life is dedicated to it. But one life is not enough. No single man can free Aristotle from his chains. The task is immense. It isn't simply a translation of Aristotle into Latin."

"It couldn't be", said Thomas breathlessly. "For even Aristotle was not always right."

"Son," shouted Albert jubilantly, "that sentence alone proves that you are the man to do it." In his elation he jumped up and began to pace up and down the tiny room. "Aristotle was not always right", he repeated. "Do you know that there is probably no man alive who'd dare to say that in public? Of those who have read Aristotle, I mean. For the others, and especially a few theologians I could name, are firmly convinced that the whole of Aristotle is the work of Satan himself. Can you imagine that? Good men crossing themselves when the very name of the

Stagirite is mentioned. But you, son . . . oh, I love you for it . . . you have read him, and neither do you shrink from him, nor do you bow to him without reservations."

He stopped abruptly. "Here is where we enter the fairy story, son . . . you and I, with our plan to unchain the giant and bring him back to his senses."

"The great Jews will be of help", said Thomas eagerly. "And especially Rabbi Moses ben Maimon. His *Guide of the Perplexed* . . . "

"You have read that?" asked Albert, surprised.

"Oh, back in Naples", admitted Thomas. "They had a good copy at the university. Rabbi Moses was a great man, and a good one."

"And he also does not regard Aristotle as infallible. Son, son, do you realize where this leads?"

Thomas nodded. "The Christian will be able to say: 'By the Grace of God I believe; I have faith. There is much in my faith that surpasses reason but nothing that contradicts it.' "

"Exactly", shouted Albert. "Exactly." He controlled his enthusiasm. His voice became quiet, but there was a harsh tinge to it as he said: "I warn you of one thing, Thomas: our own people are going to make things difficult for you. The most intelligent Franciscan I ever met, Friar Roger Bacon . . . not the best, mind you, but the most intelligent . . . laughed at me when I told him my idea. He said it was impossible. It couldn't be done."

"We shall find out", said Thomas.

"But the worst opposition will not come from him. It will come from the narrow-minded, the chicken-hearted, the sterile . . . and some of them are very powerful. They are going to besiege you like the bulls of Bashan. And they will speak with formidable authority. They'll quote the great saints against you, aye, and even the Fathers of the Church themselves. They'll crush you with St. Gregory, with St. Bernard, with the greatest of all, St. Augustine . . . "

"It doesn't matter who said it", interposed Thomas. "What matters is what he said."

Albert stared hard at him.

"By the love of God," he said, hoarsely, "I believe you mean it."

Thomas stared back, in blank surprise.

"I could not say so, surely, unless I meant it."

The little man, before whom they all trembled, said in a muffled voice: "Tell me, son . . . have you ever been intimidated by anyone?"

"Oh, yes", said Thomas.

"I don't believe it. By whom?"

"By Our Lord . . . on the altar."

Chapter XI

THE NEWS of the defection of Parma reached Frederick the Second halfway between Verona and Turin. To a man of his genius it was clear that the Parmese would not dare a thing like that unless they knew, and knew for certain, that they would find strong support. From Mantua most likely, and from Ferrara, but it might well be worse than that. Unless this was stopped at once, rebellion would flare up in a dozen, in a hundred, other towns.

His astrologer, Bonatti, had told him more than once that his true greatness would show itself in times of adversity, because he was born with the sun in Capricorn and the rising sign in Scorpio. He was living up to that prophecy now.

In his first terrible anger over the result of the Council

of Lyons he had accepted and even welcomed the role of Antichrist. He had even gone so far as to demand of his court that he be addressed as "Holy Lucifer", and he had given orders to strip all churches, monasteries, and convents of their riches. "Riches" meant everything that was made of gold, silver, or precious stones. He saw the entire issue as a gigantic duel between himself and the Pope, and his first idea had been to march against Lyons and capture his archenemy. He saw himself as the "Prince of the World" of the Gospels, as the "Beast" of the Apocalypse, and he gloried in the idea.

The defection of Parma brought him to his senses. He came down from his metaphysical heights and showed himself once more as the shrewdest, the most cunning, and by far the most energetic and resourceful ruler of his age. He made the army turn about and marched not to Parma but to Cremona, where he was joined by Eccelino of Romano with over six hundred Burgundian knights and their retinues. He drew all garrisons together to prevent them from being attacked and overcome one by one. Then he let his cavalry loose—in strong detachments—to race across the peninsula and prevent uprisings. He himself appeared before the walls of Parma only two days after the meeting with Eccelino at Cremona and thus began one of the strangest sieges in the history of mankind. The art of siege, so highly developed under imperial Rome, had degenerated. High walls and stout defenders on them were an almost insuperable obstacle to armored knights. To conquer a heavily walled and well-defended town, one had either to cut its water supply or to starve it out. Parma's water supply was plentiful. Starvation, then, was the only possibility. Frederick's cavalry cut all the communications. A strong detachment under Margrave Lancia succeeded in conquering the north end of the Appenine pass. But it was clear that it would take many months before Parma could be forced to surrender.

Within a few weeks Frederick knew that Mantua and

Ferrara were supporting Parma. He had every Mantuan his men could get hold of hung . . . three hundred in one week. When the news came that Reggio, deep in the south, had revolted, too, he was beside himself with rage. In an outburst lasting more than three hours, he told his stunned court that he was going to crush all resistance and then leave Italy and the Occident to erect his rule in the Orient instead. There alone they were worthy of a real ruler. "*Felix Asia,*" he exclaimed, "you alone know how to obey."

His troops burned down half of Reggio and executed a hundred of its most respected inhabitants. To deter further rebellion, they were first blinded.

The news of insurrections multiplied quickly. In ten, twenty, fifty, in hundreds of towns the lily banner of the old Guelf party had been raised.

He had six towns burned down, and another twenty revolted. He sent troops against Arezzo and razed it to the ground. He had Bishop Marcellin of Arezzo hanged. As an answer to such sacrilege Florence now rose against him, too. And still Frederick remained undiscouraged. Over the Alps came a steady trickle of German knights, each one a little fortress by himself, to reinforce the imperial armies in the field. The very soil of Italy groaned under the hooves of their armored horses.

The religious character of the insurrection became clearer and clearer. In many towns mendicant monks and friars preached holy war against the deposed Emperor, the atheist ruler of a Christian country, the freethinker who believed in his own divinity, who scorned the priesthood and called himself a priest, who was a scourge of God but proclaimed himself to be the new Messiah, who talked incessantly of freedom and was yet a tyrant the like the world had never seen since the days of ancient imperial Rome.

But Frederick's captain, Marinus of Eboli, defeated the defenders of Viterbo, and the fortress of Sala had to surrender to another imperial leader.

Frederick himself remained with the army besieging

Parma. Parma had been the first to revolt, and he himself was going to punish it.

Regardless of the tempest raging all over Italy, he stayed where he was. Important prisoners were taken to his headquarters, where he presided at their trial, after which they were handed over to the "sons of Vulcan", his Saracen executioners to whom cruelty was a pastime. But the Emperor himself dictated the punishment. Most were mutilated, blinded, or at least whipped before they were led to death. Many he had drowned in the river Po, conveniently near for such purpose, and some of those who had incurred his wrath more than others he had sewn into a sack together with a poisonous snake; the sack with its content . . . living, dying, or dead . . . was then thrown into the river. It was the punishment that oriental potentates sometimes inflicted on unfaithful wives of their harem.

Yet he was bored with his inactivity, until the idea occurred to him that it was unworthy of a great ruler to spend so much time in a mere tent camp and that it might be just as well to build a new town, as Parma would have to be razed to the ground in a few months' time. At once he gave orders for thousands of workmen to be brought to the camp; architects had to devise their plans, and almost overnight the foundation of a new town was laid, to which he gave the name of "Victoria".

In the very sight of the Parmese the houses, municipal buildings, and palaces of the new town arose as from nothing, until they disappeared again behind new fortifications. There were the palace of the Emperor, a dainty pavilion for the Saracen dancing girls and their eunuchs, a magnificent building for the imperial treasury, huge sheds for the stacking of weapons and war equipment of other kinds.

There was no church. The only bell of the town, an enormous one, was hung in a small watchtower. It was an alarm bell, to be rung whenever the Parmesans made a sortie, as they frequently did to get hold of foodstuff somewhere in the vicinity. For by now, after a siege of almost a year, food was very scarce in the besieged town.

Frederick had given strict orders that every sortie must be repulsed at once, and if the detachment of Parmese managed to break through, they must be pursued and driven back into the town. "The more mouths they have to fill in there, the earlier their food will give out."

Time and again food transports arrived from other towns, and time and again Frederick intercepted them and paraded the wagons and carts in front of the starving defenders on the walls before storing them up in his own sheds in Victoria.

By now he had ceased to be interested in the building of Victoria, which was still progressing but did not need his ordering hand any longer; he spent most of his time hawking in the marshes of the vicinity, where wild birds abounded, and in writing his book *De arte venandi cum avibus.*

* * *

In Parma all was quiet. Only a very keen observer would be aware of the breath of tension in the almost empty streets and piazzas; the glittering of an eye here . . . the enforced calm of a voice there; the reflection of the moonlight on bundles of lances leaning against a chalked wall . . . a few dark figures silently crossing the street to disappear in a large building.

The clatter of hooves broke the uncanny silence as a small troop of horsemen rode up to the citadel, led by a knight in full armor. The sentinel challenged them, and the knight answered angrily: "Fool, let us through. D'ye think that six men want to storm this fortress?" But not until the leader of the watch appeared and recognized the knight could the little troop proceed.

Five minutes later Rainald stood before Landulph.

"Thank God that you're safely back, Rainald. I've been worried, more than I can say. How did you get through?"

Rainald laughed. "Give me wine, and I'll tell you. My throat is parched."

"Here is wine. Half a goblet is all I can give you. Things are not what they used to be in Parma. The first cases of death from starvation were reported last week, and it's been going on steadily ever since. I'm glad you're back . . . though I shouldn't be, really. Would have been better, perhaps, if you'd stayed away from this damned town. You know . . . if I ever get out of here alive, which is possible though not exactly probable, I shall never set foot in Parma again. I know every nook and cranny in the blasted place, and lately it's developed a particular sort of stink which I dislike intensely. Mother and the girls safe?"

"Safe enough. It wasn't easy to get them back to Rocca Secca, though. This is the strangest war I ever fought in. You never know whether the next town is going to receive you with garlands and a merry feast or whether they are going to hang you or cut off your hands or feet or something else you don't exactly wish to be without. Just as well we insisted on getting Mother and the girls out before the old demon closed his iron ring around Parma. Even so we had to fight four times on our way to Rocca Secca, and seven of our fifty men are now at their final destination, whatever that may be."

"Paradise", said Landulph simply.

"What makes you so sure of that?" asked Rainald, surprised.

"No doubt about it whatever. They died fighting for the right cause. No man can do more."

Rainald laughed. "Maybe you're right, brother mine. At least three of them were thorough rascals, though."

"Die for right, die for God", said Landulph.

And he went on: "How did young Ruggiero behave?"

"He wasn't bad", acknowledged Rainald. "Not bad at all. He had never fought in earnest, and it upset him a good deal when he ran a man through. It was a bit of a fluke, but he ran him through all right. Made the boy sob. Had to comfort him for the better part of an hour afterward, telling him that he had done what every Christian knight would do and that it was in the protection of his young wife and so on and so forth. That made him feel better. He's a tender youth."

"Too tender", said Landulph.

"He may change . . . if he gets the chance. I rather like him. Had a good deal of trouble to make him stay with the women at Rocca Secca. 'What will people say if I don't come back'—you know. Even when I assured him that his father's orders for him were to stay, he didn't want to give in. I had to tell him again the story of protecting the women. He accepted that . . . and I could feel that he was glad that he could accept it. So would I be, if I were in his place, after a few months of marriage."

"I suppose so", said Landulph, but he shook his head. "Well, I'm glad he remains where he is. He's too young for this sort of thing. Mind you, if we don't succeed here, Rocca Secca won't be safe much longer. Even as it is . . . old Lucifer is everywhere. Give the devil his due; he knows something about the art of war. How did you get through?"

"That's a long story, and yet there's not much to it. I have bad news for Parma, though."

"Have you now." Landulph did not seem much impressed. "What is it?"

"You sent the mayor to Altavilla . . . Tebaldo Francesco, didn't you? To get reinforcements."

"No. Foodstuff."

"You won't see him again. Not in this life."

"What happened? Has he turned traitor?"

"Not he. I suppose you and San Severino let him go because he had relatives in Altavilla, important people who had to be won over."

"His brother's living there, and he was supposed to meet other leaders of the Guelf party. But the main thing was to arrange for a food transport under strong escort. The last four transports didn't get through."

"There won't be any food transport from Altavilla. Frederick has stormed it. They caught Tebaldo Francesco alive."

"Poor devil."

"Yes. They blinded him, cut off his nose, one hand, and one leg. Now they're dragging him from town to town as a show piece; see what happens when you mutiny against our Emperor."

"And that is the man we served for years", said Landulph. "My God in heaven, I can't understand it. We were blind or mad or something."

Rainald laughed. "All of us . . . except for little Thomas. And now little Thomas is the only one who's safe. Sometimes it looks to me as if there is a queer sort of justice behind all the injustice of man. Is that what they call Providence?"

" 'If you serve a man who does not serve God—how can you serve God yourselves?' " Landulph nodded. "I remember him saying it. I don't remember what you answered or what I answered, though. He had a knack of saying things that stuck in your mind somehow, bless him. I'm glad he's safe. By the way, Rainald . . . you'll have to report to the war council, of course. Keep quiet about that bit of news about Francesco, will you? He's a very popular man—he was—and they mustn't get discouraged . . . not for a day or two anyway. There's something big afoot . . . something that may change our entire situation with one stroke."

"It needs a bit of changing. Frederick's getting the better of us in Italy. What's the plan?"

Landulph grinned broadly. "We have a few reliable men in his camp, and one got a message through to us: Frederick is going hawking again tomorrow morning at sunrise."

"What's so important about that?"

"In his absence Margrave Lancia will be in command."

"Well?"

"Margrave Lancia has strict orders to pursue to the

utmost of his ability every detachment of Parmese that makes a sortie."

"I think I begin to sense something", said Rainald attentively. "There will be a sortie tomorrow, of course."

"Oh, yes, there'll be a sortie. I'm leading it. You've come back just in time to come with me. We'll give Lancia a good chase. He'll get rid of some of his fat."

"And in the meantime," said Rainald, "other things may happen . . . I understand. Whose idea was that?"

"Old San Severino's. There's a man for you. Sometime I wish . . ."

"What?"

"That little Theodora had married him instead of his son."

"Him . . . or Sir Piers."

Landulph raised his eyebrows. "What on earth . . . ?"

"He loved her, brother mine. Yes, yes, I know he's not of the blood. But he ought to be."

"So that's why he left so suddenly . . . I couldn't understand it at the time, nor could Mother. I wonder where he is now."

"Somewhere in the Holy Land, I suppose. Pity. We could do with him here. You're pretty good with the sword, brother mine, but I doubt whether you could have split Brandenstein in two the way he did."

"I doubt it myself", said Landulph. "Now come with me to old San Severino. He'll want to know about his son. And go to bed early. There'll be much work to do tomorrow."

Rainald nodded. "I can do with some sleep."

San Severino received him very cordially and was obviously greatly relieved to know his son safe . . . as safe at least as one could be in Italy at the present time. "You are bound to have seen many things of great interest lately . . . but let's talk about that tomorrow night, not now. I want to keep my old head clear for . . . I suppose your brother has told you? He has? Very well then. I can feel that you have at least some bad news to tell. If we succeed tomorrow, that won't matter. And if we fail, nothing matters. You will want to join your noble brother in his sortie. God and the Holy Virgin protect you. Good night."

There seemed to be more silver in his beautifully kept black beard, and his face was haggard and of the color of wax.

"I don't think he'll live long", said Rainald, when they returned to their quarters. "I wonder why silver always reminds me of death. As a poet I could give you at least seven reasons why this should be so, but none of them is a good one."

"That's probably because you're a bad poet", grinned Landulph.

"No, brother mine. I'm not a bad poet. The trouble with me is that I'm a good one . . . I mean, I had the gift to be a good one and didn't use it. I've spent my life enjoying myself. And to be a good poet one must be something of a hermit, a saint . . . "

"Nonsense."

" . . . one must mortify the flesh, live for an idea. You can't storm the gate of paradise with a full belly. I used to believe that I could build a temple of beauty if only I collected enough marble and precious stones. But the most beautiful form is not that of women but of woman. Perhaps, if I had found the woman I was looking for in so many women . . . you see, I'm shifting the responsibility again. What was it that I was really looking for? Good God, I didn't even know that a poet had a responsibility greater than that of a commander in the field."

"What you need is sleep", said Landulph.

"I know. I'll go. At least the strength *this* sleep will give me won't be wasted. Waste, brother mine, that's a terrible word. I once dreamed of an old man who told me that the souls of all those who have wasted their lives would be melted after death to form a new soul . . . it's nonsense, I daresay, and heretical at that, but I was afraid of it for a long time afterward."

"You make me wish you'd stayed at Rocca Secca", said Landulph gruffly.

"Oh, don't worry. I'm overtired, that's all. I'll be different in the morning. Sometimes I wish I had your nature . . . all of one piece and no doubts. Good night."

"It's more honorable to have doubts and defeat them than never to have doubts", said Landulph. "Good night. And no dreams."

They shook hands, suddenly, and smiled at each other before they turned away, each to his own room.

His varlet helped Rainald to undress. On his writing table he found a plate with a piece of dry bread and a little meat, reddish and stringy. Horse meat. He shrugged his shoulders, stretched out his hand . . . and saw the eyes of the varlet, pleading greedily. He smiled. "Take it away", he said. "I don't want it."

The varlet pounced on it and rushed out of the room as if he feared his master might change his mind if he stayed on a moment longer.

Rainald threw himself on his bed. No dreams. Dear Landulph. He didn't believe in victory any more than San Severino. "It's more honorable to have doubts and defeat them than never to have doubts." Dear Landulph. How wise they can be, those simple souls. He at least had made something out of his life. Marotta, too, and perhaps also Theodora. She and little Adelasia had their lives still before them anyway. But Rainald . . . what would Thomas say to Rainald? Surely that he had hidden his talent in the ground. Or . . . or would he judge like Landulph: "Die for right, die for God . . ."

Strange how they had all been influenced by him somehow . . . even Landulph. He used to have a happy-go-lucky sort of nature, and then, suddenly, he cared so much about fighting on the right side. And now the way he talked, sometimes. And Mother, too.

But Rainald . . . what would you say to Rainald, Thomas?

Little songs to pretty women, genuine enough; perhaps,

if I had found the woman . . . if she exists at all. If she is not just one more chimaera, one more illusion in this valley, not of tears but of illusions, where man chases beauty and happiness and lets his mind color and shape what he finds so that every song seems the music of the spheres to someone, so that every girl is the Madonna for someone.

There were those who had dared to approach the Queen of Heaven herself in their song, like Adam of St. Victor.

Salve, Mater pietatis
Et totius trinitatis
Nobile triclinium
Verbi tamen incarnati
Speciale majestati
Praeparans hospitium

Ah, well—one had to be a saint to think of such a poem, to be infused with words of such majesty. It was a monk who composed it, in the crypt of the Abbey Church of St. Victor, consecrated to the Mother of God. And such was the power of this incantation that the crypt was flooded with light and the Blessed Virgin appeared to him, giving him a gracious nod for his words full of grace. So they said. And it should be believed for the sake of its beauty, if it could not be believed by faith.

And yet: in all its beauty, this was not the song of songs to be dedicated to her who was Virgin and Mother, the new Eve, the sacred symbol of all poetry. Paradise, purgatory, and hell had not found their poet yet, and neither had she, the Star of the Sea, the Gate of Heaven. Greater still, perhaps, was the task to sing her song . . . for the poet would have to climb to such heights that he could transcend even the Archangel's words when he greeted her who would be set above all the angels. To wrestle with an archangel for the palm of poetry . . . that was fulfillment.

It was worthwhile a thousand times over to stay alive for such a purpose. And that one poem would make up for an entire life wasted.

But the sortie was tomorrow.

Where find the words to be joined like pearls of equal form and size to be a necklace for the Queen of Queens? A man would have to loot the heavens themselves. The words are out of reach unless she herself carries them down to earth and blesses me with them, and I'd give her own present back to her, Rainald thought. But is not that just what happens to us in every sacrifice?

Daughter and Mother of the Child most lovable, Star of the Morning, Ivory Tower . . . Virgin who gave birth to the Spring of Charity . . . if I escape, if by your help I escape, I will sing this song.

And if I fall . . . and if the weight of what I have not done, the iron pressure of the deeds omitted, should ban me from your sight, I shall still sing it. And some friendly spirit may carry my words down from the beyond until they find the mind to give them existence on earth.

* * *

The sortie of a strong detachment of cavalry under the command of the brothers Landulph and Rainald of Aquino was made the next morning toward the south.

Margrave Lancia himself went in pursuit of them at the head of five thousand men, including two hundred knights. It took them almost seven hours to catch up with the enemy, and bitter fighting ensued, lasting through the rest of the day. In the end the numerical superiority of the imperial troops began to tell, and just before sunset a fresh attack broke the center of the Parmese.

Landulph and Rainald of Aquino were taken prisoners and with them the majority of the survivors. The rest of the detachment scattered; most of them were killed in a mopping-up operation. Only a few fought their way back to Parma.

* * *

But an hour after Margrave Lancia's departure, all the gates of Parma opened simultaneously, and out streamed the

Parmese; first the knights under the Count of San Severino; then the men on foot, hired mercenaries and the town guard; then followed what amounted to the entire male population of Parma, from boys of twelve to old men of seventy and beyond. And behind them came whole battalions of women, women of all ages.

Like streams of lava they flowed over to Victoria, where the remaining garrison was taken completely by surprise. Margrave Lancia had not made it quite clear who was to command during his absence, and bitter quarreling between the subcommanders wasted precious time. But the huge alarm bell began to toll.

Count San Severino hacked his way through the main gate to the north, and his knights clattered along the streets of the new town, opening other gates from the inside and creating havoc among the defenders on the walls, who did not know which way to turn first. Then the flood of Parmese broke in, and the scene changed from the terrible to the grotesque. Imperial knights went down under the impact of twenty, thirty women, who dragged them from their horses and clubbed them into senselessness. Hundreds and hundreds of imperial soldiers surrendered to the town guard, so as not to be torn to pieces by the yelling, screaming, half-starved, and half-mad women.

Deprived of their first object, vengeance, the women at once concentrated on the next: food. With incredible speed they had the heavy doors of the warehouses open and were swarming over the huge piles of foodstuff, all the provisions of the imperial army, and the transports that had been intercepted. Some of the more intelligent got hold of mules or even horses, to load them with what they themselves could not carry—others just picked up the nearest things they could lay their hands on.

Yet all the time the fighting was still going on in Victoria, though by now it had become much less vigorous. Those who still resisted at this stage were all slain by embittered Parmese soldiers, who knew that most of their comrades were already looting to their hearts' content and resented bitterly that the fighting of these obstinate idiots prevented them from joining in and claiming their share.

It was at that stage that the Emperor returned.

Into the silvery sounds of the hunting bells the deep booming voice of Victoria's alarm bell had broken with desperate warning. He lost a few more precious minutes waiting for his finest Icelander to return to the glove. Then he, his son Manfred, sixteen years old and already married to a daughter of Count Amadeus of Savoy, and the fifty knights and varlets with them galloped back to the town. They had no idea, of course, that Margrave Lancia was away, much less that the town had been taken by the Parmese.

Without armor, in their hunting dress, they swept through the town, gaped at by their own soldiers and the Parmese alike, none of whom could believe his eyes, and themselves feeling that they were riding right through a nightmare. Then a few soldiers shrieked, "It's the Emperor", and after a moment's incredulous hesitation everybody surged forward.

"Out of here", commanded Frederick, "follow me. Stay at my side, Manfred."

It was easier said than done. Missiles were flying from all sides; carts, soldiers, screaming women blocked their way. The knights rode down everything in their mad flight, all the time protecting the Emperor and his son with their bodies. Eight of them fell within the first two or three minutes, then more . . . and the survivors rode on like the devil. They were melting away fast, but their horses were the best in the land, and they cut their way out . . . the Emperor, with the Icelander still perched on his glove, Manfred, and fourteen horsemen, in the direction of Borgo San Dominico.

There was something ghostlike about this interlude, and for a long time afterward the Parmese were not at all certain whether it had really happened. No more than ten minutes had passed from the moment when Frederick appeared until he had vanished again. Most of the looters had never seen him at all. Some had come across the famous Saracen dancing girls and their eunuchs; others had found the cages with the animals. Count San Severino gave orders to load them all on carts and drive them into Parma. In the case of the dancing girls he had to support his order by a few resounding blows with the flat side of his sword. "I don't think I'm preserving the virtue of any of 'em." He laughed in answer to the grin of Captain de Amicis. "But I've given the order to put fire to the town, and we don't want any stragglers. Besides, they'll have less to confess that way, the rascals."

He had sent a detachment of reliable men into the treasury building, where they had found and killed the imperial councillor, Thaddeus of Suessa. Now they came out, laden with bags and caskets of minted gold and silver. The townsmen, coming in after them, still found more than they could carry. "I've never seen anything like it", gasped one of de Amicis' knights, staggering under the weight of half a dozen bags. "All these are full of jewels." Others appeared, dressed in the Emperor's ceremonial robes, one swinging the imperial scepter, another kicking the royal seal of Sicily before him, because he had no hand free. A cripple, a well-known figure in Parmese life, whom they called *"Corto passo"* because of his dwarfed legs, had got hold of the imperial crown, a thing too heavy for any mortal man to wear, and stumbled along with it, a rapturous smile on his ugly face. From a building near the treasury a long line of soldiers carried golden chalices, ciboria, and other precious vessels, all "confiscated" from hundreds of churches. The Count of San Severino had them put into the *carrocio di Cremona,* the Emperor's victory chariot. It took a dozen donkeys to get the overly ornate thing away with its heavy burden.

By now Victoria was burning, and the order was given

to leave the town and to return to Parma. There was not a single man, woman, or child who was not staggering under the weight of loot, with the exception of a few commanders, most of whom had their loot safely tucked away on a cart or a mule. Half an hour later they were streaming back into the gates of their home town, much to the relief of San Severino, whose eyes had searched the horizon right and left. If Margrave Lancia returned whilst they were still outside the walls, the day could have ended in disaster.

As it were, Lancia returned only in the middle of the night . . . a night lit by the flames of Victoria. By now it was quite impossible to extinguish the fire. In the morning Frederick's new town was a smoldering heap of ruins.

Book Three

Chapter XII

THE SANTA MADDALENA had landed in Naples harbor only an hour ago, but the news she had brought spread like wildfire.

She had come straight from Egypt, from Damiette—and she was the first of many ships to follow.

The crusade was lost. It was incredible, but it was true. The crusade was lost, although it had been led by King Louis of France—and the King and all his army had been captured by the Moslems. They had been forced to pay a whole mountain of gold for ransom—and now they returned, or what was left of them.

Half Naples streamed into the taverns in the morning, hoping to find a few of the crusaders there—anybody coming back from the desert was likely to be thirsty. And groups formed around the men in tattered coats with the black cross sewn on.

In the tavern of Saint Januarius everybody listened to a tall, gaunt Frenchman with hollow eyes and yellowish skin. He told them of endless rides and marches, of flies and scorpions and attacks with Greek fire, of swarming tribes of Arabs on horses so fast that they could ride full circle around an armored knight, at the distance of an arrow's flight, before he could turn his horse. And how the best blades of Christendom had to surrender because there was not strength enough left in them to stand up when they were fully armed. Yes, he, too, had been a prisoner of the heathens.

"They often killed those who were too ill to walk—but some of them were decent enough. There was an old Saracen, a fierce-looking man with a long, curved sword, he took a fancy to me. I had a wound across both my knees and couldn't walk, and I very much feared they'd kill me, too. They say it means paradise at once, but my faith was just not good enough, I suppose—I thought there are a few things which may not be washed away just by getting an Arab knife through my gullet. So I was afraid. But the old Saracen, he came and brought me food, and twice a day, believe it or not, he carried me on his back to the place where even the Emperor will go on his own feet . . . "

They roared with laughter.

"The trouble was", said the crusader, "that twice was not enough. We were all suffering from dysentery. Yes, you laugh . . . may it be spared to you to experience what it feels like. You think you're having a baby every half hour. Well, to go on with my story . . . the strangest thing was, the Sultan who had demanded and obtained our surrender was murdered."

"By whom?"

"By some of his own amirs . . . that's the heathen word for Count . . . they had formed a conspiracy against him and smoked him out of his house with Greek fire, and when he fled, they pursued him, and they reached him, where do you think?"

"How do I know? . . . go on, tell us . . . "

"Well, he threw himself into the river and swam for his life, and they caught up with him and killed him in the water, and one amir tore his heart out and then boarded a ship, and it was our ship, a whole transport full of prisoners, and King Louis himself was on board, and so was I."

"Man, you're lying."

The crusader touched the tattered cross on his tunic. "I'm speaking the truth", he said quietly. "I know it sounds incredible, but believe me, you get accustomed to things unbelievable where we come from. The amir went right up to King Louis, his hand still bloody, and said: 'What will you give me for having killed your enemy who would have killed you if he'd lived longer?' And the King did not utter a sound, just looked at him, and the amir turned away. No one can bear it when King Louis looks at him that way. It's like . . . like looking at your own mother when you're still a child and have done something really nasty. You can't stand it."

"They say he is a very saintly man."

"He's more than that. He's a saint, if you ask me. That's what he is, a saint, and if the Pope doesn't canonize him after all he went through, then the Pope doesn't know his business. That's what I say."

"And then?"

"We all thought our last hour had come, now that the Sultan had been killed, and as there was no priest on board our ship, we all confessed to each other, and thus I heard the confession of the Sieur of Montignard—I, a simple man of Soissons and my father a peasant—and I gave him absolution with what power God gives a Christian in the moment of death when no priest is there, and then I knelt down next to him and confessed to him, and he absolved me. It would have been much more fitting had he been able to confess to a man of his own standing, but he was wounded and could not get through to the other part of the ship, where the nobles were with the King, and he said when it comes to this, a peasant is as good as a knight and maybe better. And do you know what was the strangest thing of all? When I got up, I'd forgotten everything he had confessed to me. I didn't remember a single sin of his."

There was a pause of quiet awe.

"They didn't kill us after all, as you see", went on the crusader. "In fact, the amirs stuck to the treaty the King had made with the Sultan they'd murdered. And just to show you: the Sultan had asked for five hundred thousand pounds in gold and the town of Damiette, and King Louis had accepted. When the Sultan heard that, he exclaimed: 'By my faith, this Frankish king is a generous man not to bargain at all about such a large sum. Go and tell him I will be content with four hundred thousand.' And the King made all the rich nobles pay for themselves and paid out of his own pocket for all the simple men."

"I wish I were a Frenchman", sighed a Neapolitan citizen. "Or that the Emperor were a little more like your Louis."

"Or", said another, "that we had a few amirs in Italy who know how to deal with a Sultan . . . "

"Shut up; do you want to have us all in prison?"

"Why, we're all good friends here . . . "

"You never know. They hanged another hundred and fifty in Messina the other day, and they may be working on the lists in Naples right now, friend or no friend."

"Hasn't he hanged enough people? Surely now that the great rebellion is over . . . "

"It isn't all over in his opinion, it seems."

"You've had a rebellion here in Italy?" asked the crusader. "Tell us about it. I've done all the talking so far."

"Friend, we've passed through hell all these months and even years. First it was Parma and half a dozen other towns in the north and then Reggio and Messina and everywhere, and the Emperor's soldiers were sweeping through Italy like birds of prey. Wherever you looked, something was burning. But the worst came when the Parmese had defeated the Emperor and burned down his camp or town or whatever it was and took away all his precious things and thought they had won the war."

"They hadn't, apparently?"

"Oh, God, no. There's something about the Emperor: when things go wrong for him, he somehow grows and grows and is more terrible than ever. He had escaped with his bare life and a handful of men, and yet a week later they say he was stronger than ever. The great princes in the north came to his aid, of course. Eccelino of Romano and his son Enzio and his son Conrad, whom he made King of Rome, and all his other sons, and he has so many you lose count, and they all assembled at Cremona, and he borrowed twelve thousand pounds of Pisan silver at eighty percent interest, and the Greek Emperor sent him money, and the

Germans sent him mercenaries. Piero della Vigna had deserted him when the news of his defeat came, and now he caught him, and della Vigna ran against a wall with such force that he smashed his skull . . . the Emperor's chancellor he had been, and he knew only too well what would happen to him, so he left life good and quick."

"Suicide", said the crusader, horrified.

"Ah, yes . . . but I don't know what's worse, hell or being taken prisoner by the Emperor when you've done what della Vigna did."

"Hell lasts longer", said the crusader, shaking his head.

"Anyway . . . he won back Ravenna, and he defeated five leaders of the Guelf party in succession, and his Margrave Pallavicini routed the Parmese, and there they got hold of the Count of San Severino and killed him in a cruel way, the old one; my wife's sister had seen him often, and a very fine man he was, she says, and a great knight, but there it is; you can't stand up against the Emperor and live."

"And that was the end of it?"

"More or less. The Emperor had regained the March and the Romagna and Cingoli and Spoleto . . . and he was master of Italy again, and he made lists of all those who had been fighting him, and they were dealt with . . . they still are being dealt with. Now I heard only this morning there's troops assembling somewhere near Naples, it's all very secret, but they say it's an attack on the Aquinos or rather what's left of them; they were for the Emperor all the time but then went wrong, too, and two of the sons are supposed to be in the Emperor's prison in Verona, they were caught at Parma or in Parma, I don't know for sure . . . "

"Oh, stop it, Carlo, all these names can't mean anything to our friend here; I'm sure he has never heard of Aquino in his life . . . "

"They're very great names in this country anyway. And I tell you, I *know* the troops are going against Aquino and

Rocca Secca; my sister's husband is with them at that place, although he's not allowed to say where it is, but they'll march tonight or tomorrow, and that's the end of that family, too."

"All right, Carlo, all right . . . but now let our friend here tell us some more about the end of the campaign in Egypt."

"I'll tell you about it", nodded the crusader. "But where have the two Englishmen gone?"

"Who?"

"The two Englishmen who came with us on the *Santa Maddalena*—a knight and his varlet, though you wouldn't know the difference now, with all of us in rags. They came in with us . . . they were sitting over there in that corner, not saying a word. Englishmen are either mad or mute and often enough both. It was the same on board ship. But they're good fighters. Where have they gone? Well, never mind. The amirs let the King and many of the nobles return to Damiette, so as to collect the ransom, and they had to weigh gold for days. And when the treasurer told King Louis that he had succeeded in making the bags appear full weight but that he had 'saved' about ten thousand pounds, the King became very angry and insisted that the missing amount be paid at once and he would not board his ship before it was done."

"There you are, Livio", said a Neapolitan. "Follow his example. Full measure, Livio, full measure."

"Haven't you heard what he said?" asked the tavern keeper, frowning heavily. "He said King Louis is a *saint.*"

* * *

"Quicker, Robin", said Piers. "Quicker."

"Not on these horses", growled Robin Cherrywoode. "We'll be lucky if we get there at all."

"We'll get there, because we must. Don't you see that this is the Providence of God? We arrive just when she . . . when Aquino is in danger, we hear about it as soon as we have landed, and we have still money enough to buy the horses . . . "

"One can always get horses somehow", muttered Robin Cherrywoode. He would have liked to say a good deal more: that it was the height of foolishness for two men, not yet fully recovered from the Eastern fever and the strain of a long sea journey, to ride unarmed in succor of a family to which they no longer owed allegiance and to which the Emperor, apparently, had sworn extinction. That it was silly to talk of the Providence of God, just because they had heard somebody talking of the Aquinos without being asked about them . . . when they would have got the same information anyway by asking; and that it was most likely not the Providence of God at all but rather the scheming of the foul fiend in hell, to whose realm taverns and tavern keepers were supposed to belong anyway. But of what use would it have been? Ever since that first day when they had arrived at Rocca Secca, the master had been bewitched. And they would land in Naples, of course . . . near enough to Rocca Secca. It was scarcely worthwhile to have escaped the bugs, Arabs, gnats, Turks, fevers, Greek fires, and various other amenities of the crusade to ride straight into the Emperor's nearest dungeon now. But then, if it hadn't been for that little lady, they would probably never have joined the crusade. They'd be in merry England and . . .

"Master . . . "

"I've seen them."

But it was too late to try to escape. This was not the desert, where the enemy was visible when he was still a long, long way off, a whirling little cloud of sand, rushing up from a leaden horizon . . . until the glitter of a spear blade or the raucous cry *"Allahu akbar . . . Allah il Allah"* made it certain that here came a foe who desired to get a step higher in paradise by killing a *giaur,* an unbeliever, as they called the Christians.

Here the enemy simply rode forward from behind a few

houses, a dozen men on horseback, led by a knight. They barred the road.

Piers saw that there was no emblem on their armor except for the shield of the knight, showing three leopards, couchant.

"Stop, you two", said the knight. "Where are you going? And where do you come from?"

Before Piers could answer, Robin said plaintively. "We're crusaders, most noble sir, as doubtless you would have seen were it not that our habits are torn so miserably. We are returning from Egypt . . . "

"On horseback?" asked the knight caustically.

"Ah, no, most noble sir, the horses we bought in Naples with the last of our money, so as to get home quicker. It is a long way to France, most noble sir. Wish we had never left it."

"France." The knight frowned. "Subjects of good King Louis, are you? Ride on, then."

"Thank you, most noble sir", said Robin. "And honor and victory to you."

They rode on, the knight's men giving way before them.

"There are more over there, beyond the hillock", murmured Robin. "And still more on the other side. Emperor's men."

"Who gave you permission to talk to that knight and tell him a pack of lies to boot?" said Piers angrily.

"Well, master . . . the way we look, he couldn't know you were a man of his own rank, and that was all to the good . . . for had he known it, you would have had to talk to him, and either you would have told him the truth—in which case he might have known you as a former knight of Aquino, and that would have been the end of both of us—or you would have had to tell a lie, too. And if it's a matter of lying, it's better the servant lies than the master."

Piers could not forbear a grin. "But why tell him we are going to France? And why wish that rogue honor and victory?"

"He might have wished to put us into the Emperor's service, master. As subjects of King Louis we were safe. As for honor and victory, I added in my thoughts 'if ever you go on a crusade'. No harm wishing him honor and victory against Saracens, is there?"

But Piers was in no mood for jokes. "Three to four hundred, at the very least", he said. "Not enough to storm Rocca Secca. But . . . perhaps they are only the vanguard. And they are halting and camping now, in the best riding time. They are waiting for something: either for reinforcements, or . . . how long is it from here to Rocca Secca, Robin?"

"Three hours, on a good horse. Four and a half on these creatures".

"I think you're right. They're waiting for reinforcements or for the dusk. They may want to attack at night. Quicker, Robin."

* * *

After little more than four hours Rocca Secca came in sight. Once more Piers was struck by the strength of the fortress, with its double walls and proud turrets, just as he had been when he saw it first, so many years ago. To take a place like this with only three or four hundred men was madness. But where were the defenders? He could see no spears, no halberds, no cross-bows. There seemed to be somebody on one of the turrets . . . or was he mistaken? Here was the steep way up to the main gate. Again no guards were visible.

For one moment an icy fear gripped Piers. Had the castle been taken already? Was he too late? Were the soldiers he had seen returning from their conquest instead of waiting for the right time to attack?

Then he saw the little window in the heavy gate open. The head of an old man became visible, and a tired voice asked what they wanted.

"Is the most noble Countess of Aquino here?"

"The most noble Countess died three months ago. Who are you that you do not know that?"

"We are crusaders, back from Egypt", said Piers in a shaking voice. "Is . . . is the young Countess of San Severino here . . . and the Count?"

"What concern is this of yours?" asked the old man suspiciously.

"Is she alive . . . is she well?" asked Piers.

And such was the tone of his voice that the old man glanced at him once more and said: "She is alive and well, praise God."

Piers took a deep breath: "Tell her, then, Sir Piers Rudde is here at her service, if she so desires."

The old man gaped with surprise. "Now I recognize you, noble sir . . . I will open to you . . . in an instant I will open to you."

But it took a long time before one side of the heavy gate began to open, creaking like the door of the underworld. Amazed, Piers saw that the old man had done it alone. Where were the guards, the soldiers, the knights of the household? The old man had tears in his eyes. "It's good to see you back."

Before Piers could answer, he saw her coming out of the women's wing, a flurry of black velvet; she was there before he could steel himself; she was holding both his hands and smiling up at him—the smile that had haunted his sleep and his waking all these years. She was talking to him, wildly, full of a shining joy, and he did not hear a single word. He was gazing at her, not with the greedy eyes of starvation but with a kind of incredulous awe—"so you do exist, you live, my love, my sacred love, you live."

Slowly, slowly the gentle murmuring was transformed into words . . . she was in black, he had never before seen her in black—ah, the Countess, of course . . . what was she saying? He knew he ought to speak . . . what rudeness! he had not even bowed to her; and somebody was coughing all the time—Robin was coughing; and there across the courtyard came a young man, slim and boyish, the young Count of San Severino, and she turned her head, still not relinquishing his hands—she turned her head toward her husband: and now Piers did hear her say: "Ruggiero . . . it's Piers, Sir Piers. Everything's all right now. Thank the Holy Virgin, everything's all right now."

Ruggiero approached, a shade of anxiety slowly ebbing from his face.

"Welcome to Rocca Secca", he said, a little breathlessly. "Forgive me, but I did not recognize you at once, Sir Piers."

"Small wonder", Piers heard himself say. "I look like a scarecrow, and so does Robin here. Most of King Louis' army do . . . what's left of it."

Ruggiero nodded. "We heard the news."

"A crusader", exclaimed Theodora. "So that's why you left us so suddenly, when . . . " She broke off. Only now did she let go his hands. A thin red mounted to her face and forehead. "Of course," she said hastily, "there's the cross on your tunic, I . . . I didn't see it at once."

"There's not much left of it either", said Piers. "Countess . . . your poor dear mother . . . God rest her . . . "

Theodora nodded, her eyes suddenly far away. "She died very peacefully . . . like a saint. We were all with her, Adelasia and I and Mother Maria of Gethsemani . . . that's Marotta's name now. All her daughters—but none of her sons . . . "

"It is true, then, about Count Landulph and Count Rainald."

"They're in Verona . . . as prisoners. That's all we know. And poor Ruggiero's father . . . "

"Don't, dear heart", said young San Severino. There were tears in his eyes. "I am glad it's all over for him, though God alone knows what he must have suffered."

"He was a fine man", said Piers. "God rest him." The spell was broken now, and he began to look about. "Where are your men?" he asked.

"Ah, well, you see", began Ruggiero. "That's just it . . . I do not really understand it at all . . . there were over thirty men left yesterday, and . . . "

"Sir Piers," interrupted Theodora, "the truth is that the men have left us. There were two hundred three weeks ago, with three of our household knights. *They* were the first to go, each one under a different pretext. The last thirty men simply deserted yesterday night. It's the same with the women. I cannot blame them . . . after what has happened to so many of us."

"And you let the men go?" asked Piers grimly.

San Severino avoided his eye. "What could I do?" he murmured. "I talked to them more than once and promised them more money—but their fear was stronger than money. I . . . couldn't force them to stay, could I?"

"No, I suppose you couldn't", said Piers. He had great difficulty to make his voice appear even and calm. "This is bad news", he went on. "Who is left in Rocca Secca?"

"Only we two and old Paolo here and Giulia in the kitchen", said Theodora, exactly like a child who has to own up to some silly mistake.

Piers took a deep breath. "Where are your sisters?"

"Adelasia is with Mother Maria of Gethsemani in her convent near Padua . . . we thought it was better for her not to stay here. I was afraid the Emperor might send for us—that's what the men were all afraid of."

"Naturally", said Piers drily. He cleared his throat. "You must leave at once", he said. "There are imperial troops on their way here. We've seen them. About three to four hundred. I wondered why there were so few. Now I know there are far too many. They didn't seem to know that all your men have gone, but they didn't seem to expect too much resistance either. You must leave at once."

"Of course", said Ruggiero in a wavering voice. "But . . . where to?"

"We'll talk that over later", said Piers. "Get all the valuables you can carry—but no more than you can carry yourselves. Let the two servants go wherever they like and be ready as soon as you can."

"Won't you . . . won't you come in with us and get yourself new clothes?" suggested Ruggiero timidly.

Piers felt his heart soften to the poor young man, burdened too early with such grave responsibilities.

"I think we'd better keep the old ones", he answered. "Crusaders may get through where others can't. But arms . . . if you have a few helmets and swords and shields left in the armory."

"Oh, many of them", said Ruggiero quickly. "Come and take what you like."

"And horses", said Piers. "I hope they haven't taken them all away."

"Most of them", admitted Ruggiero. "But there are some left—not exactly the best. About six or seven. We could put some of our belongings on the back of the spare ones."

Piers looked at the sun. "Another two hours before dusk", he said. "You must be very quick about it. We'll help. Come on."

* * *

When Rocca Secca was out of sight, Piers began to breathe again.

Up to the last moment he had feared that the soldiers might suddenly turn up. The sun was sinking fast now. For a while they rode silently, Robin in the vanguard, leading a heavily laden spare horse, then Theodora and Ruggiero and Piers bringing up the rear with another spare horse. Theodora had pleaded for a last visit to her sisters in the Benedictine convent near Padua, and after short reflection Piers had agreed. Padua was not far, and they would have to spend the night somewhere. At the convent at least they would be safe. The nuns would not give them away. An inn was far too dangerous in this region.

“But where shall we go tomorrow?” asked Ruggiero a little plaintively. “My father’s castles in Sicily . . . ”

“Impossible”, said Piers. “You would be seized before you got there—and if you got there, you’d find them occupied by imperial troops. You might just as well have stayed at Rocca Secca . . . or at Aquino or Monte San Giovanni. I must get you to Naples somehow . . . and on board a ship. I know all the ships in the harbor and the time of their departure and where they are going. We enquired about *that* before we heard of the danger threatening Rocca Secca.”

“Leave Italy”, murmured Theodora.

“He’s right, dearest”, said Ruggiero sadly. “We are exiles.”

“I wish you were”, said Piers almost brusquely. “I haven’t got you out yet. But we’ll discuss all that at the convent. I must keep my eyes open now.”

Again they were riding in silence.

Suddenly Robin raised his hand, and they saw him force his horses into the laurel bushes on the left of the narrow road. “Follow him . . . quick”, whispered Piers, and they obeyed. He, too, drove his horses into the bushes. He could see the crossroads a little farther down, and there they came, five, ten, twenty . . . about fifty soldiers, their helmets flaming like torches in the dying sun. “Hell’s agents”, he thought grimly. Sixty . . . seventy . . . a hundred. Then nothing, for a while. But now he could hear the clatter of hooves. There was the knight they had encountered on the way; he could just see the three leopards on his shield. Cavalry followed. Fifty . . . seventy . . . a hundred . . . and still they came. Two . . . three . . . four hundred. Then silence. Endless silence.

“Robin . . . have a look at the road. Give the Count your spare horse.”

After a few minutes Robin came back, grinning. “The road’s clear, master. But they’ll be in Rocca Secca in an hour’s time . . . or a little more.”

“I know. By then we’ll be in Padua. Let’s go.”

He saw Theodora looking at him, her eyes swimming with tears, so full of gratitude that he felt his heart turning in him. With a superhuman effort he forced himself to look aside and said gruffly: "Keep your eyes on the road, my lady; you're riding a bad horse."

It was true, too. The god-forsaken scoundrels had left only half a dozen wretched mares in the stables, not much better than the hacks he had bought in Naples and those on which old Paolo and the equally old Giulia had left for their villages, after a tearful farewell.

As soon as they reached the main road, Piers let the horses fall into a canter. Bad as they were, they could stand it for the rest of the way . . . they would have to.

They reached the convent of St. Benedict two hours before midnight. To Piers' relief it was just outside the town, so there had been no need to pass a gate where Theodora might have been recognized.

As it happened, her presence was as much of a help here as it would have been a danger at the town gate. The good nuns would not let them in until one of them recognized Theodora and summoned Mother Maria of Gethsemani, who embraced her sister fondly.

"She'll be welcome," muttered Robin, "but what about three men and six horses? I can't sing in the choir, and I'm sure the horses can't either."

But a moment later Mother Maria of Gethsemani was in full command of the situation. There was a stable with a number of cows, where the horses found accommodation and the men were asked to come into the refectory, and to sit down at the long table, with nuns buzzing around them like bees, some with cold food and wine, others arranging three primitive beds with rugs and a few cushions.

"You will have to sleep in the refectory, I'm afraid", said Mother Maria of Gethsemani. "Even that is against the rule, of course, but these are times of emergency . . . and I cannot very well let you sleep in the stable . . . even if that was good enough, once, for Someone of far nobler birth than any of us."

"She looks very much like her sister when she smiles", thought Piers. But she had changed a great deal since last he had seen her, and it was not only due to the somber, black Benedictine habit. Her face had become pale and thin, and her hands were waxen and seemed almost transparent. He did not fully realize the subtlety of her words: the Benedictine rule demands that every visitor is to be received as if he were Christ himself.

Then Theodora came back with Adelasia, and they all ate and drank, Mother Maria of Gethsemani looking on and filling their goblets as soon as they were empty. It was nothing new for Robin to eat at the same table with his master . . . it had happened often enough during the war in the Holy Land . . . yet he felt a little uncomfortable about being served by a nun who was a countess.

When they had finished their meal, Mother Maria said: "Theodora, my dear, you must go to bed now . . . no, no, I will have no argument. I am the older sister, and besides" —again that lovely smile—"here you are under my jurisdiction. Whatever there is to be discussed will have to be discussed in the morning, when you'll be fresh and strengthened. Show her the way to her cell, Adelasia."

She waited until the footsteps became inaudible. Then she turned to the three men. "There are fires burning in the north", she said quietly. "I could see them from our little tower. Three of them. Rocca Secca, Aquino, and Monte San Giovanni. The Emperor is quick."

Ruggiero gasped. Piers nodded glumly.

"Is there any way of getting you out of the country?" asked Mother Maria. "Either to France or to Spain. An uncle of yours lives in Barcelona, I believe, Ruggiero?"

"Yes . . . Mother Maria."

"There is a ship leaving for Barcelona on Friday", said Piers. "Friday night. But how do we get them to Naples?"

"If you travel only at night . . . "

"We would arrive too late. We must leave tomorrow morning—as early as possible."

"The roads to Naples are always full of people. Both Ruggiero and Theodora are known to many . . . "

"And there are spies everywhere", concluded Piers. "I know. I've been thinking and thinking ever since we left Rocca Secca how I can get them to Naples without being recognized."

Robin gave up chewing his thick, yellow moustache. He cleared his throat. "The roads would be safe for a couple of nuns, I suppose?" he asked innocently.

"What do you mean?" asked Piers.

"Well . . . the most noble Count is not very tall, and he's young, and if he'd wear lady's dress, he might easily pass for a girl . . . no offense meant", he added hastily. "But in a nun's habit one doesn't see very much except a bit of face and the hands, and even those not often."

"Robin", said Piers, shaking with laughter, "you've found it. By all the . . . beg pardon, Mother Maria. You've found it, Robin. It is the perfect solution."

"Really, I don't know." Ruggiero was smiling a little uneasily.

But Mother Maria nodded emphatically. "I think your man is quite right, Sir Piers. We have a number of spare habits here, too. And we could give you a cart, and you and your man could be the drivers. No one will suspect a few poor nuns on their way to Naples. It is a good idea, no doubt. It will suit you quite well, too, Ruggiero."

Ruggiero blushed. "Well . . . if you really think it will help . . . "

"There's no doubt whatever", said Piers firmly. Somehow the idea gave him a strange sort of satisfaction; he did not himself know why.

"All is settled, then", said Mother Maria. "As for Adelasia, I can keep her here for the time being . . . until things change, as change they must and will." She walked toward the door. "If you are sensible, you will go to sleep now, too", she said. "Good night and God bless you."

"Good advice again", said Piers. He got up and made himself as comfortable as he could on the primitive bed. It was better than the little hole in the *Santa Maddalena* where he had been sleeping for weeks. Ruggiero and Robin followed his example. The excitement and danger of the last hours had made the young Count tired enough to fall asleep almost at the moment his head touched the stiff leather cushion. It was just as well, for very soon afterward Robin started his usual night music, with its enormous range from an eerie little piping to a deep, hollow rumble like the deepest tone of a big trumpet.

Piers was accustomed to it. But tonight he could not find sleep. Again and again he had to chase his thoughts away, fierce, demanding, ugly thoughts, unworthy of a Christian knight, unworthy and forbidden. She was more beautiful than ever. Often enough he had told himself that her picture in his mind had been exaggerated by his imagination, that he was thinking of a creature so perfect that she could not exist among mortals, and now the picture had paled to nothingness and her beauty prevailed, rich, triumphant, glorious beyond all dreams. The look she had given him when they had escaped the soldiers, near the crossroads . . . fool, it was gratitude, gratitude that you had saved her and her dainty husband; you would have got the same look had you been an old man of seventy and a hunchback to boot. Not one moment, not a word of hers ever exceeded the bounds of what was right for a great lady to give to one who had chosen her as his lady. There was no sin even of thought in her. Would you have it otherwise, you of the unholy thoughts, would you like her to be assailed by the same demons that assail you? Would you drag her down into the mire and yet still pray at her shrine?

He rose; quietly he slipped out of the refectory and walked on tiptoes along the dark, high-arched passage and past the heavy door into the courtyard, where the moonlight had changed the stone walls to glistening silver, leaving the flowerbed in the middle a dark, amorphous mass. Stairs were leading up the wall, and he climbed them and stood on the parapet. Yes, the fires were still visible, all three of them, the three fiery claws of the imperial eagle.

Just in time, he thought. Oh, God, just in time. He would get them safely to Naples now. It was unthinkable that he should be allowed to arrive from Egypt at the very hour of danger to save her and then be defeated in the last minute.

A gentle noise, no more than a slight swish, made him turn round.

Mother Maria said: "I see you are not a sensible man after all."

"I could not sleep, Mother Maria. But what about yourself?"

"I need very little sleep. It's still burning, I see. Poor Rocca Secca. Mother loved it dearly . . . much more than Aquino. Theodora, too. Don't tell her . . . it would make her sad, and she won't have an easy time as it is, the poor lamb. I wish I could keep her here, as well as Adelasia, but she must go with her husband, and I couldn't very well keep him here"—a warm little chuckle—"not even as a nun."

"He'd make a very good nun", said Piers drily.

She said nothing, but under her steady look he felt a little uneasy.

After a while she went on. "I feel sorrier about Monte San Giovanni."

"You were born there?"

"No, we were all born in Rocca Secca. And yet, in a way I was born there . . . into my new life."

"And . . . does it make you happy, this new life of yours?"

"Now, only, I know what happiness means . . . at least I am as near to it as I can be in this life. The approach to God, however slow and imperfect . . . " She broke off, shyly.

"And . . . you do not miss anything?"

This time her smile was positively mischievous. "Neither Adelasia's clothes nor Theodora's husband", she said. Then, suddenly very serious again: "My brother Thomas taught me to be content only with the supreme Good. With nothing less than that."

"Mother Maria," said Piers with a twinkle, "where is your humility, pray?"

"Just that *is* humility", said the nun simply.

He shook his head. "I don't understand."

"Think, then . . . what does it mean to be content only with the supreme Good? In other words, to want God, God himself, nothing less? It means that you must recognize first that you are in need, in a great and dire and terrible need of him, so much so that nothing else matters. Then that in this need of yours you cannot help yourself at all . . . that you need the help of Another, of God. Then, that you have no claim on such help . . . none, none whatever. And worse still, that you are unworthy of that help. *Domine, non sum dignus.* And thus you empty yourself until nothing is left, no desire, no wish, no hope, except for him alone. You die to the world; there is nothing left in you but that which awaits him; you are a vessel to be filled but with him. Our Lord himself . . . as Man . . . emptied himself in such a way, obedient . . . even he . . . unto death. His was the supreme humility, and him we must imitate. But there can be no true humility unless you aspire to the supreme Good."

After a long pause Piers said gently: "Now for the first time I think I know what a nun is."

"Or a monk, a friar . . . or any true servant of God, whether in a religious order or not."

He shook his head. "How can a layman follow that way? He would never succeed."

She said, smiling: "There is no such thing as success- . . . only fulfillment."

"Or failure", he thought with a sudden bitterness arising in him. Was that the difference between a nun and a knight? Or was it merely the difference between Mother Maria and Piers Rudde? In any case he owed her an apology.

"I shouldn't have said that Count San Severino would make a good nun", he said, avoiding her eyes. "It's . . . far above him. Or me", he added with a rueful smile.

"It was not a good remark", she admitted, "but then, we are so apt to make bad remarks when we are hurt."

"Hurt?"

"Dear Sir Piers . . . "

There was a pause. "She knows", he thought, almost in a panic. "She knows. How have I given myself away?"

"You are a most honorable man, Sir Piers, and God must love you very dearly. Most likely your life is itself the answer to your question how a layman could follow the way I was talking about. What humility demands is the renunciation of the self and also a readiness to serve. And surely you are fulfilling both demands."

He gave a bitter laugh. "It's just as well that you do not see what's going on in me, Mother Maria. Why, the very reason why I couldn't sleep . . . " He broke off as she raised her hand, waxen, almost transparent.

"Sir Piers . . . you have served under King Louis, whom all Europe is calling a saint while he still lives. Imagine that we both are his captains: and to me he gives his fortress of Melun to guard for him . . . it's near the capital, and there is peace, and I guard his fortress with all the necessary skill and care; but to you he gives one of his strongholds in the Holy Land, and you must ward off the attacks of Saracens and Arabs every day, and you are wounded, and there is little food and scarcely enough water to quench your thirst, and yet you hold out. We are both doing our duty, but whose is the greater merit?"

There was light again in his eyes. "Mother Maria . . . Mother of Good Counsel . . . you have a right to bear that name."

"I am Mother Maria of Gethsemani", she answered gravely. "And much as I have prayed, the chalice will not pass from me."

"But . . . you said you were happy."

"I am happy in my new life, yes. Especially as it will not last very much longer."

"Mother Maria . . . what do you mean?"

"The physician says I have not long to live."

Piers drew in his breath sharply. "He . . . he may be wrong."

A good-natured smile thanked him for his wretched comfort.

"Promise me that you will not tell Theodora . . . she at least shall be as happy as possible in *this* life."

"I'll gladly give my life for that."

"I believe you", said Mother Maria. "You promise, then?"

"I promise."

"She will hear about it later, of course. About me and even before that, perhaps . . . about Rainald and Landulph." The frail little face was rigid with pain. "*That* is the chalice", she whispered. "I . . . I go gladly . . . but they . . . delivered to the beast, kept in prison only to die a tenfold death from torture . . . oh, Lord, have mercy on us."

"If they're not dead yet, something may still be done", said Piers with such vehemence that she looked at him as if she could not believe her ears.

"But . . . they are in the Emperor's main prison, in Verona."

"Never mind where they are", said Piers truculently.

Sadly she shook her head. "They are beyond human help, I am afraid. To see those suffer whom one loves most of all living creatures: that is my chalice . . . and even more so that of Thomas."

"Thomas . . . I've often thought of him."

"That happens to everyone who met him."

"But why . . . why does he suffer even more than you do?"

"His is the greater love. And love is the measure of true suffering. Besides . . . he knows about my illness."

"You have written to him?"

"No. But he knows."

In the silence that followed, Piers could hear his own heart beat. At long last the nun said: "And I know what he says to everything you and I have been talking about."

"What does he say?"

"That there is nothing to unify God and the soul but the Cross."

* * *

On Friday, in the early afternoon, a little cart drawn by two mules rumbled through the streets of Naples in the direction of the port. It halted only when it had reached the quay where the *Conchita* was awaiting the hour of departure. She was a fairly big ship, clumsily built and very dirty.

The driver of the cart and his companion jumped down. But when the two young nuns made a move to follow suit, the driver stopped them. "Just a few more minutes, my Mothers . . . I'd better go and fix the passage for you with the captain." Obediently they waited. "Keep your eyes open, Robin", whispered the driver and walked over to the ship.

It took the better part of half an hour before he came back.

"All is settled and well", he said, handing the taller of the two nuns a little leather bag. "Here's the rest of the money, Mother Beatrice. Now listen: the captain did not want to take you at first . . . he doesn't like women on board, and he's not particularly fond of nuns either, it seems. So I said he needn't worry; the passage would be paid in good solid gold pieces. That defeated his prejudice against women, but he still wanted to know how poor nuns could pay in gold. So I told him that you are both of good family and that your uncle is a grandee of Aragon, and if he did not see to it that you get to Barcelona safely, he would soon find out how long Don Pedro d'Alcantara's arm is. Just as well you told me your uncle's name, Mother Beatrice. It worked like magic."

"You are the greatest friend I ever had", said the smaller nun.

The taller one stammered: "Does that mean . . . does that mean that I must remain like this during the whole voyage?"

"And until you get into your uncle's house", nodded Piers. "You will find that it is just as well. There are always a good number of rough people on board of these ships, and there is no one to protect you—and Mother Lucia here—except your habits and the captain's fear of your noble uncle."

The taller nun groaned, but Mother Lucia said wide eyed: "But aren't you coming with us? Oh, Piers, Piers, come with us . . . "

There was no banter left in his tone as he whispered: "It cannot be, my lady. It must not be. God bless you and keep you. You must go on board now . . . take your bundle . . . here is yours, Mother Beatrice."

He helped them to get out; he whispered last instructions in great haste: "Never show your gold or jewels to anyone. Fasten a rug at your cabin door to make sure that you are not being spied upon through some hole in the wood. There is a sailor called Miguel, a big, swarthy fellow . . . I've given him a gold piece and told him to watch over you. I've also told him that if anything happened to you, Don Pedro would have him skinned alive. But the fellow looked reliable to me. Careful now, don't stumble . . . and don't forget, you are Sisters, you two . . . "

"Piers, Piers . . . "

"God be with you, dearest lady."

He turned away and walked back to the cart. Robin had mounted it already. Piers sat down next to him, took the reins, and turned so viciously that some men had to jump for their lives. Their curses followed until they had left the quay. Still in sight of the *Conchita,* Piers halted. It was over two hours before the *Conchita* left the harbor and all that time they sat in the cart, watching. But no soldiers turned up. Slowly the *Conchita* became smaller and smaller.

"Let's go", said Piers hoarsely.

"Assuredly", nodded Robin. "But where to?"

"To Verona, of course."

"To Verona? What on earth for, master?"

"To pay a visit to the prison there."

"To . . . "

As the cart rumbled back through the streets of Naples, Robin chewed the end of his moustache. Mad. Quite mad. Hopeless. The only good thing about it was that Verona was just a little nearer to England.

Chapter XIII

THE COURIER with his bag full of secret letters reached the Emperor and his retinue as they were riding south.

"You can stay with us", said Frederick, "take his bag, Manfred, and read the letters to me. Ten gold pieces for the courier if the news is bad, thirty if good. Read, Manfred. No . . . just give me the content of each letter."

"From the Count of Caserta", said Manfred. "The Papal Legate Peter Capoccio has made an attempt to invade Sicily . . . he was beaten off. Lost two thousand men. Two of his nephews have been taken prisoner."

Frederick nodded, the unblinking eyes gleaming strangely in the pale, beautiful face. "One hope less, Holy Father. Go on, Manfred."

"Conrad is coming", said the boy, frowning a little. There was little love lost between the Emperor's sons, all by different mothers. Manfred was eighteen now and Conrad twenty-two . . . worse still, Conrad had received the title of king—King Conrad IV . . . and ever since had looked down on his brothers even more than before. "He has finished the Rhenish campaign", said Manfred sullenly. "A truce has been concluded with the archbishops on the Rhine."

"Good again", said Frederick. "If Conrad makes a truce, he is certain to fleece them. He's a sharp one. Go on."

"Avignon and Arles have renewed the oath of allegiance to the Emperor," said Manfred, "and there are well-confirmed rumors that the Pope has written to the English King for asylum in Bordeaux."

"That is the best news of all! Fifty gold pieces for the courier! Boy, do you know what that means? It's almost the end of my struggle against the King of the superstitious. Bordeaux! After that there is only Britain left for him and then the ocean. To the fishes with the successor of the Fisherman. Not even the pious Frenchman can stop it now . . . he will take years to recover from the thrashing he got from my Moslem friends. This is my moment, Manfred. I've got him where I want him. The rest is easy. Berard . . . where is Berard?"

"Here I am, my Emperor." The Archbishop of Palermo had not seen his archdiocese since he had been excommunicated together with his master, whom he followed almost everywhere with doglike loyalty. He was a very old man now, and had to be carried in a litter most of the way.

"Berard . . . send off that letter I asked you to prepare the other day . . . the letter to Duke Albert of Saxony. Unless the Saxonian painters are the worst flatterers in the world, his daughter must be very pretty."

"You're not going to marry *again,* Father?" asked Manfred angrily. "Why, you'll be fifty-six this very month. Haven't you sired enough sons by now?"

Frederick stopped his horse. "You're Prince of Taranto and Vicar of Italy . . . at eighteen", he said acidly. "What have you to complain about? I shall get myself as many other whelps as I like. Be quiet! I will not have this day spoiled by anybody. Out of my sight now."

Very pale, but still angry, young Manfred turned his horse and rode back into the glittering cavalcade that followed the Emperor at about fifty yards' distance.

"The young devil", said Frederick with a bitter smile. "I know what he wants . . . and what Conrad wants, too. In a way they're all alike, my dear sons." He was breathing heavily, and his face was flushed. Suddenly he drove his horse off the road, halted and began to vomit. Spasm after spasm ran through his powerful body. He slumped in his saddle.

After a brief moment of consternation, the cry, "Physician! Physician!" ran along the cavalcade and John of Procida came hurrying up to his master, still a fairly young man despite his great professional reputation, with the face of an intelligent monkey and brand-red hair under the black cap. He helped the Emperor dismount—no one else had thought of that in the general commotion—and from the way he had to support the body of his master it was evident that this was not an ordinary attack of nausea; there had been no relief, apparently. "Two men to support our lord", cried the physician. That brought them forward with a rush. "A litter", ordered the physician. "There must be no more riding. A litter." But the only litter available was that of the Archbishop, they pleaded. "Then get the old incense swinger out", cried John of Procida. Knights and courtiers looked at each other. One could call an archbishop almost anything at Frederick's court, but Berard was a personal friend of the Emperor.

"Get him out, I say", yelled John of Procida. "I want that litter for my lord, and he's going to have it. Never mind the superstition seller."

The Emperor was only half conscious. But when Manfred

came up to him with a great show of worry, he turned his head away, and Manfred withdrew again.

By now the old Archbishop had climbed heavily out of his litter. He had not heard the physician's words, and if he had heard them, they would not have upset him much. He knew John of Procida and his views about matters spiritual. Quite innocently he came forward and offered his litter to Frederick. He was horrified to see the Emperor's face. It was yellowish and mottled, the eyes sunken and circled. He seemed to be in pain, too, and was leaning heavily on the two knights who now supported him.

They carried rather than led him to the litter, helped him in, and covered him with the Archbishop's rugs.

"Who's in charge now?" bellowed John of Procida. "Whoever it is, I'll have him know that there can be no more traveling. Where is the next place where my lord can have a decent roof over his head?"

But the next town was over two hours' ride away, and the physician shook his head energetically. "Quite out of question. What's this thing over there?"

The thing over there was a small castle just above a few olive groves. No one knew its name or the name of the owner.

"Whatever it is and whoever owns it, that's where we go", said the physician. "Up, litter."

"You are adopting a rather high-handed manner, Messer physician", said Pietro Ruffo, master of the royal stables. "My orders were . . . "

"I'm your servant, noble lord, at any other time", interrupted John of Procida. "Something has happened since you had your orders, as you can see. The Emperor's health is my responsibility, and it is endangered. I would be grateful to you . . . and so, I'm sure, will be our lord . . . if you'd make certain that we are suitably received at the castle."

He was so obviously right that Ruffo shrugged his broad shoulders and commanded a dozen knights to ride up to the castle and see to it that everything was prepared for the arrival of the imperial patient.

They sped off, and the rest of the cavalcade followed. It was quite impossible, of course, to find quarters for over twelve hundred people and six hundred horses at so small a place.

Later, Pietro Ruffo tried to find out how long it would be before the Emperor had recovered sufficiently to proceed with the journey. The physician's answer was a shrug.

Well, then, when would there be a chance to talk to the Emperor and ask him for instructions? A shrug again. Perhaps tonight. Perhaps tomorrow.

Ruffo passed the meager report on to the nobles, and it was decided to make camp where they were and to wait for the Emperor's orders.

Some of the knights came back from the castle to report that the owner—Count Torrani—was in Rome with all his family and that his servants were, of course, already preparing the Count's rooms for the august patient.

An hour later the Emperor was in bed, turning restlessly from one side to the other. "Leech . . . "

"My Emperor?"

"Have I been poisoned, Leech?"

"No, my Emperor. Not, unless you have eaten something when I was not present, and I don't think you have. I've tasted everything you had."

"What . . . is it . . . then?"

"I don't know yet."

"My belly's on fire . . . and so's my head."

"This will make you sleep, master. Drink it."

Frederick drank the poppyseed mixture with a grimace.

There was no swelling and no acute spot of inflammation. But he had been hawking again in the marshes, day after day, and the marshes were dangerous; they bred all kinds of fevers. The pulse was fast and irregular. John of Procida decided to stay in the room and tell Ruffo and everybody else to keep out.

After about half an hour Frederick fell asleep. The physician sat watching him gravely. The finest, the most wonderful brain in the world was given into his care. He had admired the Emperor during his boyhood when he heard people bless and curse him for his astonishing deeds. His worst enemies had to concede that he was brilliantly intelligent, and intelligence was what John of Procida had admired most, even as a boy. Soon he had discovered that his idol hated and despised priests and that he did not believe in the tenets of the religion Pater Filippo was teaching at school. And Pater Filippo and all the other paters made wry faces when he mentioned the Emperor. Yet to his eager questions they rarely gave an answer other than "you must believe that if you want to be a good Christian". Must. Must. Why? If these stories were true, why couldn't they explain? And if they weren't, why should he believe them? The little redhead was a rebel at school, pointed out to other boys as a warning example and of course worshipped by them for it. At the University of Naples and later at Toledo he lost the last remnants of faith. Religion was superstition. Reason and faith excluded each other. In fact, the intelligence of a man was in direct proportion to his lack of belief. When he became the Emperor's physician, he was supremely happy. He had never lost his boyish admiration for the most brilliant man of the century, and even at close range his idol did not disappoint him. The Emperor's wit, his caustic remarks about the solemn-faced fools in surplice and stole, his cunning and bold ways of putting them exactly where they belonged, never ceased to delight the physician as much as did his master's phenomenal knowledge.

The Emperor slept until late in the evening, then woke up in renewed spasms of pain. The fever was higher than before, the eyes glassy, the skin dry and very hot. John of Procida sent word to the Prince of Taranto and the nobles that the Emperor was gravely ill and would take several weeks to recover. Vomiting recurred, too. But the heartbeat was still strong. The physician worked like a madman. Poultices had to be made and renewed every ten minutes—he selected two young women of Count Torrani's household to see to that, while he changed the adjacent room into a veritable alchemist's tower. He succeeded in making the Emperor sleep, fitfully, through the major part of the night. After sunrise the fever was a little lower, and John of Procida decided to have a few hours of sleep himself. He had only just gone to bed when he heard a terrible raucous cry from the Emperor's room. He jumped up and rushed in. Frederick was sitting upright, his eyes protruding from their sockets, his mouth distorted.

"Leech . . . leech . . . get me away from here."

"Calm yourself, master, please, calm yourself. What is it?"

"Get me away . . . quickly. . . . "

"No, no, master, not yet. The fever is too high for you to travel. But why? What is lacking here, that . . . ?"

"Fool, fool. Ah, . . . you don't know. What a cheat fate is, what a cheat. . . . "

He began to laugh, a hoarse, desperate laughter that would not end.

"What has happened?" asked the physician in a whisper. The two young women were so frightened that he had to repeat his question several times before one of them said in a whining tone: "Nothing, my lord, nothing at all. He . . . the Emperor asked us what the name of the castle was and I told him and he screamed."

Frederick's terrible laughter was still going on. It ended in a long-drawn groan. "I'm dying . . . I'm dying. . . . "

"No, master, no," protested John of Procida. "I have seen this kind of fever before and treated it. You will not die, not for a long time."

"Sub flore," whispered Frederick. "Michael Scotus was right . . . *sub flore.* I shall die *sub flore.* Do you know what this place is called, leech, do you know? Castello Fiorentino . . . Castello Fiorentino . . . "

A spasm went through his body and he pressed both his hands against his stomach. "All the time . . . I avoided Florence . . . never . . . went there . . . never tolerated . . . flowers above my head . . . and they take me to Castello Fiorentino . . . "

"You don't believe that", exclaimed the physician, horrified. "You can't believe that, my Emperor, not you!"

"I am dying", said Frederick. "Call . . . them in . . . all of them." He began to vomit again and the attack was peculiarly painful, as he had not eaten anything during the last thirty-six hours. As soon as it was over, he repeated his order and John of Procida had to obey. A few minutes later they came in, terrified, shaken to the core by the sight of the man who only a short time ago had been the very symbol of strength and self-assurance.

He began to dictate a number of state documents. To the physician's astonishment his mind seemed to be clear and his thinking concise and logical. How was it possible then, that he could believe in this idiotic prediction?

John of Procida knew, of course, that there had been astrologers and occultists at the Emperor's court, but then there had been Saracen dancing girls and wild animals, too; he loved playing with every kind and form of life without placing undue importance on any of them.

There was no doubt that he was gravely ill and there was the possibility that he might die. But this illogical, this unscientific idea of having to die because the accursed castle's name seemed to bear out his star gazer's prophecy was laming his will power and thereby the strongest factor for recovery. Superstition, superstition; not even the most brilliant mind in the world was free of it. Or . . . or could it be that there was such a thing as getting a glimpse of the future? A kind of memory forward instead of backward? There had been intelligent men in Toledo who believed that and experimented with it. It was easier to imagine than that the great Frederick's mind had kinship with that of old women of either sex. Perhaps it was all simply due to the fact that the Emperor knew more and not that he believed in such things. Even so it was harmful knowledge; it diminished his powers of resistance. Could . . . could knowledge really be harmful? The superstition sellers said something of the kind, babbling of a tree of knowledge from which man had eaten the fruit of death. But then they'd say anything to keep people stupid and to rule over them.

Document after document was dictated, written, signed, and sealed.

Honors were conferred, titles and positions of power. John of Procida did not understand much of such matters, but enough to know that in this little room the whole of Italy was divided in zones of power, each under a son of the Emperor. Italy had become the family possession of the Hohenstaufen family.

Other letters went to the German princes, to the King of France, the Duke of Burgundy, to King Henry III of England, to the Amir of Tunis. Hour after hour this went on. Frederick's voice was weak and hoarse, sometimes sinking to a whisper. But his thoughts were clear and his hands cool to the touch, as if the impact of imminent death had frightened his fever away. At last, in the midst of a letter to Spain, Frederick fell asleep. Some of the nobles broke into tears, thinking that he had died, but John of Procida shook his head and asked them to leave the room, which they did, dumbfounded, wretched, helpless, frightened children rather than rulers. Half an hour later Frederick began to murmur incoherent words. From time to time he gave a short, mocking laugh or a groan. The fever was back in full force.

Once he sat up without help and said in a clear, metallic voice: "I have come to fulfill the law."

Then he sank back and began to mutter again incoherently.

* * *

After four days of fighting, John of Procida knew that there was no more hope. The symptoms were unmistakable: the skin had become clammy, the face had a bluish tinge, breathing had become difficult, and at long last the heart began to rebel.

Fully conscious, Frederick gazed at him, the ghost of a smile on his bloodless lips. "The truth . . . leech . . . d'ye hear me? The truth. How . . . many more . . . hours . . . have I got?"

The time for caution was past. And it was impossible to deceive these eyes. "Not many more, master."

Frederick nodded imperceptibly. "Berard . . . " he said. "Call Berard."

Sullenly the physician sent one of the women to fetch the old man. But when Archbishop Berard entered with two acolytes carrying a table with cruets of oil and water, a covered chalice, and two burning candles, he jumped to his feet and protested angrily, although in a subdued voice.

"Quiet, leech," said Frederick, "your work's finished . . . his work starts now."

John of Procida stared at him, horrified. "My Emperor, . . . you are not going to . . . you don't mean you will let him . . . you can't believe in . . . in this. I know you can't. Why, all your life you . . . "

The unblinking eyes fixed him and forced him to silence.

"Young man," said Frederick, "it is not you who is going to die."

John of Procida fell on his knees. "My Emperor, oh, my great Emperor, I have loved and admired you always. You were the symbol of the highest thing I knew, the human mind; you were the apex of the human mind, unfettered and free. You saw through the fallacies and hypocrisies of the superstitious. You were the Emperor of the mind, the strong, courageous mind. Let it not be said of you that you, that even you, gave in at the crucial hour, that the greatest realist of us all needed the comfort of illusions . . . "

He was sobbing now.

"My poor fool," said Frederick gently, "the highest thing a man knows is . . . what we call God. So I . . . was your god . . . and now . . . your god is dying. It's a grim and sad thing . . . when God is dying. You're right . . . it is the *crucial* hour."

He took a deep, painful breath. "You don't know . . . what dying means", he said almost in a whisper. "It isn't fear. It is . . . beginning . . . to see. To see . . . without illusions. Happy the man . . . who can bear it . . . if there is such a man." Another deep breath. "Go now, . . . good fool . . . "

Crying, John of Procida fled from the room, where his god had fallen.

The unblinking eyes fixed their stare on the Archbishop.

"Berard, my old friend . . . your loyalty to me . . . has brought about your . . . excommunication. Tell me . . . can you still . . . validly . . . hear confession and give absolution?"

"I can, in an emergency", said the old man in a trembling voice. "And this hour will make up for all the pain I have endured. I can hear your confession and give you the Viaticum. The consecration of a priest is forever . . . however much he may sin!"

Frederick nodded. "Good . . . good. Send these children away."

The acolytes left silently.

"How long have I been here, Berard?"

"Five days, my Emperor."

"Five years . . . fifty years", said Frederick. "Believe it . . . or not . . . I have lived my whole life all over again. Everything I did and said and thought . . . it gives you a foretaste of . . . eternity. And do you know . . . I committed only one sin . . . one single sin: I wanted to be God."

Berard nodded. "There is only that one sin, my son. There is no other. Adam's sin. To take the law into our own hands, to be a law unto ourselves. To be like God. It is the sin of our ancestors, and it is our own. You are Adam; I am Adam."

"I wanted to be God", whispered Frederick. "Even as a

boy, when I was poor and had to beg for my food, in Palermo . . . I wanted to be God, great and powerful . . . all-powerful. And when *he* came to my help, that terrible old man . . ."

"Innocent the Third . . ."

" . . . I hated him for it. I did not want to owe anything . . . to anyone except myself. From the very beginning. I hated him and all he stood for . . . and his successors . . . and he . . . were one. How else could I be the Emperor, unless I reigned . . . supreme? And always . . . an old man in Rome . . . held up a law . . . against me, a law that was not . . . *my* law. One of us . . . had to go. But he was tenacious . . . and when he died . . . another came as tenacious as the first. Only five days ago, Berard . . . five days ago I thought . . . I had won . . . and now look at me . . . dying in my own vomit . . . in my own mud . . . like what they said I was . . . like Herod . . ."

The Archbishop raised his head, his eyes swimming with tears. A mountain of human pride had crumbled into dust and rubble.

"Not like Herod", he said softly. "For you repent."

* * *

The Emperor died an hour before sunset.

A strange story made the round of the Empire soon afterward: it came from Sicily. A Franciscan monk saw the Emperor at the head of a great cavalcade of knights ride across the sky and disappear in the fiery crater of Mount Aetna. It was just an hour before sunset on the day of Frederick's death. Many people believed it, and many did not.

* * *

Two days after the Emperor's death King Conrad arrived at Castello Fiorentino with a large retinue, a slim, brown-haired young man in golden armor; his eyes were pale blue and piercing, his mouth firm, with thin lips, his chin jutting. He was in vigorous health.

Within half an hour of his arrival he had countermanded most of the orders young Prince Manfred had given. Almost the only thing he approved of was that his father's body should be taken to Palermo, where a magnificent sarcophagus of dark red porphyry—Frederick's own choice—was awaiting it. Then he sat down to study the documents the Emperor had signed at Castello Fiorentino.

"What is this?" he asked with a frown. "The Church to recover all her possessions if she will render to Caesar what is Caesar's? And all prisoners to be released except convicted traitors? Our glorious father cannot have been himself when he signed that."

"He was more himself than ever", said Archbishop Berard firmly.

King Conrad's smile was dangerous. "Fortunately for the state it is I who has to decide whether or not the Church is rendering to Caesar what is Caesar's. And it is I also who will decide who is or is not a convicted traitor. Every man who fought against our glorious father must die. And we shall certainly see to it that our treasury is not depleted at the very beginning of our reign."

"The sun of the world has set", said Prince Manfred. "I can think of nothing else."

"It has not set in our hearts", said King Conrad. "We shall give orders that our subjects may pray to the great spirit of our father. He was immortal, and what is immortal is divine. Quiet, Archbishop . . . we shall not listen to any dogmatic objections. A throne in heaven to our father and death on earth to those who committed treachery against him. These are our orders."

Chapter XIV

IN THE CHAPEL of the convent of St. Jacques on the hill of St. Geneviève in Paris, Friar Thomas of Aquino was saying Mass. There was no congregation. It was six o'clock in the morning of a fairly cold day in early March. The chapel itself was icy. The friar's hands, lifted up for prolonged periods, as the ritual demands, became numb. It was almost impossible to turn the pages of the missal. The silver of paten and chalice seemed to burn at the touch. Outside it was still so dark that the two candles on the altar and the dim glow of the eternal lamp provided the only light.

Friar Thomas had read the epistle and the Gospel of the day. He always felt a little pang of loneliness when he said Mass on a day that was not the feast day of a saint as today, the seventh day of March; he felt deprived of a heartening and encouraging company, left alone to reiterate the tremendous sacrifice of Calvary, and somehow today that feeling was especially strong, until the thought descended upon him on silent wings that he shared his very loneliness with that of the First Sacrifice.

There was joy now in his gesture as he took up the paten and the host and then the chalice.

As he went on, he did not hear that the door opened and a wizened little friar came in, whose huge head was in such striking contrast to his body that it looked as if it had been mounted straight away on his legs. Silently Master Albert slipped into the last bench and began to pray. His face was very grave.

Friar Thomas did not see him even when he turned round to exhort an invisible community to pray that "my sacrifice and yours may be acceptable to God the Father Almighty". As often, when he spoke the words "*Orate fratres*" into a void he thought of his own brothers.

Whenever that happened, he prayed for them with particular fervor when he had reached the commemoration of the living. But today, to his anguish, he felt himself bereft of all fervor as he pronounced, in a whisper, the names of Landulph and Rainald; a strange, flat silence was in the air—no, not in the air, in his own heart it was and with it the thought, dark and leaden, that their place was no longer here but at the commemoration of the dead, with his mother and Marotta, of whose death he had been informed three months ago by the Benedictine nuns of Capua.

Bracing himself, he prayed for his sister Adelasia, for his sister Theodora and her husband, for all the people of Aquino, Rocca Secca, and Monte San Giovanni, for Friar John of Wildeshausen, Magister General of the Order, for Friar Reginald of Piperno, for Master Albert, for his Franciscan brothers, Frater Bonaventure from Italy and Frater Roger Bacon from England, for the Prior and the friars of St. Jacques and for the people of Paris, and especially for old Madame Fourchon, who had lost her three sons in the crusade and was very ill, and for the student of theology Etienne Fripet, that his memory and understanding should increase and enable him to pass the examination, as Thomas had promised Madame Fourchon and the Sieur Fripet he would do when they had asked him to after Mass on Sunday.

Meanwhile three other friars had entered the chapel and started saying their Masses, and the murmur of their voices came up to him like the consolation of good friends at a sad hour.

Then the moment approached for God to descend upon his altar incarnate in the forms of bread and wine, and as Thomas' hands moved over the oblation and he whispered the ancient formulas, all other things paled into nothingness. And God descended in a sweet and tranquil joy, filling the world with his blessing and the foreknowledge of priceless things comprehensible only in the world beyond the senses, in the world of Reality, of which earthly life is only the shadow.

Friar Thomas adored. He prayed that his sacrifice "be carried by the hands of thy holy angel to thy altar on high". And he beseeched God to "be mindful . . . of thy servants and handmaids who are gone before us" and whispered the names of his mother and of Marotta and of old Friar Lotulph, who had died a fortnight ago.

It was then that it happened. All sound ceased. There was movement between him and heaven. Without lifting up his eyes, he saw the roof of the chapel recede into cloudy distances. All darkness was poured out of the realm in which he moved and had his being. The purple veil of the tabernacle grew and grew, paling into a milky white and thickening to the solid and radiant form of a book, a book of pages as many as the stars, and there was writing in it, and the writing was luminous and alive. And all that was written here in letters of dancing azure and throbbing gold were names, and though there was an infinite number of them, he could read only two, and they were the names of his brothers, Landulph and Rainald. Immediately the book dissolved again as the swift revelations returned to their Author, darkness poured back into the chapel, and once more the two candles on the altar and the dim glow of the eternal lamp were the only light.

Striking his breast, as the liturgy demanded, Friar Thomas prayed that to him and all other sinners God might grant, in the multitude of his mercies, some part and fellowship with his holy apostles and martyrs. After the slow and quiet majesty of the Our Father, the prayer for delivery from evil and for peace, and the threefold invocation of the Lamb of God, he proceeded to the union with the Lamb.

A few minutes later he was back in the sacristy, where other friars were robing for their Masses. He had only just finished disrobing when Master Albert slipped in. He waited a few moments, until two friars had left for the chapel.

Then he said gently: "There is news, my son . . . and it's grave news, I'm afraid."

Thomas nodded. "My brothers are in heaven."

Albert stared at him hard. "You knew?"

"I knew."

"Since when?"

"Since . . . half an hour ago."

They both crossed themselves.

"King Conrad had them executed", said Albert.

"Landulph was a rough man, but good at heart", said Thomas softly. "And Rainald was very gifted . . . there was a time when I hoped . . . when I very much hoped he would write a really great poem . . . about great things. About the greatest thing of all, perhaps. I prayed for that, too, many a time. Now he will sing it in heaven. This is joy for Mother and for Marotta."

Albert pressed his hand and turned away abruptly to robe for his own Mass.

Quietly Thomas returned to the chapel for his thanksgiving and from there to his cell. Then only he wept.

* * *

"You can go and see him now", said Master Albert, and he added with a deprecating gesture, "I am sorry that it was not possible yesterday evening, when you arrived. It was the hour of silence."

"You have told him . . . Father?" asked Piers in a low voice.

"Yes", said Albert, looking straight ahead. "I have told him. Take your man with you, if you wish . . . I am sure he will be happy to see him again, too . . . take the third door on the right; it leads to the garden. You will find him there."

Piers bowed instinctively to the strange little man with the enormous head. He knew nothing about him, but no one could meet Master Albert without feeling something of the spell that had made him a legendary figure in his lifetime.

It was just as well that he had told him where the garden was . . . it was easy enough to lose one's way in that cluster of grey and yellow buildings that was the convent of St. Jacques. The lay brother who had let them in had guided them through a maze of corridors, orchards, shrubberies, and doors. The third door on the right, then.

There was little green in the garden . . . it was too early in the year. But a mild sun had come out, and there was a glow in the air, pale and virginal, a first promise, a first stirring.

He saw a few friars walking up and down the many little paths, some reading their breviaries, some fingering strings of what seemed to be little pellets, which he had seen before and knew were some new way of concentrating on certain prayers. None of the friars spoke, and except for the soft music of the gravel under their feet there was no sound. It was like walking in a dream, utterly removed from the world as he knew it.

The large friar approaching them now, with his massive head shorn except for a circlet of glossy brown hair, interrupted at both sides of the forehead and with a little forelock in the middle, was a stranger until Piers saw his eyes—Theodora's eyes and yet not hers. And there was that smile—unchanged—that lit up the round face, still young, though no longer that of a boy, a smile that somehow made one feel a better man than one was. "He's not like her brother", thought Piers. "He's like her father and more than her father." But already his thought gave way to other thoughts, one more irrational and bewildering than the other. He found himself wishing that this huge, gentle man were his own father . . . felt that in some strange and unaccountable way he was coming home and was welcomed home with hands stretching out to him as if he had been awaited a long, long time. He wanted to go down on his knees as if he were the prodigal son; he wanted to unburden himself utterly and completely. Shaking all over his body, he burst into tears.

"Welcome to a very dear friend", said Thomas. "And God bless you for all you have done for those I love."

Blinded with tears and in agony Piers heard himself say: "Father . . . Father Thomas . . . where is God? Where is God?"

"Very near to both of us at this very moment."

"I tried so hard to save them, Father Thomas . . . " With a great effort Piers regained control over his voice, "Twice it looked as if we might succeed in getting them out; we had found someone to help us with money, and we had bribed the jailer and his two assistants, but they took the money and did nothing in exchange; then the rumor came that on his deathbed the Emperor had granted an amnesty, just when I had got hold of fifty men who were ready to risk an assault on the prison, and we decided to wait two more days, and the very next day came the news that the Emperor's amnesty had been cancelled by King Conrad, so we made the assault, but it was too late: they had been killed, together with many others. We found it out during the fighting. Then troops came, and we had to ride for our own lives."

He broke off.

After a while, Thomas asked softly: "Why did you try to save them, friend?"

"Why?" Piers frowned, wrestling with the answer. "I . . . I had been one of the knights of your family. I had seen the grief of your sisters . . . I wanted to spare them still more grief; they had lost so much . . . all of you. And you were in your monastery, and Count San Severino was very young, and besides he had to look after Countess Theodora. They at least were safe; I had news in Verona that they had arrived in Spain."

"Yes, thanks to you", said Thomas.

"But I failed her . . . I failed you all in Verona . . . "

"Surely not", said Thomas gravely. "There is no such thing as failure or success where a man does all he can do. You fulfilled your mission."

"That's . . . that's how your sister spoke one night . . . Mother Maria of Gethsemani."

"That is how she would speak. For it is true. Cease reproaching yourself for that which is not your fault . . . and begin to reproach yourself for that which is."

"What is it, Father Thomas?"

"You asked: 'Where is God?' What you meant was: Why did God allow Landulph and Rainald to be killed? And perhaps also: Why did God not help me to liberate them? You asked that *your* will be done in heaven and on earth, because that which you wanted to achieve appeared to be good in your mind. But his ways are not our ways. He wanted Landulph and Rainald in heaven."

Piers hung his head. "You haven't seen what I have seen, Father Thomas. Madness is ruling in Italy. The big eagle has gone, but the little eagles are almost worse. Wherever you look, you see tears and despair and bloodshed. I felt that my own life was senseless. And I may as well admit it: I am no longer certain that God exists."

"I needn't exist", said Thomas calmly. "You needn't exist. But God must exist, or else nothing else could. You can scarcely doubt your own existence . . . it's a violation of the law of contradiction: for if you do not exist, who is it that holds the doubt? So you do exist, but not in your own right. You have received existence: from your parents and ancestors, from the air you breathe, the food you take in. A river has received its existence, and so have mountains and everything, not only on earth but everywhere in the universe. But if the universe is a system of receivers, there must be a giver. And if the giver has received existence, he is not the giver at all. Therefore the ultimate giver must have existence in his own right; he must *be* existence, and this Giver we call God. Can you contradict that?"

"I cannot contradict it", said Piers. "But it does not satisfy me. Nor will it satisfy anyone who suffers."

"Your question, then, is not whether God exists, but why there is suffering. But what is suffering? What are its causes and consequences? It is caused when parts that belong together are separated and prevented from joining each other. And its consequence is pain. A sword cut severs tissues that belong together, and thus suffering is caused and leads to pain. Or two people who love each other are separated and prevented from joining each other: suffering is caused and thereby pain."

"But what", thought Piers, "if the parts that belong together, if two people who belong together remain separated for all time? If the barriers between them are unsurmountable, are so high that they do not even realize that they belong together . . . until it is too late and both their lives are wasted?"

And he said: "But why must it happen? Why must that which belongs together be separated in life? You explained to me what causes suffering and that pain is its consequence. You did not explain why God permitted the cause."

"All human suffering", said Thomas, "goes back to the archetypal suffering . . . the separation of man from God."

Piers stopped in his tracks—and only then realized that they had been wandering up and down the garden. He saw Robin sitting on a wooden bench at some distance—he had forgotten all about him. Thomas, watching, read him like a book. He knew Piers had not seen Robin and him smiling at each other delightedly . . . much less Robin's anxious twinkling and nodding "for goodness' sake, do something for my poor master; he is in a bad way."

Thomas said, lightly: "The sun will do him good." Piers began to walk again. After a while he said: "The separation of man from God. That means the story of the Fall in paradise, does it?"

"Yes."

"It's so long ago, Father Thomas. What has it to do with you and me?"

"God is beyond time. It was yesterday. It will be tomorrow."

"I don't understand that."

"You will, very soon. We are told about the Fall of man in Genesis. The Greeks and other peoples remembered it:

they called the time in paradise the 'golden age'. Do you remember the words of the serpent, 'Eat . . . and you shall be as God—'? We ate . . . and by that act of rebellion cut ourselves off from God. We broke the link between the natural and the supernatural. That was the separation."

"And were driven out of paradise. And had to die and to suffer. That was God's answer."

"No, friend. That was the inevitable consequence of our own act. But God did give an answer, and his answer was Christ."

There was a pause. Piers sighed, and in his sigh were England and Foregay and old Father Thorney's impatient voice, cracked with age: *"Agnus Dei qui tollis peccata mundi: miserere nobis";* and Mother, gravely reading a missal she knew by heart and little Piers wishing it were all over and time to break the fast.

But Thomas said: "Our Lord took upon himself the total pain of that separation. The union between God and man is the Cross."

Piers' eyes widened. "Mother Maria of Gethsemani", he thought. And then: "Father Thorney . . . and Mother Maria of Gethsemani. They are separated by more than twenty years of time and yet living in my mind together. Perhaps there is a world outside time . . . "

"Supernatural life was restored to man", said Thomas. "And thus God is like the precious soil into which the seed, man, is sown. And the seed branches out into three roots by which it clings to the soil: the roots of faith and hope and charity. And all three are acts of our will—the will to accept the truth as revealed by God—the will to trust the promises of Christ—and the will to see in God the supreme Good."

"I think I understand that", said Piers. "It's like . . . like an oath of allegiance to the love of God."

Once more he saw that irresistible smile that seemed to confer an honorable accompliceship.

"You see now," said Thomas, "suffering means sharing

with Christ. If you love him . . . how can you renounce suffering? No lover will renounce the pain of his love."

"True", said Piers hoarsely. "True."

"Man loves so many things", said Thomas. "Wealth . . . or power . . . or a woman. But if you had to name what all men desire, whatever forms their desire may take . . . what would you say?"

"Happiness", declared Piers after short hesitation.

"Yes. Happiness. But what is happiness?"

"I . . . I don't know. I know what it is for me."

"There is then something you desire more than anything else."

"Yes. But I shall never have it."

"And if you had it, you would be happy?"

"Yes, of course. But . . . "

"But if you had it and so had to fear that it might be taken away from you again—would you still be happy?"

"N-no, I suppose not. Not entirely."

"Therefore . . . shall we agree that happiness is the possession of the desired good . . . whatever it is . . . without any fear of losing it?"

"Yes . . . I think so."

"But in this life on earth we have not only the fear but the certainty that we shall lose it. For one day we must die. Therefore true happiness . . . lasting, everlasting happiness cannot be our lot on earth. Nor could it be otherwise. For everlasting happiness is only another name for God."

Thomas' eyes shone. "Do you see it now? The urge for everlasting happiness is still in man, in all men. But since the Fall it has been misdirected, and like fools we see our happiness in this or that—in the accumulation of gold or of power or in the union with another creature, when in reality it is in God alone. The love of God is the true quest of man. 'Love and do what thou wilt', said St. Augustine. And our Lord said: 'Seek ye therefore first the kingdom of God and his justice, and all these things shall be added unto you.' "

"Father Thomas," stammered Piers, "I . . . I feel as if I were thinking for the first time in my life. Don't go away. I mean . . . let me stay with you. Let me stay here."

"It is part of what we are doing here," said Thomas joyfully, "to teach people how to think. Don't overrate it, though. Our faith is not founded on reasoning but on the most solid teaching of God. But it is good to know that reason is on our side and not against us, as so many false philosophers would make us believe."

From the little tower beyond the shrubbery a bell began to ring.

"He's calling", said Thomas with dancing eyes. "Come, friend."

Robin rose from his bench and followed them. Friars came from all sides of the garden, unhurried, and yet speedily enough.

Piers saw that they were forming a double row and fell back a little to let Thomas take his place with them. Robin caught up with him."

"Master . . . "

"Yes?"

"He looks quite cheerful. You must have comforted him."

Piers gazed at him. He laughed, for the first time in many months. Robin grinned broadly.

Then they entered the chapel.

Chapter XV

THE RUE DE LA HARPE was swirling with people.

"May I have a word with you, Father?" asked the tall young man courteously.

The Dominican stopped, skillfully avoiding a vegetable cart. "Your servant, messire, but I am not a priest . . . only a lay brother and not much of one at that."

"Well, I'll admit that the first thing I thought about you was that you carried your habit like a soldier rather than a friar . . . "

The Dominican nodded. "I've been a soldier most of my life, messire."

" . . . And the second thing I thought was that you look like an Englishman", said the young man with a cheerful twinkle.

"I am that, messire. Yours are sharp eyes for one so young . . . you are not twenty yet, I believe."

The young man laughed. "No . . . but I am something you are not: a married man. Oh, I have said the wrong thing, and I am sorry. I did not wish to hurt your feelings."

"And you didn't."

"I hope not. When I saw you passing by in this street full of so many foreign faces I felt happy to meet a countryman of mine."

"So you are English, too? I wasn't sure."

"Indeed I am . . . and visiting this astonishing city for the first time in my life, Brother—what may I call you?"

"I am Brother Peter now . . . that's what they call me at the convent. It used to be Piers . . . "

"Oh, don't tell me. Brother Peter is good enough for me. So when I tell you that my name is Edward, it will be good enough for you . . . ah, that made you laugh. Good. Paris is a bewildering city. Do you know it well?"

"I have been here four years", said the Dominican slowly.

It seemed as if he wanted to add something, but he did not.

"I wish you could show me some of the things a stranger would not see without a guide . . . but perhaps your duties do not allow you that, and I have already presumed on your time." The young man smiled very pleasantly.

"You are most courteous, Messire Edward. I am, in fact, on my way to the university—ah, not to study there, my brain is not good enough for that, I fear, but to bring these manuscripts to one of our fathers . . . he forgot to take them with him when he left."

"They are springing up everywhere now, the universities", said the young man thoughtfully. "It's the same in England, especially since you friars have come over, and the Franciscans, too. I'd like to see what yours is like. I've heard a good deal about it. It was founded by the King's own chaplain, I believe."

"Yes, Father Robert de Sorbon. He should be happy enough, with all the teachers there now."

"Yet, there is some sort of a war going on at your university at present, they tell me. . . . Why does that make you chuckle? Look here, you must be on your way. May I accompany you?"

"I shall be honored", said the Dominican with a little bow. "Yes, there is a war on amongst the learned men, and a strange enough war it is. A few of the students had a brawl with some good citizens . . . both sides were too full of wine for their own good, and there wouldn't have been much harm in it except that the students thought fit to fight the municipal guard, who tried to restore the King's peace. So they were arrested, and the Rector of the university demanded their instant liberation . . . which was refused. Now all this has happened before, a long time ago. At that time the university simply left Paris, and with it ten thousand students . . . so the municipal authorities gave in. But this time there was dissension about the issue. The secular teachers wanted to leave Paris again or at least suspend all teaching, but the Dominican and Franciscan teachers declared that they would not stop spreading knowledge just because a few students had behaved badly. They put it all much better than I can do it, but that is the gist of it, I think. So now the friars are the only ones who are teaching, which is about the last thing the secular teachers wanted. That's the war you mentioned."

"And here is the university. May I enter with you?"

"Surely, Messire Edward."

"Faith, how noisy they are in the hall over there."

"There's a Quodlibet going on, under Master Alexander of Hales. Anyone can ask any question he likes, and, my, the questions they ask sometimes."

"Let me have a look into this other hall . . . who is the Master there? A Franciscan, it seems. Never have I seen a finer face."

"That must be Brother Bonaventure . . . yes, it is. He's to the Franciscan Order what Friar Thomas is to the Order of St. Dominic."

"And that is?"

"The heart, Messire Edward".

"He looks . . . he looks as if he had been born without original sin, Brother Peter."

"Aye, Messire Edward. It's the same with Friar Thomas, though you couldn't find two people who look more different."

"They know each other?"

"They are great friends . . . so much so that people say they know each other's thoughts without saying a word."

"I'd like to stay and listen to Master Bonaventure for a while."

"I must deliver my manuscripts, Messire Edward."

"Ah, yes, I forgot. Perhaps on our way back—look at that multitude down there on the square: What are they doing? There must be at least fifteen hundred of them. I know . . . it's an assembly of those protesting against the friars."

"No, Messire Edward . . . that is one of Master Albert's regular lectures. He has to go out into the square because no lecture room will hold his listeners. They're so accustomed to that by now that the square is called the Place Maubert . . . the square of Maître Albert. He's that little man on a chair just on the right of the well; can you see his habit?"

"This is indeed a new age . . . "

"What did you say, Messire Edward?"

"Nothing. And is this Master Albert also such a holy man?"

"I think so, Messire Edward, though there are many who doubt it, because he is so often browsing over books that are dangerous . . . about alchemy and the black art and suchlike. So they're afraid of him. And over there is another man many people are afraid of . . . "

"That crusty fellow in the brown habit? A Franciscan again . . . "

"And a countryman of ours—Brother Roger Bacon".

"What is he putting on that other man's nose? It looks like two iron rings with a handle on each. Is he explaining an instrument of torture?"

"No, Messire Edward, though it's said to give the wearer a bad headache after a while. It's a contraption to make him see clearer."

"Magic? Surely a Franciscan should not indulge in that."

"Well, you never really know with Brother Roger Bacon. They say he tries everything he can think of, and that's saying a great deal. But this is not a magical thing. I had it explained to me: there is a little glass window enclosed in each of the two iron rings, and the glass is cut and polished in a certain way, so that a man whose eyesight has become weak from illness or old age will see things clear again. Master Roger has given one of them to our old

Friar Gudaric, and now he can read his breviary again, though he always gets a headache from it."

"And Brother Roger invented that contraption?"

"I don't know for sure, but he's certainly inventing new forms of it all the time. This is the fourth or fifth I've seen so far. They say he's always inventing things, and there is such a stink in his rooms at the university that no one likes to come and see him there. But I think it's not only the stink that keeps them away. He's a deep one, and I wouldn't like to swear that he's invoking Our Lord's help before every new *experimentum,* as he calls it. Once, in the middle of the night they heard a clap of thunder coming from his rooms . . . "

"Good Lord in heaven . . . "

"Aye . . . for quite a while they didn't dare to go and look, but in the end they did. They found the whole room devastated as if a dozen foul demons had trampled through it and Brother Roger lying in a corner with his face and hands burned and covered with blood. He babbled something about a great new discovery, but they didn't like it, and the Rector ordered that his room should be cleaned and all the poisons he kept there taken away. Six weeks later it was all astink again. He never has any money, of course, being a Franciscan, but he has a great gift for begging, and in the end he always gets what he wants. Lately he has been steeping himself in mathematics because he says that's what God is most interested in, too. But yesterday he said to Friar Thomas he felt sure he could design a contraption that could make a man fly like a bird."

"He must be mad."

"No doubt he is, but it's a clear-sighted madness. Master Albert loves him, though they quarrel fiercely about things with names as long as the cathedral is high. Friar Thomas loves him, too, but then he loves everybody, I think . . . except when someone is insincere. He can't bear that."

"Where is that Friar Thomas of yours?"

"In the next hall . . . here we are at last."

"Go and deliver your scripts, friend. I'll wait here for you."

"I'll be back at once."

"Don't hurry. I'd like to listen to the questions and answers."

"Master," said a thin voice, "what is the definition of life?"

"Self-motion", came the answer from the pulpit. "That which moves by itself is alive. You must die, so as to be moved by God instead of self."

Another student popped up.

"Master, I have a friend who is in constant danger of sinning against purity and chastity. He is fighting his base desires, but they seem to increase rather than diminish."

The huge friar hesitated a moment. Then he answered, very gently: "When a dog attacks a man and the man turns to fight the animal, it may tear him to pieces. But if he turns his back to the dog and walks on steadily, the animal will desist. Tell your friend to stop fighting his base desires, as they tend to increase the more he concentrates on them." The friar leaned forward, with a smile, big and round like the sun. "Tell him to concentrate on Our Lord instead, and he will find the power of his will strengthened beyond his own means."

"Here I am, back again, Messire Edward. Shall we go?"

"I'd like to stay on, but this man makes my brain whirl as if a giant were drumming on my helmet with a seven-foot sword."

"You are a soldier then, too, Messire Edward?"

"Wait . . . what is the little redhead asking him?"

"Master, how can we *know* that there is such a thing as truth? I know a man who doubts everything."

"You are mistaken; you cannot know such a man. A man who doubts everything would also have to doubt that he doubts everything. He would have to doubt his own existence, but if so, who is doubting? Also, you must admit that his life is in constant contradiction to his theory: doubting that there is food, he will eat it. The position of the complete sceptic is an impossible one; therefore there is no such person as a complete sceptic. There are, however, people who pretend to themselves that truth cannot be recognized, because the recognition of truth would encompass the necessity of moral obligation. Pontius Pilate asked, 'What is truth?' Shortly afterward he condemned a Man to death of whom he knew in truth that he was innocent."

A lean young man with eager eyes jumped to his feet. "Master, what is the definition of truth?"

"The conformity between the view of the intellect and the thing. And error is the nonconformity between the view of intellect and the thing."

"But are we able to know the whole of the truth about a thing?"

"No. Only God knows that." Was there a tinge of regret in the priest's voice? "But this by no means implies that our partial knowledge is not true. Assume that you find a piece of tin in the street. If you think, 'This is silver', your thought is erroneous. But if you think, 'This is metal', your thought is true and it remains true, although you do not know that I dropped the piece of tin and that it was once the part of a goblet. On the other hand I know both these things, and my knowledge is true, although I do not know that you will come and pick up the piece of tin. But God knows your facts and my facts and all other facts about it. He knows where it ultimately came from and where it ultimately will go to and every single stage in between. He knows all its properties, many of which may be entirely unknown to us, and he knows exactly what part it has in the purpose of the universe. And still your knowledge and mine remain true, incomplete as they are." The giant friar seemed to grow even larger. There was a deep rumble in his voice. "Beware, friend, of any philosopher who tells you that truth is not within the scope of our cognition.

Whatever his views are, they will lead to nothingness and perdition, and it is of such a man that St. Paul said: 'Take care not to let anyone cheat you with his philosophizings.' "

"Come, Brother Peter. This is all I can take in on one day. He's a large man, but even so I wonder how he can carry the weight of his brain. I'd rather fight fifty infidels single-handed than your Friar Thomas in an argument."

"Yes, it's heavy going if one isn't accustomed to it. It's above my own poor head anyway. But it's good to think that there are such brains in defense of what we believe in. It makes it easier for you when you get doubts of your own. It would be different if these men were vain and just trying to show off."

"Your Friar Thomas is not vain, then?"

"All he knows about vanity is its definition."

"Don't give it to me. I believe you. But you . . . you said it's above your head. Are you happy where you are?"

"Happy enough. It has set my thinking right and my feelings at rest. They both needed it badly. I do a good deal of gardening, among other things . . . I and Brother Robin. He used to be my varlet when we were in the world. Now we are equal in station, and I often think that he's a much better man than I am in many ways. He had no reason to live this kind of life, except that he wanted to be where I am. And it was far more difficult for him to call me Brother Peter than for me to call him Brother Robin. He didn't like having his moustache cut off, either."

"And . . . are you going to stay Brother Peter for the rest of your life? Ah, I think that was a sigh. Have you taken the vows already?"

"No. They wouldn't let me do that, though I wanted to when I entered."

"Perhaps one day you'll wish to exchange the garden shovel for a sword and your habit for armor again. There is happiness on the back of a horse, and I doubt whether you are cut out for a monk. You haven't taken the vows. That means you could leave at any time, doesn't it? And I can think of someone who might be glad of your service, Sir Piers Rudde."

The Dominican made a step back. "You know my name?"

"You were a knight in the retinue of my uncle, the Earl of Cornwall. Later you fought in the crusade under King Louis, my very gracious host. I am Edward Plantagenet."

"I knew that, too, my Prince. I have seen your royal father many a time in London. I wasn't sure at the beginning, but when you asked me to call you Messire Edward, I gathered that my Prince wished to see Paris in his own way."

The Prince smiled happily. "I am indebted to you for what you have shown to me. Think over what I have said to you. And if you ever need my help, let me know. It's yours for the asking. Thank you and good-bye, Sir Piers."

"God bless you, my Prince. And give my love to England."

* * *

William of St. Amour, Canon of Beauvais and Doctor of the university, sat sunk in his beautifully carved chair. He was a slight man with a keen, mobile face and cool, grey eyes, rarely free of a sparkle of irony. Neither his sober-looking friend Christian, who came from William's home town, nor Odo of Douai, massive and sagging, doubted the superiority of his mind not only over their own but also over that of the Rector of the Sorbonne, Jean de Gecteville, who was sitting on top of his large desk, wrapped in his wide black gown as though in a thundercloud.

"I wonder what the Pope will do", said Jean de Gecteville.

"My dear friend," said William of St. Amour, "we all know your astonishing talent for saying the obvious in an obvious way. Your sermons excel in it, and it has given you the reputation of being sound. We all wonder what the Pope will do. We've spent the last six weeks trying to think with his mind; at least I have. The trouble is that he's got his own troubles. King Manfred has proved in many ways a worthy son of the great Frederick. He's probably a greater nuisance to the Holy Father than his brother Conrad would have been if he hadn't died so conveniently only one year after his sire."

"There are rumors that Manfred had him poisoned", interposed Christian.

"There were the same rumors when Frederick died", shrugged William. "And why not? It is always difficult to believe that a tyrant has died a natural death. I must admit, though, that I had a sneaking kind of liking for Frederick. He was a magnificent old brute . . . the last great megalomaniac."

"Really?" asked Jean de Gecteville softly.

"Besides, he was witty, Jean, and I can forgive a man a great deal for that. Remember when he attacked the ships on which all the prelates sailed . . . it was a ghastly thing to do, no doubt, but do you know what he said when old Berard of Palermo reproached him for it? 'What could I do? They just would not walk on the water.' "

Odo of Douai threw his head back and laughed. The other remained impassive.

"I wonder whether you would have walked, dear Jean", said William. "However . . . Italy is in as bad a shape as ever."

"Yet King Louis refused the plea of the Pope to send the Duke of Anjou to Italy", mused Christian.

"Everybody knows that King Louis has a good heart. He did not wish to have the Italians chastised with scorpions", said William gently.

This time they all laughed.

"Alexander IV is new and has his hands full with little Manfred", resumed William. "He may not wish to make major changes within the Church at such a moment . . . and there's no doubt that the abolition of the mendicant orders will be a major change. Therefore we must prove to him that these beggars are not only a very disturbing influence but an actual danger to the life of the Church. That is why I called my treatise *About the Dangers of Modern Times.* At a time when the Church is assailed from without, she cannot afford such disruptive activities from within."

"I don't like saying it," grunted Jean de Gecteville, "but it's the most brilliant treatise I ever read. And thank God, it isn't witty."

"We had to wait long enough", said William bitterly. "I could have sworn that the holy beggars would stab us in the back when the university gave the only suitable reply to the impudence of the municipal authorities. But that alone was not good enough. The Pope is not Rector of the Sorbonne. He doesn't understand that with us the university comes first . . . the Holywaterfrogs might have won the day, saying that nothing must stop the spreading of knowledge. But now we've got them."

"Of fifteen masters, nine from the mendicant orders", said Jean de Gecteville. "It really is unbearable."

"Yes, I couldn't get a post for my own nephew", growled Odo of Douai.

"We've got them", repeated Christian. "That means the Franciscan General's treatise on the Eternal Gospel, I presume. What's ridden John of Parma to write that kind of thing, and in his position, too?"

"Whom the gods want to destroy, they strike with blindness first", smiled William. "There's enough heresy in the blessed thing to smash up half a dozen mendicant orders. The Dominicans will be swallowed up with their brown brothers, and good riddance. As you know, I have admitted in my treatise that they had their purpose and that the Church was wise as well as kind to permit their existence for a while. But now there is no more need for them. Bishops and parish priests are the real shepherds and teachers and not these friars. Why, the very next thing would have been that they wanted us to live on nothing, too. I, for one, refuse to go begging. It has never been the custom in my family. And believe me, we shall find strong support in the Holy Father's headquarters. If it were not for the political situation, I would not have a shred of doubt about the outcome of the issue, great as it is."

"When do you want us to be ready for the journey?" asked Christian.

"The beggars will receive their invitation to go and see the Holy Father today, just as we did, I suppose. The one thing that matters, the only essential thing, is that we are there before them. Not too long before them, but long enough to prepare a hot reception. The thing to do is to let them depart first."

"But you just said it was essential that we are there first", said Odo, shaking his massive head.

"And so it is, my slender friend. But it's no good arriving several months before them. I don't think they'll walk all the way, rule or no rule. The invitation of the Holy Father is ground enough for a dispensation even for their narrow minds. But even so, what kind of horses do you think they'll have?"

"Mules", said Odo with a fat chuckle.

"Exactly. And my Burgundian horses have no equal in France. Let them depart . . . we are bound to know when they leave, because they'll have to send their best men, and they'll be missing at the university. We shall depart the day after. Which means that we shall stand before the Holy Father at least one week before they arrive. Just right."

"Magnificent", said Christian. "You've thought of everything. They're lost."

"Amen", said Jean de Gecteville.

"I loathe them", said William. "I loathe their false humility, their asceticism . . . it's nothing but negative lust of the mind; the insane, insatiable curiosity of Roger Bacon; the way they all melt before little Bonaventure and that fantastic idea of Albert and Thomas to teach Aristotle the catechism. Good night, friends. I go before I sin against charity."

"Before!" laughed Odo. "But he really means it all, I believe."

"Yes . . . in spite of all his irony our William is an idealist," said Christian, "apart from being the finest brain of the time."

"I don't care what he is, as long as he and you smash the mendicants", said de Gecteville. "What matters is the university."

"Friend, this issue is bigger than the university", said Christian.

"There is no such thing", said de Gecteville emphatically.

* * *

There is nothing better than digging when a man cannot rid himself of his thoughts and when they are the kind that go in circles and swallow their own tails—and Brother Peter was digging away with a will.

He did not even look up when Brother Robin came to join him, and for a while they both worked, silent and intense, until Brother Robin could no longer keep back the secrets that were gnawing at his vitals.

"There's a storm on . . . something big. It's about the war with the university men."

Brother Peter only growled unintelligibly.

"Brother Kitchenmaster says there is danger that the Order will be dissolved by the Pope . . . he has it from the Prior himself. Doctor William of St. Amour has written an accusation against the Order and against the Franciscans, too, and sent it to the Pope, and it's very serious, says the Prior, says the Brother Kitchenmaster."

Brother Peter grunted something in which the name of William of St. Amour could be recognized; the rest was inaudible but in all likelihood not exactly charitable.

"And now the Pope has invited Big William to come and see him at Anagni and Master Albert and Master Thomas, too, and they'll set out tomorrow after the second Mass."

Brother Peter heaved up another shovelful of good, rich, brown earth. Then he paused for a moment and asked: "And the enemy? I mean . . . St. Amour? When is he going?"

"I don't know, ma . . . Brother Peter."

Suddenly Brother Peter rammed his shovel into the earth as a soldier might ram his sword into the heart of an enemy and walked away. Five minutes later he stood before Master Albert.

* * *

"I am not going to ask you how you know all this", said the great little friar with a weary smile. "I've been living in convents too long for that. No, we are not going on foot; it would take us too long, and His Holiness is urgent about the matter. We'll take the mules, and there is an old carriage in one of the outbuildings."

Brother Peter swallowed hard.

"Shall Brother Robin and I be allowed to be the coachmen, Father?"

"Would you like that? It is a good idea, I think. You've been here four years now; you can do with a little movement."

"Thank you, Father. But . . . the coach is *very* old and ramshackle, and Cunigonde and Portiuncula are just like the coach. Cunigonde is lazy, too, and Portiuncula is very fat and very obstinate."

"I suppose so, Brother Peter, but what can we do?"

"Doctor St. Amour has got good horses, Father; I've seen them. Burgundian breed."

"Doctor St. Amour is a fortunate man", said Albert stiffly.

"But, Father . . . he'll arrive long before us, and if I know anything about him, he's going to make the most of it."

"I am fully aware of that," said Albert, "and it is most regrettable. Unfortunately, there is nothing we can do about it. We have no money to buy horses and carriage. We are a mendicant order, Brother Peter."

"Yes, Father. May I have the afternoon free to . . . prepare things for the journey?"

"You may."

"Thank you, Father."

As the door closed behind Brother Peter, Albert thought for a fleeting moment that Brother Peter seemed to be up to something and that for once he could not guess what it was. But at once his thoughts were again engulfed by the worry and anxiety over the most vicious attack ever launched against the Order. He had not yet been able to see a copy of the *Dangers of Modern Times*—St. Amour was a wily opponent: he had sent it only to the Pope and to King Louis. From the Pope one copy had gone to the Master General of the Order, now the venerable old Humberto de Romanis, who did not dare to send it on to Paris. It was a lengthy document and would have taken a long time to copy. Thus all the Master General could do was to write to him and mention the tenor of the whole thing in his letter. Until they had arrived in Anagni, neither Albert nor Thomas could do anything. And there St. Amour would be waiting for them, and he and his friends in Italy would clamor for speedy settlement. Apart from the Master General's letter, the only available material was the Franciscan General's *Introduction to the Eternal Gospel,* and that wretched treatise was decidedly a step in the wrong direction. St. Amour would try to make the most of it, trust him for that. And if he succeeded, it was the end of all the work of St. Dominic and St. Francis . . . it was the end of his own lifework, the work of Thomas and Bonaventure and Roger Bacon. It was the end of the glorious imitation of Christ's poverty . . .

The end of the Order.

With his heavy head sunk on his folded hands, Master Albert prayed more fervently than at any time since he had entered religious life, over thirty years ago.

Brother Peter had by then left the convent of St. Jacques far behind him. When he had reached the palace, he turned to the left a little and marched straight into the courtyard of the royal stables. There he got hold of an official who had more tassels on his coat than the others and asked him to kindly convey a message to His Highness Edward of England. The stable official appraised him sharply. He had never before heard of a Dominican brother being drunk; why, they even watered the beer in the refectory until it was no more potent than a *tisane.* But what else could be the matter with him? However, they were big children and did not know the ways of the world.

"These are the royal stables, Brother."

"I have not lost either my eyesight or my sense of smell", said the friar, a trifle less patiently than was becoming to his cloth.

"But the entrance to the palace is over there, don't you see? And if it is a matter of begging, the time for that is at eight o'clock in the morning, when the King comes back from Mass. He's feeding four hundred every time."

"Friend, may the saints give me patience and you a little more intelligence. I know the difference between the palace and the stables, and I know the Christian habits of the good King, God bless him. I want nothing of him. All I want is that you send somebody to the King's guest, Prince Edward of England, and let him know that Brother Peter is here and would be happy if the noble Prince would spare him a few minutes of his time."

"You mean . . . you want His Highness of England to come here to the stables?"

"Exactly."

"He won't come."

"Why not let him make his own decision, friend?"

The stable official cleared his throat. But he remembered in time that the King had a very definite liking for mendicant monks; it was known that he had received some of them at his own table. Besides, the English had notoriously strange manners; perhaps it was a natural thing for an English prince to meet a beggar monk in the stables. In any case, it seemed to be the only way to get rid of the beggar monk.

"Very well", said the stable official. He instructed one of his men—with the friar listening attentively—and returned to his duties.

The friar had a good look at the horses, whistling softly through his teeth as he walked from one to the other. Burgundian breed took some beating. He was still examining proud heads and powerful limbs when a cheerful young voice asked: "Where is that friar of mine?"

"Here I am, Your Highness."

Prince Edward was a very different man from Messire Edward. Instead of a simple black coat without fur trimmings, he wore an undercoat of precious blue velvet, trimmed with white ermine and an overcoat of the same color, set with sapphires.

"I didn't think I'd see you again so quickly, Brother Peter, but I'm glad I do. Now tell me for what reason you stopped me from dancing with the beautiful ladies of this court."

It was the mildest of reproaches.

"My Prince has assured me that I could come to him whenever I needed his help . . . "

"Faith, so I did. What do you want of me?"

"You remember Master Thomas of Aquino at the university . . . "

The Prince laughed. "I'd find it difficult to forget him if I tried . . . his definitions have cost me many an hour of sleep."

"He must travel to Anagni to see the Holy Father. His Order has been calumnied by some of the secular doctors, who demand that it should be dissolved. I have to drive him to Anagni . . . in a carriage that looks as if it had been built from the remnants of Noah's Ark, and it is drawn by two mules who match it in age and quality. Whereas Doctor William of St. Amour has a fine carriage with Burgundian horses . . . and if he arrives first, he'll move heaven and hell against us."

"Charles!" shouted the Prince. "John!"

His men turned up as from nowhere, caps in hands.

"One of my best carriages, traveling, not ceremony. And two of my own horses . . . take Falcon and Terzel. Quick."

Charles and John ran.

"By Our Lady", said the Prince. "This man St. Amour may have the advantage in weight, but it will be of small avail to him. There are no horses in France to beat Falcon and Terzel except my stallion Boreas. I wish I had someone to bet with me. Do you think that fellow St. Amour would hold a hundred pounds in gold against me?"

"I doubt it, most gracious Prince", said Brother Peter, grinning. "God bless you . . . ah, the lovely creatures! Ah, the marvels!"

They were chestnuts, as graceful as they were strong, and they threw their fine heads up proudly as the Prince caressed them.

"This is Terzel, and this is Falcon. They are yours as long as you need them. I make one condition, though. When your mission is accomplished, you must bring them back to me yourself."

Brother Peter's eyes gleamed. "I am not my own master at present, as you know, my Prince. But when my mission is accomplished, I shall ask my superior for permission to bring Falcon, Terzel, and the carriage back to your service . . . and myself in the bargain."

"Faith," said Edward, "this is better than any wager. I hold you to it, Brother Peter. Give my respects to Master Thomas of Aquino and tell him we shall be happy to see him in England one day if his duties will permit it. And it won't be only the Black Friars in London and Oxford who'll be honored but the whole country."

"My Prince," said Brother Peter, "this is the finest present of them all."

"Off with you", laughed Edward. "And send that villain of the beautiful name where he belongs."

The horses were harnessed to the carriage. Brother Peter jumped on the driver's seat, took the reins and whip from Charles' fingers, shook his head with sheer delight, made a swift flickering movement with the reins, and off went the noble horses with such speed that a couple of stableboys near the entrance had to jump for their lives.

A few minutes later the carriage rolled into the large courtyard of the convent of St. Jacques, and it was perhaps not exactly sheer coincidence that they stopped just in front of Master Albert's window.

The great little man leaned out. "What have we here, Brother Peter?"

"Carriage and horses worthy of their fare, Father", said Brother Peter.

"I hope His Highness of England knows about that", said Master Albert.

"He does . . . and he wishes us well. But how did you know . . . ?"

"You'd better take his crest off the carriage", said Albert drily. But his eyes shone, and suddenly he broke into a chuckle. "If we do as well as you did with your 'preparations', we'll win", he said.

"I guarantee that we'll be in Anagni before Doctor St. Amour", said Piers, feeling on top of the world.

"It isn't exactly a humble statement, but I welcome it", said Albert.

* * *

Four cardinals, enthroned on a dais, their long, red trains flowing around them like molten lava, and in a wide semicircle before them a flowery field of ecclesiastics of all ranks, seculars and regulars, prelates, abbots, officials of the curia, and masters of theology and philosophy. Red and black prevailed to such an extent that the white of the Dominicans and the brown of the Franciscans seemed to stand out like alien elements. It was the purpose of the court to find out whether they were just that.

The Franciscan delegation consisted of the General, John of Parma, Frater Bonaventure, two abbots from Rome and Milan, and a few younger brothers of the Order; the Dominican delegation of the Magister General, frail old Humberto de Romanis, Master Albert, and Thomas of Aquino.

The Brothers Peter and Robin were sitting behind them, overawed and somewhat ill at ease.

Master Albert had invited John of Parma and Frater Bonaventure to share their journey in the fast carriage at their disposal. The Franciscan Order was not much better off for transport facilities than their Dominican cousins had been originally, and the invitation had been gratefully accepted.

Of Doctor William of St. Amour and his delegation there was no sign. "Unless they fly like birds, they will not catch up with us", Brother Peter had sworn, and Falcon and Terzel had made his words good.

As a reward he had asked permission for Brother Robin and himself to be present in court... "You won't find an Englishman who doesn't want to see a good fight" ... and Master Albert had procured it for them from the General.

It was as if the curia had decided to outdo even Falcon and Terzel's efforts in speed. They had only just reported their arrival when a letter came from Cardinal Eudes de Chateauroux asking them laconically to appear before the court within thirty-six hours. There seemed to be little doubt that this would only be a first hearing, but this first hearing could very well be decisive.

Thirty-six hours, and they had not even seen, let alone studied, the treatise demanding the dissolution of the mendicant Orders . . .

But Humberto de Romanis had had it copied several times. He gave one copy each to Master Albert and to Friar Thomas. They received it kneeling and returned at once to their cells.

At seven o'clock in the morning Brother Robin entered Thomas' cell with a pitcher of fresh water. He found Thomas on his knees in front of the crucifix. On the writing desk the copy of *The Dangers of Modern Times* was still rolled up. The bed was untouched. Thomas had spent the first twelve hours of his precious thirty-six in prayer. Only now he rose, gave Robin a friendly though somewhat absent-minded smile, and sat down to work.

The twelve hours of prayer were followed by twelve hours of work, and that by twelve hours of sleep. On the morning of the fateful court session he was ready. And here he was now, just in front of the two lay brothers, calmly waiting to be called up. Master Albert looked smaller than ever beside him, but there was so much magnetic power stored up in the tiny body that those around him . . . Thomas excepted . . . found it difficult to sit still. Yet Albert himself did not move at all. The old Master General sat slumped in his chair.

It started in the usual way, with the invocation of the Holy Ghost and the prayer to be protected from error.

Then Cardinal de Chateauroux spoke, white haired, round eyed, looking a little like an owl, Piers thought. But not a benevolent owl. Cardinal John Franciago, next to him, had a friendly, worried, round face. It was clear that he strongly disliked sitting in court. He would be at his best when feeding and clothing the poor or, as papal legate, persuading a disgruntled prince to try a little Christianity as the remedy for his troubles. Yet there was obstinacy around the corners of his small mouth. The mild man who didn't like to be taken for a mild man. The kind man, fearing all the time that his kindness might be traded upon. In fact he was a stern disciplinarian for just that reason.

Cardinal Hugh of St. Cher, tall, lean, bony, with an enormous forehead over dark, bushy eyebrows, the eyes perpetually half closed, a longish, heavy nose and thin lips, not the kind of man one would like to meet if one had a bad conscience, Piers thought.

And Cardinal John of Ursini, thickset, sturdy, with a pair of brilliant black eyes that seemed to observe everything, one of the Church's best experts of canonical law, his mind sharpened like a knife; he was the youngest of the four judges.

"... therefore we call up in defense against the aforesaid treatise Friar Thomas of Aquino, of the Order of Preachers."

Piers' chest heaved in an inaudible sigh.

Thomas rose, in his hand a sheaf of papers, rolled up, which made them look like a baton or a short scepter. Yet there was nothing of the general or ruler about him. A huge, big, kindly man was speaking in a clear, even voice.

Four years as a lay brother do not give a man much of philosophical and theological training. Piers did not understand even half of what Thomas said. But most of his life had been soldiering. He had seen the attacks of knights in full armor, galloping headlong into crashing collision; he had seen the wild, furious, lightning-quick *jihad* of Arabs and Saracens and many a single combat between warriors renowned for their strength and bravery. Never had he seen anything like this.

It seemed to him ... and not to him alone ... as if there were a gigantic, smoky, cloudy figure looming between Thomas and the four judges, the veritable materialization of the *Dangers of Modern Times.*

Into this specter sailed the huge, big, kindly man Thomas and began what could only be described as an act of demolition. He did not hit it. He did not stab it. He did not seem to be in the least angry against it. He just dismantled it, bit by bit, showing the pieces to the judges as if in deep regret that they were made of such bad quality. Piece after piece flecked off the body of the giant. Thomas dislodged its brain, scientifically and with the utmost care, and demonstrated, as a matter of objective interest, that it was eaten up by a cancerous growth. He removed its heart and exhibited it as a mass of synthetic little falsehoods instead of a working organ. Wherever in the *Dangers of Modern Times* there had been a quotation from Scripture, he plucked it out like a precious thing that had become soiled and sullied by its surroundings, and he seemed to lay it before the judges as something that now had to be purified, before he returned to go on with his quiet, systematic, murderous work.

There was no need for Piers to understand theological terms or to follow the trend of thought in order to see how the battle went. He saw Thomas' completely unruffled attitude, the spare but significant movements of head and hand. He saw Cardinal de Chateauroux nodding a few times and each time checking his nod hastily. Cardinal Franciago blew up his round cheeks, like a man laboring heavily under the impact of a terrific weight. Cardinal Ursini's gimlet eyes seemed to bore holes into the speaker, but his mouth was opened a little in utter fascination. Only Cardinal St. Cher's long, stern face remained impassive.

The work of demolition went on inexorably. The name of Doctor William of St. Amour was never mentioned; his personality was never touched. Not he but his treatise was the only object of attack, and of that gigantic, smoky, cloudy thing only shreds were left. Thomas set out to tear them into little pieces and then to pulverize the pieces, and all that with a devastating kind of angelic patience. Not once did he raise his voice.

At the last stage he seemed to be a man weeding a flowerbed very thoroughly and finding, in the end, that there were no flowers at all. Whereupon he stepped back, leaving between him and the judges not ruins, not even rubble, but something like a little heap of ashes, some specks of moldy substance to be cleaned off with a broom.

Then he bowed to the judges and sat down.

Cardinal de Chateauroux could not help looking at Cardinal Franciago next to him, only to meet the latter's eyes, sharing his own expression; quickly he looked away.

Piers had to make an immense effort to restrain a grin of huge dimensions. Brother Robin beside him and in exactly the same trouble stared steadfastly at the ceiling.

But the most difficult task was that of Master Albert. He had followed not only every phase but every shade of the fantastic battle. He had been watching the work of logic as a weapon of destruction, of logic personified, and of such force as even he had never encountered before. He would have liked to jump up and hug the pupil who had surpassed the master. Instead he had to sit where he was and wait for his own cue. He managed it. But the eyes in the enormous head were sparkling.

At long last Cardinal de Chateauroux recovered.

"The court will now hear Frater Bonaventure of the Order of Friars Minor."

The slender young monk, of whom everybody already said that he was a saint, rose, stepped forward, and bowed. On the very ashes of the enemy he began what was not so much a speech but a song. And this song had little if anything to do with the accusers of his Order. Brother Bonaventure did not fight anybody. He praised Christ who in his servant St. Francis had formed anew his own life of poverty. It was the most precious treasure, that divine poverty. No wonder it was envied. But he pleaded that he and his brethren would be allowed to keep it, for in the service of our Lady Poverty, St. Francis' ideal spouse, their hearts and minds were free for the love of Christ.

John of Parma wept. This was the glory that was St. Francis, God's most beloved fool, court jester of high heaven. Rightly they said that he had been able to speak the language of birds: for like all birds, he had only one song, the song of love, and death alone could make him cease singing it.

When Frater Bonaventure went back to his seat, Cardinal de Chateauroux bowed his head a little in the direction of the Franciscan General, a courteous gesture of acknowledgment; the defense of the Order of Friars Minor had been heard. Then he called up Master Albert.

The great little man needed only a few minutes to have the whole assembly under his spell. He alone made a reference to Doctor William of St. Amour and his friends, and only one: "These are the kind of people who killed Socrates", he said. Then he conjured up the tremendous picture of the Order in its entirety: of the work done every day in so many convents and in so many countries, of buildings built and books written, of sermons preached and sacraments administered, of missions undertaken and missions planned. And he asked whether all this, the life-work of St. Dominic and his sons, should be sacrificed and what values the accusers had to offer the Church, in order to make good a loss of such dimensions.

When he sat down, John of Parma looked up as if expecting that his turn would come next. But to his surprise Cardinal de Chateauroux shook his head and rose.

"The court will adjourn for council. His Holiness the Pope will be informed of our findings."

A short prayer followed. Then the four judges walked out.

Piers saw them passing in front of Thomas. He thought he saw Cardinal de Chateauroux give him a little nod, he felt almost certain that Cardinal Franciago blinked at him, and he could have sworn that Cardinal Ursini not only smiled but grinned cheerfully. Only Cardinal St. Cher walked by as impassive and deadly serious as ever.

But when the judges were alone, with the heavy doors closed behind them, St. Cher said: "I wonder whether the Blessed Trinity will ever have better representatives than the three defendants today."

After a council lasting little more than an hour, the judges announced to the Pope their decision that no further hearings of either side were necessary. One by one they made their reports.

And the Pope published the bull condemning the treatise *About the Dangers of Modern Times* as iniquitous and criminal. It was burned publicly in the presence of the Pope.

Three days later St. Amour and his friends arrived in Anagni.

* * *

"Christian of Beauvais, Odo of Douai, and Jean de Gecteville have signed their submission to the bull", said Humberto de Romanis.

"And St. Amour?" asked Albert.

"He refused."

"That means he is barred from all further teaching."

"Yes . . . and exiled to his estate in Burgundy. But I have more news for you, my son. John of Parma has been informed by the curia that his treatise *Introduction to the Eternal Gospel* will be given to Friar Thomas of Aquino for further report."

Albert winced a little. Then he said: "I understand. They do not wish to condemn anything on the instigation of St. Amour and his friends. It is a gesture of great courtesy to the mendicant orders."

"There will soon be a new General of the Order of Friars Minor", said Humberto de Romanis quietly. "Perhaps his name will be Bonaventure."

"He is only in his thirties . . . but they could not make a better choice."

"Friar Thomas will be made Master of Theology as soon as he has returned to Paris." The old Master General broke into a smile.

"Then I shall have to prepare him for the shock", said

Albert. "He cannot bear anything in connection with rank and dignity."

"I know how he feels", said Humberto de Romanis. His smile broadened. "It was the best I could do for him. The Holy Father wanted to make him an archbishop. It's taken me a long time to talk him out of it."

* * *

"Father Thomas," said Piers, "I've come to say good-bye. Master Albert has released me and Brother Robin. He says you will return to France by sea. And I must take the horses and carriage back to Prince Edward. From what I hear he has left Paris. I shall find him in London."

"You will enter his service there?"

"Yes, Father Thomas."

The round, black eyes were thoughtful.

"I am a soldier," said Piers, "and I have not seen my country for a very long time. As for poor Robin, he's been homesick ever since the chalk cliffs of the British coast went out of sight."

Still there was no answer.

"You once quoted to me," said Piers shyly, " 'Love and do what you like.' Don't you remember?"

At last Thomas smiled. "I shall miss you", he said simply.

Piers began to beam. "I have an invitation for you, Father Thomas: Prince Edward charged me to give you his respects and tell you that he will be happy to see you in England one day if your duties permit it. And he said that it won't be only the Black Friars in London and Oxford who will be honored but the entire country. Will you come, Father Thomas?"

"I hope so", said Thomas. His eyes were her eyes once more.

Piers knelt down. "Your blessing, Father Thomas."

The voice that had destroyed St. Amour prayed over him.

Piers rose. "No man can have a better shield", he said. "Don't forget me." And he rushed out of the cell.

Robin was waiting in the corridor.

"Just a moment, master", he said and dived into the cell Piers had just left. He reappeared again a few minutes later, looking very red in the face and trying to chew a moustache that wasn't there. Piers did his best not to notice it. But as they walked toward the tiny stable of the convent, Robin said hoarsely: "About Father Thomas . . . I can't understand it."

"What is it you can't understand?"

"That he isn't an Englishman."

Book Four

Chapter XVI

THE SUN SHONE MERRILY on the wide square and made the stained glass of Notre Dame glow; made sport with the painted half-timber houses of the square; lit up the helmets of the King's guards and the breastplates of their horses, all neatly aligned in a double row to keep free the broad aisle from the three portals of the cathedral to the very end of the square. And as if that were not enough, the sun cast a spell on the poorest of the poor, the inmates of the Hôtel Dieu, the world's oldest hospital, just opposite the cathedral; all its balconies were full of the aged and sick, with bandages and without, and they seemed to shine in the light, as if in a foretaste of the reward for their sufferings. They certainly had the best view of all—they could see the entire square, the banners hanging from all the windows, the masses and masses of people, the glittering array of soldiers.

Little Jean Galou, deep down in the crowd, plucked at his uncle's sleeve.

"I can't see anything, Uncle."

"There isn't anything to see. They're all still in the cathedral. Now you be quiet and wait."

"But I want to see the lovely horses . . . "

"The saints give me patience—for a whole hour I've had you sitting on my shoulders."

"Give him to me, Sieur Galou", said the Widow Michard kindly.

"You'll be sorry, good lady, he's heavy—he's worn a deep hole in my shoulder. There now, be careful not to smudge the good lady's Sunday dress with your dirty legs."

"Lovely horses . . . "

"Yes, that's the King's guards. Tell me, do you know what feast we have today?"

"Course I do. Corpus Christi".

"That's right", nodded the Widow Michard. "And who's given it to us?"

"The Holy Father."

"Right again. And what's the Holy Father's name?"

"Why have the guards no shields, Uncle?"

"They don't wear them on parade. Answer the lady's question, Jean; show that you've learned something. What is the Holy Father's name?"

"Clem—Clement."

"Well, yes, my boy, it's Clement, Clement IV. That's the present Holy Father, Pope Clement IV. But the feast was given us by the Pope before him, Urban IV, and before *him* came Alexander IV . . . "

"My, but you are well informed, Madame Michard . . . "

"You flatter me, monsieur."

"Well, you certainly know your Popes backwards. But forgive me if I correct you: the Holy Father established the feast, that's true enough, and such is his business, but given to us it was by our Master Thomas."

"Well, yes . . . "

"What do you mean, 'well, yes', madame?" The bowlegged little man became excited. "Without him it would have remained a little local feast up in Liége. But when our Master Thomas came back from England a few years ago, he was called to Italy, and the Pope wanted to make him a cardinal for all the work he'd done, and he said, 'Thank you a thousand times, Holy Father, but you just leave me as I am; me, I don't want a red hat.' So the Holy Father said that was too much modesty, and Master Thomas said no, it wasn't, on the contrary. 'How so?' says the Pope. 'I want much more than to be a cardinal', says Master Thomas. 'Why,' says the Pope, 'do you want to be Pope instead of me?' 'God forbid', says Master Thomas. 'I want this feast Corpus Christi to be made a feast of the universal Church from now till the end of the world', says he. Now Pope Urban IV, bless his memory, he came from simple stock, with his father only a cobbler just as I am, and simple people, they know how to drive a bargain, because they have to, so he made a great show of thinking it over, and then he says, 'Master Thomas,' he says, 'it's a big thing . . . but I'll give it to you, yes, I'll give it to you on the condition that you write me the liturgy for the feast.' 'Holy Father,' says Master Thomas, 'I'll do that and gladly', and was as pleased as can be, being what he is, a glutton for work. And that, my good Widow Michard, is how we've been given the Feast of Corpus Christi."

"I've never seen so many people . . . it's all black right up to the Seine."

"Well, you don't often get to see so many princes in one heap as there are today in Notre Dame."

"They say they've come because there'll be another crusade", said an old stonemason.

"What? Not under King Louis?" cried a shriveled little woman.

"Yes, they say he's going to take the Cross again."

"Hasn't he had enough from last time?"

"Well, that's sixteen years ago."

"That hasn't made him any younger. He looks pale, and he isn't in good health, if you ask me."

"Not another crusade, for the love of God . . . "

"Don't wail, Mother; you've had sixteen years of blessed peace, haven't you?"

"Yes, and why?" interposed a red-faced baker. "Because we're keeping the infidels at bay, quite apart from fighting for the Holy Places."

"But the infidels are far away, across the sea. Why not leave them there in peace? . . . That's what I say."

The baker smiled condescendingly. "Because you don't know better, Mother Culepin. They aren't only across the sea, and they aren't so far away either. They're holding the better half of Spain, and that's near enough. They've made a ring around us from one end of the world to the other, and unless we pierce it from time to time, they'll strangle us."

"Ah, bah, keep me away from politics."

A black-coated lawyer turned round, with a certain amount of effort.

"Well, then, Mother . . . how would you like it if a troop of turbaned heathens settled down in Paris, and you couldn't go to Mass at Notre Dame because it was turned into a mosque for Allah and Mohammed?"

"What nonsense, Maître Gaspard. I'd go and hit them over the turban with my frying pan, and so would everybody else. But that couldn't ever happen."

"Maybe not. But do you think that Notre Dame is a holier place than Bethlehem and Nazareth?"

"He's caught you there, Mother Culepin. Ah, yes, lawyers have brains. You better shoulder your frying pan and go with the others on crusade."

The stonemason shook his head. "You don't need to go on a crusade if you want to meet Moslems and pagans and heretics . . . you can have that here in France, too. What do I say, in France! Here in Paris, and the learned men are sometimes the worst."

"Did you hear that, Father?" asked a thin-faced little student.

"Yes, and I'm afraid it's quite true." The priest looked grave. "The Moslem poison is working. I've heard professors of the university teach the Averroist heresy to Christian men: that the world is eternal, that God cannot bestow personal immortality, that there is no such thing as Divine Providence . . . "

"What? Then what are we all praying for?" asked Mother Culepin shrilly.

"Exactly. The trouble is that there is no one to *prove* them wrong."

"Don't you know Master Thomas, Father?" The little student's eyes shone. "I've been to his lectures many a time, and I've heard him deal with those well poisoners . . . oh, the beautiful fighting it was. He got them down on their knees every time."

"I wish he'd try himself on Master Siger of Brabant", sighed the priest; "that's the most dangerous of them all. There hasn't been such a dialectician in the world since Abelard!"

"But Master Thomas has challenged him, Father . . . challenged him publicly . . . and he didn't accept."

"I don't know—perhaps it is better so. I've heard Master Siger speak . . . I can't imagine him beaten in an argument."

"That's because you haven't heard Master Thomas", insisted the student.

"It would be much better if they'd leave all that arguing and go back to simple faith", said the priest impatiently. "Why can't they trust the saintly men of the past, like St. Augustine, and St. Gregory, and St. Chrysostom? They knew what they were talking about."

"Yes, but they're not here to defend what they said. And even a saint needn't be infallible."

"Now, that's a very audacious thing to say, young man: Where did you pick that up, if I may ask?"

"From Master Thomas, Father. And he says you can't keep reason in chains all the time. It's been given to us by God so that we should use it, but use it in the right way."

"I'm not sure whether that's not very wrong, my dear young man. When an argument starts by doubting the saints, that is a very dangerous sign. I'm not sure whether there is much difference between Master Siger and your Master Thomas, if any at all."

"Better go and listen to him, Father. You needn't argue with him . . . if you don't feel up to it. Just listen . . . "

The priest shook his head sadly.

"I was at his Mass this morning . . . a very wonderful

thing it is. It would be a great pity if he turned out to be a heretic."

"If Master Thomas is a heretic, I'm a heretic myself."

"Careful, young man, careful . . . "

"Look, they're coming out."

The cheers were deafening as the tall, gaunt figure of King Louis became visible in the middle portal of the cathedral, but again many people remarked on his paleness, enhanced by his coat and surtout of red velvet, trimmed with ermine. As usual he was wearing an old-fashioned and formless hat. The Parisians never ceased to joke about this eccentricity and Queen Margaret's horror of it.

An army of glittering figures followed, led by Prince Philip, the King's son.

"Who's the tall, fair noble in the blue coat, friend?"

"I don't know . . . might be the Duke of Anjou, the brother of the King."

"Now, don't you give a stranger wrong information, Jacques . . . the Duke of Anjou isn't in France at all; he's been made King of Sicily and is teaching King Manfred good manners in his own way."

"Ah?"

"Yes . . . and that means I wouldn't like to be King Manfred. The noble in the blue coat is Prince Edward of England and a very good friend of our King, I may say."

"I am greatly obliged to you."

"For nothing, friend. One can't know all the princes, can one? A very fine young man, Prince Edward, and a great warrior, they say. Most likely he's come over to join the crusade, though he's only just settled a civil war in his own country."

"There's Bishop Tempier."

"Those are Spanish nobles, aren't they?"

"Look at the lovely lady, all in red."

"She's not Spanish; she's Italian. I saw her at Mass the other day with her husband . . . he's the elegant man just behind her with the beautiful hair. And do you know who she is? Father Lefebvre told me: she's a sister of our Master Thomas."

"Of my Master Thomas?" The young student leaned forward eagerly. "Let me have a look at her . . . by Our Lady, she's almost as lovely as his mind."

A tall knight stopped abruptly. "Take this for what you've just said." He smiled and went on.

"What is it? What has he given you?"

"A whole purse of gold!" stammered the student. "Six—eight—ten pieces!"

"Lucky boy", said the Sieur Galou. "What are you going to do with it all?"

"I can't believe it. Now I can buy my own books and really good paper and sleep in a clean bed. I can't believe it . . . "

"You didn't even thank him", said the Widow Michard reproachfully.

"I had no time . . . he said and was gone, and here is all this gold."

"Who was it, anyway?" asked the stonemason.

"I don't know. He spoke without an accent, but the cut of his dress was like that of an Englishman. Perhaps he's one of the nobles of Prince Edward's retinue."

"You're right", nodded the lawyer. "He was dressed in blue, as they all are."

The baker shook his head. "But why should he give a little student of Paris a whole purse of gold?"

"Are you seriously asking me why an Englishman behaves as he does?" The lawyer snorted. "Master Thomas himself couldn't answer that question."

* * *

"My Lord King," said Prince Edward, "permit me to present my cousin Henry of Almaine . . . Lord Rudde of Foregay . . . Sir Geoffrey Langley . . . "

"What an unhappy king I am", said Louis with his slow, winning smile, "to meet such splendid knights and yet to be deprived of their help now that I set out again to beat the enemy of the Cross."

"I regret it no less than you, my Lord King," said Prince Edward, "but the wounds caused by the civil war in Britain are still too fresh for me to join you at once. My father will not let me go as yet. In a year or two, God willing, I shall join you, though, and I hope you will leave a few of the circumcised dogs for me, my knights, and my archers."

"Your great-uncle Coeur-de-Lion could not have given me a more royal answer. I am told you resemble him in action as well as words."

"King Richard", said Edward, "could split a steel mace into halves with one stroke of his sword." The unmistakable envy in his tone broadened Louis' smile.

"He was not your age when he performed that feat. And when he was your age he had not yet conquered a rebellious town as you have. You were the first on the wall of Northampton, they tell me . . . and you spared young Simon de Montfort's life."

"He almost lost his own over it, Royal France", exclaimed young Henry of Almaine.

"In that case," said Louis, "Lord Rudde of Foregay cannot have been near him, or he would have prevented the danger somehow."

"It is true", said Lord Rudde. "I was fighting half a mile away on that day. But I very much fear my presence would have changed very little. I was with my Prince when he opened a safe road between London and Winchester . . . which meant that we had to defeat the most dangerous outlawed knight, Adam Gurdon and his men. He was more of a Goliath than an Adam. And my Prince insisted on single combat."

"Adam Gurdon had the right to single combat. He was an outlaw, but of knightly stock."

"My Prince had knights enough with him who could have served for the purpose."

"Piers," said Edward, "you are just jealous, that is all. He always wants to do my work for me."

"He has not changed much, then", said King Louis. "He did the work of seven knights when he fought under the oriflamme at Damiette."

"My Lord King remembers me", said Piers, astonished.

"I would remember you if you had been a lesser man than you were", said Louis quietly. "You were Sir Piers Rudde, then, and you had with you an English varlet, tall, with a fair moustache."

"It is a little grey now, my Lord King, but Robin Cherrywoode is alive and with me still", said Piers, shaking his head in genuine if unceremonious admiration.

"I was lucky", laughed Edward. "I picked Rudde up here in Paris at my first stay . . . in the black and white habit of the Friars Preacher, together with his precious Robin. Even so I had to settle the issue with my uncle Cornwall, in whose retinue he had been a very long time ago."

"You, a lay brother, Lord Rudde? I wonder how you could find your way back into the world then", said Louis, and for the first time his voice did not sound quite steady. "Why, if my duty did not keep me where I am . . . may you never regret it that you left. Which convent was it? St. Jacques? The Prior will be here at our banquet presently, Friar Hugh of Soissons, and with him Master Thomas of Aquino."

"I know Master Thomas, my Lord King", said Piers.

"How they all begin to beam when his name is mentioned . . . myself included", smiled Louis. "Tis a great man, and today we have more reason than any other day for being grateful to him. By the way, his sister is with us too today—the Countess of San Severino, with her husband. You know her too? Have you already offered her your respects?"

"I only saw her with her husband in the cathedral, my Lord King."

"You will find them in the Venetian hall, I believe", said Louis kindly, and Piers bowed, feeling, rightly or wrongly, that the King was reading him like a book.

Louis began to talk to Sir Geoffrey Langley, and soon afterward Prince Philip came to present a number of nobles from Flanders.

"He's getting old," said Edward when they were out of earshot, "but what a man he is. I wish we could join him straightaway. Go and see your friends, Piers; I know you'd like to, and there may be little opportunity for you to exchange words with them during the banquet."

"Thank you, my Prince."

Where was the Venetian hall? Ah, yes, the very next one, full of Venetian mirrors. He felt his heart thumping alarmingly. How one could lie while saying what was true . . . he had indeed seen her only during Mass in the cathedral. But . . . it had been an event more stirring than the assault on Northampton. She had seen him, too, and she had given him her smile, for one breathtaking moment, before her eyes were fixed again on the altar, where her brother celebrated his own, his very own Mass. And in that one moment they had met again and had been close to each other and glad of each other's existence. In that one moment the space across bowed heads and bejeweled necks had been filled with all the sights that made the picture of his life, and she had looked upon it and judged that it was good. "I only saw her with her husband in the cathedral . . . "

And there she was, and he would see her from very near now. Perhaps there was a little grey in her hair by now—there had been much of that in the circlet of hair around her brother's head and in his little forelock when he turned round to embrace kings and beggars in his benediction. She was not so much younger than Thomas, though he had aged before his time.

"Piers! Sir Piers . . . no, they've made you a baron now; I beg your pardon. Ruggiero . . . here is Piers. I told you it was he in the cathedral. I am glad . . . I am so glad . . . "

She did look changed. Ripened, not aged, slender and full-blown, her eyes sparkling.

He tore himself away to greet Ruggiero, magnificently dressed and smiling courteously, and somehow he found himself saying: "Faith, how different you look, you two, than on the day we saw each other last. I can still see two venerable little nuns boarding the *Conchita* . . . "

Theodora's laughter was just a trifle uneasy. Ruggiero smiled coldly. "Much has happened since then", he said. "I hear your Prince is not taking the Cross with the rest of us."

"At least not at once . . . " Piers gave him a surprised look. "Are you . . . I mean, are you yourself considering . . . ?"

"I am not considering. I am taking the Cross. Does that surprise you, my Lord Rudde?"

"Not from the son of your father", Piers bowed to him. He did not look at Theodora, but he knew now that all was not well and that it would be difficult, perhaps impossible, to find out more.

"Did you arrive from Spain?" he asked lightly.

"No, from Rocca Secca", replied Theodora. "We have had it rebuilt."

"King Charles has been most gracious and helpful", drawled Ruggiero.

That was the Duke of Anjou, of course . . . one had to get used to all these new titles, including one's own.

"Thomas will be at the banquet," said Theodora, "but I don't know where they'll place him; there are hundreds of guests, and it's very formal . . . there goes the trumpet."

It was blown by a herald dressed in a tabard embroidered with the lilies of France.

Other heralds and palace officials tried to get the King's guests into formation; it was not an easy task, for they had to maintain all the courtesy and formalities due to personages of high rank, and yet it had to be done quickly.

"I don't think I shall be able to talk to Thomas", said Theodora. Ruggiero and Piers had already bowed to each other, and she saw that her husband was becoming impatient. She added hastily, "I shall pay him a visit at his convent tomorrow morning." Piers saw her eyes flash upward as he bowed to her. When he raised his head again, she was already walking beside her husband, staring straight ahead.

It was time to resume his place in the retinue of the Prince, he thought. But there was Edward, entering the Venetian hall himself, followed by his cousin and Sir Geoffrey . . . of course, the banquet hall was on the other side, and the guests were entering in accordance with their rank, the lesser ones first, and the King himself last, so that at the moment of his entry the banquet could commence at once. Only now it occurred to him how often he had pictured to himself his first meeting with Theodora as equals in rank—though of course both the names of Aquino and of San Severino were not only older but also related to royal and imperial blood—and now it did not seem to matter at all. Tomorrow morning she was going to visit her brother Thomas in his convent. Ruggiero, too, had changed. There was something at once petulant and mulish about him . . . or was it just hurt dignity because he hated to be reminded of "Mother Beatrice"? There was still something of the spoiled boy about him.

The banquet hall was huge and oblong, with the seat of the King under a canopy at one of the narrow sides. Four to five hundred guests flanked the tables, graced by an equal number of dishes, half hidden under beautiful flower arrangements. There was a silver goblet, knife, and spoon in front of every guest and a chased silver platter between him and the guest opposite. Liveried attendants filled and refilled the goblets, presented the dishes, and perfumed the air from time to time with little bellows of incense. The chairs, though elaborately carved, were stiff and straight . . . to the secret regret of the elegants who preferred to recline on couches at their meals.

"One would think", sighed the beautiful Countess of Chatillon, "that our dear King were ruling Sparta instead of France."

The Sire de Joinville, opposite her, caressed his moustache.

"I'll wager our dear friars do not think so", he said, grinning cheerfully.

"Oh, they . . . poor men, how glad they must be to get this kind of food for once." With dainty fingers she wrenched the white meat off the breast of a magnificent peacock, whose head and tail with all its feathers had been put back after the roasting, bathed it in the spicy sauce that filled a little ship of silver, and began to eat.

About a hundred such peacocks were spaced out all along the table at regular distances.

The minstrels in their gallery began to play, and as long as the first onslaught on the food lasted one could hear them playing. Later, after the third or fourth filling of the goblets, the conversation became too animated for that.

Piers thought: tomorrow she is going to visit Thomas at the convent of St. Jacques. Tomorrow morning. Did she tell him that because she wanted him to be there? Did it mean that this would be an opportunity for them to talk alone? That Ruggiero was not coming with her? Or was he flattering himself, and her remark had no significance beyond the fact it had stated?

She had been uneasy, and it had been due to her husband's presence. Something was wrong between them—or so it seemed. She was worried . . . and she could not say, could not say before San Severino, what it was about. But tomorrow morning she would visit her brother at the convent. Yes, she wanted him to be there. She wanted him to be there for a reason.

There was no question of flattering oneself. Her reason was not Piers Rudde. Her reason was that something was wrong between her and her husband. But what use could he be to her in such circumstances?

It was understandable that she should go to see her brother about it—who was not only her brother but also probably the wisest man of his age. And Ruggiero went on the crusade . . . Now if . . .

"Piers! Piers!"

"Yes, my Prince . . . ?"

"We thought you were falling asleep. Do you know I've called you five times? You don't eat, you don't drink. We've been in Paris only one day, or I would say you've fallen in love."

"The last time I fell in love", said Piers, and he managed a smile, "was very many years ago."

"And it has made you the sworn enemy of women, it seems. Ah, it's no good denying it. I tried hard enough to open the door for the many lovely ladies in Britain who wished to become Lady Rudde of Foregay, and yet . . . "

"My Prince . . . "

"But at least you might eat and drink . . . you're as bad as Master Thomas; look at him . . . "

Master Thomas was sitting fairly far away, but Piers could see that he was far away in more than space. He was sitting upright in his chair, a mountain of black and white, and his side of the silver platter was untouched. He could not have heard Prince Edward's words . . . nor could Theodora, although she and Ruggiero were sitting nearer: they were engaged in conversation with a knight and a lady, neither of whom was known to Piers. Looking back at the Prince, Piers saw that he was now talking to the King, and he heaved a sigh of relief. His fondness for Edward had grown to as deep and valuable a friendship as their difference in rank permitted, and it had been strengthened by all the joys and worries, triumphs and disappointments they had gone through together. Edward was a master anyone could be proud to serve, just, courageous, loyal to his friends—but his teasing was not always in the finest taste, especially after his attempt to make the noble Lady Edith Norham Lady Rudde of Foregay had failed, which had made him sulk angrily for several months.

The Lady Edith Norham was a lovely creature, elegant, witty, and of great wealth. It was incomprehensible that a man in his senses should refuse point blank to marry her.

King Louis was having his goblet filled . . . half with

wine and half with water, as was his wont. It was a monastic habit. But then, he might have been the abbot of a monastery, stern and benevolent, his justice equal to his mercy, and both excelled by his charity. There was no doubt that he would have liked to live for God alone and that only his sense of duty kept him on his throne. Piers dimly remembered how Master Thomas had once shown him a book by Plato in which the sage said that the best ruler was he who did not really wish to rule at all, and several people had told him about a mysterious monk who had visited Louis at his castle in Hyères and told him that no empire had ever gone down or changed its ruler but for lack of justice in the land. The King had spent many hours with the monk alone and then beseeched him to stay on, but the monk had departed the same day, never to return.

Everyone could appeal to Louis' jurisdiction directly, from the street beggar to the highest noble. But no one would do so unless he felt certain that he had right on his side.

"And despite all your burdens," Edward had once said to him, "despite that tremendous amount of work, government of the state, administration, supervision of all your officials, jurisdiction, official and private charities, audiences, receptions, forming of new laws, care for your own family, and a hundred things more, you still find time to listen to the Horae, to hear Mass twice a day and Vespers and Compline."

"Not in spite of it," King Louis answered, "because of it. Without that I could never do my work."

The huge, golden banner of France was hung up just behind his seat; and Piers could not help thinking of the many pictures of saints he had seen in old churches in Italy, painted in the Byzantine manner on a golden background. There were many who talked of Louis as being a saint, though perhaps it was wrong to talk like that about anybody who had not yet been born in heaven.

A long way further up the table, the Prior of St. Jacques

was becoming seriously worried. Friar Hugh of Soissons was a strong believer in doing the right thing at the right time. When he prayed, he prayed. When he worked, he worked. And when he was . . . for once . . . invited to the King's table, why, then he behaved as was expected from a guest. He had eaten well, he had had two goblets of watered wine, and he had exchanged polite words with old Madame de Nangis on his right and the King's Almoner on his left. Whereas Master Thomas, opposite him, was doing what he so often did in the refectory . . . he was dreaming. What was more, he did not even hide that he was dreaming. He was sitting there, towering high over everybody else, with his eyes half closed; from time to time he toyed with his goblet; once he had muttered something to himself . . . but when the poor good lady on his right had eagerly asked, "What did you say, my Father?" he had given her no answer. It was most irritating. In the refectory Friar Reginald of Piperno would see to it that he had his food. But one could not very well reach across the table and take his arm, not at the King's banquet. Now he was making curious little gestures with his fingers, this way round, that way round, this way round . . . as if he were weighing up something. Fortunately, very fortunately, no one seemed to pay much attention. Still, it was worrying. He had had that habit for a long time, but it seemed to be becoming worse and worse.

What Prior Hugh of Soissons did not know was that a battle was being fought in the banquet hall . . . the battle of one man against a huge specter that had stalked through the world for hundreds of years, causing misery, strife, and bloodshed wherever it passed. As so often in the world of thought as well as of action, the battle had been started by a tiny, trifling incident. The Countess of Chatillon had offered Master Thomas a piece of roast peacock. He had declined the offer with an apologetic smile, but he had looked at the peacock.

Peacocks. Was it not Master Albert who had mentioned

in *De avibus* that they had come from Persia? That the kings of Persia kept thousands of them in their gardens, walking flowerbeds, incredibly beautiful, perfect to look at, but their voices were horrible, and . . . they could not fly. A glittering, dazzling thing . . . until it showed its imperfection. Like so many things, like so many ideas that had come from that same region. Like the thought of Manes, the mystic who had committed the crime of all crimes: to divide the kingdom of heaven into black and white. He had condemned nature as evil, a creation of the black kingdom; he had thus accused God, the black God, of being the author of evil; he had preached that marriage was an abomination because it was legalized impurity. Again and again new children were born to this ghastly heresy. Pope Leo I in the fifth century had had to combat a belief, which, if spread over the earth, would lead to the end of man, to his uncreation. And it was in order to fight it, when it had gained life again in the Albigensians, that St. Dominic had founded the Order of Preachers fifty years ago. They talked of purity when they meant sterility; they talked of God when they meant Satan. Holy Scripture stood against them like the sword of an archangel; marriage was sanctified by the presence of Christ at the wedding feast of Cana; St. Paul had testified for it not once but many times. Human nature was redeemed through Christ, who had "not disdained to partake in it". Human nature had overcome death in Christ. And just as nature had been good in the beginning, when God "looked on all things and saw that they were good", so human nature was to be brought to the glory of the Resurrection. Thus the difference between Christians and Manichees was the difference between joy and woe, between triumph and despair.

But how to prove the error of this heresy to those who did not accept Holy Scripture as the measure? How to prove that evil was not what it seemed to be, an entity of equal strength, perhaps of equal right as the Good?

It was at this stage that Prior Hugh of Soissons saw

Master Thomas' fingers move as if they were weighing something. King Louis was still talking to Prince Edward. De Joinville was laughing at a witticism of the pretty Countess of Chatillon. The wine, mixed with honey and spices, had loosened all the tongues. The minstrels in the gallery ceased to play. They had been inaudible during their last two songs.

But the general noise was inaudible to Thomas.

Entity. Being. Entity. But . . . but was evil an entity at all? What caused evil? Imperfection in activity . . . imperfection of matter . . .

It could not stand alone. It could not exist by itself. It had to use a preexisting Good. It was an imperfection of the Good, a privation of the Good, a perversion of the Good. By itself? By itself . . . it was . . . nothing. By itself it had no being. It was *not* an entity . . .

The Prior's eyes widened, first in bewilderment, then in downright horror. De Joinville saw it and broke off in the middle of a sentence. Astonished, the Countess of Chatillon looked in the same direction, and others followed her example. Thus an island of silence was formed, and it spread rapidly. Within a few seconds there was silence in the entire hall, though no one really knew why, as so often happens in large assemblies.

The Prior's horror was not without justification. For the immense friar opposite him had slowly raised his right arm up to heaven and his hand closed to a fist. And then this fist, like the club of Hercules himself, came down with an earsplitting crash in the middle of the table, which it shook like an earthquake. Plates and goblets rattled, saucers jumped, the poor Prior jerked his chair back to escape from an avalanche of cooked river trout pouring over the tablecloth.

"And *that* settles the Manichees", thundered Thomas.

Breathless silence. Then a short titter here and there. No one dared laugh outright. Everybody was staring at the stern, quiet face of the King . . . everybody except the culprit, who still seemed to be a man in a dream.

Louis looked at Thomas. He saw the huge face of the friar, rapt in joy, beaming, supremely happy, utterly unaware of a breach of etiquette the like of which the hall had never seen before.

The King leaned back. "Briancourt", he said.

The name was not familiar to the majority of the assembly. Had the King asked for the captain of his guards?

A lean man in simple black dress appeared and made obeisance.

"Briancourt, go to Master Thomas over there—and take down the argument he just found lest he forget it."

Obediently the secretary walked up the aisle until he reached Thomas. And such was the strength of the King's personality that even now there was silence.

Thomas woke up at last. He saw Briancourt with a writing table in his hand. He knew him for what he was. Briancourt explained in a whisper. Thomas looked at the King and bowed, this mountain of a man, with the natural grace and elegance of a great noble. The King inclined his head.

Piers saw it all. He felt, strangely, that there was a special and personal kind of understanding between this King who might have been a friar and this friar who might have been a king. That they had something in common in which no one else in this hall had a share. That everyone else was dwarfed by them, almost to the point of nonexistence. And across these feelings zigzagged, swift as a silvery fish, a queer thought which seemed to have no relevance at all: that there was bound to be great courtesy in heaven.

Calmly Thomas began to dictate to Briancourt a sequence of thoughts which tore evil from its throne of being an entity, a principle in its own right, and relegated it to the status of a parasite.

Conversation was resumed, sporadically at first, but soon in full force.

The Countess of Chatillon shook her pretty head. "Upon my faith, I do not understand. Why, it all started with me offering the good friar some of this excellent peacock. A peacock! Now what can that have made him think of, I wonder?" And she laughed, a little shrilly.

Not without difficulty, de Joinville swallowed the obvious answer.

* * *

When Theodora arrived at the convent of St. Jacques, at the official visitors' hour, she was made to wait a long while. It did not improve her temper. She had looked and looked at the gate, but there had been no sign of Piers. Hadn't she made it clear enough that she expected to see him? And now apparently she could not see her brother either. "I shall tell him at once", the Brother Doorkeeper had said, but that was half an hour ago, or so it seemed to her. She began to pace up and down the small, meagerly furnished visitors' room.

At long last the door opened . . . but it was not Thomas who came in. It was a pale, middle-aged monk with frightened eyes.

"I am Friar Reginald of Piperno, most noble lady. You are waiting for your brother, Master Thomas of Aquino."

"I have been waiting for him for some while now, yes . . . Friar . . . "

"Reginald. Reginald of Piperno. I know you have been waiting. It is . . . he is . . . he will be here very shortly . . . I hope."

Suddenly she saw that his hands were trembling.

"For the love of God, I hope nothing has happened to him?"

"N-no . . . that is to say . . . "

"He is not ill, is he?"

"No, no, he is not ill, he . . . he will be here very soon now, I think . . . if you will excuse me . . . "

Friar Reginald fled. She could hear the hasty pat-pat-pat of his feet on the stone floor outside.

She sat down on one of the heavy, artless chairs. She was

frightened herself now. Something must have happened. She had never seen a more terrified man, except Ruggiero that night on board the *Conchita* when the drunken sailor had tried to enter their cabin at night. But it wasn't the same kind of terror. The friar had looked, as if . . . as if he had seen a ghost. She crossed herself, murmured a quick Ave, crossed herself again, pushed her little chin forward, and sat bolt upright, waiting for what was to come. It was exactly what her mother would have done in the circumstances. Without knowing it, she was becoming more and more like her.

Footsteps? Yes . . . and this time not the hasty pat-pat-pat of Friar Reginald. She jumped to her feet. As Thomas came in, she rushed up to him, the words tumbling from her. "Oh, there you are, thank God! What was it? What has happened . . . are you well?"

He patted her hands. "I am quite well. I am sorry you had to wait. I was . . . detained in the chapel."

"I'm so glad . . . " she had tears in her eyes now. "Friar Reginald came to tell me . . . "

"What did he tell you?" asked Thomas, staring at the window.

"He said . . . you would be here shortly; but he seemed so strange . . . so frightened of something; I got quite frightened, too."

He turned to look at her. "There is nothing to be frightened about", he said. He sat down. He began to smile, an easy, natural smile. "I am sorry I made you wait", he repeated. "And now I have only a few minutes left."

She made a face at him. "I shall complain about you to the Prior," she decided, "and then you will be in disgrace. I imagine he has not yet forgotten that you tried to smother him with fish and to smash King Louis' best table. Now, dearest, if you dare to look contrite about it, I shall never forgive you. If I were an intelligent woman I would ask you what it was that you found, but as it is, I shall carefully refrain from asking."

He chuckled. "You will never grow up, Theodora."
"In a minute I shall quote Scripture at you", she threatened.
"Flippant girl." He leaned forward. "I believe you have painted your face. You have, too."
"Well, yes. Sinful, isn't it?"
"What do you do it for?" he asked gravely.
"My lips are too pale, and so are my cheeks. I suppose I have not got as much blood as you have, dearest. And I wish to look my best."
"You wish to please your husband?"
"Yes", said she quietly. "I wish to please my husband."
"It is not sinful", said Thomas thoughtfully. "I know that some of the Fathers will not agree with me, but I cannot regard it as sinful."
Her eyes were dancing now. "What if I were unmarried? Would it be sinful then?"
He pondered over that in all seriousness.
"For a *good* reason it should be permitted", he decided.
Somehow she felt touched. "You are the best, dearest brother a girl can have. Fancy you having time for my trifling nonsense. I was so proud of you yesterday in the cathedral. They tell me you wrote the hymn, too, that they sang. I have started learning it; I don't know it by heart yet, but I will. It's so . . . so full of joy. *Sit laus plena, sit sonora, sit jucunda, sit decora mentis jubilatio.* . . . That's what I love most about you; you are like . . . like a cherub, a big, large, enormous cherub; don't laugh at me! I mean it. And you have done what Rainald could not do . . . what he should have done, perhaps."
"Rainald is happy", said Thomas quietly.
"You've done it for him", said Theodora. "I know you have."
"Rainald is happy", he repeated. "But you are not, little one. Why is that?"
There was a silence for a while.
"You wouldn't understand", said Theodora. Suddenly

she began to laugh again. "I'll wager no one has said that to you before. Still . . . " Her laughter died.

"I wonder", he said. "I was asked once by a student what in my opinion was the greatest grace I had received from God, and I answered: that I had always understood every page that I read."

"I'm not a book", said Theodora. "I'm a woman."

She crossed over to the window, turning her back to him.

"You know Ruggiero is taking the Cross", she said.

"Yes. But surely . . . "

"He is in God's hand there as he would be at my side. And we are a family of soldiers."

"It isn't that, then."

"No, it isn't that. At least . . . that's only part of it. But why, why, why is he taking the Cross? God wills it, they say. Ruggiero is a good man. In his own way, he is a good husband, too. I should be a very happy woman."

He waited patiently. And it came.

"There is something else", she said in a low voice. "He is not taking the Cross because God wills it. Or . . . not only. I don't think he knows that, though."

She turned round. "You see . . . he is not really a very courageous man . . . he is sensitive, and he hates everything that is ugly and painful. He knows it, too. His father . . . used to tease him about it, not in a friendly way, and he resented it. But he knew it was true, all the same. A San Severino . . . and a . . . and not courageous . . . "

She stamped her foot. More than ever she looked like her mother.

"And . . . does he know that you know that?" asked Thomas gently.

"But that's just it . . . " She bit her lip. "I . . . I must have made him feel that I knew. Ah, what is the good of pretending: I did make him feel that I knew. He has never forgiven me for it. Not in his heart. He knows I cannot stand . . . lack of courage. I'm an Aquino. And now, you see, he is taking the Cross . . . "

" . . . because he wants to regain your respect."

"Yes. And his self-respect. I . . . I am his mirror. I reflect his picture. He didn't like what he saw. He wants to change it."

From somewhere came the thin sound of a bell. Thomas rose, mechanically.

"Now if something happens to him . . . " she broke off. "You must go . . . no, don't say anything, please don't. Pray for me. I . . . good-bye, Thomas." She rushed out. When he followed her to the corridor, she had gone.

She rushed down the stairs, across the small courtyard, past the doorkeeper's lodge, and into the street, where her carriage was waiting.

"Your servant, my lady", said Piers.

Her hand flew up to her heart.

"You've come after all."

He only smiled.

"I shouldn't have asked you", she murmured.

"You didn't", said Piers.

"Not in so many words, no, but . . . it was foolish. Worse. It was unjust. Oh, I don't know what to do."

She has been crying, he thought. He turned pale. Instinctively his fingers closed hard round his sword hilt.

"Who has hurt you, my lady? Tell me who has hurt you!"

She shook her head. "No one." She managed a faint smile. "You talk as if you were still a knight of Aquino."

"You have never ceased to be my lady", he said tonelessly.

"I wish it were as you say", she murmured. "No, do not misunderstand me. I believe you. But it is not right and meet . . . I can never thank you enough for what you did in the past. I . . . I wish to ask your pardon for my husband's words yesterday . . . for his attitude rather than his words. He . . . he is at war with himself, and I am worried about him . . . more than I can say."

"It is not he who has hurt you, then", said Piers.

"Oh, no, no . . . I told you, no one has."

"There was a time", he said, "when you saw in him your worst enemy."

"Yes." The memory made her smile a little. "And you offered to kill him. What children we were, Piers. Instead, you killed that dreadful German who threatened him, and God bless you for it. And you helped us to escape when all was lost, and I know how hard you tried to save Landulph and Rainald, too. Truly, you have done enough."

But with a lover's intuition he knew what she did not dare to say.

"You are worried about . . . him, taking the Cross."

Tears welled up in her eyes again.

"He will never come back", she said. "I know it."

"Theodora . . . my lady, how can you know such a thing?"

"He is not really a soldier . . . he . . . I just know it."

He nodded, pensively. "I suppose", he said, "if I talked to Prince Edward . . . he would let me join now instead of later. Then I could look after him."

She stared at him wide eyed. "Holy Mother of God," she said, "how can anyone despair of the world if there are people like you and Thomas."

"Thomas", said Piers, "is a saint. I am an ordinary man. I love you. I have loved you from the first moment I saw you. It has always been hopeless . . . but at least I can serve you. Set your mind at rest. I shall join now. God bless you."

He fled. A little farther up the street a varlet was waiting, mounted, and holding a spare horse. Perhaps it was old Robin. An instant later the two were speeding away.

She stood, motionless, she did not know for how long. Then, very white and shaken, she ascended the carriage steps.

* * *

"Master Thomas," said Reginald, "there are a number of notes here—fresh ones, I think: Do they belong to the *Summa,* or are they something else?"

Thomas glanced at them. "*Summa*", he decided.

"Good", said Reginald.

"You are always pleased when something belongs to the *Summa,* son, and you always make a face when it doesn't. Why is that?"

"Oh, well . . . I suppose I'd like to see it finished." Reginald was a little embarrassed. "It's such a wonderfully large thing, the sum of all Christian theology. They can't let that pass by quietly. You'll see, you'll be offered the red hat for it again. I know you don't want it. But all the same . . . you should think of your family. Such an honor should not be . . ."

"Of my family only two sisters are left. I don't think they care so very much whether their brother is a cardinal or not. Only my little brother Reginald cares about that."

" 'Whether it is permissible for a woman to paint her face' ", read Reginald, not without astonishment. " 'That the interpretation of dreams is permissible in order to acquire knowledge about the disposition of a patient . . . the influence of the stars stronger on the masses than on individuals . . . about work and pleasure . . .' "

"This will all be treated in the *Summa*", said Thomas. He was playing with a fresh quill, his eyes downcast. Reginald knew what was coming, and he shifted uneasily in his chair.

It came. "Reginald . . . about this morning in chapel . . ."

"Yes . . ."

"You . . . you saw, did you?"

"Yes." Reginald was trembling now.

Thomas looked up. "Reginald . . . my dear son: promise me not to talk about it to anyone . . . to anyone! . . . before I die."

"I promise", said Reginald. Then he burst into tears.

Chapter XVII

REPEAT AFTER ME", said the mullah sharply. *"Allah il Allah, we Mohammed rassul Allah."*

Most of the two hundred prisoners howled something that might well be taken for the sacred formula of Islam if one did not listen too carefully, especially as the first three words came out fairly clearly. The prisoners had long agreed among themselves that there was no harm for a Christian in saying that God was God. To confirm that Mohammed was the prophet of God was quite a different thing, though, and so they just howled some inarticulate syllables until they came to the word "Allah" again, which they shouted as loudly as possible.

The performance would never have taken in one of the learned imams of the Sultan of Tunis, where most of them had spent the first two years of their captivity; there, however, no one had insisted on it. In the capital a slave was a slave, and whether he prayed to the Christian God or to a fetish did not matter to the master.

But El Mohar was not Tunis.

El Mohar was a tiny oasis, a few thousand palm trees, a spring, and the *kasr,* the fortress, which the prisoners had to build around the spring; that was all.

There was a garrison of seventy Arabs under their caid, Omar ben Tawil, and there were a few dozen huts for them to sleep in until the *kasr* was ready. The prisoners, of course, slept in the open and were chained together at night. Nearly fifty of them had died, but there were still enough of them left to get the *kasr* ready. There was no hurry . . . the Frankish *giaurs* had taken such a beating that it would be years before they could be ready to renew their attack. Caid Omar ben Tawil was fairly certain about that, and he knew the Franks and their ways . . . his grandfather had served under the great Saladin, and he himself had fought at El Dimiat, which the Franks called Damiette, against the same Frankish *melek* who had been defeated before Tunis. Giant bodies, these *giaurs* . . . but as sensitive as women. Allah breathed at them with the fiery breath of the desert, and they wilted like flowers. The Frankish king himself had wilted—and died, and the Franks claimed that he was now a *marabout,* a saint.

The mullah was a very holy man, too, no doubt, but he was a fool, nevertheless, to try and teach these uncircumcised dogs the truth of Islam. He might as well teach it to camels or goats. Still, teaching was his business, and with Allah nothing was impossible, though the great Saladin had said that when a Christian was ready to become a Moslem, he was bound to be a bad Christian, and a bad Christian was not likely to be a good Moslem.

Caid Omar grinned to himself and, eating a handful of dates, watched the mullah at his daily effort. They had not answered too well today, and so he made them repeat the formula again and again.

"*Allah il Allah . . . we wawawawawa* ALLAH!"

"Now I know what he looks like, my lord", whispered a tall prisoner. "Been trying to find out a long time. Just like a very old hen . . . "

"Quiet, Robin."

" . . . with a beard."

"Shut up . . . he's looking at you."

"Wish he were", growled Robin. "But it's *him* again."

Piers groaned. Twice before the old priest, or whatever he was, had singled out Ruggiero to make him speak the sentence alone. He had refused, bless him, but there had been fear in his eyes, and the old man had seen it. Ever since he had had his eye on him. He could not use violence . . . the Caid needed his workmen and would not stand for that. But he might incite him to give an answer regarded as blasphemy or as an insult against the great ruler of Tunis, and then the Caid himself would have to punish the offender. Robin had tried to divert the mullah's attention

... but without success. Piers bit his lip as the old man advanced on Ruggiero and began to whisper to him. Threats ... perhaps promises. Either way had succeeded at times. At least five or six of the prisoners had embraced Islam since the mullah had started his efforts. They were made to "renounce the errors of the past, the worship of the man Jesus and of three gods instead of the One", to pronounce solemnly the formula of their new faith, and to recite the first sura or chapter of Alcoran. Then they were circumcised. Thus they acquired the right to wear the turban and ceased to be slaves ... no "true believer" could be a slave. They were either sent to Tunis or remained here as foremen or supervisors of the others. There was no doubt that they could be trusted ... they usually responded to the contempt of the Christian prisoners with the worst hatred there is: the hatred of the weak man who knows himself to be guilty.

Piers knew how tired Ruggiero was ... only last week he had had an outburst of despair, a frequent enough thing at El Mohar, and always dangerous. It had been at night, and fortunately Piers had been near enough to talk to him ... with only two men chained between them. He had talked and talked, and somehow he had pulled him through again, as many a time before. But there was no doubt that his resistance was very low and that the old mullah was well aware of it.

"He's stepping forward", whispered Robin.

"By Our Lady," roared Piers, "get back, Ruggiero."

The mullah turned to him, his eyes blazing: "Who has permitted you to speak, *giaur?*" He spoke the lingua franca, and Piers answered in the same language. He had learned it on his first crusade, and the last three years had given him ample opportunity to make progress in it.

"Shame on you, oh, Mullah," he said, "it will be said that you could persuade only those who are half dead with fatigue and more than half starved to become interested in your faith. Have this man given double rations and exempt him from heavy work for a month and then ask him again and see what he'll answer you."

"Dog and son of a dog", snapped the mullah. "You were conceived by a whore from a galley slave."

"What that fellow needs is a sense of logic", said Robin between his teeth. "Surely it could be only the one or the other."

Piers nodded. "When two theses contradict each other, either one or both of them must be wrong." They had not been lay brothers at the convent of St. Jacques for nothing. "He won't catch me that way."

But the mullah did not give up so easily.

"By whose name did I hear you swear just now?" he asked loudly. "Was it not a woman? Everyone knows that the men of Frankistan have become as women since they went so far in their idolatrous practices as to worship a woman . . . "

"My lord, it's a trap, don't fall for it, my lord, he just wants . . . "

" . . . and to invent all manner of lies about her purity and . . . "

"Down with you", said Piers in a strangely calm voice, and he rushed forward. In the next instant his fingers closed round the scraggy throat of the mullah. Half a dozen Arabs jumped at him, and Robin plunged forward like a mad bull, knocked one down whose scimitar was nearest to his master's head, and grappled with the others. It could not last long, of course. A minute later the mullah was free, Piers and Robin were in heavy chains, and thirty arrows were ready for any prisoner rash enough to come to their help.

The Caid strode forward. "These two men will be flogged", he said sulkily. "Thirty strokes with the kurbash to each of them. Kamil and Achmed—you'll do it. Have you now finished with the others, oh, Mullah?"

Rubbing his neck, the mullah began to talk again to Ruggiero. But the young man's mood seemed to have changed. He raised his hand, waved it in a gesture of finality, and stepped back into the ragged front.

"Well done", shouted Piers. "I wish Adam had behaved like that in paradise."

Robin grinned broadly, but the Caid said: "Five strokes more for that man." He added, under his breath: "See to it that they are not unable to work."

They started on them then. As it would soon be over, the Caid let the other prisoners watch the procedure.

"Dear fool," said Piers, "who asked you to butt in on my little talk with the mullah?"

Robin gave only a snort.

"Sorry that I got you into this", said Piers quietly. Then the kurbash—a whip made of rhinoceros hide—came down, and he gritted his teeth.

"One", said the Caid . . . "and one. Two . . . and two."

"He'll make a bad end", grunted Robin. "The clerical infidel I mean, my lord."

"Certainly. We'll find a way. No one can say what he said and live."

"Three", counted the Caid impassively. "And three. Four . . ."

When he came to eighteen, Piers said in a clear voice: "It's all right, Ruggiero—it's all right." Then he fainted. Three strokes later Robin fainted, too, a good varlet, always following his master wherever he went.

"Enough", said the Caid. "There is no use in flogging a dead camel. Take them to my hut. I shall decide later whether they'll get the rest of the strokes or not. Abdullah—lead the prisoners to work. By the Caaba, we've lost time enough with all this. *Jallah*—get on with it."

When Piers came to, he found himself sitting on an old couch, propped up with cushions. His back hurt badly, and his hand went to it instinctively, only to find that it had been bandaged. Looking up, he met the eyes of the Caid, who was sitting on another couch opposite him, sipping a goblet of sherbet. Ah, and there was Robin, an anxious, fully conscious Robin, bandaged, too, and . . . also sipping sherbet.

"Blessed be Our Lady", said Robin.

Piers grinned at him and then looked back to the Caid.

"I had to have you flogged", said the Caid gruffly. "You, who used to be a commander among the *giaurs*—you would have done the same thing. Have some sherbet."

"You are not a bad man, Caid Omar ben Tawil", said Piers, drinking. "If someone had blasphemed what is holy to you in your presence, you would have jumped at his throat also."

"I have blood in my veins", said the Caid. "We both did what we had to do. You will not get the rest of the strokes—nor will this man here, who is as faithful to you as the mullah is to Alcoran. Mullahs", he added slowly, "do not often have breadth of spirit. They only know one kind of truth—their own."

It was still difficult to breathe—the long weals hurt at every movement of the body.

"One kind of truth", said Piers. "I think I have heard that before. You think there is more than one truth, oh, Caid?"

"There are two truths", said the Caid placidly. "The truth of religion and the truth of philosophy. If they come to different results, it only goes to show the great variety of Allah's world."

"The error of Averroes", said Piers.

"Ibn Roshd", nodded the Caid. "I was introduced to his writing by a wise *alim* in Tunis. But you are wrong, Franki, Ibn Roshd has never committed an error—neither has *his* teacher, the Greek."

"Aristotle. He also was wrong at times", said Piers. "Mind you, oh, Caid, Averroes, or Ibn Roshd as you call him, taught that there were not only two kinds of truth, but three: the truth of the philosopher, who required proof; the truth of the theologian, who only needed probable arguments; and the truth of the simple man, who believes what he is told and is satisfied with it."

"Allah!" exclaimed the Caid. "How do you know all that, Franki? I knew there was a third kind of truth, but I didn't remember what it was. Are you a disciple of Ibn Roshd yourself? There are men who teach his wisdom in Frankistan, I believe."

"Yes, there are . . . and the greatest of them is a man called Siger of Brabant who is teaching in Paris."

"It is true, then, Allah be praised. At last the infidel nations are beginning to look for true wisdom. Soon they will find out that it tears down all their false beliefs and that it is madness further to resist the spreading of the true faith. When I read Ibn Roshd I thought: if only the infidels could read this, they would shed their errors and there would be one world under the green flag of the prophet. You are a disciple of this man Zikr—what did you call him?"

"Siger of Brabant. No, Caid, I am not his disciple. But I have been for some years the disciple of a Christian mullah who had studied both Aristotle and Ibn Roshd and discovered where they went wrong."

"Impossible."

"He wrote a *kitab,* a learned book about it which he called *Summa contra Gentiles;* and he challenged Siger of Brabant to fight it out with him at the school of philosophy in Paris before the highest imam of the city."

"But he was beaten, of course?"

"So great was the power of his very name that Siger tried to avoid the fight. But in the end he was forced to face his opponent so as not to be laughed at by his own disciples. Mind you, he was a formidable fighter, and there were many learned men who thought he had not his equal in all Frankistan and beyond."

The Caid's eyes gleamed. "I know that learned men can fight with their brains as I fight with javelin and scimitar- . . . and though you do not see blood flow . . . at least not often and not much . . . it is no less a fight without mercy. What happened?"

"The fight took place just before I left with the army of the Great King. It lasted for seven hours without a pause, and Siger was beaten so thoroughly that the Grand Imam who presided at the fight declared his teaching to be null and void."

"By the Caaba! By all the Califs—that man Zikr cannot have known the teaching of Ibn Roshd, or he couldn't have been defeated."

"He knew it well. I witnessed the fight myself. Siger fought well. But no one on earth can stand up against Thomas of Aquino, brain against brain—and win. He wrote another *kitab* in which he tears the Averroist theory into little pieces, especially the idea that there is only one single intellect, manifesting itself in all men . . . "

"Allah is great, he knew about that, too, then . . . this Mullah Thumash . . . and so do you!"

"I had my fill from the crumbs that fell from his table", said Piers.

The Caid sighed. "This Mullah Thumash must be killed quickly if Islam is to conquer Frankistan from inside—yet I would give my second best filly if I could have him here and ask him questions. Are you strong enough to walk now, Franki?"

Piers rose, wincing a little. "I can walk, oh, Caid."

"And your man here?"

Robin got up without apparent difficulty.

"It is well", said the Caid. "You will rest from work today and begin again tomorrow. If you will swear by all that is holy to you that you will not try to escape, I shall leave you unchained at night."

"I swear", said Piers, "by all that is holy to me that I shall certainly try to escape as soon as I have an opportunity."

The Caid smiled. "It is a pity. But I would have said the same thing if I were your prisoner. Go now . . . and see to it that you do not rouse the anger of the mullah again. I may not always be able to protect you."

* * *

When they were chained together again, that night, Ruggiero was too far away for an exchange of words, but he gave Piers a weary smile and made a touching attempt at a sign of the cross . . . the chain was too short for it.

"He's getting very weak", murmured Piers.

Robin nodded. "He won't last long, my lord."

Piers groaned. "I promised I would look after him, Robin . . . I promised . . . "

"It wasn't you who suggested the attack on that day, my lord. You hadn't even been asked to join it."

"What else could I do? Ruggiero had joined it."

"Will you stop chattering, you scum", bellowed one of the supervisors. "Perhaps your backs are not sore enough yet?" It was one of the renegade Christians, a Frenchman. The prisoners had a silent agreement never to answer anything they said. Piers and Robin remained silent. They did not sleep much that night; their backs hurt abominably.

From fairly near came the noises they had become accustomed to: the bleak, high-pitched laughter of a hyena, circling cautiously around the oasis; the hoarse bark of the jackal; the stirring of the horses in their long, well-built shed. Horses were much too precious to be exposed to the dangers of the sharp air of the Tunisian night.

The worst, thought Piers, was that every new day diminished the chances of an escape. At first when work started at El Mohar he had had hopes. They were three times as numerous as their guards, and once they had managed to find out on whom one could rely, there might be the possibility of a mutiny, led by the right elements. But the heavy work and bad food had weakened the prisoners very quickly, and there was nothing definite one could promise them even if the mutiny succeeded. Between them and Europe was the sea, and the sea was ruled by the swift ships of the Arabs. The sea was near. But they would have been caught long before they had got hold of a vessel in one of the smaller ports. And the punishment for mutiny and flight was death . . . and not a particularly easy death either.

A dozen, perhaps two dozen men among the prisoners would be ready to risk it in spite of that; the others would not. All one could do was to wait for an opportunity.

There was, of course, the possibility that ransom would be offered for them by Prince Philip, now King Philip of France . . . perhaps even by Prince Edward. But that possibility was very remote. Rumors had come through that Prince Edward was fighting in the Holy Land, at Acre. It was most unlikely that he could do anything even if he had heard of his vassal's captivity—and that was most unlikely, too. And King Philip was not King Louis. Even if he had heard of the fate of the men captured in that last, senseless attack before the great withdrawal, he might well forget about them; most certainly he would not be eager to do something for prisoners who were not even his subjects. A few bold men had escaped in Tunis . . . the Sieur de Murailles among them, a very brave man. But whether they had reached France no one knew this side of the Mediterranean.

So one had to wait . . . to wait for an opportunity . . . and even if it came—Robin was right: Ruggiero would not last much longer. Perhaps it was better to stay and die with him than to escape when he had died. El Mohar was purgatory. But even purgatory was better than the terrible, the unmitigated hell of standing before Theodora and telling her that once more her knight had failed her and that her husband had died, as her brothers had before him.

* * *

It was about three weeks later that the sentinel on the first completed tower of the *kasr* gave the sandstorm warning.

Immediately the supervisor drove the prisoners off their work and made them take cover behind the wall. The Arabs led their horses to the shed. The Caid mounted the tower. "A sandstorm, Yacub? At this time of the year?"

"See for yourself, oh, Caid. It might be a fast-moving

caravan of very many men, but the caravan from the salt lakes cannot have left there yet, and this is coming from the north . . . "

"From the north? By Allah, your father was a one-eyed breaker of the law, and your mother had no nose. There is metal shimmering behind the sand. It's an enemy."

"How could it be an enemy, oh, Caid? There is no one now, who . . . "

"To arms", roared the Caid. "Mount, you sons of heroes, you chosen ones of Allah, you glorious swords of Islam—get ready to fight, you ill-begotten lepers, you seedless cripples, you droppings of a camel without hump—my horse, Ali!"

He could see the enemy now, and they were Frankish knights without the shadow of a doubt; huge armored horses and huge armored men, one with a triangular flag at the end of a young tree. But there seemed to be no more than about fifty of them, though the cloud of dust they raised was covering a very large space. Hastily he climbed down and found Ali waiting for him with his horse. He mounted. Turning in the saddle he saw his men streaming up to him from the shed on their horses, baffled, but ready.

"Jallah," he shouted, "they must be escaped prisoners—we are more numerous than they are. Follow me."

They thundered out of the half-finished gate of the *kasr,* a compact mass of men and horses, yelling, whinnying, clattering, brandishing arms.

"I don't believe it", said Robin, his face split by a huge grin.

All the prisoners were looking over the wall to their fate, coming up, armored, in a cloud of dust.

"Blue", said Piers breathlessly. "Blue and . . . by all the saints, it's the flag of Edward Plantagenet. He's a thousand miles away at Acre. I'm dreaming this. I'm dreaming this."

"Too good for a dream", said Robin. "Do you think these chains might be any use, my lord?"

"You're right, of course." The chains they wore during

the night were handy weapons. He was just going to shout to the prisoners to arm themselves, when he heard a fever-cracked voice screaming: "San Severino!"

Turning swiftly, he saw Ruggiero rushing madly at the mullah.

He leaped to his help, hoping against hope that he would not be too late. For the holy man had drawn a long, curved dagger, and one of the renegade supervisors came running up, whip in hand.

Under Ruggiero's assault the mullah went down, but he had not lost his knife, and . . .

Beside himself, Piers came down on the mullah like a thunderbolt, smashing his face with his right fist and tearing him from under Ruggiero. He did not even bother to look for the renegade . . . Robin could cope with three of that kind, weakened as he was. Again and again his fist came down on the man who had blasphemed Purity itself and killed the man who had been under the protection of Piers Rudde. When the mullah had gone limp, Piers staggered to his feet and went over to Ruggiero. He found him in Robin's lap, and from the expression on Robin's face he knew that there was no hope. Then he saw that the mullah's knife had gone deep into Ruggiero's left breast.

He bent down: "Victory", he whispered. "You won. You won."

The flicker of a smile went over Ruggiero's face, still so strangely young, still boyish. With his ear at Ruggiero's mouth, Piers could hear a name very sacred to him and—scarcely audible—the Christian plea for forgiveness. Then agony set in, and both Piers and Robin crossed themselves and prayed the prayers for the dying which evoke all the powers of heaven to come to the aid of a departing soul.

And Ruggiero died.

They were still praying when the very soil began to tremble under them. Looking up, they saw what at any other moment would have been the sight of their lives. Armored knights on armored horses came streaming into the courtyard of the *kasr.* The prisoners around them were yelling and jumping up and down like madmen. And the tall, lanky figure in silvery armor on a beautiful chestnut . . .

"My Prince", said Piers, rising with tears in his eyes.

Edward Plantagenet dismounted and embraced him. For a while no one spoke. At last Piers found the strength to say: "I thought you were at Acre, my Prince. How on earth did you find us here?"

"I was at Acre. We delivered the town from its siege, and I marched as far as Nazareth. We're on our way back. But a message had come from the Sieur de Murailles . . . "

"God bless him for it."

" . . . that you were a prisoner of the Tunisians and with you a shiploadful of Christian men. So I thought it was a good idea to land and have a look for you and break a lance or two in memory of King Louis at the same time. Prisoners we made told us where you were likely to be found, and here we are."

"The battle is won?"

Edward laughed. "It wasn't a battle, scarcely a skirmish. They thought we were about fifty strong; couldn't see the main force coming up behind us. There are five hundred of us and another five hundred covering our retreat by sea. Eight large ships stopped for your sake, my Lord Rudde. We caught the headman of these fellows, I believe . . . "

"Caid Omar?"

"That's what he calls himself. Did he ill treat you? By my faith, if he did . . . "

"No, my Prince". Piers smiled wearily. "He is a keen student of philosophy", he said. "Take him to France or wherever we sail so that he may learn more about the single truth. He is a good man. But we have three renegades here and an infidel priest."

"With permission, my lord", said Robin respectfully. "The three renegades have already arrived at a place still hotter than Tunisia."

"The mullah", said Piers, "has blasphemed Our Lady."

"Not a fellow with a green turban?" asked a young knight of the Prince's retinue.

"Yes. I knocked him down to save my poor friend San Severino, but I was too late."

"Knocked him down?" asked the knight curiously. "With your bare fist? Why, the fellow looks as if a hundred horses had ridden over his face. He's very dead, my lord, and if you ever come across me in a joust, I hope you'll use a blunted spear and go easy at that."

"It seems you didn't leave us any work to do here", laughed the Prince. "We'll get water for our horses and ourselves, and then, Piers, I think we better leave this kingdom of sand and scorpions before the Sultan in Tunis wakes up. What is the matter with you, man? Won't you be glad to see England again?"

"God bless you for what you've done, my liege", said Piers. "But there's no gladness left for me in life. It were better if I were dead."

Chapter XVIII

BROTHER REGINALD OF PIPERNO was blissfully happy. His happiness had started when he walked at the side of Master Thomas into Naples, and ever since everything had gone just as if he had ordered it so. The very entry into the city had been a triumph without precedent.

Never before had a newly nominated Doctor of Theology been received by tens of thousands of people, lining the streets, yelling with enthusiasm, throwing flowers, blowing kisses.

Thomas, of course, had looked back, as if he expected that the man who had evoked all this was someone else, marching or riding somewhere behind him, perhaps the Duke of Anjou, or rather the King of Sicily as he now was, and he had felt most uncomfortable. As if anybody would yell with enthusiasm when the King of Sicily made his somber appearance. They had never taken to him, the Neapolitans, although he certainly had made short shrift of the last eaglets of the Hohenstaufen. Everybody knew what he had answered King Manfred at Benevento when Frederick's son had sent a messenger to him for last-minute negotiation of peace. Manfred's troops were mostly Saracens of his father's famous colony of Moslems in the very heart of the kingdom of Sicily, around Lucera.

"Bear this message to the Sultan of Lucera", said King Charles grimly: "God and the swords are umpire between us; and either he shall send me to paradise or I will send him to the pit of hell."

From which it could be seen that Charles of Anjou knew exactly where he was going, or thought he did. Anyway, he was as good as his word, and before night fell the Saracens were dead and King Manfred with them.

And when young Conradin, last of the Hohenstaufen, came sweeping down into Italy to avenge Manfred and to re-establish the empire of his father Conrad and his grandfather Frederick, Charles met and beat him at Tagliacozzo, made him a prisoner, and had him executed in the market place at Naples.

The Neapolitans were a cheerful people. They did not like tyrants, whether they came from Germany or from France.

Somehow they never quite forgave Charles of Anjou

for liberating them, though they might have forgiven him if he had then proceeded to liberate them of himself as well. Of that, however, there was but little likelihood.

There would be no flowers for King Charles, and if they yelled when he passed by it wouldn't be a sign of joy.

Later they heard that the King had very carefully enquired about the reason for such incredible popularity of a mere Doctor of Theology. He knew, of course, who Master Thomas of Aquino was, but then who didn't? He knew not only that the Aquinos were the rightful owners of half a province north of Naples but also that Master Thomas was *persona gratissima* with King Louis, who was then still alive and about the only man whose anger the King feared. So he sent a very courteous, a honey-sweet letter to the Dominican convent, welcoming "the illustrious new Master of Naples' university whose fame had spread all over the Christian world, the friend and adviser of his royal brother of France" and assuring him that "he shared to the full the joy which his Neapolitan subjects had shown at the entry of their beloved teacher into a city which had the proud and justified claim to be called his home town".

"Of course," snorted the old Prior of the convent, "if someone must be more popular than he is, he'd rather it be a mendicant friar than someone who might become a rival."

His rule worsened considerably after the death of his great and saintly brother. He was afraid of no one now, with the single exception, perhaps, of the new Pope, Gregory the Tenth, an Italian Pope after three Frenchmen. Teobaldo Visconti of Piacenza had been a close friend of King Louis. It had been very difficult to dissuade him from going with the King on his last unfortunate crusade and to make him remain in Liége, where he was archdeacon until he was called to the throne of St. Peter.

Now the new Pope had issued an encyclical, a few days after his coronation, that proclaimed a General Council to be held in Lyons to deal with the Greek schism. It was supposed to start on May the first of the next year, and today was the sixth of December. There was little doubt that Master Thomas was going to be invited to participate in it, and this time they would give him the red hat whether he wanted it or not—just as they had done with Brother Bonaventure. And that was one of the reasons for Friar Reginald's happiness.

Another was that the time between now and the journey to Lyon was just sufficient for Master Thomas to finish the most massive, the most profound and glorious work of his entire life . . . his *Summa Theologica.* The first two parts were finished, and he was working on the third and last, the part dealing with the Redeemer himself, *De Christo.*

And here in Naples he was not so busy fighting the errors and faulty arguments of others; he did not have to combat Averroists in the morning and Augustinians in the afternoon before he could settle down to his writing. Naples was not Paris. The only person he visited from time to time was his poor sister Theodora, whose husband had disappeared in that unfortunate crusade which had cost King Louis' life, too. At long last Master Thomas had time to concentrate fully on his own work.

Thus all one had to do was to see to it that he had all the books he needed, that his papers were in order, that he ate properly at midday, and that all minor disturbances were kept off. Here was bliss indeed.

There was, of course, no paradise without a serpent. However, the Neapolitan serpent was a very small one. Its name was Brother Dominic. Brother Dominic was the sacristan of the convent, a dry little man, whose thin lips seemed to be made for a perpetual ironic smile—though that was perhaps only due to an attempt to hide a very complete lack of teeth. He had been sacristan at the convent and the church of St. Nicholas well over thirty-five years, and he was no respecter of persons. It was known that he had given—well, very energetic answers even to the Prior, and the worst was that he knew his business so well that he was usually right in the matter at hand. His beady little eyes were everywhere and saw everything.

Brother Dominic was the only man whom Friar Reginald had not been able to convince of the importance of Master Thomas' work. Or at least not as much as Friar Reginald wanted to. And when Master Thomas, deep in thoughts, marched off in the wrong direction and went to the courtyard instead of the refectory or was just a moment late at Vespers, Brother Dominic raised his hairless brows with an expression that cast grave doubts on the great philosopher's state of mind.

At the same time he always knew exactly how much liberty he could take and how far he could go. One could not catch him out, not Brother Dominic.

"Brother Dominic . . . did you lay out a larger set of vestments this morning for Master Thomas?"

"Can't lay out a new set in the middle of the week."

"But, Brother Dominic, you know as well as I do that Master Thomas is of unusual build physically . . . "

"I cannot be made responsible for that, Friar Reginald."

" . . . as well as in other ways. I didn't say you were responsible for that. But you are responsible for laying out the right vestments."

"Sixth of December", said Brother Dominic. "Feast of St. Nicholas, patron of the church. Bishop and Confessor. White."

"Yes, yes, I never doubted that you know your duties. All I wish to point out is that Master Thomas has been gravely inconvenienced more than once by a set of vestments that might fit me or even you, but not a man of his size. It is an appeal to your imagination as well as to your good heart, Brother Dominic. Master Thomas cannot raise his arms properly if the chasuble is too tight for him."

"I've been laying out sets of vestments for over thirty-five years in this church, Friar Reginald . . . "

"Yes, yes, I know, but . . . "

" . . . including High Pontifical Masses, celebrated by His Eminence the Cardinal-Archbishop of Naples . . . "

"What's that got to do with . . . ?"

" . . . and many other princes of the Church, and there have never been any complaints."

"I did not complain, Brother Dominic. I only appealed to . . . "

"Imagination", said Brother Dominic. "Thank the saints, I never had any of *that.* Thoroughness, Friar Reginald; know your details; never forget anything. Know where everything is or should be, unless the acolytes have got there after me. If I had imagination, I'd have lost my post thirty-five years ago."

Friar Reginald gave up and returned to Master Thomas' cell to see whether everything was neatly arranged for the morning's work.

Brother Dominic sauntered over to the Church. Master Thomas must have finished his Mass by now. Extinguish candles, book back to sacristy, clean the cruets and the dish, take the towels away . . . order. Order. Not imagination.

Snorting a little, he entered the church. To his dismay he saw that Master Thomas had not finished his Mass yet. He was still at the altar. The next thing he became aware of was that Master Thomas looked quite unusually tall. So tall, in fact, that his head was on equal height with the foot of the crucifix. Brother Dominic's tidy mind deduced that there must be something wrong with the crucifix and that Master Thomas had got himself a footstool so as to reach up and put it right again. This, however, was not Master Thomas' job. It was Brother Dominic's job, and no one was going to do it for him.

He approached, decidedly annoyed now.

Then he saw that Master Thomas was not touching the crucifix; his arms were spread in the gesture of adoration.

And only now Brother Dominic saw that there was no footstool.

There was nothing between Master Thomas' feet and the ground. And the nothing between his feet and the ground was almost a yard high. One could see the full breadth of the shabby, red carpet and the white marble steps. One could see the full breadth of the altar itself.

Brother Dominic blinked. This was impossible. A man could not stand on air. But then, Master Thomas did not stand on air. He was . . . he was floating, floating in the air. The soles of his shoes were fully visible.

"Imagination", thought Brother Dominic in sudden terror. "I have been stricken with imagination." But the tough common sense in him denied at once any relation between his little self and this terrible sight in front of him, this huge mass of priestly clothing, dangling feet, hands stretched out, head thrown back, floating, immobile.

Brother Dominic began to gasp. He made a step backward and half turned as if to flee from the awful sight. But his feet seemed to rebel. He could not leave. His eyes, too, rebelled, fixing themselves on that enormous skull thrown back in . . . what was it? Anguish? Fear? Torture? He had to know. He had to know. He didn't in the least want to, but he had to. His feet made little, uncertain steps until they reached a place, well in the shadow, at the side of the altar. And now Brother Dominic could see the face of the skull, and it was Master Thomas' face no longer. It was long drawn and open mouthed, its eyes shining with a fierce and terrible light. It was not the face of a man who is seeing a sight of great beauty. It was the face of a man who sees the Person he most loves walking toward him across a wide abyss . . . "Come, come, come to me, but don't stumble, don't fall . . . " No. It wasn't that. It was something of that, but it wasn't that.

Suddenly and for no apparent reason Brother Dominic was again six years old and hearing, for the first time, the story of Moses, as God shows him the Promised Land and tells him, "Thou hast seen it with thy eyes and shalt not pass over to it." And little Dominic had cried because poor

Moses, after all his labors, was not allowed to enter the Promised Land.

That was how this man, who had once been Master Thomas, looked now—like the man who saw the Promised Land and could not enter it.

And Brother Dominic, still small, though no longer a child after sixty-two years of life and thirty-five of them as sacristan of St. Nicholas, bit hard into his hand not to stop himself from crying, for that he could not help, but not to be heard crying.

The white-golden cloud that was Thomas was still hovering high over the altar steps. But his face changed. From a rapturous, intent, pain-racked longing it changed to complete, utter ecstasy. The doors of limbo were torn open, and at long last Moses was allowed to enter the Promised Land. Here it was. Here it was. The outstretched hands closed together. He was praying now. But if this was praying, Brother Dominic had never seen anyone praying before. It was a child running into its mother's arms; it was a bride looking up to the beloved; it was a man who had discovered a treasure, a hero who saw victory, a leper who found himself cured. It was a man being born anew into a new world. It was all that, and it was not that at all. For Thomas knew nothing of himself in this moment. Suspended in midair, he was like a moon, gleaming in reflected light. And the light came from the crucifix on the altar.

Brother Dominic fell on his knees. The last conscious thought he had was that it was, perhaps, for the sake of his tears, as a child, when he had wept for poor Moses, that he was now allowed to see this glory and that nothing he had done afterward was worth one of those tears.

But then all thinking had ceased before what happened, and what happened was such that it engraved itself on him for the rest of his life. He heard. Words. Clear words. Spoken from the altar, from the crucifix on the altar.

"Thou hast written well of me, Thomas. What wouldst thou have as a reward?"

And the voice of Master Thomas, answering: "Only thyself, Lord."

Then, slowly, very slowly, he began to sink back to earth.

So, in a way, did Brother Dominic. He scrambled to his feet and staggered out of the church and back to his cell.

* * *

Early in the afternoon, Brother Dominic came to see Friar Reginald and told him that in future Master Thomas would always get the largest set of vestments available. And was there anything else he needed? There wasn't? Well, if there was, would Friar Reginald please let him know at once?

Bewildered, Friar Reginald took notice of the fact that there was no more serpent in paradise. Bewildered— and just a trifle suspicious.

When he entered Master Thomas' cell half an hour later with a manuscript—a treatise on penance by St. Bernard—he found him at his desk as usual. But there were no papers on the desk, no books, no quills, no ink. Nothing but the crucifix.

"I . . . I've found the St. Bernard after all", he said. "It's quite complete and a good copy, too, so if . . . " His voice trailed off.

"Reginald", said Thomas, "Reginald . . . it is you, isn't it?"

Friar Reginald became very pale.

"Of course it's me", he said. "What is it . . . are you ill?"

"No . . . no . . . Reginald . . . take that manuscript back. And these, too, in that corner."

"Back? Why? You need them, surely, for . . . "

"No. I shall never need a manuscript again."

"Thomas! You *are* ill. I shall go and see the Prior at once. You need a few days' rest, a week at least. I have never seen you so pale and . . . Oh! It's happened again. I can see it. Like on that day in Paris, when . . . "

"Quiet, Reginald. You promised not to talk about it until I am dead. It won't be long now, I think."

"Don't say that, Thomas, please, please, don't say that. You will have a rest. You will get well again and finish the *Summa* and then . . . "

"I shall never write again, Reginald. Everything I have written is like straw . . . in comparison to . . . what I have seen. Go now, old friend. I must be alone."

Reginald withdrew. Not only the serpent was gone. Paradise had vanished, too.

Chapter XIX

War was not such a terrible thing, once you got over the first ugly shock of seeing, quite suddenly, what a man looks like from the inside. When you know what entrails are like and brain matter and blood coughed up from the lungs, you were over the worst. And if it happened to oneself, well, either one wouldn't know much about it or there'd be pain. But pain was something one could deal with. Grit your teeth and take long, deep breaths and grin; better still, do all that and at the same time offer it up as a Christian knight, your mite in the alms box of heaven. And if it grew too strong, well, then you lost consciousness and all was well again.

Captivity was not such a terrible thing either. Later on, you were almost glad you had experienced it. All the hopes, smashed or sustained, the holding of the fort against the attacks from within. The starry heavens above you when you go to sleep. And the jerking, tearing joy when liberation was in sight.

There was only one truly terrible thing: the suffering of the beloved. The suffering of the beloved that you have caused . . . and you can do nothing about it but stand and look on, a large, clumsy fool, a monster.

The vision of that specter had been with Piers, an inseparable companion, since El Mohar. It had ridden with him to a tiny port, where Prince Edward's ships were waiting. It had sailed with him, first to Spain, then to France. It had traveled with him to Italy on horseback, sitting behind him in the saddle and stabbing him again and again.

He had doubled up under it when he reached Rocca Secca. He had sighed with relief when he was told that the Countess of San Severino was not there but at Magenza, a castle belonging to her niece, Francesca Cecano. It was the stupid, instinctive relief of a man whose execution has been postponed for twenty-four hours. He spent the night at Rocca Secca. It was a rebuilt, new Rocca Secca, but from every corner memories kept creeping up to him. The hall where he had seen her first . . . the wall on which he had kept watch. It was a new hall and new walls and yet . . .

He slept very little. He heard her voice, her laughter. He heard Rainald's lute; the swish of the old Countess' robes; Landulph's deep-throated roar, ordering more wine; Mother Maria of Gethsemani, too, was there, all black veil and quiet resignation. Of the living only she was there, she to whom he had to bring the news of another death, to her the most painful of all.

It was a bad night.

The mild February sun found him wide awake. Today. Irrevocably today. In a few hours he would be in Magenza.

Robin brought the horses; he did not look up when he murmured his greeting. "Grey", thought Piers, "he's become very grey. An old man." He smiled at him and nodded.

* * *

They reached Magenza in the afternoon. Varlets in the Cecano livery helped them off their horses; yes, the Countess of San Severino was with their mistress; the noble lord would be announced at once to both ladies.

Francesca Cecano appeared, a shy, worried-looking young woman with a restless smile; words were murmured, the inevitable little courtesies. The hall and a room, where some people bowed, knights of the household, ladies of the household. Francesca Cecano was fluttering alongside with her painful little smile; by now she knew, of course, and by now she, too, knew that he and Robin had come . . . alone.

Another room. A little figure in black. Francesca Cecano murmured something and fled.

The little black figure remained immobile.

Piers felt that the whole room was filled with his own heartbeat. It was an act of supreme courage to march forward until he stood before her. He went down on one knee.

"My lady, I have failed you."

There was no answer.

He made a last, overwhelming effort and looked up. For the first time he again beheld the face of the woman whose prisoner he was in freedom and captivity. It was as beautiful as ever . . . and yet it had changed again, changed in a terrible way. It was bloodless and thin, the eyes unnaturally large, and their expression . . .

He could not read their expression. There was compassion, pity, anguish . . . there was pain, so heartrending, so excruciating that he felt his breathing stop and his limbs go numb. And yet that was not all. There was something else, something behind it all, a deep and solemn secret he was not allowed to share. She was before him, and she was far away, with land and ocean between them.

"My lady, can you not forgive me? I tried . . . hard."

The pale little mouth began to move. And he heard the words: "May the saints bless you. It is not you who have failed."

Acquitted. Acquitted. But there could be no joy before the pale, ghostly shadow of what had once been Theodora.

"My lady . . . no man can have a more beautiful death than Ruggiero de San Severino."

"He . . . died bravely?"

"I never saw a braver deed. He attacked, unarmed, an infidel who had blasphemed Our Lady. He ran him down, too. But the infidel was armed, and I came just an instant too late."

"He died bravely", she repeated tonelessly. Once more he saw that strange, enigmatic expression in her face. She nodded to herself, as if this were the news she had expected . . . but also as if it had been the worst part of it. It was inexplicable.

He cleared his throat. "Soon afterward we were liberated by my great liege, Prince Edward Plantagenet. We gave your husband a Christian burial. Seven hundred good men prayed at his grave. There is a cross on it. But we had to cover the grave and the cross with sand, so that it will not be found and desecrated by the enemy. And Prince Edward's chaplain said that it was well and fitting for a Christian knight of valor that his cross should be buried under the sand, just as Christ's Holy Cross was buried on Calvary for three hundred years until St. Helen found it again."

She bowed her head. She did not cry. There was scarcely anything in the world Piers feared more than her tears. And yet he felt it was a bad sign that she did not cry now.

For a long time neither of them spoke. Oh, to know what she was thinking, to be able to help . . .

At last she said . . . it was almost a whisper: "My Lord Rudde . . . Piers . . . I fear . . . I have to say something now that will give you pain. And knowing something about pain, as I do, I . . . I wish this cup would pass me by. Believe me: it hurts me just as much."

He braced himself. "What is it, my lady?"

"Piers . . . rarely a woman had so much cause to be thankful to a man as I have toward you. What man could do, you have done; and few men, if any, could have done as much."

"My lady . . . "

"There was a day when you honored me by saying that you loved me. It was an honour, although I was another man's wife. For there was nothing in your love that would be displeasing to God. Your memory and your image will be in my heart always. But we must never meet again."

He rose to his feet, trembling.

"Why, my lady . . . why?"

"That, my dear friend, I cannot answer."

"It is because I failed you . . . "

"No! No, I tell you! You did not fail me. It is I . . . Oh, Holy Mother of God, help me."

He stood aghast.

Suddenly they both turned. From the courtyard a heavy,

thunderous noise had come. It came again. And a third time.

"It is the gate", murmured Theodora. Mechanically she made a step nearer to the window. "It is Thomas", she exclaimed.

Piers approached. Two riders on mules had entered the courtyard, both in the black and white Dominican habit. But . . . something was wrong. The larger of the two friars had slumped in his saddle, and three varlets were trying to lift him off his mount. He seemed unable to move. It was as if the three men were lifting an enormous statue off its pedestal. Yes, it was Thomas . . . he could see his face now. His eyes were closed. Either he was ill, or he had had an accident.

Piers ran. Quick as he was, she kept pace with him, and they reached the hall together, just as they carried Thomas in . . . the three varlets and the other friar whom they both recognized now: it was Reginald of Piperno. Shy little Francesca Cecano fluttered in. "Put him into the guest room on this floor", she said with surprising energy. "Don't carry him up the stairs. Luigi, get Messer di Guido at once; he's in the village. Careful now . . . hold his head up."

A minute later he was stretched out on a bed, with Reginald sitting beside him. Piers beckoned the gaping varlets out of the room. Theodora crouched down at Thomas' feet, staring wide eyed at the deathly quiet face of the fallen giant. "What is it?" she whispered. "What is it?"

"He's been like this often", said Reginald sadly. "Ever since the feast of St. Nicholas. It is getting worse, I'm afraid. It used to last only a quarter of an hour, half an hour at the utmost. But this time it's been over two hours. Thank the Lord, we found some good people who helped me, keeping him in the saddle, or we would never have got here."

"Can he hear us?"

"No, most noble lady. You see?" Gently Reginald lifted Thomas' right eyelid. Only the white of the eye was visible.

"Here is Messer Giovanni di Guido", said Francesca Cecano, entering.

The physician was an elderly man with intelligent eyes and affable manners. "Your devoted servant", he said with a little bow all round. "Would my lords and ladies oblige me by leaving me alone with the patient for a little while?"

They trooped out of the room, Reginald not without reluctance.

"But what is it?" repeated Theodora, utterly bewildered.

Reginald was shaking his head. He tried to speak and could not.

"Better sit down, Friar Reginald," said Piers. He got hold of a chair just in time. "A little wine . . . "

"Here is wine", said Francesca Cecano. "Drink, Friar Reginald . . . no, a little more . . . the whole of it. That's better."

"Thank you", said Reginald, very much embarrassed to be fussed over. "Thank you, thank you . . . I'm quite all right, really. How strong this wine is!"

"Do you think you feel strong enough to tell us more about what happened?" asked Theodora anxiously.

"Oh, yes, yes, certainly. But I know very little myself, most noble lady. As I said, it started on St. Nicholas' day, on the sixth of December, though of course that wasn't really the beginning—ah, you remember, perhaps, Countess, that day when you came to visit him in Paris, and he was late . . . "

"I remember it very well. I thought that something had happened to him. You seemed so worried when you told me he would come any moment."

"Yes. I was. Even that was not the first time, though it had never been quite like that day. I am telling this very badly, I'm afraid, but it isn't easy to talk of . . . such things."

"But what things?" asked Theodora, almost impatiently. "Are you not looked after when you get ill in a convent? Surely . . . "

"Oh, yes, if it's . . . just an ordinary illness. But this

is . . . oh, I mustn't talk about it too much; he'd never forgive me. I promised not to. But I am so worried. You see, he was working on the last part of his most important book and then one day, coming back from Mass, he was quite different and . . . almost as he looks now, you see, though he was conscious, and he said he'd never write again, not a single word, after what he'd seen. And he didn't. He didn't."

"After what he had seen", repeated Theodora, frowning.

"Yes. He never wrote again", moaned Friar Reginald. "The most wonderful work of all . . . unfinished. And he at an age when Plato says that a man should then *start* becoming a philosopher! Only when the Holy Father's letter came, I could see a ray of hope."

"The Holy Father?"

"Yes, he invited Master Thomas to take part in the General Council in Lyons. He was not fit to travel, really, but he insisted on it. So we set out, with a dispensation to ride instead of walk."

"I should hope so", muttered Piers under his breath.

"The Holy Father's order seemed to have had a good effect on him", went on Reginald. "He spoke a little more and seemed quite cheerful. The King of Sicily came to see him, as the Prior would not allow Master Thomas to leave the convent before we set out for Lyons."

Again Theodora frowned. "I wonder what *he* wanted."

"Oh, I know . . . I was present. He said he wanted to wish him a pleasant journey and he hoped Master Thomas would speak well to the Holy Father about him and his rule."

"I see. And my brother?"

The flicker of a smile went over Friar Reginald's worried face. "Master Thomas said he would speak the truth."

They all had to smile . . . but at that moment Messer Giovanni di Guido came back. "He is conscious now", he announced gravely.

"What was it?" asked Theodora eagerly.

The physician looked at Friar Reginald. "It is hard to say, most noble lady", he answered cautiously. "There is nothing I could call a regular illness . . . and if it is an illness, we do not know its name."

"It is not poison, is it, di Guido?" asked Theodora in a low voice.

Everyone in the room except the physician knew what she alluded to. The King of Sicily was capable of anything if his rule was in danger.

"No, Countess", said di Guido firmly. "It is not poisoning."

"But what is it?"

Di Guido looked again at Friar Reginald. "I take it this is not the first time, am I right, Friar?"

"It is not the first time."

"I thought so. He spoke only a few words before he regained consciousness, but they told me enough to understand that this is almost exactly the opposite of poisoning."

"What do you mean, di Guido?"

"A man is called poisoned when something alien has got into him whose effect is bad, damaging, pernicious. Here it seems to be the reverse."

"You are speaking in riddles, di Guido", remonstrated Francesca Cecano. "Why can't you be plain and outspoken?"

"He is", said Friar Reginald in a low voice.

Di Guido gave him a slight nod. "I will explain as best I can, most noble lady. On the physical plane poison is usually no more than a matter of dose, of quantity. A small quantity may have a very healthy effect. A goblet of wine, for instance, will revive a weary and exhausted man. But the immoderate enjoyment of wine may do serious harm."

"What has all this to do with my brother Thomas?" exclaimed Theodora.

"On the plane of the mind and the soul it is different", said the physician calmly. "There it is not a matter of quantity but of quality. An evil passion can be called a poison to the soul. But . . . and this is my difficulty . . . what shall we call the opposite? A good passion, the highest form of passion, the passion for God alone . . . "

"Soli Deo", murmured Friar Reginald.

"But he is ill", cried Theodora. "He is weak . . . he fainted. How could this be the effect . . . "

"It could be", nodded di Guido. "We have heard of certain chosen souls whose love of God was more burning than the worst fever; the greater the love, the greater the suffering, and the more consuming. And if God . . . the Lover . . . should have revealed something of himself to the Beloved, then the soul may have only one aim: the reunion with the Lover, as soon as possible. Such a soul will only live for death."

"Is he . . . going to die?" asked Theodora, white to the lips.

"I don't know, Countess. But if he dies, it will be from Love."

There was a pause, as they tried to understand the awe-inspiring implication. Strangely enough it was Friar Reginald who spoke first:

"Is there any hope that Master Thomas will be able to recuperate . . . that he may still get to Lyons?"

"The physician has very little say in a case like this, naturally", said di Guido. "Nothing is impossible."

"May I go and see him?" asked Theodora in a clipped voice.

"Certainly, Countess. He is quite . . . from the viewpoint of the physician, he is quite normal now."

They let her go alone.

Thomas was sitting up as she entered the room. He smiled at her.

"My little one, I am sorry I frightened you. It was nothing. You see, I am quite well now. I must make my excuses to Francesca, too. Where is she?"

As she sat down beside his bed, he saw her eyes and knew that she knew. He began to play with the fringes of the silk rug, gazing, as it seemed, at the wooden beams of the ceiling.

"Thomas, my dear, dear Thomas . . . I am a very selfish person. I know I shouldn't bother you, least of all now. But I must ask you something. Perhaps it is the solution for . . . everything."

"Ask, little one."

"Thomas . . . it sounds so very stupid. How . . . how does one become a saint?"

"Will it."

She gasped. "Will it? And that is all?"

"That is all we can do. God does the rest. Love God. But remember: love is of the will. To love is to will. *Amare est velle.*"

"But what is one to do when one's will is broken?" she thought bitterly. And she asked: "What is the most desirable thing in life?"

He said very quietly: "A good death."

Perhaps it was. Assuredly it was. She had wished for it many a time, when her thoughts were gnawing at her. But she knew now that she could not follow him, that he was far away, on the summit of a mountain so high that she could not breathe there. "I have forsaken my right to happiness", she thought. "I gave it up when I refused to recognize love . . . and then punished myself by comparing everything that Ruggiero did with what *he* would have done; just a simple knight, and yet he was the measure of everything . . . and I forced his picture on poor Ruggiero, and for my sake he tried, and because of me he died. My fault, my fault, my most grievous fault."

"Little one . . . "

"Yes, Thomas . . . "

"Little one, we have no right to happiness . . . either here or beyond. It is God's free gift."

"Thomas . . . how did you know . . . ?"

"God's free gift, little one . . . but he is very generous, you know."

The enormous face was lit up by a smile, warm and round like the sun; the joy of all that is good was in it, the sparkle of intelligence, the radiance of wisdom; and it conferred an honorable accompliceship.

Then the large, black eyes closed, and his head sank back. For a brief moment she was frightened. But his breath came regularly and strong. He was sound asleep.

* * *

He was a little better the next day, talked to Francesca Cecano, and seemed glad and yet not in the least surprised when Piers came in to see him. "Brother Peter", he said. "Ah, no . . . you are Lord Rudde now, aren't you?"

"Please go on calling me Brother Peter", said Piers. "I never had a name that conferred a greater honor."

Thomas asked him a few questions about the crusade and the death of King Louis. Then he said suddenly: "You were with Ruggiero when he died, weren't you? Francesca told me."

"I was."

Saint and knight looked at each other.

"I told you once before," said Thomas, "there is no such thing as failure or success when a man does all he can do. Once more you fulfilled your mission."

Piers gave a deep sigh. "Father Thomas . . . the physician says you may be well enough, in a few days, to resume your journey. May I travel with you? You are going to Lyons . . . and I'm on my way back to England. It is the same route, and . . . " He broke off.

Thomas nodded, a little absentmindedly. Suddenly he said: "We won't have Prince Edward's best carriage this time, Brother Peter."

His chuckle was irresistibly infectious.

"Falcon and Terzel", grinned Piers. "Do you know that Master Albert thought for a moment I'd stolen carriage and horses?"

When he had left the room, he stood for a while, his lips

still broadened, his mind bewildered. He found himself thinking: "Only in there the sun is shining." Shaking his head, his smile fading, he went to find Theodora, to tell her that he was going to accompany Thomas to Lyons.

She listened, her eyes downcast.

"So," he concluded, lamely, "if you will be gracious enough to permit me to stay until Master Thomas is strong enough to set out . . . "

"You should not ask me that", she said, still without looking up. "This is Francesca's house, not mine."

Piers stiffened. "I don't think I could stay in paradise if I felt that you didn't want me there."

She said with a bitter smile: "I'm afraid I have less influence in paradise than here in Magenza." But she added quickly: "We are both being very foolish. Don't take any notice of what I say." And after a moment's pause: "It is a great relief to me to know you will be at Thomas' side."

He bowed silently and withdrew. The rest of the day was like lead.

The next morning Thomas was again better, although di Guido seemed still somewhat doubtful. The two following days showed still further improvement, and Thomas decided to leave.

It was a perfect morning when they rode over the drawbridge and down the causeway: Thomas and Reginald on their mules, then Piers and Robin and finally Theodora, Francesca, and di Guido, who had decided to accompany the travellers for an hour and then to return.

They passed the village of Campagna, where men doffed their caps and dark-eyed women lifted up their children for the friars to bless them. The smell of freshly kindled wood mingled with the warmth of the sun.

Then came the open country, lanes and soft hillocks, glistening with the shiny grey-green of olive trees.

Behind a group of pine trees, at some distance, rose the quadrangular bell tower of a monastery.

"The Abbey of Fossa Nuova", explained Francesca Cecano. "It is built upon the ruins of Forum Appii, where Christians were already living in Caligula's time. St. Paul was welcomed by a delegation of Forum Appii when he first came to Italy."

"To which order does it belong?" asked Piers with polite interest. He was both vexed and glad that a long, painful silence had been interrupted.

"They are Cistercians."

Suddenly Friar Reginald cried out. In the next instant they saw Thomas swaying in his saddle. Piers spurred his horse and was at his side just in time to prevent him from falling. Theodora arrived a second later.

"Thomas . . . dear Thomas . . . what is it?"

But it was only too clear what it was. Thomas' face was the color of ashes; his eyes seemed to have sunk in. He could not speak. Di Guido dismounted and came up to Reginald's side. One glance and he knew. "The journey has ended", he said.

"Can we get him back to Magenza?" asked Francesca in a subdued voice.

"I think so", said di Guido.

But at that moment Thomas feebly raised his hand. They saw that he was making an attempt to speak. They waited anxiously. When he spoke, it was no more than a whisper, yet they all heard the words quite clearly.

"If Our Lord . . . is about . . . to visit me . . . it is better that he . . . should find me . . . in a monastery."

"Friar Reginald," said Piers, "it will be best, perhaps, if you ride over quickly to the abbey and inform the Abbot. Robin will take your place at Master Thomas' left side. We must go slowly."

Reginald nodded and obeyed. It was no more than ten minutes' ride to Fossa Nuova, even for a mule.

The little caravan followed, Thomas between Piers and Robin, with di Guido leading the mules and his own horse. Theodora and Francesca brought up the rear. No one spoke. The blow had been too stunning. And even nature itself seemed to hold its breath. There was no sound but for the hollow clump-clump of hooves. It took them almost half an hour to reach the abbey, a huge, white building, forbidding and yet serene.

They found the gate wide open. A little group of monks in white cowls was waiting there and with them one in a black-and-white habit: Friar Reginald. Now they began to move toward them.

A few more yards and di Guido brought mule and horse to a standstill.

"Theodora", whispered Thomas. At once she was at his side.

"My little one . . . there are so many . . . to whom I shall give . . . the message of your love. Father . . . and Mother and Rainald and Landulph . . . and Marotta . . . "

"Thomas, Thomas . . . " She had taken his right hand between hers. It was icy.

"God bless you, my little one."

And then he suddenly grasped her right hand and laid it in that of Piers. His voice was clear and of almost normal strength as he said: "I want him to look after you."

They gazed at each other as in a dream, two frightened children, breathless and trembling. Neither of them could think.

When at last their hands parted, the Cistercians were already busy lifting Thomas from his mule and putting him on a rough stretcher, covered with a rug.

Piers saw Thomas' hand giving a blessing to Francesca, another to di Guido, still another to Robin. Then four sturdy, white-clad monks lifted their burden and carried it feet forward toward the open gate.

Smaller and smaller they became; they reached the gate; they passed through it, and immediately it began to close. They could hear the faint sound as clearly as if it were only a yard away.

For a while they stood in silence. Then, as if someone had given a command, they all turned and started on their way home, to Magenza.

* * *

They came back to Fossa Nuova every day, week after week. And at least once a day di Guido came to Magenza to report on his visit to Thomas, who was fully conscious most of the time.

The physician was deeply moved by what he had seen. "They are worthy that he should enter under their roof", he said. "He has been given the Abbot's cell. And everything that goes into that cell is touched by consecrated hands only. Even the firewood is collected and carried to him by ordained monks. He found out and protested, but they just smiled and continued. They love him as if he had come down from heaven instead of going there."

No one dared ask him whether there was still any hope of recovery.

When Theodora went out to Fossa Nuova, Piers followed her at a distance of three horse lengths. They did not speak to each other. At Magenza, in the presence of others, they did, with elaborate courtesy. But when they were alone, they couldn't. Thomas' last word and gesture for them had been too powerful. As so often with men whose life is that kind of imitation of the life of Christ that makes for sainthood, there was . . . or might be . . . an analogy between his words, "He will look after you", and Christ's words on the Cross, when he recommended his Mother to the care of his disciple. A sacred care. A holy guardianship, utterly beyond ordinary human relations. But, then, of course, Christ's words had meant far more than even that, had meant his parting gift to mankind. John was the representative of all men, and to all men the Redeemer had given the most priceless legacy: his Mother, who became theirs.

Both Piers and Theodora thought of that. Neither of them spoke of it.

Theodora was not allowed to enter Fossa Nuova: no woman could set foot in a Cistercian monastery and Piers did not even think of claiming a prerogative that Thomas' own sister could not share.

They halted, on their horses, in front of the huge gate and waited until one of the monks would come out to tell them what news there was. Thomas had been told that they came every day. There was no message to them, but they both felt his presence, loving and paternal, as if there were no walls between them.

They were not alone. The news had spread very quickly. Villagers came from Campagna, from other places and towns in the vicinity. Soon they came from Naples and Rome, from Viterbo and Orvieto, from Cremona and Florence, Genoa and even Milan. The Prior of the convent of Naples arrived, and many nobles from all parts of Italy, even if their relationship to Thomas was a very distant one. Only Thomas' other still living sister, Adelasia, was not present. She was in Spain with her husband, to whom she had been happily married for many years.

Whenever Piers and Theodora went to Fossa Nuova, there were always little groups and many solitary figures waiting near the gate.

Only once, on the way back to Magenza and just before they arrived at the castle, Theodora suddenly turned and said jerkily: "You never told me that you had been cruelly flogged for Ruggiero's sake."

He blushed heavily. After a while he answered: "Robin had no business to tell you that. Besides, it is not so. We were flogged because I attacked that mullah man, and Robin came to my aid . . . and I attacked him because he had blasphemed Our Lady."

"I know, Piers. But he blasphemed because you had tried to stop him from making Ruggiero do a very terrible thing."

"He wouldn't have done it in any case, weak though he was from all he had to go through. I shall talk to Robin about this."

"Don't, please", she begged. "It was my fault. I made him talk, I . . . wanted to know more. So he was flogged, too. He hadn't told me that part. You won't scold him, will you? Please!"

Without waiting for his answer she spurred her horse and rode up the causeway toward the drawbridge.

* * *

They had not given up praying for Thomas' recovery at Fossa Nuova.

Least of all, Reginald could be reconciled to losing the friend he had been mothering ever since the early days of his priesthood. Alone with Thomas, he broke into tears, stammered how much he had hoped that they would reach Lyons after all and with it the certainty of "great glory to the Order and high honors".

Thomas talked to him as to a child. God had granted him what he had always asked of him, by taking him out of the world as he was. "He gave me light and grace at an earlier age than others, so that he might mercifully shorten my exile and admit me the sooner to his glory." When Reginald stared at him, still unconvinced, Thomas said gravely: "He himself in his goodness has made me know that." For a while they remained silent. The March sun brought in the smell of sweet, warm grass. From the chapel came the chanting of the monks.

"If you love me," said Thomas gently, "rejoice with me. For my consolation is perfect."

That same day four Cistercians came to ask him for a great favor. Would he give them a commentary on the crown of all mystic writing, the Canticle of Canticles in the Old Testament?

He frowned a little. "I have given up writing."

But they went on pleading. Of course he needn't write

down anything. They would do that. They would write down every comment he would make. One of them, a very young man with eager eyes, dared to remind him that St. Bernard, too, had worked to the very end.

Thomas smiled. "Give me St. Bernard's spirit, and I will do likewise."

But the idea had taken root in him. It was a song of love, *the* song of love. Suddenly he agreed.

They beamed with happiness. Perhaps the renewed interest in work was a sign of recovery after all. Perhaps it would *make* him recover.

He began to dictate the commentary to the greatest of all love songs, praising prophetically the union between Christ and his spouse, the Church on earth and in heaven. When he fell asleep, they withdrew on tiptoes, to return again the next morning.

When he came to the seventh chapter and read out the words "Come, my beloved, let us go forth into the field", the book dropped from his fingers and he fainted.

Di Guido was fetched, and after a little more than an hour Thomas regained consciousness. "Reginald", he said quite clearly. "The sins of my whole life . . . "

They understood that he wished to make a general confession and left him alone with his Dominican brother.

A short while afterward Reginald staggered out of his cell, his face streaked with tears. "The sins of a child of five", he whispered. "Oh, my dear God, in all his life the sins of a child of five . . . "

Only then he saw the Abbot standing before him with the Viaticum and behind him in a double row the whole Cistercian community. He knelt down before the Sacrament and let them pass into the cell.

From inside came Thomas' voice, loud and strong, vibrant with exaltation: "Thou are Christ, the King of eternal glory."

* * *

On the sixth of March the crowds before the gate were denser than ever. News had come that Thomas was sinking and that he had received Extreme Unction.

But the day passed and nothing further happened. When dusk fell, the crowds began to disperse.

"I shall stay", said Theodora as Francesca Cecano moved up to her. "You go back, Francesca. Please, do. I must stay."

Francesca stayed on for another two hours and then returned to the castle. It was a cloudy night, with only a few stars visible. Here and there a solitary figure remained, an old shepherd, a couple of young girls.

Theodora sat down on the grass. She could not pray any more. She could not think. Her life had come to a standstill.

A few paces behind her Piers stood, leaning on his sword. At some distance the horses were grazing.

In the darkness the monastery looked immense, as if it had expanded to hold the spirit of the dying giant.

Piers thought of what the Abbot had said to him the day before, when he had come out for a moment to greet Thomas' sister.

"His highest achievement is that he has made philosophy a weapon in the service of Christ. It is not only that he has made a happy synthesis between Aristotelian and Christian wisdom. He has done far more: he has given to philosophy itself the sacrament of the Holy Spirit." The philosopher, the theologian, the metaphysician, the learned Doctor. If only they did not forget the *man* . . . the most lovable, the kindest, gentlest man who was Thomas.

A tinny bell proclaimed midnight. The seventh of March . . . that was the day on which Piers had gone to him, so many years ago, in Paris, with the news that his brothers had died.

Another bell began to toll . . . and still another . . . and now the big ones, seldom heard, fell in. The night was filled with the mighty sound.

Theodora rose to her feet.

Piers took a step forward.

They both knew. They crossed themselves and prayed until at last the bells ceased their tolling.

Then Piers went to fetch the horses. She mounted without a word, her face dark and serene.

In silence they rode. But after a while she held her horse for Piers to join her, and he did, his eyes burning, his heart turning in him. Suddenly she stretched out her hand to him, and as he seized it, she let her weary head drop onto his shoulder.

He broke a living silence.

"Now I know", he said.

"What?"

"That he has started his work in heaven."